GUNSLINGER GIRL

JIMMY PATTERSON BOOKS
FOR YOUNG ADULT READERS

For exclusives, trailers, and other information, visit jimmypatterson.org.

GUNSLINGER GIRL

LYNDSAY ELY

JIMMY PATTERSON BOOKS
LITTLE, BROWN AND COMPANY
New York Boston London

Copyright © 2018 by Lyndsay Ely
Foreword copyright © 2018 by James Patterson

JIMMY Patterson Books / Little, Brown and Company
Hachette Book Group
1290 Avenue of the Americas, New York, NY 10104
jimmypatterson.org

First Edition: January 2018
First Paperback Edition: December 2018

JIMMY Patterson Books is an imprint of Little, Brown and Company, a division of Hachette Book Group, Inc. The Little, Brown name and logo are trademarks of Hachette Book Group, Inc. The JIMMY Patterson Books® name and logo are trademarks of JBP Business, LLC.

The publisher is not responsible for websites (or their content) that are not owned by the publisher.

The Hachette Speakers Bureau provides a wide range of authors for speaking events. To find out more, go to hachettespeakersbureau.com or call (866) 376-6591.

Library of Congress Cataloging-in-Publication Data
Names: Ely, Lyndsay, author.
Title: Gunslinger girl / Lyndsay Ely.
Description: First edition. | New York : Little, Brown and Company, 2018. | "JIMMY Patterson Books." | Summary: In a post–Second Civil War lawless West, sharpshooter Serendipity "Pity" Jones stars in, and lives at, the Theatre Vespertine, but there is a dark cost to her freedom that Pity may not be willing to pay.
Identifiers: LCCN 2017015174 | ISBNs: 978-0-316-55510-4 (hc) | 978-0-316-55524-1 (pb)
Subjects: | CYAC: Gunfighters—Fiction. | Loyalty—Fiction. | Freedom—Fiction. | West (U.S.)—Fiction. | Science fiction.
Classification: LCC PZ7.1.E473 Gun 2018 | DDC [Fic]—dc23
LC record available at https://lccn.loc.gov/2017015174

10 9 8 7 6 5 4 3 2 1

LSC-C

Printed in the United States of America

*Dedicated to irrepressible girls
and persistent women*

FOREWORD

A girl who can draw a pistol faster than any man. A United States devastated by a Second Civil War. A decadent city teeming with vice and a peculiar kind of virtue. This is the Wild West as you and I have never seen it.

Lyndsay Ely imagines a new West where teenage gunslinger Serendipity "Pity" Jones seeks her fortune. She's not looking for a fight, but she sure knows how to finish one. And you won't be able to put this book down until you finish Pity's thrilling story. I know I couldn't.

—James Patterson

PART ONE

CHAPTER 1

THEY DRAGGED IN THE DEAD SCROUNGER IN THE FADE of the afternoon, tied to the last truck in the convoy. Dust clouds billowed after the vehicles like a fog, blanketing the compound's entrance in ochre twilight.

Pity squinted and pulled her bandanna over her nose. She wandered into the commotion, eyes half scanning the jumble of vehicles and riders for her father but mostly letting her feet carry her over to where the scrounger lay. Flies alighted on him and on the trail of wet muck he had left behind. The body was face-down, though when one of the convoy guards kicked him over, Pity reckoned that was no longer an apt description, as there wasn't much face left to speak of. She swallowed the sourness that rose in the back of her throat.

The guard, dressed in a weathered Transcontinental Railway

uniform, sniffed and spat. "Shoulda left the trash outside for the crows."

"What'd he do?" Pity toed the scrounger's mangled hand. There wasn't a lot to be made of the body. Male, certainly. Maybe young. Maybe not.

"Thief. Found 'im sneaking around camp this morning. Nearly made off with an armful of solar cells."

Brave, she thought, *but dumb.* It was one thing to pick through the abandoned landscape, another to steal from a Trans-Rail convoy.

A hand clamped around her arm. "Get yer ass away from that!"

She grimaced beneath the bandanna, careful not to let the emotion touch her eyes as she turned to her father. Three days' worth of dust and grime from riding motorcycle escort to the convoy did nothing to diminish his chill air of authority. The guard mumbled a quiet "Sir" and hurried off, but her father's slate-hard gaze never left her. Pity took an involuntary step back and spotted the commune mayor, Lester Kim, standing behind him, along with a sharp-featured man she didn't recognize.

The stranger's eyes slithered over her. "This her, Scupps?"

Her father nodded. Pity flinched when he reached out again, but he only yanked the bandanna down. Strands of acorn-brown hair fell across her cheeks. She pushed them back.

"She don't look much like you."

"Serendipity favors her mother." Lester's head bobbed up and down on his scrawny chicken's neck. "In the good ways, mind you."

"You mean like my aim?" Pity stifled a smirk as Lester

stiffened. She also pretended not to notice the narrowing of her father's eyes, a sign that she should be silent.

He shoved his pack at her, sending a fresh cloud of dust into her face. "Get home and clean my gear. We're back on the road tomorrow morning."

She hesitated, eyeing the stranger still considering her like a piece of livestock.

"You gone deaf while I was away? Go!"

Pity obeyed, plunging into the mess of workers unloading crates, each one etched with the Confederation of North America seal and destination marks for Pity's commune, the 87th Agricultural. The smell of exhaust tinged the air, clamorous with labor and barked orders. It was a familiar enough scene, save for an aberrant oasis of order at the center of it all. Set away from the rest, a pair of sleek black trucks idled, gold logos emblazoned on their sides. Pity slowed.

Drakos-Pryce.

Corporate cargo.

She wandered closer, curious. In matching black uniforms— none of which looked like they'd seen six months on the road— the Drakos-Pryce team moved with precision and order, stacking their delivery in neat piles. The commune and TransRail workers gave them a wide berth, tossing only the occasional awed look their way.

Except for one.

Hale looked up as she spotted him, waving her over to where he stood before an open case. "Pity! Take a look at these."

"What—" Her breath caught as she spotted the rifle. It was a model that couldn't even generously be called recent, but it was still better than anything she had seen in person. "Those are for the commune?"

He nodded. The settlement's head firearms instructor, Hale was also responsible for everything that came and went from the armory. "Security upgrades."

Pity's hands itched as he lifted the gun out of its container. She longed to feel the exquisite balance, to look through its scope and gently wrap her finger around the trigger.

Inhale, aim. Exhale, shoot.

The memory of the words came with the pungent scent of cheap home-still, along with the vague sensation of her mother's touch as she made some small adjustment to Pity's form. Pity could still feel the warmth of the sun bleeding into her skin, see round after round of targets as she cut them down. Never quite as well as her mother, not yet, but creeping closer and closer with every—

No. Pity's hands tightened around her father's pack, an anchor to reality. Her mother was gone, and her daddy would sooner grow feathers and lay an egg than allow her anywhere near a weapon like that. Not that he'd get one, either. They'd be issued to the wall-walkers, the men and women who patrolled the commune ramparts and crop field fences. Her mother had been one of them once—the very best, sober or not.

The old ache rose within her, the anger and frustration at her exclusion from the commune's defensive forces. She'd inherited her mother's eye and skill with a gun. But as mayor, Lester Kim made the labor appointments, and Lester listened to her father so much that people joked about who really ran the commune.

At least riding escort keeps him gone half the time.

Hale caught wind of her thoughts. "Come down to the range when he's gone. It'd be irresponsible not to test these out before distributing them, right?"

A smile found her lips. Hale had been her mother's friend once, and he had no qualms about letting her practice shooting when her father was gone. At least she'd been able to keep her ability from withering away.

"Don't look around," Hale said abruptly, keeping his voice conversational. "Your father is coming this way. Go on, before he gets any closer. If he asks why we were chatting, tell him I was passing along your brothers' range scores."

She couldn't resist. "Are they any better?"

"Well, they can hit a barn...provided it don't move too quick."

Pity swallowed a chuckle and ran off, leaving the fuss of the convoy behind for a cluster of squat administration buildings. Beyond them lay the commissary shops and, finally, the neat grids of worker homes. The identical rust-colored structures were mostly deserted, their residents still at work in the fields or barns, but a lanky arm waved from the porch of one.

"Pity! Thank goodness. Save me!"

As Pity angled over, arguing voices drifted out from within the house. "What's going on?"

Finn glanced over her slumped shoulder. "Well, so far as I can tell, Rena Harrow is pregnant." Pity's best friend ran a hand through her cropped wheat-hued hair; an untidy nest of dirt, oil, and whatever else had been dripping on her that day. "And her mother is none too happy about losing her first grandchild, so she's trying to get Rena to fess up and marry its daddy before she's whisked away to a mothers' home for nine months of luxury incubation."

Pity winced as somewhere inside the house a door slammed so hard that the windows shook. Despite the values preached, CONA didn't try to stop people from doing what they were going to do—not with birthrates still so low, a lingering remnant of the bioterrorism years that had preceded the Second Civil War. But children born out of wedlock were considered wards of the government and adopted out to couples who couldn't conceive in the natural way.

"I'm guessing Rena isn't too happy about planning a wedding?"

Finn shook her head. "Which is no business of mine"—she nudged the bag of tools beside her—"'cept that the block's generator is belly-up again, and I need to check each house to see if they're over-drawing power. I've been sitting out here for an hour, waiting for those two to cool down."

"The generator's down *again?*" Pity grimaced. "This is the third time this month!"

"Well, all I can do is keep patching it up until I get the right parts. Oh, geez, you just got that look."

"What look?"

"The one where your face scrunches up and your cheeks go so red I can barely see all those freckles."

Pity tried to smile but her mouth turned down instead. "I can make do with cold water to wash, but *he's* not going to be too happy about bathing in it."

Finn's expression curdled as she spotted the pack, only to

brighten an instant later. "Wait, the convoy's back?" She jumped up. "C'mon!"

"Where?" Pity stayed put. "I need to get home before—"

"The belts I ordered come in with this convoy! I can finally finish the Ranger!"

Excitement flickered within Pity. The Ranger was Finn's baby, her mechanical firstborn. It had started as an old frame for a plains buggy, scavenged out of the junk pile, but since finding it, Finn had begged, traded, and scrounged for every wheel, clamp, hose, and gear. It would never win a prize for looks, but her friend swore it would be faster than a jackrabbit when she was done with it.

"And with the Ranger ready to go"—Finn leaned in closer, whispering—"we can finally start making real plans to—"

"Standing around when you should be working, squirt?"

They both started at the new voice. Two long shadows approached, attached to Pity's brothers.

"Yeah, squirt," Billy parroted. "Dinner ready yet?"

Pity frowned. "You're early."

"Outgoing crop shipment needed to be loaded up by tomorrow, so they called all the crews in." Henry adjusted the rifle slung over his shoulder and eyed the pack. "You seen Daddy?"

She nodded.

"Then don't you think you should be cooking?"

"Generator's down again, boys," Finn said. "Dinner's gonna be late."

Henry and Billy frowned in unison, looking almost like

twins with their dusty brown hair and field tans. At eighteen and sixteen, they hated being called *boys,* and Finn knew it.

"Again?" said Billy. "I thought you were supposed to be good at fixing those things, *Josephina!*"

Finn bristled. "I ain't a miracle worker."

"I'll manage something," Pity interjected. "You go on, Finn. I'll stop by the workshop later if I can."

"A busted generator ain't Pity's fault. Y'all remember that." Finn shot Billy and Henry an acid look as she headed off, tool kit slapping against her thigh.

Pity stared after her, tight with impatience. *Six more months,* she told herself. In six months she'd be a legal adult.

And as soon as that day came...

Not giving her brothers a chance to make more demands, Pity turned on her heel and headed to the last house in the line. Inside, stale silence met her as she threw her father's pack into a corner of the kitchen and began knitting together a meal. Billy and Henry entered a few minutes later, clomping up the stairs to clean up before dinner. Pity had just grabbed a wet rag and started work on her father's gear when he, too, arrived home. He leaned his rifle beside the door and sat at the table. When Henry and Billy joined him a moment later, all three folded hands.

"Thank you, Lord," her father intoned, "for your blessings on our fields and our stock so that we may feed the mouths that depend on us back east. And may they continue so, amen."

For a while, the only sounds were chewing and the clink of utensils against plates. As Pity rinsed out a canteen, Henry and Billy traded furtive glances.

"Heard y'all got a scrounger," Henry ventured finally.

Their father chewed a mouthful of cold chicken. "We did. Caught and dealt with. Nothing to speak of." Her brothers' disappointment at the brevity of the story was tangible, but they knew better than to press. "Pity, bring me some water."

She grabbed a glass from the shelf. "I made some lemonade if you—"

"I said water."

He stared at her as she brought the glass over. She kept her own gaze carefully downcast.

"My gear gonna be ready by morning?"

"Yes, sir."

"Good. I'll only be gone a day or two. While I'm away, get your own things packed."

Halfway back across the kitchen, she faltered. "What?"

"You best learn to hear better than you been, girl. That nonsense isn't going to be tolerated where you're headed." He took a sip of water. "The man who was with me at the convoy is from the 34th Mining. You're going back with him when I return."

"But—" Her guts twisted into a sick knot. "Why?"

"Why do you think?" Billy smirked. "There's only one thing a place like that would want from you, and it's between your—"

"You shut your goddamn mouth!" The retort snapped out before she could stop it.

"Pity!" Her father's face turned rosy. "You will not blaspheme in this house!"

"Sorry!" She took a step backward, reflexively conscious of possible retreats—the stairs, the back door—but he remained at the table. "I...I just don't understand."

"What's unclear? You're headed to the 34th. Lester's already approved the transfer."

"But that's not...I can't..." A shiver of realization raced through her. She should have seen it coming. Six months and she'd be lawfully released from his control. But he couldn't let that happen easy, not him. Her jaw tightened. "You sold me off, didn't you? You and Lester."

Bridal bribes, they called them. CONA rewarded communes that met their birth quotas, so it hadn't taken long for an underground market to arise between those that had an excess of fertile young women and those that didn't. Her transfer might come under the guise of a worker exchange, but Pity knew exactly what it was. Was the stranger intending to force her into marriage, Pity wondered, or was he only her ferryman?

"How much did you get for me?"

Her father didn't answer. He stood slowly, fingertips pressed to the table so hard that they were white. "You will do your duty to the Confederation, and you will obey me."

Pity tensed with anger. And though her heart pumped cold fright, it didn't stop the words that came out next. "Momma never would have let you sell me off."

"Your *mother*"—her father's face went from rosy to red as he said the word—"was an insurgent and a drunk. And if she hadn't gotten herself killed, she'd have sent you wherever she'd been told to send you!"

"No, she wouldn't!" Pity took three shaky steps toward her father.

He gave a derisive sniff. "Lord knows she had no trouble selling herself, now, did she?"

"And look what kind of heartless, godforsaken son of a bitch she got stuck with!"

She didn't register the pain until she was on her knees, staring at the wood slats of the floor. She lifted one trembling hand to the side of her face. It came back slick with crimson.

"The 34th is more than you deserve." Her father's voice fell on her like a rain of gravel. "You *will* be ready to leave when I return. And if I hear one more word of dissent, I will go to Lester and make sure you're sent to the very farthest edge of the settlements. And you don't even want to *know* what brand of sons of bitches they send out there. You hear me?"

Cheek throbbing, Pity raised her head. A few feet away, within easy reach, was her father's rifle.

He followed her gaze. "Go ahead," he said. "Try. They'll all say how ironic it was that your mother bargained her way out of the noose only to have you end up in it."

She swallowed hard, the coppery taste of blood coating the inside of her mouth. Trembling with fear and adrenaline, she got to her feet and met her father's eyes.

Glacial indifference stared back.

Pity inhaled sharply, then turned and bolted out the back door, not slowing a moment for the cacophony of shouts that trailed after her.

CHAPTER 2

"DAMMIT," FINN GROWLED. "I TOLD THEM THE GENERATOR wasn't your fault!"

Though she doubted pursuit, Pity locked the door of the workshop after her. All concrete floor and corrugated metal, it was little more than an old shed wedged into the back corner of the garages, just large enough for a tool bench and the Ranger. She wiped at her eyes. "It's not..."

"Hey, stop!" Finn grabbed a clean rag and doused it with alcohol. "You're smearing the blood around. Let me."

Pity winced at the sting of disinfectant.

"Well, you don't need stitches," her friend said at last. "But you're gonna have a helluva bruise. What happened this time? You forget to fold Billy's underpants?"

Pity drew a breath. Simply thinking the words made her tongue go stiff. "I'm...being sent to another commune."

"What? *Where?*"

"A mining settlement that needs fertile women. He and Lester schemed it up."

Finn stared in disbelief. "That...that..." She grabbed a wrench and pitched it across the shed. It clanged against the wall, leaving a dent. "When?"

"When he gets back from the next transport." Pity slid into the Ranger's passenger side. The patchwork seat embraced her, as it had a thousand times before. Still fuming, Finn climbed in opposite. She fished out a flask from beneath her seat and offered it.

Pity reached, then hesitated.

"A little. For the pain," said Finn.

She winced at the potent, evocative scent that escaped as she unscrewed the top. It was good for pain, all right—Pity's mother had applied it liberally and regularly. But it wasn't drink that had faded her to the shade of the person she should have been. It was misery—the despair of a wolf trapped in a tiny cage when it should have been free. That and the man who had been as much a jailer as a husband, who never touched a drop of alcohol and was a monster anyhow.

Pity took a sip and grimaced. The home-still went down like liquid flame.

"What did you say to get that, anyway?" Finn crossed her arms. "A smart man should know better than to mess with the face he's trying to sell."

"Who said he was smart?" There were many words she might have used to describe her father—cunning, obstinate, righteous—but not smart. "I called him a heartless, godforsaken son of a bitch."

Finn let out a snort of laughter.

"It's not funny! He said things about my mother..." Fresh anger crested, white-hot. "He called her an insurgent and a drunk."

"Aw, Pity—"

"And Lord knows it's true—she was! But he always...he always has to..."

Finn scowled. "And how many others in the commune were on the losing side of the war? Plenty. Your mother was a good woman, Pity. She could have made a run for the dissident camps out west—they'd never have caught *her*—but she didn't. She made a deal and she kept it."

"I know," said Pity. *Because of Henry and Billy.*

And me.

The guilt tinged every memory of her mother. But it had served as a catalyst, too, stoking her resolve to avoid a similar fate.

Six months.

A few hours ago the thought had been a promising breeze, a hint of spring after a long winter. The Ranger would be complete, she and Finn would have enough currency and supplies squirreled away to keep them comfortable for a while. No one telling them what they could and could not do with their lives, and the entirety of the east open for them to explore. They could visit the cities, see the ocean—anything they wanted.

Now that dream was gone, set behind an unreachable horizon. Six months on an unfamiliar commune with no friends or allies—Pity had little doubt of her father's and the stranger's intentions. Whatever situation she ended up forced into, there would be only one way to escape it entirely.

She stared down at the flask.

On the day her mother died, the clouds had been a black line rushing toward the commune, the afternoon going from sweltering hot to shivering cold in the space of minutes. Rain pummeled the ground like bullets; lightning split the oldest tree in the orchards. After it passed, they found her mother beneath the wall, lying at the base of the ladder from which she had fallen, blank eyes staring at the clearing skies. They blamed the fury of the storm, of course, but even the torrent of rain hadn't washed the scent of home-still from her lips. What no one had said out loud was that it was a small miracle she hadn't fallen long before.

"I don't care," said Pity. On the opposite wall of the workshop, a faded CONA poster depicted happy, smiling families before the soaring skyline of Columbia, CONA's capital city. Nothing like the family her mother had bartered her life for. Nothing like what awaited Pity. "I don't care what's been arranged, I'm not going."

"Of course you're not." Finn's mouth was a hard line, her face shadowed by the canvas tarp that served as the Ranger's roof. "We planned to run, and that's what we're going to do."

"How? We've got nothing ready. The Ranger isn't even done."

"Oh?" Finn reached for the steering column and pressed the ignition switch. The vehicle rumbled to life.

Pity straightened. "Did you—"

"Yup. Purrs like a barn cat, right?"

"But we don't have supplies yet, and my father—"

"Will be gone for a couple days." Finn ran a hand over the steering wheel. "I have enough currency to get us on the Trans-Rail, so long as we don't mind riding freight. After that, well, we'll figure it out."

Pity shook her head. "No. This isn't fair. You don't need to do this. You've got some promise of a future here."

Finn scoffed. "Like what? Fixing engines and swapping solar cells until the day I die? I want to do more, *see* more—Columbia, Savannah, New Boston. Like we always talked about. Might be sooner than we expected, but you're not leaving me behind. If you go, I go."

Pity searched for an argument, some reason to spare Finn from troubles not her own. But a crack had already formed in her doubt, letting a trickle of hope leak in.

And, fueled by that hope, came the beginning of a plan.

Pity took a deep breath. "It's now or never, isn't it?"

"Yup," Finn said. "We've got our reason, and we've got our ride. So where are we going?"

Tears filled Pity's eyes again. She blinked them back.

"Anywhere but here."

Morning dew still clung to the grass as Pity gingerly climbed the back steps. At the door she paused, senses straining for the sound of her father's voice, his footsteps, his presence. When it opened suddenly, she jumped, but it was only Henry.

"You can come on in. Daddy's gone." He clutched a mug of coffee. "And *pissed,* with dirty gear to boot. I suspect you got one last good thumping when he gets back."

"You gonna pretend you care?" Pity pushed past him into the kitchen. From the table, Billy gave her an oatmeal-specked grin. "You swallow whatever you're about to say, Billy Scupps. I ain't in the mood!"

The smile faded. Pity stared him down as he struggled for a retort—Billy had never been particularly quick—but in the end he scowled and went back to his breakfast.

"Where have you been?" said Henry, as if he didn't know the answer.

"Finn's."

"She must be heartbroken." Billy shoveled another spoonful into his mouth. "Did she cry when you told her?"

Pity was halfway to the table before she stopped herself. Upending the bowl onto Billy's head would mean he'd have to wash. *Get rid of them,* she thought, *just get rid of them.*

"You know what your problem is?" Henry came up behind her, so close that icy wariness rippled over her skin. "You got too much fight in you. Think you'd know better by now." He went over to Billy and slapped him on the shoulder. "C'mon, we're gonna be late."

Billy sneered at Pity as he and Henry grabbed their rifles and disappeared out the door.

The instant they were gone, a keen impatience shivered through her. It was sheer will that forced her to sit at the table and wait a few minutes in case they came back. On the wall, a small display screen—one of the few luxuries her father allowed—quietly broadcast the daily news update. Pity stared at the front door, paying only passing attention to the coverage: a new trade pact signed with the African Unification, the narrowing field of the upcoming presidential election. Above the display screen, the hands of the clock crept forward at an agonizing pace.

At last, she couldn't wait any longer.

Their plan was simple: head for the TransRail, keeping away from the main roads, and pick it up a few stops past where anyone might be looking for them. Her footsteps echoed hollowly as she went upstairs, dug out her mother's old pack, and filled it with clothes, her meager stash of currency, and her good knife. Downstairs, she packed a week's worth of food and water purification tablets.

After that, there was only one task left, one thing she couldn't leave behind.

Well, two.

Her heartbeat turned from a dull throb to a pounding drum as she fingered the cutting tool in her pocket.

It's now or never.

She went back upstairs. This time she entered her father's room, pushing the door open with the tips of her fingers. It creaked like a coffin lid. A long chest sat tucked between the bed and the wall. She wrapped her hand around its steel padlock, hesitating.

After this, there was no turning back. Even if she chickened out and managed to replace the lock, she knew her father would somehow realize what she'd done.

She flicked a switch, and the cutting tool flared to life. A moment later, the lock banged to the floor. On the top shelf of the chest was one of her father's spare rifles, which she placed on the floorboards beside her. They would need it, but it wasn't what she was after. She continued searching until she found the box, buried at the very bottom.

Hands trembling, she placed it on her lap.

Inside, on a bed of red velvet, lay two shining revolvers. Modeled after guns from a time long gone, their chased metal barrels gleamed, contrasting with the black ebony grips inlaid with silver and mother-of-pearl. Only six shots each but deadly accurate.

A lump formed in her throat. The last time she saw these weapons her mother had still been alive. When she picked one up, it was as familiar as pulling on a pair of old boots. The guns had been a gift to her mother from the remnants of the United Patriot Front, who had fielded the fiercest guerrilla fighters in living memory but lost the war anyway. They were also the only things her mother had brought with her to the 87th, save the clothes on her back.

And Pity had no intention of leaving them behind.

She pulled out an old gun belt and wrapped them in it before grabbing the rifle and as much ammo as she could carry. Then she bundled the whole lot in a blanket, not bothering to close the gun chest. She wanted her father to have no doubts about what had happened when he arrived home. The bedroom door she made sure to shut, though; letting her brothers make the discovery would be a waste of a good surprise.

At the back door, she took one last glance around the kitchen, trying to muster a happy memory, one good thought to attach to the house she'd spent her entire life in. The specter of her mother surfaced, bringing a holiday dinner to the table. She smiled down at Pity, eyes bigger and browner in memory than in real life as she placed a bowl of mashed potatoes in front of her daughter. Pity had reached for them. Years later, she could still feel the grind of bones in her wrist as her father grabbed it.

"You will wait for grace," he had said.

Pity picked up her pack and strode out the door.

"Aw c'mon, Rawley." Finn flashed the smile she saved for when she was getting what she wanted, come hell or high water. "We're not going far. Just a little ride and a picnic to celebrate her maiden voyage."

Rawley stuck a finger under his hat and scratched. "I don't know. Lester say it was all right?"

Finn tapped the steering wheel pointedly. "I've been working on the Ranger for *years.* Do you think I was gonna let him tell me no? He even gave me the outer gate code so I could try her out on the plains."

Pity marveled at the ease with which Finn spun her lies. It was Hale who had provided the code. A calculated risk, but Hale, bless him, had taken one look at her face and given it over. No questions, no comments. She said a silent thanks to him as she kept her gaze straight ahead, certain her expression would give them away. Her heart felt ready to beat right out of her chest.

After an elongated moment of thought, Rawley reached for his radio. "I better check in with—"

"Wait!" cried Pity.

He paused and gave her a quizzical look.

She faltered, mouth still open. *Say something!* She sat straighter in the passenger seat, letting the fear within rise to her face. "Lester gave Finn permission...but not me. And if *he* finds out I went with her, then..." She turned her head so the swollen, purple bruise on her cheek was more visible.

Finn caught on. "It's just a little fun, Rawley. Everyone is allowed that, huh?"

Rawley wrestled with the problem. Her father's temper was no secret, Pity knew, but gambling on sympathy wasn't a tactic she liked having to employ. Shame joined her apprehension.

"Fine," Rawley yielded. "But be back before quittin' time." He went over and opened the front gate.

"Of course!" Finn winked at him, then hit the accelerator.

Relief melted Pity back against her seat as fallow brown fields enveloped them. An overnight rain shower had dealt with the worst of the dust, but even so, when Finn turned and drove them off the main road, an earthy cloud followed in their wake. Finn maneuvered a bit, winding over the bumpy, weedy ground, but kept them moving steadily toward the outer fence. If anyone was watching, by all appearances it would look like they were joyriding. And, Pity supposed, Finn actually was. Her expression was pure delight.

Pity, on the other hand, could only focus on watching for commune vehicles. Oily fear filled her stomach, growing stronger as scenarios played out in her thoughts: Rawley could decide to radio Lester after all, or they could cross paths with a crew of field hands. And there were the wall-walkers, too; at any point, they could pass by on their rounds.

Beneath Pity's coat, the comforting weight of her mother's guns pressed against her hips like a vow.

I'm not going to die here, too. I'm not.

Finally, Finn returned to the road and Pity spotted the gate, the last barrier between them and the unsettled wilds of the CONA territories. Finn slowed to a stop and jumped out. Pity leaned out the open window of the Ranger, blood pounding in her ears as she took one more look around. In both directions along the fence, she saw no one. With a hiss of hydraulics, the gate began to slide open.

"Sit down," said Finn, returning. "It'll close after us."

For a moment, Pity couldn't move. Her limbs might as well have been concrete.

No one was watching them.

No alarms had gone off.

No one was going to stop them.

"Pity!"

She slid back into the Ranger. The wind that hit her face as they barreled through the gate was cool and fresh. Cooler and fresher than the air they had just left. At last, she smiled. Then she smiled wider and stuck her head out of the Ranger. "Whooooooooo!" she bellowed.

Finn laughed and added her voice to Pity's. They howled like wolves as the Ranger picked up speed, tires rolling over the pavement with an invigorating reverberation.

"Good-bye, 87th!" yelled Finn.

Pity twisted in her seat and looked back, unable to hold her elation in. "Good-bye, 87th!" she repeated, screaming at the top of her lungs. "And good riddance!"

CHAPTER 3

PITY SCANNED THE HORIZON WITH THE RIFLE'S SCOPE.

"How much longer you gonna do that?" Finn twisted a wrench, tightening something on the Ranger's frame. "I don't know what you're expecting to see. Rawley forgot about us the minute he went off duty. Your brothers will think you're hiding out with me. And even when everyone realizes we're gone, how d'you think they're gonna find us?"

"There's more to worry about than my father."

"Sure," said Finn. "Those deer we saw a few miles back looked like the menacing sort."

"There's no harm in being careful." She did another sweep.

Her initial elation was receding, leaving her unable to shake the itch of pursuit. They had left the main road almost immediately, the Ranger taking on the grassland with faultless mechanical grace. Here and there they had passed the skeletons of structures, the cracked remnants of old roads, but mainly the terrain had been flat, repetitive. At dusk they had made camp near a line of trees following a stream.

"Let's go to Columbia first," Pity said, changing the subject. "Just to see it. My mother used to say she'd take me there someday."

"Really? I'm surprised she'd want to go anywhere near Columbia." Finn tossed the wrench back into her bag. "Given who some people think she was."

"Stop it. There's no secret there. Everyone knew she was a sniper, and if she hadn't been fertile they would have strung her up with the Patriots they tried for war crimes. Anything else is old gossip."

"Gossip or not," said Finn, "some folks swear she was a Reaper."

"They say that about anyone who is a half decent shot."

"And you think she would have told you if she was part of the deadliest, most hunted squad of assassins in the war?"

"Yes." Pity lowered the rifle. "I do."

Did you kill people?

Pity didn't remember if it was the first time she had asked the question, but it was the time that stuck in her mind. The war had been over for a decade by then yet as ever present as the harvest, visible in scars and missing limbs and endless, haunted stares.

To her credit, her mother had replied honestly. *Yes.*

How many?

Enough. At first, Pity hadn't thought she'd say more. Her

mother had been quiet about the war, saying little more than she had guarded supply depots until near the end, when the conflict had crested to such ferocity that fighting was unavoidable.

I tried not to kill anyone who didn't need it, her mother had continued, words sober, shared at a time when she still held the advantage in her battle with the drink. *But when an entire battle came down to a moment—to when taking one life might turn the tide and save a hundred—well…that's when a decision needs to be made.*

"By all accounts, the Reapers were vicious, unrestrained," Pity said to Finn. "My mother was a lot of things, but she wasn't that kind of killer."

Finn shrugged. "Columbia it is."

Pity raised the rifle again and sighted the empty bean can she had set up two hundred yards off. Its contents simmered over the fire next to her.

"What?" said Finn.

"What do you mean 'what'?"

"Something is still bothering you."

Pity steadied the rifle. "It's nothing."

"Liar. You tell me."

She sighed. "What currency we've got between us isn't going to last long. We've got no contacts and no official transfers. There's always need for a good mechanic, but what am I gonna do? I kept house and worked in the dairy sometimes. There are no cows to milk in the cities."

"I'm no expert," Finn said, "but that doesn't look like a cow's udder in your hands."

The bean can floated in the crosshairs. "There are no walls to walk in the cities. And I'm not joining the military. That doesn't leave too many options."

Finn rolled her eyes. "Serendipity Scupps, whatever you find can't be much worse than what you left behind, right? So stop worrying and—"

"Don't call me that."

"What?"

"Scupps. I don't ever want to hear that name again." She thought for a moment. "My mother's name was Jones. I can get a new name along with a new life, can't I?"

Finn gave an approving nod. "I suppose you can. Serendipity Jones... Can't say I hate it."

Pity repeated the name in her head as she tightened her finger on the trigger. Briefly, it was almost like her mother stood behind her, as she'd done years ago.

Inhale, aim. Exhale, shoot.

She pulled the trigger. The can flew off the rock and disappeared in the grass.

The world turned from light to dark as they ate. Stars appeared, and when the chill settled in, they huddled back-to-back beneath blankets, staring at the endless pinpricks of light.

"Pretty," said Finn.

"Mmm-hmm." Beneath Pity's pillow was the hard, comforting outline of her mother's guns.

Finn shifted, turning over so that she spoke to the back of Pity's neck. "When we get to the cities... we're gonna be okay, y'know? We'll figure it out together."

Pity turned as well. The fire had burned so low that Finn was hardly more than a darker piece of the night, but Pity could sense the weight of her and pick the faint scent of machine oil out of the air. "I'm sorry to fuss. I know we will. Like you said, can't be any worse than what we left behind, right?"

"Right. G'night."

"'Night." Pity pulled the blanket tighter and pushed her fearful thoughts away. They didn't matter, not right then. Because as she felt Finn's warmth beside her, listened to her friend's breaths grow slower and more rhythmic with sleep, she couldn't remember the last time she had felt so hopeful.

Icy water tickled Pity's ankles as she dipped the mouth of the canteen into the stream. The midmorning sun warmed her shoulders and danced across the ripples as a faint breeze sent the leaves whispering. Earlier, she had woken to a sunrise that felt unfamiliar, like a sight she had never seen before. It had taken her a while to figure out why.

Pity closed her eyes. *This is what it is,* she thought, *to be outside the cage.*

This was what it felt like to be free.

A twig cracked.

She opened her eyes and spun, drawing her gun in the same movement.

Downstream, a turkey strutted out of the brush. It took a few jagged steps, stopped, and considered Pity.

She considered it right back.

"You'd make a good meal, Mr. Turkey." She aimed for the

loose red flesh of the bird's neck. "But Finn's probably done packing camp by now, and I don't feel like taking the time to dress you." She slid the gun back into her holster.

On the shore, she pulled on her boots and started up the steep bank of the stream. The thick undergrowth tugged at her clothes as she navigated it, retracing her steps until she reached where the trees thinned.

Mid-step, she froze.

Something was different.

When Pity left the camp, Finn had been whistling a cheerful tune that didn't quite match the song it was supposed to be. Now that sound was gone, replaced by one she knew too well: engines.

Motorcycles. She dropped the canteens and ducked into the brush. *More than one.*

Was it possible? Could her father have found them already? No, he wouldn't be back at the commune yet. Had Rawley raised the alarm, then? Her throat tightened, but it still didn't ring true—she and Finn had taken a wandering route, and the Ranger left hardly more trail than a bobcat.

She inched forward through the brush, a single thought pounding in time with her heart.

Finn.

By the time she reached the edge of the tree line, another distinct rumble could be heard. Fifty paces away, beyond where the Ranger sat, a truck rattled up to join the two motorcycles that flanked their camp. A man jumped from its cab and joined the dismounted riders. Beside the remains of the fire, Finn stood, stiff-backed. She took a few cautious paces backward as the men approached.

Trembling, Pity cursed silently. Her rifle leaned against the side of the Ranger.

"Mornin'!" one of the men called out, his voice carrying to where Pity hid.

She inspected the trio. They were young but with a coarse, dirty look to them, the kind of rough that didn't wash off. Not commune workers, then, and she didn't see any CONA patches on their clothing. All three were armed, the riders with handguns on their belts. As for the truck driver, Pity didn't see a gun, but strapped across his chest were half a dozen grenades. She eyed the truck.

Metal scraps. Wiring. A pile of mismatched tires.

Scroungers.

They could be looking to trade, she told herself. Being armed didn't mean anything out here. But she remained crouched as Finn responded to the greeting, her words too faint to make out.

The men looked at one another. One pointed at the rifle and said something. Finn started for the gun, but he put himself between her and it, a split-wound grin on his face.

Pity's heart slid into her stomach. Her free hand drew. Scroungers, maybe, but something about them was old-milk sour. She gauged the distance between her and the men, cursing herself again for leaving the rifle behind. With it, she could have sent warning shots at the intruders—or worse maybe, if they refused to take the hint. But this far away, and with three against one, her pistols were a chancy proposition at best.

What do I do?

If she broke cover now, they'd be on her in an instant. And for all that she would have joined the commune's defenses in a heartbeat, she had only ever shot at targets, never a live human. Her palms began to sweat as the sick sensation in her gut spread.

"Go on!" Finn spoke loud enough for Pity to hear this time. "Take it and go. I ain't got anything else worth stealing." She waved dismissively and set her hands on her hips, back still to Pity.

She knows I'm close. A line of sweat slid from her forehead to the bridge of her nose. *Why hasn't she called for help? She isn't so much as glancing in this direction.*

Realization bloomed in her like a frost.

They think Finn's alone. They have no idea I'm here.

And Finn was trying to keep it that way.

The grinning rider grabbed the rifle. When Finn took an angry step toward him, the man closest to her drew his handgun. He grabbed her arm and twisted, shoving her to her knees. She went stone-still as he shoved the muzzle against her temple.

"You stay right where you are, now."

Pity read the words on his lips as much as she heard them. Her muscles screamed to move, but she felt no more mobile than the surrounding trees. A primal direction rooted her, a fear-soaked sense of preservation.

Don't . . . Her thoughts were hard to hold on to, the pounding blood in her veins drowning them out. *Wait. Think. Don't toss away what advantage Finn's bought you.*

Now that Finn was partially turned toward the trees, Pity could see her eyes running back and forth over the brush, blank fear painted on her features.

I'm here, Pity thought, jaw aching with desperation to cry out. *Finn, I'm here.*

An idea struck her. She raised her gun, angling it so that sunlight winked off the silver plating.

I'm here.

Finn locked on the signal. Pity flashed one more time and dropped her arm, before the scroungers could take notice.

"Anything good?" Finn's guard called to his companions, who had begun rooting through the Ranger.

The driver pulled Finn's tools from the vehicle and tossed them to the ground. "Nothin' that'll buy you the moon, but not bad." He straightened, a cross air about him. "Finish up and come help, would you? We're not doin' all the work this time!"

Finish—

Terror prickling her skin, Pity snapped back to Finn. Her friend stared directly at her.

"For sayin' you do all the work, you two sure never get your hands dirty!"

Move! The word screamed through Pity's mind, but her body refused. Every inch of her felt carved from ice. In her hand, the gun she could pick the petals from a daisy with remained half raised, heavy as a concrete block.

Finn's gaze never left her. But the fear in her eyes was gone, replaced by soft resignation. As Pity watched, her head slid back and forth once, the movement barely perceptible. Her mouth formed a single word.

Run.

Pity ripped her other gun from its holster.

A moment later, a shot cracked the morning into shards.

CHAPTER 4

IN A MIST OF CRIMSON, FINN SLUMPED TO THE GROUND.

With a scream like a piece torn from her soul, Pity bolted from the brush, firing three shots in rapid succession and closing half the distance before the scroungers saw her coming. One of the shots took Finn's killer in the leg, toppling him. The others were lost to the frantic haze.

Taken by surprise, the two unscathed scroungers retreated toward the truck. Pity fired twice more before one turned and shot at her with her own rifle; a bullet whizzed by her ear, another tugged on her jacket. She angled toward the Ranger and threw herself behind it. Blood pounded in her veins. *Finn, get to Finn.* The thought ricocheted off the inside of her skull, obliterating every rational thought that tried to form.

"Where the hell did she come from?" one of the men yelled. Another cried out in pain.

Pity leaned through the open doors and fired. "Finn!"

More shots answered hers. One dinged off the metal above her head, clear as the chime of a bell.

In an instant, coherence returned. The world's colors were too bright, the edges of her vision too sharp, but Pity registered that both scroungers had reached the truck, and the third was nearly there, hobbling on his injured leg. Her brief advantage was spent. She was outgunned and pinned behind the Ranger. She looked around. Open ground surrounded her. Her chest tightened.

There was nowhere to go.

"Finn..." she said again, knowing no response was coming.

Too late. Only heartbeats had passed, but Pity was already far, far too late.

"Idiots! I'll handle her."

She peeked back through the doors in time to see the truck driver rip a grenade off his chest strap and pull the pin.

He readied to throw.

With no time to think, Pity sprang to her feet and aimed over the top of Ranger.

Bang!

Bang!

Her shots caught the driver in the shoulder. The grenade slipped from his fingers.

She had just enough time to register the shock on the scroungers' faces before the air exploded.

The first thing was darkness.

On its heels followed a high-pitched whine and an acrid burning smell. Finally came the pain. It was everywhere, like the whine and the darkness. Her head pounded with it, sending shock waves of nausea through her. She tried to swallow and tasted...dirt? The damp earth lay beneath her, bits of grass poking her in the face.

What...?

She tried to move her legs. A cold stab of panic shot through her when she couldn't. She tried again and realized that it wasn't her legs that weren't obeying—something was pinning them. She lay still instead, skull throbbing with each beat of her heart. The darkness wasn't night. Something was draped over her. She smelled canvas and wax among the char and scorched oil.

The roof of the Ranger. But before she could fathom why it was on top of her and not on top of the Ranger, she heard another, unmistakable sound.

Footsteps.

Her thoughts slammed into place.

The scroungers.

A moment ago her guns had been in her hands. Now they held nothing. She slid one arm outward. The movement sent a bolt of pain up her side. She cried out.

The footsteps stopped. "Hey!" said a muffled voice. "Someone's still alive!"

There was no time. Pity shifted her other arm, bracing for

agony, but it responded without complaint. She pawed blindly at the ground around her.

"C'mon, over here!" More footsteps.

They were coming.

Her fingers brushed steel. Pity grabbed the pistol, slipping her finger into the trigger and cocking the hammer as the debris pinning her began to shift.

One chance.

Light flooded in, scorching her vision. She angled the barrel up as the canvas was lifted and tossed to the side.

She fired.

"Holy shit!" A blurry figure tumbled backward.

The shot had gone wide. As her vision broke apart and came back together, Pity raised the gun again, but a lightning sear of pain shot through her wrist. The gun flew from her grip as it was wrenched to one side. Another silhouette appeared, quickly lost as a gray fog of unconsciousness enveloped her again.

"She's waking up."

Her ears still rang. Everything still hurt. And this time Pity couldn't move at all. Not a finger or a toe. Her eyes cast around helplessly. She was in a room but could see nothing except a metal ceiling above her and a blank wall to her right. A clipped yelp escaped from between her frozen lips.

"Hey, shhhh." A face appeared in her field of vision: a young man around her age, dressed in filthy clothes. He was milk pale, a feature amplified by his spiked hair dyed oil-slick black. Except for the tips, which were cyan. At least a dozen silver rings and studs pierced his eyebrows, lips, and ears.

Another scrounger?

"Don't try to move," he said. "We didn't know if you had internal injuries, so we gave you a paralytic to be safe."

A paralytic? Pity took a sharp breath. Where would a scrounger have gotten paralytics?

"You were lucky. A mild concussion, a lot of bruises and scrapes, but you're alive."

"Move, Max." He was replaced by an umber-skinned woman at least a decade his senior. She had a square face and dimpled cheeks, with dark eyes that would have been beautiful had they carried any hint of softness. "I'm going to un-paralyze you now. *You* are going to behave yourself. If you don't, I'm going to shoot you in the knee. Blink twice if you understand."

Pity blinked twice. She felt the prick of a med injector in her neck.

"Try to sit up," said Max.

"Slowly," warned the woman.

Pity lifted herself onto one elbow, muscles waking slowly. Her other arm ached like the devil, but she could move it without much effort. She lay on a narrow cot. There was another like it nearby, along with a small seating area built into the wall and a tiny kitchen. The rest of the space was occupied by storage containers of all sizes. There were no windows. A wave of pain radiated through her body. She closed her eyes and leaned over the side of the bed, afraid she would be sick. It was then that she noticed the vibration—a distinct, subtle turbulence.

This wasn't a room...it was a vehicle.

And it was moving.

"Finn!" Her eyes flew open. "Where's Finn?"

The woman stepped away, crossing her arms as she leaned against a counter littered with bandages and a portable medical scanner. A row of metal cabinets with coded locks ran above her head. "Was Finn one of those bodies back there? Because they're right where we left them."

"Geez, Olivia!" Max perched on the edge of the bed beside her. What she had taken for filth on his clothing were actually streaks and splatters of paint, in all colors. "We saw the smoke. What happened?"

"Finn and I...we..." Pity grasped for the words. "Scroungers attacked our camp. They...they killed..." The room wavered as her lungs emptied. She fell back onto the bed. *No.* The word beat in her head, worse than the pain. *No, no, no.* "They killed her and...and you just left her there?"

Max's brow furled. "There was nothing we could—"

"Did you bury her? Did you do anything?"

"She was *dead*," said Olivia.

"You just left her there!" Pity shot up again, oblivious to her injuries, only to have Max push her back down.

"We had to," he pressed. "It was dangerous to linger, and you were hurt."

She shoved him away, searching for something to say but finding nothing.

Too late. A scream built in her chest, unable to go anywhere. *She was right there, and you just watched them—*

The thought refused to finish.

"It's not all bad," Olivia said. "These survived." Pity looked over to see her dangling the gun belt in one hand and brandishing a revolver in the other. "They're awfully nice."

Pity's cheeks burned with anger. "Those are mine! Give them to me!"

"Not a chance." Olivia stashed the weapons in a cabinet above her head. When she closed it, the touch pad flashed red. *Locked.*

"They belong to *me.*"

"And I say they're good payment for saving your life."

She glared at Olivia, who glared right back and let a hand fall to her side. Strapped to her hip was a leather whip, coiled in a tight circle. Pity recalled the pain from before and looked at her wrist. Ringing it was a wide bruise.

Max sighed. "Olivia, please..."

"We don't know her from Adam, Max. And she tried to kill you."

"I didn't—" Pity began, but the vehicle's vibrations suddenly tapered off and ceased.

A moment later a door opened at the front of the compartment. A massive, densely muscled man ducked through it, carrying a rifle.

"My turn to drive?" said Olivia.

He shook his bald, round head. Other than a thin strip of dark hair on his chin, he was clean-shaven. "Time to swap out the fuel cell. How's our guest?"

Olivia swatted a hand. "She's fine."

"Is that true, miss?" His voice was deep but smooth.

Pity grimaced. "No."

"Of course not." When he approached the bed and reached

out a huge, flat hand, she eyed it warily but shook it. "Santino Quintano," he said. "Santino, por favor. And you are?"

"We hadn't gotten there yet," said Max.

"Serendipity." Her voice was as hollow as an old bone. "Jones. Everyone calls me Pity."

"Pity," Santino continued, "you were very lucky today. We can drop you at the next outpost or commune we pass. They will have real medical facilities and—"

"No!" she cried. "I mean, I can't..." She hesitated, thoughts tangling. *Finn...her guns...* The pounding in her head intensified. She pressed the heel of her hand to her forehead. When she looked up again, everyone was staring at her.

"Hmm." Santino tipped his head. "Judging by your clothes, I'd guess you're off a commune?"

She nodded.

"And where were you headed?"

"East."

"Just east?"

"Yeah." She cooled her tone. "Just east."

Olivia snickered. "Runaways. Cute. Did you think you were going to stroll into Columbia and find the streets paved with gold and all the prosperity you could carry? You would have been lucky to find a bed to rent in the lower slums. What were you thinking?"

"We were thinking"—her voice cracked—"that we had to get away from where we were." *No,* she thought. *I needed to get away.* Pity swallowed at the lump that had formed in her throat. "It doesn't matter. But I...can't go back there."

"Comprendo, chiquita," said Santino. "But you can't come with us."

"Why not?" balked Max, getting to his feet.

"Max—"

"She's hurt and alone, with nothing. Her friend is dead and she says she can't go home. So why can't she come with us?"

"I do have something," Pity interjected. "I've got my guns."

Olivia snickered. "Hon, you ain't even got that."

"If she's a good shot," Max pressed, "Beau might take her on. He's always complaining about the lack of—"

"Max," Santino warned. "We have a job to finish."

"The job's done," he countered.

"The package still needs to be delivered."

"And it will be, whether she's with us or not," said Max.

"What makes you think a girl like her is going to want to go where we're going?" Olivia said.

"Why?" Pity spat, irritated at being pecked over like a bit of corn by crows. "Where *are* you going?"

"End of the world." One side of Max's mouth turned up proudly. "We're headed for Cessation."

CHAPTER 5

HELL, AS PITY HAD HEARD THE CITY DESCRIBED, SOUNDED exactly like what she knew of Cessation: hedonistic, ungodly, full of sinners. Outside the CONA embrace, where there was no government, no morals, and no law. As different from the communes as it could be—a city dedicated unto itself.

"Sounds great," she said.

Max brightened. "Really?"

"No. But I don't have much choice, do I?" She stared at the locked cabinet. *And I'm not going anywhere without my guns.*

Santino looked at Olivia, who shrugged. "I say we dump her at the nearest CONA outpost. And that's only so we didn't waste our time saving her sorry ass."

Pity waited as Santino deliberated her fate. It was his decision to make—that much was obvious. Her heart pounded harder with every passing moment, each beat like a shard of glass piercing the back of the eye, but she forced herself to hold his golden-brown gaze. What if he decided to leave her? Were they anywhere near the 87th? By now her father might know they—

A different sort of pain stabbed her.

—*she* was gone. Pity didn't know how much dust he'd kick up over her, but she had a good idea what would happen if she ended up back within his reach.

At last, Santino took a deep breath. "Stopping might mean curious officials, and we don't need that. So we take her with us. But Olivia holds on to her weapons, and, Max, she's your responsibility. Now and when we get home. Me entiendes?"

Max nodded.

"Great—Maxxy gets a pet and we get another damn passenger." Olivia stomped over to a storage crate and typed a code into the lock. It clicked open. She drew out a squat metal cylinder. "C'mon, I'll help you swap the cell."

Santino checked his rifle. "Let's be quick. Way things have gone today I don't want to be idle any longer than we need to. Keep an eye on her, Max."

"Both eyes," said Olivia as they exited the front of the vehicle.

"Thank you," Pity said when they were gone. "For not letting them leave me."

"No problem." The rings at the edge of his mouth twitched up. "I know something about needing to get somewhere other than where you're supposed to be. How are you feeling?"

"My head hurts." Everything hurt: her bones, her skin, her

soul. *Finn's dead.* The thought gored her over and over—*Finn's dead, Finn's dead.*

And it's all my fault.

"Here, hold still." Max pressed another med injector into Pity's arm. The pain washed away like dust in a summer rain. "Better?"

She nodded, not trusting her voice. Without the pain to keep them at bay, Finn's final moments flickered in memory. Why hadn't she done something? Why had she just *watched?*

"It's okay. You don't need to hold it in."

"I'm...not..." She curled forward, chest tightening. The room wavered through the gathering tears.

Finn.

"I can't leave you alone, but I don't really need both eyes on you, either." Max put on a pair of headphones and then grabbed a sheaf of papers and some pencils. He sat down at the seating area, turning slightly away. "If you need anything, I'm right here."

He began to scribble. True to his word, he didn't so much as glance back, not for the several minutes Pity watched.

Finally, she rolled toward the wall and let the tears flow.

Pity slept. When she woke, Max made her tea. She cried and slept some more, grief and exhaustion coming in shifts. She remained bedridden until the following morning, when, with careful steps, she hobbled over to where Max was washing dishes. They were nearly the same height, and their eyes met when he looked up from the indentation that passed as a sink. For a moment, Pity faltered. His appearance was still an oddity to her, but Max had a disarming air to him, a trait that served to both calm and unnerve her in equal measure. Despite the kindness he'd shown, he was, Pity reminded herself, a stranger.

"Can I help?" She shifted her weight from one foot to the other. "I can't lie there any longer."

"You can dry." He handed her a towel. "Any better this morning?"

She grimaced. "My body feels like one big bruise."

"What about the rest of you?"

The question hung in the air.

"Sorry," he said, "I didn't mean to—"

"It's okay. But can we talk about something else?"

"Like what?"

She wiped the water from a plate. "Like who y'all are. You're not scroungers, and you don't strike me as drifters."

"No, we usually stay put in Cessation."

"Were you born there?"

"No." Max laughed and scratched the back of his head. His hair was so dark that Pity half expected his hand to come away stained inky black. "But who is? Cessation is someplace you end up, not where you start."

A weak smile crept onto her lips. "And this vehicle—it's a mobile command, isn't it? From the war?"

"You've seen one before?"

"Not in person, but I've heard about them." Metal fortresses on treads, mobile commands were predecessors to the near-impenetrable TransRail train cars. It would take a missile strike to even scratch one. Pity thought of the Ranger and felt like a fool. How could she and Finn have thought they were safe? "Where did you get it?"

"We're only borrowing it." He handed her a bowl. "My turn for a question. Why did you run away? You *did* run away, right?"

"Yes." She lowered her gaze. "My father was trying to send me to another commune."

"Why?"

Pity shrugged, wincing at the pain that accompanied the gesture. "Spite, mostly. He hated my mother, never mind she's been dead for years. Not that there was much in the commune for me anyway...except...except for Finn." Her breath snagged in her lungs and trembled there, trapped. She gripped the edge of the counter.

"Hey." Max dropped the cup he was washing. "You're shaking."

"I'm fine." She gasped, unable to get enough air. "It's...it's just she..."

"Sit down," he ordered. "You shouldn't be on your feet yet."

Pity backed up against the cot and collapsed, hardly feeling the pain that rippled through her. Tears filled her eyes once more. "She shouldn't have been with me." The leaden words tumbled from her tongue, unbidden. "She should be on the commune right now, elbow-deep in an engine. That life was killing me, but she was the one who ended up dead. It's all my fault."

"Don't say that." The sharpness in Max's tone pierced her daze. "You weren't the one who pulled the trigger."

"But I didn't do anything to stop it, either. And now..."

Pity shuddered as reality bit deep, a warped inversion of her brief, hopeful dream. First east, now west—from the stalwart CONA cities to the biggest den of sinners on the continent. Her brief, hopeful dream was as dead as Finn. Even her guns weren't in her possession anymore. "Oh, Lord, what am I going to do?"

Max went down on one knee beside her. "You're going to come with us," he said calmly, "and figure things out from there. Cessation is...It's not like what you've heard. I mean, it *is,* but it's more. There are all sorts there—dissidents and drifters, Ex-Pats, CONA citizens, and free folks. Don't worry. There's always work for a girl who—"

Her head snapped up.

"That's not what I meant!" He searched for a moment. "Look, if you change your mind when we get there, I'll put you on the train myself. I promise."

His gray eyes were earnest, without a hint of malice, but Pity recoiled. Everything suddenly seemed like a terrible idea. Maybe it wasn't too late to go back. Maybe her father *wouldn't* kill her.

"Why are you being so nice? I don't know you...any of you."

"You don't," Max said quietly. "But we helped you when we could have left you behind."

The door to the cab opened, and Olivia stepped through. She stopped short. "Did I interrupt something?"

"No." Max got to his feet. "We were discussing what Pity might do once we get to Cessation."

"Oh, yeah?" Olivia went to a storage bin and fished out an apple. "Did you get around yet to telling her what you do?"

"No," Pity said, tensing with suspicion. "He didn't."

But Max swelled with pride. "I'm with the Theatre."

She waited. "The Theatre?"

"Don't they know about us in the communes?" Some of the pride evaporated. "The grandest show since before the Pacific Event? Cessation's crown jewel of entertainment?"

"Sorry, no."

"Damn, I really thought you would have heard about us…"

"Heard about *who*?"

Max threw out his arms with a flourish. "Halcyon Singh's Theatre Vespertine."

The name meant nothing. "So…you're an actor?"

Olivia snickered and took a wet bite of apple.

"Uh, no," Max replied. "I mean, it's not that kind of theatre. I do costumes and painting—backdrops, sets, skin."

"Skin?"

"Some of the costumes are…unconventional."

"What about you?" Pity said to Olivia. "Are you with the Theatre, too?"

"Me?" The woman chewed and swallowed. "Nope. I'm just a bartender."

Without another word, Olivia returned to the front cab, closing the door after her. The click of its lock was a grim reminder that, for all intents and purposes, Pity was in a cage. Where she was going—and what she was going to do when she got there—wasn't entirely in her control. Which meant that she needed to bide her time. Falling to pieces wouldn't bring Finn back or get her anywhere at all.

"I'm sorry," she said to Max, "for getting worked up. Y'all have been nothing but kind to me…more or less."

Max smiled. "Olivia is slow to warm to strangers. Give her some time."

"Sure," Pity said aloud, staring at the locked cabinets.

I don't want her warmth, she thought. *I want my guns.*

They hit the desert a day later. Though she remained confined to the back of the vehicle, Pity didn't need to see it. She was familiar with the parched, empty steppe shown in CONA broadcasts, the edge of the lifeless scar left by the Pacific Event more than fifty years before. To this day no one knew exactly what had happened—the nature of the weapon or who had unleashed it or even whether it had been an intentional act. Only that it had left huge portions of the world uninhabitable and erased civilizations that had endured for millennia.

The bleak history that led up to it was well documented, though: escalating global conflicts, overpopulation-driven biological terrorism that left so many infertile. The aftermath of the Pacific Event was little better, the desperate exodus eastward too much for an already strained nation to bear. In comparison, the conflict waged between the Confederation of North America and the United Patriot Front hardly seemed worth spilling a tear over. Bloody as it had been, it was an ugly sort of proof that life could, and would, go on.

Is it the same for you? she asked herself. *How much can you lose and still go on?*

Without windows in the vehicle, Pity measured time in meals. It was morning when Max made breakfast, night when he said it was time for dinner. She helped him cook, though there wasn't much to it: open a pack, heat something up, add water to something else. Still, the work helped to quiet the grim ruminations that stumbled through her head like drunks: where she was going, what she was going to do, and what an artist, a bartender, and a soldier were doing in the middle of nowhere with a mobile command.

And Finn, left behind to rot.

In late afternoon on the third day, the door to the cab opened.

"We're almost at Last Stop," Santino called, still strapped into the driver's seat.

Max, fussing over the status display on one of the larger storage containers, looked up. "Can I bring Pity up front?"

"Why not? Olivia, you drive. Pity, take her seat."

Pity put down the rag she was wiping the counter with. "Last Stop?"

"The last station on the TransRail, ten miles outside the border of Cessation." Santino slipped into the back. "Cargo five-by-five, Max? I want it ready to move as soon as we get to Cas."

"All set." Max took Pity by the arm and practically pushed her through the door.

A curved control board took up half the front cab. The rest of the space was filled with the operators' seats. Pity climbed into the empty one.

Max leaned in over her shoulder and pointed. "There's the station."

"And more," Olivia said as they drew closer, her tone grim. "Might want to close your eyes, kid."

It was too late. Pity had seen the station. With the TransRail line running into the center, it was little more than a sprawling

mass of dark buildings growing darker as the sun set. But there
was no mistaking what lay just outside its razor-wire fencing.
From a scaffold hung half a dozen bodies, their shadows goug-
ing long, dark fissures across the baked earth. As the mobile
command passed by, Pity could see a painted placard above
them, bearing the CONA seal and one word: CRIMINALS.

She suppressed a shudder, thankful for the black hoods hiding the corpses' faces. "What did they do?"

"Who knows." Olivia accelerated, leaving the ugly sight
behind. "Murdered a whole squad of CONA soldiers. Stole a
heel of bread. It's not the crime that's the point. It's the warning."

Max sighed. "Even though they have little presence this far
out, CONA authority officially ends at Last Stop." A note of bitterness crept into his voice. "A fact they like to remind Cessation
of. Step one foot over the line and... Well, I'm sorry. That's not
what I wanted you to see."

Pity remembered the scrounger. "I've seen worse. It's just
that... I don't know."

Olivia looked at her askew. "You expected that sort of thing
from the other side of the equation?"

Pity didn't answer, not wanting to admit Olivia was right.
She would have ascribed such a grotesque act to Cessation or
dissidents long before CONA. Even the scrounger her father had
caught would never have been displayed so.

Unease filled her. It was more than the hanged men; she was
now truly beyond the world she knew, in the company of strangers. And yet...

Max put a hand on her shoulder. Maybe he was only steadying himself, but some of her distress receded. He was also

nothing like she had imagined a dissident to be. With no reason to, he'd helped her. And despite her better judgment, she was beginning to trust him.

Don't be stupid, she reminded herself. *Max might be all right, but you don't know what's coming.*

For a while there was nothing to see except desert, stained orange by the setting sun. Then, as true night descended, a haze of light appeared, bleeding out of the ground. That luminescence resolved itself into colors and silhouettes. As she realized what she was seeing, she gasped, eliciting a chuckle from Max.

Olivia rolled her eyes. "He never gets tired of this part."

In the windshield, Max's reflection grinned like a child, his piercings glinting and winking. "Welcome to Cessation, Serendipity Jones," he said. "The last place on the continent where you can do whatever the hell you want."

CHAPTER 6

OLIVIA SLOWED AS THEY CAME UPON THE CITY. TENTS—hundreds of them—were scattered on either side of the road, a drab forest of canvas flickering with the glow of cooking fires. A crowd of people gathered as the vehicle approached, all draped in flowing white robes.

"They never give up," muttered Olivia.

Pity watched as the robed figures waved signs covered in scripture and called out soundlessly from beyond the thick windshield. Some kneeled at the edge of the asphalt, hands folded in prayer. "Who are they?"

"They call themselves Reformationists," Max said. "Don't mind them. They preach on the streets and march through the city sometimes, but otherwise, they don't do much more than what you see now."

"They're masochists," said Olivia. "Who else would come all this way to squat in the desert, eat out of cans, and try to save souls that don't need saving?" She slammed a fist against the console. A horn pierced the air. The Reformationists jumped and stumbled back, faces stiff with fright.

"Was that necessary?" said Max.

Olivia chuckled. "No."

The camp ended and the city began, jutting from the soil like a fairy-tale oasis. For a moment, Pity could see only lights. There were more than she had ever seen in one place, an ever-shifting kaleidoscope of colors. Unlike the eastern cities she'd seen on the broadcasts, there were no proud towers standing in perfect array, no sage gold domes floating above thick columns. The buildings in Cessation were tightly packed and varied, enveloping the streets like a motley cave. Pity shrank in her seat, senses overloaded.

Blinking. Flashing. Twists of shadow. Words and images flickered and disappeared—a snippet of a news broadcast; a beautiful woman with wet, pouting lips. Signs sizzled and drenched doorways in red and purple and green. Laser-writ words appeared on the sides of buildings—advertising drinks, entertainment, and things Pity didn't comprehend—only to disappear a few seconds later.

And the people...

The street steadily filled until there were so many pedestrians that Olivia had to reduce their speed to a crawl. Folks strolled or walked or ran, paying little attention to the massive conveyance rumbling in their midst. A woman danced in front of their headlights, wearing a gown that shimmered like the ripples in a lake. She nearly collided with a man in rags, who yelled at her, his mouth full of stained teeth.

On one corner, Pity spotted a band of men and women astride motorcycles, brandishing rifles and razor-edged stares. Patches marked them as Ex-Pats—former United Patriot Front fighters and their supporters. Unwilling to accept defeat, even after two decades, they still attacked CONA outposts from time to time. Seeing them stirred an odd sensation in Pity. Had any of them fought alongside her mother? If her mother hadn't been captured, was this where her life's path would have led? Pity stared until they were out of sight.

Gilding the chaos, hawkers weaved among the crowd, proffering their goods and services. Booths, erected in every bare spot on the sidewalk, displayed trinkets and food and things Pity didn't recognize. But she could almost hear the sizzle of the hot fat, smell the roasting meat.

Beyond the booths were alleys, where the lights abruptly ceased. Some folks gave these a wide berth. Others slipped into them, alone or in groups, the shadows swallowing them like dark water.

A series of thumps sounded on the roof.

Olivia slammed on the brakes. "What the hell?"

Two youths slid into view, dressed entirely in crimson. Grinning madly, they clung to the top of the vehicle with one hand. With the other, they banged on the windshield of the cab.

"Goddamn Old Reds," Olivia said through gritted teeth.

The blond girl dangling in front of Pity waved in a way that was anything but friendly.

"One of the gangs," Max explained.

The girl pointed a finger at Pity and then put it in her mouth. Pity started as she bit down hard. As blood dribbled from the wound, the girl drew a smiley face on the windshield.

"That's it," said Olivia. "I'm gonna shoot those little—"

Something out of sight caught the Old Reds' attention. They traded a look of manic desire and jumped from the vehicle, bolting away like wolves after prey. Pity's stomach clenched, the cold fear returning. Before her, the bloody smile ran in rivulets down the glass. *Is this a city,* she thought, *or an asylum?*

"Should have left her in back," said Olivia. "Look—her mind is going to break into pieces before we even make it to Cas."

Pity stiffened. "No, it's not."

"You'd better keep your wits—it doesn't get any easier than this."

"I'm *fine.*" She stared straight ahead, her jaw set. "Who's Cas?"

Max pointed. "Not who, where. It's home."

Ahead of them the structures ceased, creating a circular perimeter around a large, open area. At the center stood a bone-white building flooded in light, dwarfing everything around it. The road they were following split and circled around a massive marble fountain before joining again at the building's entrance. Above that, written in lights that blinked and chased one another into infinity, was a single word.

CASIMIR.

Despite her unease, Pity felt a twinge of disappointment when Olivia steered them off the main road and onto a plainer, narrower avenue. It snaked around the side of the building, where they turned onto a ramp that descended into a concrete tunnel. The open air and bright lights disappeared, replaced by sour yellow incandescence and vague claustrophobia. Finally, they entered a sprawling garage. The mobile command pulled off to one side and ground to a stop.

"Let's move." Olivia shoved the cab door open and leapt out, Max on her heels.

Pity was descending with more caution when a skinny, dun-haired man in oil-stained coveralls appeared.

"Baby! You're back!" he cried.

Pity glanced at Olivia.

"Oh, no, he is not talking to *me*. Relax, Widmer, we brought her home safe and sound."

"You damn well better have!" He ignored Pity completely, hands running over the mobile command's treads and exterior armor. "Why is there *blood* on the windshield?"

"It'll wash off, Wid." Santino sauntered up from the back of the vehicle. In one hand he carried Pity's gun belt. Her heart jumped, but he tossed it to Olivia, who strapped it around her waist. "Call the porters. Big crate in the back. We're heading upstairs."

Widmer dipped his head. "You got it."

Pity trailed behind as they crossed the garage, the click of their steps echoing through its vast expanse. At the back wall was a set of elevators. It was a short ride—smooth and silent, nothing like the silo elevators on the commune.

The doors opened into a crescent-shaped room, all fresh cream and silver trimming. To Pity's left was a line of glass doors, through which she spotted the fountain. Enraptured by Casimir's entrance, she stumbled as she stepped from the elevator and sank into lush carpet. She stared at her boots, simultaneously embarrassed that they were filthy and filled with the urge to pull them off and go barefoot. She had never walked across anything so sumptuous.

Opposite the entrance was a throng of people, crowded before a set of gilded doors.

"Excuse me." Santino's huge form parted the press of chattering bodies with ease. Pity kept her nose practically planted in Olivia's back as they moved forward.

"Hey," said Max. "From here on, stick close to me, okay?"

She glanced back at him. He looked almost normal, his blue spikes and silver rings dull compared to the garishness that surrounded them. "Why?"

"Because right now you're a stranger. But you're less of a stranger so long as you're with us. Understand?"

"I . . . Yes."

They broke free from the pack. Before the gilded doors stood half a dozen men in gray uniforms with rifles and shock sticks, and eyes as hard as diamonds. Two silver stars were pinned to their collars.

"Tin Men," Max whispered. "Casimir's security force."

"I do not accept this!" A shrill man in an absurd grass-hued suit squared off against the guards. "I came all the way to this dusty shit hole, and if I want in, I'm getting in!"

"Sir," said a bald man the size of a bear, his tone unyielding, "step away."

"The hell I will!" Green Suit poked the behemoth in the chest. "I want to talk to your boss."

The Tin Man grabbed the digit that prodded him. Pity winced at the audible crack that followed. "Noted," he said over the scream of pain. His gaze rose to Santino. "Sir?"

"Toss him," replied Santino.

Another Tin Man seized the offender by the collar and dragged him, whimpering, back into the now significantly quieter crowd.

"Home sweet home." Olivia smirked.

The bald Tin Man nodded at Pity. "Sir?"

"With us," Santino replied.

"Welcome to Casimir, miss." He opened the doors.

Welcome was not a word Pity would have used to describe how she felt in that moment. With Max at her side, she steeled herself as the cream and silver gave way to red and gold, velvet and burnished wood.

It did little good. Luxury unlike any she had ever seen assailed her. At least three stories high, the room they entered was so deep that the back wall was lost to dusky lighting and a haze of cigar smoke. Numerous as ants in a hill, people stood at tables, dealing cards and tossing dice, moving markers and tapping screens. They lounged in rounded booths or on the myriad of sofas and plush chairs scattered about. A hum of gaming, laughter, and the clinking of glasses enveloped Pity. Music played somewhere, its tune lost among a buzzing cacophony of delight.

Pity followed Max down a carpeted staircase, hardly watching where she put her feet as she struggled to take everything in. At the bottom was another fountain, a miniature twin to the one outside. Light shifted below its waters, and atop its center sat a golden mermaid with long hair and bare breasts. As Pity stared at it, the mermaid turned her head and winked.

Pity froze. She looked around the room again, eyes flitting from person to person, truly seeing this time. Her gaze fell on a woman in a tiny skirt, a feather boa, and nothing else, with her arm locked through that of a suited gentleman. A young man in fluttering azure trousers sauntered past the couple, beckoned by a woman reclining on a velvet chaise.

"Max." Her voice cracked. "Casimir...is it a brothel?"

"It's...a lot of things."

"These people are prostitutes." Pity took an involuntary step backward. *Harlots...low people...*From the orations on the commune, she knew there were prostitutes in Cessation. She simply hadn't expected so *many.*

Max grabbed her hand. *Hard.* "It's a brothel, sure, and a gambling hall and about a hundred other things. It's also the safest place in the whole city. Casimir runs Cessation. Out there"—he pointed to where they had come from—"you take your chances."

She glanced down at the fingers encasing hers. The pace of her heart, already faster than normal, quickened. "Why didn't you tell me this before?"

"Because all that matters is that as long as you're with us, you're safe." Max let go.

Pity wished he hadn't. For a moment, his touch had seemed to carry the safety he promised. "Are you certain?"

"More or less."

That was all the assurance she was going to get, apparently. Pity looked back at the line of guards at the door and then to the brothel floor, where Santino and Olivia were waiting. The heel of Olivia's hand rested on the butt of one gun. Pity's jaw tightened. *Get your guns. Then worry about everything else.* For the thousandth time in the past few days, she wished Finn were beside her. Finn would have laughed at the spectacle—and at Pity's reaction—before diving right in.

"Everything okay?" Santino called.

"Peachy," she snapped, striding past Max.

They weren't fooled.

"Don't worry," Olivia said. "No one bites unless you pay them to."

Her face burned.

"Hey, San." A lithe male figure pounced on Santino and wrapped his arms around the big man's neck. He had short flaxen hair and angelic features—an innocence that stopped at his neck. The sparkling corset and tiny shorts he wore made Pity's eyes plunge to the floor. "It's been *forever*. You coming to see me tonight?"

Santino gave a wry smile and pushed him down, though not without affection. "Still on the job, chico."

The young man pouted. "You know what they say about all work and no play." He tossed a wink in Max's direction as he strode to where a young woman with long dark hair and a handsome copper-skinned young man lounged. When he said something to them, they turned toward the new arrivals. The young woman grinned and blew a kiss at Max, who waved back.

"Well, there are our little lost lambs!"

Pity's attention turned to the woman flouncing over to them. Her butter-yellow ringlets bounced as she approached, as did her bosom, which threatened to spill over the top of her pink dress, cinched so tightly that Pity wondered how she could breathe. With its skirt of white ruffles and lace, she looked like a disturbingly sensuous doll.

"Evening, Flossie." Santino pecked her on the cheek. "How's business?"

"Brisk as always, sugar." Her voice lilted like a bell.

"You seen Halcyon tonight?"

"Oh, yes," Flossie purred. "He's upstairs. With Miss Selene."

"Hmm," said Santino. "Can you let them know we're—"

"She already knows," said Flossie. "She wants y'all there, pronto."

Santino indicated Pity. "We picked up a stray. Can you have someone take care of her until we're done?"

"Oh, honey, you know I'd make sure she had the *best* of care…" Flossie sauntered over to Pity and eyed her. "But Miss Selene said *all* of you. And when she says *all*, you know she means *all*."

Pity turned to Max, whose face was tinged with apprehension. "Who's Miss Selene?" she whispered.

"Someone," he said in an equally low voice, "we shouldn't keep waiting."

CHAPTER 7

PITY'S GAZE FLITTED BETWEEN SAFE AND UNSAFE AS THEY traveled through the room: the luxuriously patterned carpet... a pile of cushions swarming with bodies...Santino's broad back...a couple in a booth furiously grasping at each other. Her body roiled with nervousness, embarrassment, and a twisted knot of other sensations she didn't want to dwell on.

They came to another elevator, with more Tin Men positioned on each side. Pity pressed herself into the back of the space, feeling her stomach drop as their ascent began. There were no buttons for other floors, only a single display that ticked up steadily. Finally, the doors slid apart to reveal a vast floor of black marble. It was so polished that when she stepped onto it, Pity locked eyes with a reflection of herself.

This room was as large as the one they had left but nearly

empty, its dark floor stretching to meet bleached white walls with high, arched windows. Plants in massive stone pots were positioned at intervals—ferns, bushes, even small fruit trees. The only other fixture in the room was a desk, set before an open terrace. Gauzy curtains floated in a light breeze.

Two men flanked either side of the desk. The one on the left, wearing an immaculate gray suit, had pale eyes in a handsome but severe face. Not a hair on his head was out of place. *Clean* was the first word that popped into Pity's mind as his raptor's gaze tracked them. *Dangerous* was the second. But it was the lanky man on the right who invariably drew her attention; he was dressed in a purple-and-orange-striped tuxedo.

It wasn't until the woman behind the desk stood that Pity took note of her, though it was the tuxedoed man who spoke first.

"Santino, Santino, Santino, my good man! Wonderful to have you back." The long tails of the tuxedo fluttered as he approached them. "Dear Olivia! Cessation was a drearier place without your presence."

Olivia snorted.

"And Max! Without Max the color was all gone. Everything was gray, cloudy, dismal—"

"Halcyon."

A single word from the woman quieted him immediately. He backed away, smoothing his dark hair as she stood.

"It's good to be home, Halcyon." Santino bowed his head respectfully to the woman. "Miss Selene."

In a sleek black dress, her petite form moved with feline poise, eyes downcast as the tips of her fingers trailed across the desk. Pity could make out the digital displays set into it, reflecting off a shallow bowl filled with decorative glass spheres set on a corner of the surface.

"Everything went smoothly?"

"Yes, ma'am," said Santino. "The porters—"

"Delivered your package moments ago." She flicked a hand at a transport container nearby. "And it appears you acquired an additional body as well. Who is she?"

Pity felt the woman's eyes sear into her before she found the courage to meet them. Once she did, she was afraid to look away. Full-cheeked, with a delicate nose and golden skin, Miss Selene had the look of a predator considering its prey, trying to decide if she was hungry or not. From the strands of gray in her deep brown hair and the faint lines that crimped the edges of her eyes, Pity guessed that she was a few years older than her mother would have been, had she still been alive.

"Your show, Max," said Santino.

Max cleared his throat. "We found her on the plains, ma'am. Scroungers killed her friend. She was injured."

The careful subservience in his voice unnerved Pity even more. *Who was this woman?*

"And why," Selene continued, "did you bring her here?"

"Well, because, uh…" Max faltered.

"Because I asked them to." Pity brushed by him, taking a few steps toward the desk. In a flash of movement, a handgun was leveled at her head.

"Stay right there," said the gray-suited man. His tone was civil but as chilly as a winter wind.

Pity took a slow step backward. Common sense told her

to keep quiet, but an explanation bubbled out anyway. "I had nowhere else to go."

Selene moved around the desk, paying no attention to the man in the gray suit as she crossed in front of him. He sidestepped deftly, keeping Pity in his sights. A cold sweat broke out on the back of Pity's neck. She said a silent prayer for intervention— from Santino, Max, the good Lord himself—but had the sudden and distinct feeling that she was on her own.

Selene's expression was pleasantly neutral as she came closer, a hint of perfume preceding her like a warm breath. "Too rough for an easterner, too well fed to be a dissident. Commune worker?"

Pity nodded once.

"Seeking your fortune far from the dirt and hard work?" Selene smiled faintly. "Cessation has seen its share of runaways. Most don't last long. Perhaps you should reconsider your stay here, Miss—?"

"Pity."

"Pity?" Her head tilted in curiosity. "Not a very well-fortuned name."

"It's Serendipity, actually. Serendipity Jones."

"Those two names are rather polar," said Selene. "Which, pray tell, do you tend toward?"

"Right at this moment, ma'am? I'm hoping for the luckier one."

Selene's laugh was surprisingly melodious. "Take my advice," she said. "Return home while there is still time to forgive your youthful foolishness. I'm sure you're missed."

Pity's fear shifted to frustration. "With all due respect,

ma'am, the best thing I've got waiting for me back there is a beating I may not walk away from. And if I do, things will only get worse."

Selene stared at her for a moment, her long-lashed eyes blinking once. Without looking away, she called back over her shoulder. "Beau, would you put that thing away."

The gun disappeared into his jacket. The intensity etched on his face did not. Pity was certain the weapon would reappear in a heartbeat if needed.

"So," Selene continued, "you want to stay in Cessation."

"I...do." It was a half-truth at best, but if Selene noticed it, she gave no indication.

"And how do you expect to make your way? I'm sure a CONA-raised young lady such as yourself knows that little in this world comes free." She lifted Pity's chin with one dark-nailed finger. "How old are you? Has Flossie gotten a look at her yet?"

Pity jerked her head away. "I'm not interested in selling myself, ma'am."

A flash of amusement crossed the woman's face. "It's not a calling for everyone, I suppose."

"I didn't run from hard work," Pity said. "I'll scrub toilets if that's where the need is."

Selene raised an eyebrow. "And that's the best you have to offer?"

She felt her cheeks redden. "No. My mother was a sniper in the war. She taught me to shoot."

A small smile appeared on Selene's lips. "We do learn so

much from our mothers, don't we? Marksmanship is something you're proficient in, then?"

There were better times for humility, Pity decided. "I'm the best." *So why didn't you save Finn?* The thought slithered into her mind before she could stop it, searing with accusation. She fought to remain focused on the opportunity presented. "But Olivia took my guns."

It was a gamble, but one that was rewarded when Selene gestured. "Bring her weapons here, please."

With unenthusiastic obedience, Olivia unclasped the belt and put it on the desk, then returned to her place beside Santino.

Selene removed one of the revolvers and held it gingerly. "Lovely." She eyed Pity again and returned the gun to its holster. "Santino? This would be a good time to complete our other business, I think. The package, please."

Confused, Pity waited for Selene to say something more to her, but the woman's attention had shifted. Selene returned to her seat behind the desk. The guns sat on its edge, scant feet out of Pity's reach. Beau, noticing her interest, cleared his throat. Pity stepped back another pace and risked a glance at Max. He reached out and gave her arm an encouraging squeeze.

At the container, Santino knelt down and tapped the control display. With a low hiss the top of the box cracked open. White smoke spilled out of it, crawling over the black stone floor like a fog. When Santino flipped the top open all the way, Pity recoiled in surprise.

Inside was a body.

It was a man, average-sized and rough-looking, with an

untidy brown beard. His skin was pale and hung around his face.

What's going on? Pity tried to telegraph the question to Max with a look, but he shook his head and put a finger to his lips.

Beau drew his gun again. Meanwhile, Santino pulled a med injector from his pocket and thrust it into the neck of the dead man, then backed away.

A heartbeat later, the eyes flipped open. The corpse sat up straight, a strangled cry ripping from its throat. As the sound died away, the man looked around wildly, shocked and uncomprehending...until he spotted Selene. With a lurch, he tried to stand, but his legs went out from under him and he plummeted to the floor, landing half in and half out of the box.

"Don't try to run, Beeks," said Santino. "Beau will shoot you if you do." All the warmth in Santino's voice was gone, and Pity hardly recognized it. "Get up. Slowly."

Beeks looked around again, the hysteria in his face fading to a simpler terror. But he did as he was told. "Now, Miss Selene," he croaked, limbs shaking, "I know what you're—"

"Be. Quiet," said Selene. "Do you know why you're here, Beeks? Do you know why I had to send Santino halfway across this godforsaken continent to drag you back to Cessation? Hmm?"

Beeks shriveled. "Ye-yes, ma'am. I do."

"Say it."

His face drained of what little color it had. "I—I stole from you...ma'am."

"Very good! And you know how I feel about people stealing from me."

"Yes, ma'am," he replied. "You—you can't abide it."

"No," said Selene. "I can't. That currency was supposed to go to our friends in the east to ensure a new port was built exactly where our friends in the south wanted it. As you might imagine, it took no small amount of work for me to smooth that situation over."

Though her words were calm, Beeks collapsed to his knees, eyes wet and pleading. "Please forgive me, Miss Selene, please. I knew it was wrong—I did. I couldn't help myself. I'm a weak-willed idiot. I'll do anything, *anything*—"

"Get up." She touched a hand to her brow. "I don't like begging fools any more than I like thieving ones."

He staggered back to his feet.

"Tell me something, Beeks."

"Anything, ma'am."

Selene's eyes flicked to Pity, then back to the sniveling thief. "Am I correct in recalling that you know how to juggle?"

Beeks's mouth opened and closed, but no answer issued forth.

"Halcyon," Selene continued, "you remember Beeks juggling, don't you?"

Halcyon nodded emphatically. "Why, of course! There was many an evening when his juggling garnered the rapt attention of our patrons downstairs! In fact, there was one time when he—"

"Thank you, Halcyon." Miss Selene gestured to the bowl of glass globes. "You said you'd be willing to do anything to be forgiven. Would you juggle those for me?"

"For—for you, I—" He stared blankly. "Yes, yes of course."

"Come take them, then."

Beeks obeyed, gathering five of the glass globes into his trembling hands.

"Now go stand over there," Selene instructed.

In position, Beeks looked around questioningly, clutching the globes to his chest as if they were keeping him afloat. A knot formed in Pity's stomach. A man like him might have been at home among the roughest of the CONA convoy guards, the most weathered of the war veterans. And yet the attention of a single woman had him looking like he was about to wet himself.

"Serendipity?"

Her head snapped up.

Selene indicated the gun belt. "You may retrieve your property now."

Pity hesitated.

"Ma'am," interjected Beau, "I don't think that's a wise—"

"Honestly, Beau. If she appears to be a danger, shoot her."

Pity continued to hesitate. Danger salted the air, though for whom, she wasn't sure.

"Take them!" Max whispered.

Caution fueling each step, she went to the desk, took the belt, and strapped it on. The weight of it was a comfort, but she made sure to keep her hands from straying too close to the handles.

"Start juggling, Beeks," said Selene.

Pity's hands tingled as a spark of understanding ignited.

Eyes wide as eggs, Beeks arranged the globes in his hands. One by one, he tossed them up until all five were arcing through the air.

Selene didn't even look. "No one is brought into Casimir's fold lightly," she said to Pity, "and as you can see, sometimes even I make a poor decision. But Beeks's betrayal offers you an opportunity to show me why I should let you remain here, in my employ and under my protection. Show me what kind of a markswoman you are. Do you understand?"

"Yes." Pity exhaled, mouth parched by dread. "I understand."

So did Beeks. Two rosy blotches appeared on his pale cheeks. His brow was damp with sweat.

She knew she shouldn't ask, but she did. "What if I miss?"

"Don't fret about the curtains, dear."

"I mean, what if I miss the globes? Or...hit him?"

Selene leaned back in her chair. "Then you're not a very good shot, are you?"

A whimper escaped Beeks.

Breathe, Pity told herself. *Relax.* The grips of the revolvers warmed in her palms as she timed the balls flying through the air, crossing paths but never colliding. She wondered whether it was skill that kept Beeks from dropping the globes or fear.

She raised one gun and aimed. Her hand twitched and then held steady. *Inhale, aim,* she thought. *Exhale...*

Bang!

One of the globes exploded as it hit the pinnacle of its arc, showering Beeks in glass shards. His rhythm faltered.

"Don't stop," snapped Selene.

At the last moment, Beeks regained his composure and kept the four remaining globes in motion.

"You, either," Selene said to Pity. "I've seen better."

Pity clenched her teeth. She ripped the other gun from its holster.

Bang!

Bang!

Bang!

Bang!

One by one the globes shattered. At the last, Beeks sobbed and fell to his knees, a dark stain spreading across the front of his pants.

"That good enough?" Pity spat, and instantly regretted it.

But Selene ignored the comment. "What do you think, Beau? Could you find a use for her?"

Beau considered her for a moment. "No."

"No?"

"She can shoot, but the only steel in her is in those guns."

Pity's confidence withered, giving way to another wave of guilt. *Even he sees it. If you had moved instead of freezing up, gotten to Finn before…*

Selene turned. "Halcyon, what about you?"

Halcyon was grinning like a madman. He clapped his hands together. "Yes, yes, yes! A thousand times, yes! The ideas are flowing already—Serendipity Jones! Deadliest beauty in the west! No, wait. That's *terrible*…I can think of something better…"

Deadliest beauty? Perplexed, Pity holstered her guns.

"It's your lucky day," Selene said to her, "but don't misunderstand. You've earned a chance and nothing more. Impress Halcyon. More important, impress *me*. Do that and you may stay in Casimir for as long as you'd like." Miss Selene tapped a finger against the desk. A display flared to life. "Adora, would you come in here for a moment?"

"Right away, ma'am," said a voice.

A moment later, a door opened in the wall. A young woman entered the room. Her neat navy jacket and skirt were a stark contrast to the wildly arranged magenta hair on her head. She didn't spare a single glance for the blubbering Beeks.

"Adora," said Selene, "would you please find quarters for Pity here? Somewhere in the performers' wing."

"Yes, ma'am."

"Max, go along with her as well. And get Flossie to send someone to clean her up." Selene gave Pity a final shrewd smile. "Let's see what kind of gem is under that rough."

"Follow me," Adora said coolly. She headed for the elevator, heels clicking against the floor.

Max took hold of Pity's arm and, less than gently, urged her to follow. But he was smiling. "Congratulations," he said quietly.

"Why?" she said. "What the hell just happened?"

"What do you think? You joined the Theatre!"

Behind them, Beeks finally found his voice. "Miss Selene? What about me? Am I—am I forgiven?"

"Of course not," Selene said, her words carrying across the room. "I'm giving you to the Theatre, too."

Pity winced at the howl that followed, a desperate cry that was cut off a moment later as the elevator doors slid shut.

CHAPTER 8

"THE *THEATRE?*" PITY LEANED AGAINST THE BACK OF THE elevator, muscles watery. Beeks's scream echoed in her ears. "Can't I scrub toilets?"

Max leaned next to her, grinning. "Are you kidding me? You hit the jackpot!"

"I'm not an actress."

"And I told you," he said, "it's not that kind of theatre."

Halcyon Singh's Theatre Vespertine...Meeting Halcyon only added a new layer of peculiarity to the words. "What do they expect me to do?"

"Shoot things, I suppose," said Max. "Leave that to Halcyon. He's a genius with the details."

Pity stared at her feet. "I...I don't think..."

Adora sighed. "What Max is *trying* to communicate," she

said, her back to them, "is that you have been offered a coveted position. Performers in the Theatre Vespertine are entitled to generous wages, room and board, and *all* of Casimir's luxuries."

"As I recall," Pity said, "I was offered a *chance*."

Adora turned her head, gazing at Pity with sly cat's eyes. "And you can see for what tomorrow evening. Halcyon has quite a show in store."

The elevator doors opened. For a minute they were back among the revelry of the main hall, until Adora ushered them through one of the arched exits that lined the walls. From there, Casimir became a disorienting maze of hallways and stairways.

"This way." Adora turned down a long hall, stopping before the door at the very end. She punched a code into the keypad. The door opened. "Max, show her around. I have to get back to more important things." She smiled frostily at Pity. "I'm sure you understand."

"Uh, sure," she said. "Thank—" But Adora was already walking away. Pity stared after her. "She's..."

"About as pleasant as a mouthful of sour milk?" Max said. "Don't take it personally. Adora isn't nice to anyone. But she does her job well. If Beau is Miss Selene's gun, Adora is her pen. Well, go on in."

Automatic lights flickered on as she entered, illuminating a room at least ten paces on each side. A huge bed took up much of the space, but there was a small sofa, a table, and a wardrobe against one wall.

"*This* is for me?"

"Like Adora said: luxuries. Miss Selene wants you to know what you have to gain."

"I guess so." She paused a few steps in, feeling like a trespasser. "How long does it take to get used to this sort of fancy?"

"Actually…" Max hesitated. "My room is in the basement. I tend to be messy, and no one cares if a little paint gets splattered around there. Not so impressive, but I prefer it."

The bed looked like a coat of fresh snow had fallen on it. When Pity pressed her hands into the comforter, they sank to the wrist.

"Makes you want to jump right in, doesn't it?"

"Lord, yes." Her body ached for rest. It had been days since she had slept in a real bed. Then again, her definition of *real bed* paled in comparison to what lay before her. "But it's so clean and I'm filthy."

"You're not the only one." Max sniffed his shirt and made a face. "Hazards of travel. I'd better get washed up, too. If there's a performance tomorrow, I'll have work waiting." His expression turned serious. "I'm sorry about upstairs. That's not how I expected things to play out. But you did good—really good. Selene was impressed. I could tell."

"Not that impressed."

"Listen to Halcyon. Do what he says, and she'll be begging you to stay."

Who says I want to? Now was the time, Pity thought. She had her guns back, and she had seen Cessation. It was real, and it was dangerous. Max had promised to put her on the train if she wanted… All she had to do was ask.

And where would I go? She couldn't return to the commune, and she hadn't forgotten what Olivia had said about the eastern cities. She had no supplies, no connections, and no currency.

She and Finn might have made it together, but alone? Her eyes burned.

"Max"—she pushed the words past the lump in her throat—"who is Miss Selene?"

"She's the person who keeps Cessation from descending into chaos," he replied. "Without her it would all fall apart. Miss Selene controls the Theatre, the Tin Men, and Casimir. She prevents lawlessness from taking over the city."

"I thought there was no law in Cessation."

"There's not," he said. "Except for Selene's law. Everyone knows not to cross her."

She gave him a pointed look. "What about Beeks?"

Max shrugged. "There's always an exception or two to every rule, right? Bathroom is through that door. Get some rest. I'll check on you in the morning."

"Max?"

He paused in the doorway, his gray eyes wide as he waited for her to speak again.

Ask. All you have to do is ask.

"Thank you," she said at last. "For everything."

"You're welcome. Good night."

"Good night."

The door clicked shut. Pity stood in the center of the room, alone. She remained that way for a long minute, staring down at the apple-green carpet, unsure of what to do next. Finally, she took off her belt and laid it on the table next to the bed. She might have her guns back, but how far would she make it in the state she was in? Bruised body, battered emotions, exhausted to her very bones.

A few days couldn't hurt, could it? She could rest, get her strength back. And then, if she still wanted to leave . . .

Impress Halcyon. Selene's words thrummed in her ears. *Impress me.*

Too tired to think, Pity went over and examined the wardrobe. It was empty save for a thick white bathrobe, soft as a spring lamb. She gathered it and went to the door Max had indicated was the bathroom. When she saw the bathtub, the robe dropped to the floor.

Moments later, her clothes followed.

There was a knock on the door as she was drying off.

"You decent in there?" a woman's voice called.

Pity froze, bent over, her hair trailing above the bathroom tile.

"I've *got* the code," she continued. "But I was trying to be polite."

Pity tightened her robe. She went to the door and cracked it. "Uh, can I help you?"

It was the dark-haired young woman who had blown Max the kiss. She gave Pity a pert smile, her tan cheeks shimmering with a faint gold sheen. She pushed the door in. "I'm here to help *you*, honey. Flossie sent me. I'm Luster. And you're Pity, so Max tells me."

A man entered behind her, dressed in a scarlet-and-black uniform trimmed with gold buttons. He carried an armful of long black bags on hangers. "In the wardrobe, please," Luster instructed. "Then take off." When they were alone, she gave

Pity a long look over, from top to bottom. "Well, the first thing we need to do is get you clean."

"Excuse me?"

"You heard me. In the bath." Luster kicked off her heeled shoes and strode into the bathroom.

Pity heard the water turn on again. "I spent the last half hour in there."

The bathroom was as luxurious as the bedroom, with pale blue marble and a deep, round tub fed by a golden faucet shaped like a fish. Luster leaned over it, testing the temperature of the water. Up close, she didn't look as young as she had downstairs; Pity gauged her to be at least a few years older than she was, despite her diminutive figure.

"Flossie told me to make you presentable, not dunk you underwater a few times and call it a night. Robe off, back in the tub!" When Pity failed to comply, she put her hands on her hips. "*What?*"

"Nothing, it's only..."

"Don't tell me you're shy." Luster laughed. She plucked a pair of pins from inside her bodice and gathered her hair. In a practiced instant it was twisted up and pinned in place. "Honey, you don't have anything I haven't seen a thousand times, in a thousand ways. C'mon, lose it."

Pity slid out of the robe, shivering even as the room filled with steam. *You swam naked in the creek with Finn a hundred and one times. This is no different.* Or so she told herself.

Luster whistled. "Those are some pretty fine bruises. You're more plum than peach right now. Unfortunately, I've seen *that* before, too."

As Pity slid into the water—and she had to admit, a second bath was not the worst thing she could imagine—Luster opened a cabinet under the sink, filled with soaps and oils. A wealth of smells drifted over.

"Peppermint? Wisteria? I'm partial to lavender, myself."

"Anything that doesn't smell like sweat or burnt oil." Pity sat back. The heat felt as delicious as before.

After setting the bottles within arm's reach, Luster stripped off her dress. The undergarments beneath revealed more than they covered.

Pity stiffened. "What are you doing?"

"Don't want to get it damp." She rolled her eyes. "Relax, this isn't *that* kind of work. Come over here and dip down. Get your hair nice and wet."

Pity obeyed, hesitating again when Luster ordered her to turn around. But the young woman only perched on the edge of the tub as she worked a dollop of liquid soap into Pity's hair, massaging it until a thick lather formed. It was a uniquely soothing sensation. Within a minute, Pity's muscles began to unknot and her eyelids grew heavy.

"You have lovely hair," said Luster. "Brown as cocoa...Ooh, that sounds good. You want some cocoa?" She rinsed her hands, then pressed a button on the wall Pity hadn't noticed before.

"May I be of service?" said a voice.

"Hey, y'all, it's Luster. I'm in 486. Can you send up some hot cocoa in about half an hour? And maybe some..." She turned to Pity. "Are you hungry? Kitchen does a roast chicken thing with wine and mushrooms that's tasty."

Pity's stomach gurgled at the mention of food. "If it's not dehydrated or from a can, it's fine with me."

"Send that chicken I like," Luster said. "And some wine. Actually, send that now. Thanks!"

Pity wiped a speck of lather from her cheek. "Hot cocoa? Dinner? Just like that?"

Luster winked. "One of the perks of living in Casimir. I heard a rumor that you're joining the Theatre."

News travels fast here. "From Max?"

"Oh, I never reveal my sources," said Luster. "But you're gonna love it. Great food, ample drinks. And plenty of free time in the Gallery."

"The Gallery?"

"Where you came in downstairs. Hold still. I'll hose you down."

As Luster used a sprayer to rinse Pity's hair, another knock sounded.

"I got it!" Luster popped back into the bedroom, not bothering to re-dress.

Pity heard the door open and shut. Luster reappeared, a bottle in one hand and a pair of wineglasses in the other. Pity averted her eyes. *Stop it,* she told herself. *She's got nothing you haven't seen before, either.* But there was something disconcerting about Luster's brazenness. Even the way her makeup had blurred softly in the steam seemed to carry a touch of wickedness.

Luster poured two generous measures of garnet-red liquid. "Drink up!"

"I . . . I shouldn't."

Luster pressed the glass on her. "If I looked like you do, I'd want something a lot stronger than a bit of wine." One eyebrow rose. "That could be arranged, too, y'know."

"No, this is fine." Pity took a sip. It tasted like dark cherries and left a sticky feeling on her tongue, but the moment it hit her stomach a deep warmth spread, bleeding outward to meet the heat of the bath pushing in.

Luster grabbed a sponge. "Turn around again. I'll do your back."

Pity took another swallow of wine. With every moment that passed, the tightness in her body unwound a little more. She leaned forward against the edge of the tub, arms crossed on the tiles as Luster circled the sponge over her shoulders and back, taking extra care around the worst of the injuries.

"Luster?"

"Mm-hmm?"

"Do you...like living here?"

Luster laughed. "I think what you want to ask is do I like being a whore, right?"

Pity shifted, glad her face was hidden. "It's none of my business. Sorry."

"Don't be. I asked Flossie that same question the day I stumbled into Casimir, doing my best to not look like the underfed dissident spawn that I was. You know what she said? 'No one here does anything they don't want to.' Heck, I could be a porter tomorrow if I had a mind to be." She chuckled again. "But we should all be honest about where our talents lie. Don't get me wrong, though. Casimir is a far cry from what goes on in

Cessation's alleys. I'd go back to the mudhole camp I grew up in before you'd find me there ... Well, maybe."

"Was it that bad? I don't know much about what goes on outside the CONA territories."

"Nothing more than they tell you, I'm sure." Luster sighed. "CONA called us dissidents as an insult, but in the camps it was a badge of honor. We might have lost the war, but we were free, right? No plutocrats or corporations telling us how to live our lives. Thing is, freedom doesn't put food on the table. A lousy crop meant a cold, hungry winter. Infighting was common. And even in the better settlements, fate has a cruel sense of humor. Garland—you'll meet him—came from one of the First Peoples communities. Y'know those, right?"

"Only that they stayed out of the war, and CONA trades with them from time to time."

"When it suits them, sure." Luster scoffed. "A sickness came one spring. Wiped out half Garland's community within months. Yeah, it gets pretty bad."

Pity didn't ask any more questions. For all the commune's flaws, she had never faced starvation or war, or an illness there wasn't medicine for. What others did to secure themselves wasn't for her to judge—not when their situations were dire enough to make her wonder what she might do in the same place. How bad *would* life with her father have had to be to make her jump at an arranged marriage?

Too exhausted to ponder that path, she sipped her wine and floated, letting Luster scrub away the stains of travel. Her eyes opened and closed, vision blurred by more than the steam. She didn't protest when Luster helped her out of the bath and dried her off with a downy towel, or when Luster led her to the bed and began massaging scented ointments into her bruised skin. The soft anchors of the bath, the wine, and Luster's skilled touch sank her further and further toward sleep. She roused momentarily when she heard a third knock, but her eyes closed again quickly, the faint scent of cocoa ushering her into the dark.

CHAPTER 9

MIDMORNING, MAX RAPPED ON HER DOOR.

A few hours before, Pity had woken to find herself cosseted under the thick comforter, still naked. For a few blissful moments, ignorance lay on her like a different sort of blanket. Then, one by one, memories emerged from sleep's fog. Where she was...and where she had been. She threw off the comforter, the chill on her skin nothing compared to the flame of guilt in her chest.

You're lying here, warm and clean, while Finn is rotting away somewhere in the middle of nowhere.

She sat with that guilt for a while, waiting for the flame to ignite something within her, to illuminate some hidden corner of her situation—a different path, a better idea. But when it didn't, when the feelings remained as directionless as they had on the way to Cessation, she gave in to the draw of the robe Luster had left folded at the foot of the bed. Recalling the previous evening, Pity searched through the black bags in the wardrobe. They were full of clothes—more conventional than what she had observed in the Gallery but far from the shapeless utility of commune garments. She had settled on a pale yellow shirt and a pair of caramel-brown pants, tighter than she liked but as soft as velvet. She'd even found a new pair of boots, sized perfectly.

Max, too, was cleaner but as paint-specked as ever.

"Luster did a great job, I see," he said. "You look rested." He wasn't alone. Behind him stood an older man with silver hair and baggy eyes, carrying a black leather bag.

"Thanks." Pity pulled at her braided hair, eyeing the stranger. "Stupid me, I went and fell asleep before I could thank her." Her stomach growled audibly. "Or eat dinner."

"If you can be patient a little longer, that's easily remedied." Max stepped aside. "Pity, this is Dr. Starr. He's going to give you a once-over. I'll wait in the hallway, Doc."

Starr strode across the room and unceremoniously dropped his bag on the table. "They told me about your accident. You were very lucky, it seems. How are you feeling?" He opened the kit and began searching inside. "Any new pain? Headaches?"

"No."

"Look here." He swept a light across her eyes a few times, then began prodding her around the neck and stomach. "Tell me if any of this hurts. You're from the communes, so I assume you've had the gamut of vaccines, regular examinations, all that?"

"Yes."

"Twice blessed, then. Any allergies? Are you fertile?"

"Uh, walnuts...and yes."

Starr stepped back. "Stay away from the kitchen's cinnamon rolls, then. For the other thing, we only get enough preventative meds for Flossie's crew, but if you're not interested in being a mommy someday, I can do a one-way fix for you."

"Th-thanks," she said. Sterilization was illegal under CONA law—*very* illegal. Apparently Cessation's offerings extended beyond gambling, booze, and bodies. "I think I'll stay unfixed for now."

"If you change your mind, let me know." Starr grabbed the bag. "Welcome to Casimir," he said, and departed with as much ceremony as his arrival.

Max popped his head back in. "So, breakfast?"

Unlike the Gallery, the décor of the common dining room was simple: custard-colored walls, bare floors, and wide windows. Morning sunshine streamed across tables occupied by men and women of all ages. Some sat alone, others in groups, chatting and smiling over mugs of coffee and full plates. There were no costumes or uniforms here. Pity couldn't tell if they were porters, prostitutes, or something else. They could have been workers on her commune—a thought she found oddly comforting.

"As much as Luster loves room service," Max said, "we mostly take meals here."

Along the far wall ran a buffet filled with trays. Following Max's lead, Pity grabbed a plate and piled it with eggs and bacon, toast, fresh fruit, and a mug of cocoa, to make up for the one she had missed. Her hand cramped with the weight of the plate by the time they sat down.

"After breakfast, we'll head to the theatre. Halcyon wants to see you."

He certainly doesn't waste any time. "Should I have brought my guns?"

"If you need them, Halcyon will send someone to fetch them. Just do what he tells you, and everything will be peachy."

"What'll be peachy?" The pretty blond youth who had welcomed Santino the prior evening slid into the seat across from Max. He was less pretty this morning, and less youthful-looking, his eyes tired and kohl-smeared. With him was Luster's handsome companion. He put his plate down but remained standing.

"Gone for weeks, and all we get is a wave." The blond stifled a yawn. "Good to see you, too, Max!"

"Duchess, manners." His friend reached a hand toward Pity. He was even more bitingly handsome up close, with tawny skin, dark hair, and darker eyes. "Duchess is pretending like Luster didn't fill us in already. But you were whisked away so soon after arriving, we weren't properly introduced. I'm Garland. Any friend of Max is a friend of ours."

"Pity." She put out her hand to shake. Garland took it but lightly kissed her knuckles instead, sending a flutter of warmth through her.

Duchess scowled as Garland sat. "My manners and I have been up all night. We're hungry, we're tired, and we don't have an endless supply of charm to draw from, unlike *some* people."

He nodded at Pity. "So no offense meant. Welcome to Casimir, et cetera, et cetera."

"Thanks." Pity buried her nose in her mug of cocoa.

"Normally," said Max, "you don't see these two before the backside of noon. So what was it, boys?"

Garland smirked. "Some very dedicated faro players. One was convinced Duchess was his lucky charm."

"Well, were you?" said Max.

"He lost his shirt," Duchess replied. "And not in a good way."

When they finished eating, they ferried their plates to a bin full of dirty dishes. Pity paused at the sight of it, one of the most familiar things she had so far encountered in Casimir.

"What?" said Max.

"It feels…weird." She stared at the remains of the meal. "I can't remember the last time I had a meal I didn't help cook or clean up after. The room, the bath, the clothes—it all feels so… I don't know."

Yes, you do, said a nagging voice within. *It feels kinda* nice.

"Enjoy it." Max smirked. "You'll be earning your keep soon enough, trust me."

The theatre was a whirlpool of seats, swirling down in a series of levels to the stage below. At the top were long, plain benches, followed by individual chairs, red and plush. Closest to the floor were tiers of sectioned boxes—some small, with room for only two or three people, others that could seat a dozen or more. Pity and Max passed through each section in turn, descending one of the stairways set at intervals.

"Normally we move around using the tunnels beneath the stage," he explained as they reached a door that accessed the stage level, "but I thought you might like to see it from this angle."

A tremor of nerves shook her. "I didn't think it would be this big. Everyone on the commune could fit in here, easily."

"Wait until you see it full."

While the stands were deserted, the stage was a bustling hive of activity. Everywhere people were stretching, singing, flipping through the air. She and Max came upon a group of lithe youths—two boys and three girls—with pale skin and paler hair. None looked to be older than Pity. Five pairs of icy eyes stared at her as they passed.

"The Rousseau quintet," Max said quietly. "Clare, Chrétien, Carine, Christophe, and Chloe. Acrobats and contortionists." He pointed at a man and woman next. "Eva and Marius Zidane. Knife throwers." As if by command, the pair raised their arms in unison. Two knives sliced through the air and embedded in a round target a dozen yards away.

"Not bad." Pity had tried to sound impressed, but she had seen similar skill on the commune, usually on the heels of a few tumblers of home-still.

"That's a warm-up. Their act is more...complicated."

"There she is, there she is!" Halcyon's voice cut through the noise. "Everyone, listen! Yes, listen, turn, pay attention!" He swept over to Pity. "Lovely to see you again, dear girl, and, my, don't you look rested." An arm stole around Pity's shoulders and pulled her close. "Everyone, gather round! May I introduce to you our latest acquisition, Serendipity Jones!"

The performers gathered around them. Faces stared at her,

curious but cool. One of the Rousseaus leaned to another and whispered something. They both giggled.

A woman with dark, cropped hair and olive skin broke away from the crowd. "Doesn't look like much. What does she do?"

"Why, Scylla, you should be asking what *doesn't* she do."

Scylla rolled her eyes.

"No, no, wait," Halcyon continued. "I would not withhold that satisfying morsel from you—it would be cruel, *cruel!* Serendipity here is a markswoman, finest ever trained on the CONA communes, now come to us to showcase her talents."

"A commune?" Scylla snickered. "She gonna shoot jackrabbits for her act?"

The crowd tittered. Blood rushed to Pity's face.

"Careful, Scylla," said Eva Zidane. "We don't have any jackrabbits, but we do have plenty of other creatures on hand."

The remark earned Eva an acid look, but before Scylla could retort, Halcyon released Pity and clapped his hands together in rapid succession. "Enough, enough! Back to work, my lovelies. Tonight's show draws ever closer! Go, go!" The crowd dispersed. "You, too, Max. Work to be done!"

"Sure, boss." Max shot Pity a look of encouragement. "You'll be okay."

"Well, of course she will," balked Halcyon. "We'll have a little chat, talk about her act, et cetera, et cetera."

"Go on." Pity's voice didn't quite match the confidence of her words, but she managed a smile. "I'm sure Mr. Singh will take good care of me."

"Please, my dear, call me Halcyon! Or boss, as some seem to prefer. Yes, either will do. Now come!"

It turned out that Halcyon's taste in wardrobe extended to his office. The striped walls threatened the tranquility of Pity's full stomach. Only slightly less unnerving were the orange carpet and the furniture upholstered in eggplant velvet. Halcyon plunked her onto a cushy chair before his desk, piled high with an unstable snarl of papers, ledgers, and toys. As Pity watched, a rubber ball rolled out of the mess and over to a wall plastered with maps. Pins were set in a dozen or more locations, all over the world.

"Plans," Halcyon explained. "Or hopes, I should say. Why, if I had my way, the Theatre Vespertine would be touring constantly: Columbia, Sangui City, Johannesburg—no habitable corner of the globe would remain unvisited! Sadly, here we remain tethered, a beautiful bird kept caged, unable to even move about the continent because some aspects of my show are not deemed *appropriate* for the audiences of the east. And Selene's no help, to boot. *She* doesn't want to share her treasure with the world."

Pity blinked. *This is the genius I'm supposed to listen to?* "To be honest, I'm not sure it's appropriate for me, either."

"What? Whyever would you say that?"

"Because I have no idea what you expect me to do," she said. "And I'm no performer."

"What does that matter? Performing is easy. You merely need to remember one thing."

"What's that?"

He leaned in, voice dropping low. "Give the crowd something they want to see."

"Do you..." Pity hesitated. "Do you really think my shooting is something people would want to see?"

His eyes narrowed playfully. "It will be. Ah, you still have reservations. Don't. When you step out in front of that audience for the first time, if you don't believe in yourself, no one else will. They'll smell it, like sharks smell blood."

And then you'll be out on your backside. Pity didn't need him to say it—Cessation didn't seem like a place that offered second chances. Did she even want the first? But what was the alternative? With a night's rest and a full stomach, clarity of thought had returned. Certainly she could play along for a few more days, then head east. But the prospect no longer carried the promise it once had. Finn wouldn't be east, west, or anywhere else she went. And Cessation had served up an opportunity on a silver platter; she couldn't expect the same good fortune a second time.

And isn't this what you always wanted—the chance to show what you can do? Maybe the particulars weren't exactly how she had imagined, but...

Safety. Shelter. Work.

Cessation—*Selene*—was offering her all of it. The only thing she had to do was be entertaining.

How hard could it be? she thought. *It's just shooting dressed up fancy. Finn would be tickled to see me show off for a thousand strangers.*

Finn's final moments seeped into her thoughts: the resigned, resilient look in her eyes; the nerve that came to Pity when it was already far too late.

Her breakfast curdled in her gut. *The only steel in her is in those guns.*

Beau's barb had gotten under her skin, deeper than she wanted to admit. But maybe he had done her a favor by passing her over. Security could be life or death, and not only for her.

The Theatre?

The Theatre was just a show.

CHAPTER 10

LATE IN THE AFTERNOON, A PORTER APPEARED AT HER bedroom door with a note.

Sorry, it read, a smudge of paint in one corner, *busy with the sets. Will see you tonight before the show. —Max*

P.S. REALLY sorry about Luster and the others—I told them to go easy on you.

Like the meeting with Halcyon—who had instructed her on when to return to the theatre and little else—the note left her with more questions than it answered. She pondered it as she dressed. At some point during her absence, the contents of her wardrobe had doubled. She chose an outfit from the new arrivals: a gray skirt and a black jacket that buttoned up the front, then brushed the braid out of her hair, letting it hang in waves around her shoulders.

There was a knock on the door. When she opened it, Luster, Garland, and Duchess swept into the room.

Pity didn't bother with pleasantries. "What are you gonna do to me?" she said. "And is there any way I can avoid it?"

"Not. A. One," Duchess said. "Aw, doesn't she look like a cornered kitten? I love it."

"Relaaaax," Luster purred. "We're here to help you get dressed for tonight."

"What's wrong with this?"

"Um, no." Duchess scoffed. "While, admittedly, a night at the Theatre demands something a bit more conservative than what some of us are used to"—black pants and a glittering silver shirt had replaced his outfit from the evening before—"it doesn't mean you dress like a schoolteacher on her day off."

"I do not look like a schoolteacher!"

"Not yet." Garland moved around behind her. She froze as he gathered her hair and twisted it into a bun on the top of her head. The touch sent shivers down the back of her neck. "But now you do. Oh, don't scowl like that."

Her face burned. She tried to protest, but being so close to Garland turned every objection sideways in her throat.

Luster came to her rescue. "Leave her be. Let's see what else we can find." She rooted through the wardrobe, pulling out bits of clothing and tossing them to the floor. "No, no, nope, hell nope, and bingo! Here we go!"

Pity's stomach dropped. "That's not really my—"

"No arguments." Duchess snatched the dress from Luster and pressed it on her.

"Fine. I'll try it on." She clutched the frighteningly small wisp of fabric.

"Good," said Luster. "Then we can get started on the rest of it."

"The rest of *what?*" Pity squeaked.

Half an hour later, Luster dabbed on a last bit of powder. "There. What do you think?"

"I'm..." A doppelgänger stared at Pity from the bathroom mirror. When she ran a hand down the front of the dress, the reflection did the same. Evergreen in color, it hung to her knees and sparkled faintly. *Silk,* she thought. *It would have taken me ages to save enough to buy a yard of fabric this nice.* Pity was certain she wasn't the first owner of the dress, but even if it had been torn and faded it would have been nicer than anything she had ever worn before. Around her bare shoulders her hair still hung loose, but now her eyes were rimmed with black, her lips stained berry-red. "I'm cold."

"I can fix that." Luster pranced out of the bathroom.

Pity wobbled as far as the doorframe before stopping, unsure she could take another step. Neither the heeled shoes she wore nor her resolve felt particularly steady. But it was too late. Garland and Duchess had seen her.

"Better," admitted Duchess.

"*Perfect,*" said Garland. He grabbed her hands and pulled her back into the bedroom.

She stumbled forward. "I don't know..."

"No, he's right."

For a moment, Pity didn't recognize Max, leaning against

the open door to the hall. His paint-splattered clothes had been swapped for a tailored black jacket with a gold collar and matching pants, an ensemble that fit him like a second skin. When he gave her a languorous smile, Pity's stomach tightened. She forgot Garland was holding her hands until he released them, stepping away.

"See?" he said. "If Max can dress the part of the rich elite, so can you."

Luster tossed her a gauzy strip of gold fabric. "Here, to keep you warm."

"Uh, thanks." She draped it around her shoulders.

"I've got some good news, kids," Max said. "In honor of Pity seeing her first show, Halcyon reserved us a box."

"A Finale *and* we don't have to sit with the rabble?" Duchess looped an arm around Pity's and led her toward the door. "I am suddenly so much fonder of you."

Max didn't move. "Sorry, Dutch, but if you don't mind?"

"Oh, Maxxy, I knew you'd come around sooner or later." Duchess released Pity and linked arms with Max instead, who rolled his eyes. "Oh, all right. She's all yours."

As Max led Pity into the hall, her embarrassment evaporated, chased away by a spark of excitement.

Whether it was for the show or her escort, in that moment she couldn't have said.

It began with a faint hum of music, almost too low to make out. That hum grew, vibrating through Pity, weaving among the crowd's hushed whispers and held breaths. It was impossible to tell where it came from in the dark theatre, lit only by red lights that cast everything in bloody shadows. She shifted anxiously in her seat, glancing at Max beside her. With his black suit and black hair, he seemed hardly more than a floating face. On her other side, Luster leaned against her shoulder, a huge grin on her face. Duchess and Garland were behind them, the box just spacious enough for five.

The theatre had been in a ruckus as they entered, its stands brimming with spectators. Pity had found herself assaulted by raucous laughter, colorful outfits, and scents of perfume, sweet cigar smoke, and too many bodies. But as soon as the lights dimmed, the crowd had settled, their anticipation thick and infectious.

The music continued its languid ascent. Her attention was drawn to the center of the stage, where a ring of purple and orange lights appeared, pulsing in time with the melody. Amid them, like a demon rising out of the depths of hell, Halcyon appeared.

"The sun has set, and the moon begins to rise." His voice was everywhere, like the music. "Now is the early black. Now is the time of magic and mysteries, of darkness and devilry. I welcome all of you, new friends and old, to the greatest show on the continent, to the theatre to end all theatre! Welcome"— the music rose sharply, a trembling crescendo—"to the Theatre Vespertine!"

Halcyon threw up his arms. Huge jets of sparks exploded out of his sleeves and from the apex of the ceiling, flakes of light raining down on the audience like snow. The crowd erupted in cheers as the arena flooded with light. Halcyon was no longer alone. A dozen dancers—naked save for patches of multicolored silks cut to look like feathers—appeared. They circled around him like a flock of colorful vultures before back-flipping away, bending and twisting in the air, only to land as delicately as cats.

"Tonight you will be party to some of the greatest visual pleasures known to mankind. You will be excited and tantalized, terrified and electrified, and at times—never fear!—you will not believe your very eyes!" Halcyon weaved through the dancers along the perimeter of the stage, tipping his striped top hat at the onlookers. When he passed their box, he winked at Pity. Only then did she realize that she had slid forward to the edge of her seat. She felt a hand on her shoulder—Max guiding her backward, a knowing smiling on his face.

"So sit! Relax! And enjoy all the pleasures that the Theatre Vespertine has to offer!" He returned to his ring of lights. "Tonight we begin with an act to warm your blood…though warm or cold, it makes no difference to her. Everyone, blow a hiss—pardon me, a *kiss*—to Scylla!"

The room went black. A low drumming began, soon joined by a high, reedy flute. As Pity watched, Halcyon's lights were replaced by a sour greenish glow. Fog billowed, tendrils curling into the darkness like a poisonous miasma. In the middle of the glow a body appeared, stretched supine. It rose from the fog on a rippling platform.

Rippling? She blinked, but the movement remained. Suddenly, projections of the stage appeared on the ceiling, illuminating the arena. Pity inhaled sharply.

The platform was covered with snakes.

Her vision was filled with them—big and little, striped and

scaled, copperheads and rattlesnakes, and ones she didn't recognize. And in the center of the reptilian nest, Scylla lay, still as death. Breasts bare, her skin shimmered like an oil slick. Pity shivered with a primal revulsion as the serpents slithered over Scylla's limbs, her torso—even her face.

As the tempo of the music increased, Scylla began to move, arching her back slowly before rising. In a slow, upward drift, she got to her feet, dancing seductively, her body undulating like those of her pets. The air tasted of nervousness, excitement, and sensuality. When Scylla bent forward to pluck a pair of snakes from the mass and wrap them around her neck, the audience howled with appreciation.

Pity squirmed as Scylla's eyes, ringed with green glitter, stared down at her from above. And yet she could not look away. She expected one of the snakes to strike at any moment. Instead, they slid up Scylla's legs, wound over her hips, and slipped between her thighs. She continued to dance, raising her arms above her head as the serpents coiled around them. Soon they enveloped her so completely that Scylla resembled some ancient, horrible monster.

"How does she keep them from biting?" Pity breathed.

Luster leaned in close. "Scylla's half witch," she whispered. "And the other half is snake charmer."

"Don't listen to her," Max said. "Illegal neural implants. Not that Scylla will admit it or breathe a word about where she got that done. There are some things you can't get even in Cessation."

The music stopped and Scylla froze. After a moment, it started again, lower and deeper. She began to unwind the serpents from her body, kissing each before placing it at her feet. When she plucked off the final one, a tiny black baby no longer than her forearm, Pity released the air arrested in her lungs.

Scylla spun, her hands extended toward the audience, body glistening. Applause showered down on her, continuing until her platform was out of sight.

Halcyon reappeared. "And now, from that which crawls on its belly to that which flies in the air! Your favorite quintet of gravity-defying darlings—I give you, the Rousseaus!"

"Scylla and the quints, right out of the gate?" said Garland. "Halcyon isn't holding back tonight, is he?"

"He wants people thinking about who will do the Finale," Luster replied.

Pity turned to her. "What's the—?"

"Shhh! Here they come!"

From the ceiling, the Rousseaus descended on ropes like spiders on their silk. What skin on their elfin forms wasn't concealed by gold costumes was painted in intricate, colorful patterns. Even their faces were covered.

"Did you do that?" Pity whispered to Max. He nodded proudly.

Suddenly, the five youths released their ropes. Pity started as they plunged, only to stop abruptly, a loop around one ankle keeping them aloft. The rigging holding them started to spin, and the Rousseaus extended their arms as the motion carried them outward, until they soared like birds through the air. She felt her heart rise into her throat; a slip would be all it took to catapult an unlucky Rousseau into the upper reaches of the stands. Finally, the rotation slowed, and the quints themselves began to spin, faster and faster, until they were blurs. Applause thundered in the stands. Pity stole a glance at the rapt faces of the audience, wondering what excited them more: the aerobatics or the possibility that one of the performers might plunge to their death at any moment.

On it went, a series of nerve-racking stunts filling tense minutes. For the climax of their act they launched themselves one by one through a flaming ring, bowing in midair before the ropes pulled them back up into the darkness above.

Soldiers in chariots drawn by real horses appeared next, enacting some ancient battle where men and women in shining silver armor massacred a band of iron- and leather-clad warriors. No detail was spared. When a soldier thrust a long spear into the chest of a warrior woman, the blood that exploded forth looked so real that Pity cried out.

"It's all part of the show," Max reassured her. And, indeed, the young woman danced off minutes later, along with a dozen other corpses.

"It looks so real," she muttered, embarrassed.

"It's supposed to," he said. "They're spring-loaded weapons packed with fake blood—I mixed it myself. Still haven't got the color quite right, though."

"And now, my friends," Halcyon announced. "No more masquerade. It's time for a true matter of life and death...and of love. I give you—Marius and Eva Zidane!"

The Zidanes rose out of the floor on either side of Halcyon, their backs to each other. Dressed in matching suits of black, red, and cream, with a slit skirt for Eva, both wore belts of knives strapped around their waists. The metal glinted under the bright lights. When Halcyon was gone, they turned slowly and approached each other, eyes locked. Throughout the arena, pieces of wall began to rise out of the floor. Of varying size and spacing, they were set at odd angles, like a maze with pieces torn out. A droning, exotic melody began to play, along with a slow, booming drumbeat.

Boom. Boom. Boom.

The walls locked into place.

Boom. Boom. Boom.

The music grew louder and louder, its energy drawing the anticipation in the room upward until, with a final crash—

It ceased.

Eva and Marius spun from each other and ran. As each reached a section of wall, they turned, arms arcing through the air. A heartbeat later, knives embedded in wood—one above Eva's shoulder, the other inches from Marius's cheek. They dove for cover. From there, they began to stalk each other, darting from one wall piece to another.

Pity watched as the dreadful hunt played out, cringing each time a blade came close to impaling its intended target. "Is this real?"

"Of course it is." Luster's eyes were glassy with excitement.

But Max shrugged. "Only Eva and Marius know for sure."

The audience screamed as one of Marius's knives pinned Eva's skirt. She ripped it free and lunged as another blade cut through the air she had just occupied.

The drumming began again. It beat a slow rhythm as the couple pulled their final knives. On opposite sides of the arena, concealed behind twin sections of wall, open space was all that separated them. In the same moment, the pair bolted from cover and dashed forward. Arms slashed up as they threw—

And up again as they plucked the other's knife from the air, mid-flight.

They came to a halt scant inches apart. Eva's blade was at Marius's throat; his was pointed at her chest. The audience roared their approval as the Zidanes dropped the weapons and kissed.

As they bowed and exited, Pity watched the floor, expecting Halcyon to reemerge. Instead, only his voice rang out.

"You've all been very patient." His tone was teasing, dark. "And I know you know that tonight is different. That we have a special kind of act to send you off, one that does not happen often."

The Finale? Pity slid forward again, achingly curious about what could top Scylla's sensuality, the Rousseaus' skills, or the terrifying grace of the Zidanes.

I'm giving you to the Theatre, too.

Pity's blood turned cold as Selene's words surfaced in her mind.

Suddenly she knew there was only one thing to surmount what she had already seen:

Beeks.

CHAPTER 11

"MAX," SHE WHISPERED. "WHAT'S HAPPENING?"

"Shhh. Watch." His former enthusiasm had receded, replaced by something that further curdled Pity's anticipation.

"And why is tonight's act so rare?" boomed Halcyon. "Because to have a Finale, we need a lawbreaker, and we all know that Cessation is lawless." There was a rumble of laughter. "Or very nearly lawless." He paused. "Tonight, I'm sorry to say that we have one of Casimir's own."

Luster gasped.

"Oh, hell," Garland said. "Who?"

"Someone," Halcyon continued, "who dared to cross Cessation's guardian, its protector, its patron saint. There is no law but the law that she lays down!"

The stands screamed their agreement. *"Selene! Selene!*

Selene!" they cried, the chant beating in time with the blood in Pity's ears.

"Tonight, for the crimes of theft and deception, our criminal faces his sentencing!"

There were no lights, no music, as Beeks appeared in the center of the stage. On his knees he slumped, hands limp in his lap.

"Alastair Beeks, do you deny the charges?"

"I don't." He looked into the rafters, his face as pale as old snow. "I don't, but please, Miss Selene, please have mercy!"

Pity scanned the other boxes. She saw faces rapt with attention, eyes greedy with bloodlust, but Selene was nowhere to be seen. Even so, Pity was sure she was watching, somewhere.

Halcyon replied in her stead. "Your plea of guilt is duly noted."

The ceiling lit up again. This time, still projections of the different acts appeared. Scylla, the Zidanes, the Rousseaus, and others floated above the heads of the audience. The images began to rotate, faster and faster, until they were only streaks of color.

"Honored guests, here is where you weigh in. Tell me, what shall be the manner of his punishment?"

One image popped out as the others continued to spin. The Rousseaus. The crowd cheered. When another image appeared beside it, this time of the Zidanes, they cheered even louder, some stamping their feet in the stands. Then Scylla's image appeared, and all hell broke loose. The noise was deafening, the stomping shaking the entire theatre.

"Ugh, rough draw for Beeks," said Duchess. "They chose Little Miss Tits and Snakes *again.*"

"You're only saying that because you're afraid of snakes!"

Luster tossed back. "Personally," she said to Pity, "I hate the Rousseaus. Last time they dangled the guy on a noose and toyed with him before dropping him from the top of the theatre. The sound he made when he hit the floor...bleah, it still makes me cringe!"

Pity barely heard her. Everything was muted, distant. There was only Beeks, caged in a spotlight, close enough that she could see the glaze of sweat on his forehead. He looked like he was going to be sick. She sympathized, bile rising in the back of her throat.

"Our champion is chosen!" Halcyon cried. Scylla's music began to play again. "Alastair Beeks, you have been judged and sentenced. May whatever power you pray to have mercy on your soul...because Scylla won't."

Beeks finally panicked. He leapt to his feet and darted for the edge of the ring. A door opened in front of him. He froze as Scylla appeared. At her feet, a river of green and black and beige slithered out, spreading around either side of him. He stumbled backward, trying to get away, and nearly trod on a cobra. It struck out; he barely avoided the attack. The crowd roared.

Scylla took her time. She strolled around the perimeter of the stage as the audience cheered her on, traipsing among the snakes like they were summer flowers. She didn't look at Beeks, who had retreated to the center of the stage, only watched her pets lovingly. At one point she stopped and ran her fingers over the back of a thick white python. It curled up her arm and over her shoulders.

Only then did she approach Beeks. With each step, the snakes she passed turned and followed her. The rest of the serpents slithered toward the center of the stage as well. Beeks's island of safety began to shrink.

"Miss Selene, please!" His body shook as he screamed. "Scylla, sweetie, beautiful—you know me! I made a mistake. Don't do this. Call them off. *Call them off!*"

Scylla's step never faltered. She glided closer to Beeks as the audience began to chant her name, stopping a few paces from him. The snakes formed a dense ring around the pair. Scylla petted the python around her neck. Then, slowly, she lifted one hand and pointed. Beeks shook and fell to his knees.

Scylla snapped her fingers.

One by one, the snakes attacked. They struck at Beeks's arms, his legs, his chest. One launched at his neck. Beeks batted it aside, but two more latched themselves on to his forearm. Somehow he managed to get to his feet, face pink and already beginning to bloat. Scylla signaled again. The snakes stopped and slithered back. Teetering, Beeks stumbled forward two steps, reaching out for Scylla. White foam bubbled from his mouth. On the third step, he fell, face forward, onto the floor.

His body shuddered a few times and stilled.

When the riotous clapping began, Pity joined in automatically, her hands moving back and forth mechanically to applaud the final act of the Theatre Vespertine.

Pity yanked the scrap of fabric tighter around her. It did nothing to stop the shivering. She leaned against the wall for support as they waited in a passage beneath the stands. Above them, hundreds of feet pounded against the ceiling, as loud as the applause minutes before. She could feel the eyes of the others upon her.

"Are you okay?" Luster asked.

Pity stared at the ground, unsure how to answer. The show had left her with a distressing snarl of emotion—energized, excited, disgusted...and terrified.

"Leave her be," said Duchess. "Her delicate sensitivities aren't used to—"

The feelings burned away in a flash, fuel for the anger that coursed through her. "You think I've never seen a dead man before? You think the communes don't have their own sort of justice?" She stalked over to Duchess and stabbed a finger at him. "Just because we don't kill folks for entertainment where I'm from doesn't mean we're 'delicate.' So don't you tell me what kind of sensitivities I do and do not have!"

"Whoa, calm down." Garland wrapped an arm around her waist and pulled her away. "He didn't mean anything by it."

Clutched against Garland, Pity was more unsettled than ever but no longer shivering. Heat rose in her cheeks, and she was instantly ashamed for having such a reaction after the morbid event she had witnessed.

"You're not the only one who got a shock," Garland continued as she disentangled herself. "I take it that's what you and Olivia and Santino were up to, Max?"

"Yeah. I would have warned you, but..."

"But it wouldn't have done a lick of good." Duchess tossed his head. "Beeks crossed Miss Selene. He knew better."

That no one asked what Beeks had done didn't escape Pity's notice.

"Well," Luster sighed, "after that, I think all our sensitivities could use a drink."

The Gallery was crowded and raucous by the time they arrived. They elbowed their way to the long bar that ran along one wall, where Max wrangled a stool for Pity.

Luster wriggled in beside her and leaned across the polished wood. "Hey—hey, Olivia!"

Olivia sauntered toward them, in finer clothes than the last time Pity had seen her, though her whip remained coiled on her hip. She smirked at Pity. "Hardly recognized you. Nice dress. Almost covers the bruises."

"Drinks, Olivia, strong ones." Luster kicked up a heel and balanced it on the bar, her dress riding high on her hips. When the patron beside her gave her an appreciative once-over, Luster winked at the woman in the mirrored wall that ran along the back of the bar.

Olivia frowned. "Not when you ask like that, missy."

Garland gave a winsome smile. "Please. The word she forgot was *please*."

Olivia rolled her eyes. "Anyone ever said no to that face, Gar?" She eyed Pity. "Performers drink free, though you're not really a performer yet, are you?"

"C'mon, Olivia," said Max.

"Fine. I guess she might as well enjoy herself as long as she's around. Although *others* are supposed to be working for their keep."

"One round and we're on the clock," Garland promised.

"Horseshit." But Olivia filled five tumblers from a pitcher, sliding the first over to Pity.

Pity hesitated, body tight with unease. A few hours ago she had begun to relish the possibilities that the Theatre offered. But now? She took a polite sip. "Thanks. It's good."

"Really?" said Olivia. "Because from the look on your face, it tastes like old spit."

Pity stared into the tumbler. The ice cubes knocked against one another woodenly. "I'm not much of a drinker is all."

"Interfere with your aim?"

"Don't know." Her eyes locked with Olivia's. "Never messed up my mother's, though, no matter how many empty bottles she left behind her as she walked the wall. Her balance, on the other hand…"

A pall fell over the group, a knot of silence in the surrounding revelry.

"I'm sorry," she said. "I don't know why I said that."

"It's okay, honey," said Luster. "You just watched a man die. Something like that always stirs up old ghosts."

"New ones, too." Pity leaned over her drink, thinking of Finn's flask the night before they ran. *For the pain,* she had said. Pity took another long swallow.

"I'm sorry," said Max. "I wanted to say something, but I was afraid if I did you might get a bad idea about the Theatre."

"A bad idea?" Pity shoved a stray piece of hair out of her face. "Max—they executed a man! With *snakes!* Is that a normal thing here?"

"No." He shoved his hands into his pockets. "Look, a Finale

is pretty rare. Only the very worst end up there—the ones who do more than enjoy the absence of law, who step over the line and keep going."

"Yeah, like this." Duchess pushed closer and lifted his silver shirt to reveal a jagged, florid scar. Pity's chest tightened as he twisted around to give her a better view. It started above his left hip bone, hooking around his waist and up to the middle of his back. "Not the prettiest thing about me, huh?"

"Where...did you get it?"

"A present from an admirer who liked to break his toys when he was done with them. This was before Casimir, when I was living on the streets." He let the shirt fall. "Those of us who worked the alleys knew it was happening. Didn't know who was doing it, but, well, we had to eat, right? I was lucky. I got away. But I didn't hide or look for a doctor. I came here. Walked right in the front door with my guts nearly hanging out because I knew what Selene would do about it." He paused. "They patched me up, took me in, and soon enough my admirer was the Theatre's featured attraction."

"Still..." Pity searched for the right words, embarrassed at having scolded him earlier.

"Still what?" Duchess drained his drink. "He got what was coming to him."

"What he's saying is that no one ends up in a Finale unless they deserve it," said Max. "And there are some people the world is better off without."

Did Beeks really deserve to die? Pity took a deep breath. Magnanimous or not, Selene was clearly not a woman to cross. "Is Halcyon going to ask me to do that? Because I'm not sure I could."

Max nudged her. "You didn't show this much reluctance when you nearly killed *me*."

"That was different. It was self-defense!"

There was a sudden, high cry. Pity and everyone around her turned toward it. A few yards away, in a padded red booth, a man clutched a young woman in white lingerie. She was pushing him away, a frantic look on her face.

"Son of a—"

Olivia launched herself onto the surface of the bar and leapt off, landing among scattering patrons. With a flick of her whip, the man in the booth was clawing at his throat; a yank tumbled him to the carpet. The woman in white retreated behind Olivia as the bartender's boot descended on the man's hand with an audible crunch. He howled.

"You got a bad memory or something? You've been warned already."

The man glared, his face half pain and half sneer. "What do you care? I'm a paying customer, aren't—"

Olivia ground his hand into the floor with her heel. Pity flinched as his argument turned into a scream. "This is *my* hall, and you will follow *my* rules when you're in it. Understand?"

Flossie materialized out of the onlookers, all peachy skin and bouncing pink lace. "Problem, Olivia?"

"Not anymore." The bartender whistled. A pair of Tin Men ran over. "Give him a shot."

One of the Tin Men jabbed the man with a shock stick. He bucked as every muscle contracted at once, a cry of pain trapped behind clenched teeth.

"Your turn," said Olivia.

Flossie addressed the offender. "I'm sorry, sir, but your patronage is no longer welcome in Casimir. Olivia, sweetie, you want to bust his other hand before they toss him out?"

Olivia shrugged. "Why not?"

"No!" he cried. "No, I'm sorry, please don't!"

"Oh, don't apologize to me, hon. Apologize to Kitty."

The man sniffled at the young woman. "I'm sorry, Kitty. I swear I am."

"Now, sir." Flossie leaned closer, her smile as doll-like as the rest of her. "If you ever try to come here again, Olivia will shoot you. *Happily*. Understand?"

He nodded vigorously. At Olivia's command, the Tin Men dragged him away.

Flossie put her arm around Kitty. "Come here, sweetie. You wanna take the rest of the night off?"

"Thanks, Flossie. I'm okay." She rubbed the tops of her arms. "He wouldn't quit pinching me. It hurt! I told him that wasn't my thing and someone else would be happy to accommodate him, but he just wouldn't *stop*."

Olivia returned to her spot behind the bar. She picked up the pitcher and pointedly refilled Pity's and Max's glasses.

"Message received," said Duchess. He and Garland wandered off. Luster was already engaged with the appreciative customer, sitting on her lap and offering a pill from a silver tin.

Pity raised an eyebrow at Olivia. "You're pretty dangerous for a bartender."

"Well, bartender *and* deputy head of security." Olivia grabbed a bottle. "For all the professions I've pursued in my time, they all seem to come down to the same thing eventually."

The same thing. The thought echoed in Pity's mind. Selene...
Casimir...they didn't hesitate to protect their own. She saw
Finn fall again, murdered by thieves who cared no more about
putting a bullet into her as they would a rabid dog. *Would you
have hesitated to see them executed for it?* The answer came
quick and clear: *No.* But what did it say about Pity that she'd
leave the difficult part to someone else?

The only steel in her is in those guns.

That wasn't true. She might not be tough enough for security work, might have failed to save Finn, but she wasn't a coward. She *wasn't.* And Max was right. There were some folks the
world was better off without.

She turned to him. "Okay. I understand."

"Understand what?"

"What Olivia just did...and the Theatre and Beeks. It's all
different kinds of justice, right?"

He thought for a moment. "That's a good way of putting it."

Justice, she repeated to herself. *I can handle justice.*

"Look," Max said, "even if you're in a show with a Finale,
what are the chances the audience would pick you? A bullet is
fast. Simple. The Theatre's audience? They want a *show.*"

There were no clocks in the Gallery, and Pity had no idea what
time it was when they finally stumbled back to her room. She
was exhausted and barefoot, shoes dangling in one hand.

"How in the world does Luster get around in these? My feet
are killing me! Wearing them is like trying to walk on river

stones!" Despite nursing her drinks all night, Pity felt warm all over. Words tumbled recklessly from her mouth. "Have you ever walked on river stones? You know how they get all mossy and slippery?"

Max laughed. "I can't say I have. Have you ever gone swimming in the ocean?"

"Are you kidding? I think Cessation is as close to an ocean as I've ever been." She unlocked the door and tossed the shoes into the corner. "Good riddance."

Max pointed. "Looks like someone left you a present."

On the table was a small satchel with half a dozen boxes on top of it. An orange note sat beside the pile.

"'Dearest Pity,'" she read, affecting dramatic intonation. "'A little something for tomorrow's rehearsal. See you at noon, sharp! Ever yours, Halcyon.'" She picked up one of the boxes. It rattled when she shook it. "I know that sound!"

Inside, bullets were stacked in neat layers. She picked one out. The smooth, cool casing was oddly soothing.

"Halcyon gives the best gifts." Max took the note from her hand. She felt a fresh flush of warmth when his fingers brushed hers. "Noon? I should let you get some sleep."

Pity gripped the bullet. She didn't want to sleep. And she didn't really want Max to go, either. Her earlier anxiety was gone, replaced by an unfamiliar energy, and she knew that if Max left, if the night ended, then the energy would, too.

But there was Selene's mandate to keep in mind. Pity hadn't earned her place in the Theatre yet. And if she failed in that, she'd be saying good-bye to Max for more than a few hours.

"You're right," she said. "It's late. And if I want to stick around, I better be able to shoot straight, right?"

Yet when he was gone, Pity lay wide-awake in bed, rolling the bullet back and forth between her fingers, back and forth, until it was so warm it felt a part of her.

CHAPTER 12

HALCYON WAS WAITING WHEN SHE ARRIVED AT THE arena the next day.

"We never hold rehearsals the day after a show," he explained, "so it is the optimal time to begin your acclimation."

Pity examined the deserted stands, hand resting on the satchel of bullets beside her gun belt. The ecstatic screams of a thousand voices sounded in her memory. *Will they cheer for me?* she wondered. Scream for her the way they screamed for Scylla and Beeks? Her eyes sought the spot where he had died, but all evidence of the previous night's show was gone. Pushing the dark thoughts to the back of her mind, Pity drew one of her guns and aimed it into the seats. She spun around slowly, letting herself get a feel for it.

A head popped up in one of the boxes—Widmer, the mechanic from the garage. "Not quite yet, please!"

She flipped the barrel toward the ceiling. "Sorry. I wasn't going to fire."

"No, but the enthusiasm is appreciated." Halcyon grinned his mad grin. "So tell me, what did you think of last night's performance?"

"It was"—she chose her words carefully—"like nothing I've ever seen before."

"Of course not!" He scowled. "That's because you can *only* see it here! Never mind, never mind, let's get started. Widmer, how are we coming?"

"Almost done. Just a few more adjustments." Widmer stood. "There!" He climbed over the lip of the box and lowered himself down to the stage floor. "Let's give it a try."

"Give what a try?" said Pity.

"The device that's going to keep you from killing the audience," Halcyon said. "As dramatic as that would be, I do believe it would affect the long-term viability of the act."

Widmer fiddled with a display screen he carried. "I've always wanted a reason to use this tech. Sadly, the amount of power it draws doesn't make it good for much."

He pressed the display again. There was a sudden shift in the air around them, a low vibration, so faint that Pity wondered if she imagined it.

Widmer pointed at the stands. "Take a shot now."

"There's no target."

"Just aim into the stands like you were before. Go on."

Pity raised her gun.

Bang!

Sparks exploded midair, at the boundary where the stage ended and the boxes began.

"Brilliant!" said Halcyon. "Pity, do it again!"

She fired over and over, until her gun was empty. Every bullet detonated like the first. "That's amazing."

"Runs all around the edge." Widmer smiled proudly. "And wait until you see what else I've got rigged! Get ready now."

A tube appeared out of the floor and spat three glass globes into the air. Pity hesitated for only a heartbeat. She drew her second gun and fired. The globes exploded. At the opposite edge of the floor, another three launched. She felled two, but her third shot missed and a sphere landed on the floor, rolling to a stop a few feet away.

"Dammit." She rubbed her eyes. "Guess I'm still a little worn around the edges."

"Nonsense!" said Halcyon. "No performer is perfect *all* the time. Why, we used to have a young man who swallowed swords…" He stopped. "Actually, you don't need to hear that story. Tsk—such a tragedy. But my point is that practice makes perfect!"

Pity reloaded. "So am I going to be shooting at launched targets all the time or—" She stopped. Halcyon was staring at her.

"Well, that won't do," he said.

"What?"

"That! It's rather slow and dull isn't it?"

She looked down at the half empty cylinder. "Well, if you want me to keep shooting I'm going to need to reload sometimes."

"I know, I know, but there's no showmanship to it!" He waved a hand erratically. "We shan't worry about that right now. I'll get Eva to work with you—she's got a good head for choreography. Now back to work!"

Halcyon and Widmer retreated to a box, giving Pity the run of the arena. At first, the globes launched at regular intervals, and she picked them off leisurely. Then Widmer upped the pace. Soon she was moving back and forth in the ring, spinning and twisting, ears straining for the faint *thwip* that accompanied each launch. Her heart pounded, but her fatigue was forgotten. She stayed focused on the challenge, rushing to reload between each volley. She wasn't always fast enough, but by the time Halcyon called to her to stop, she had destroyed a score of targets for each one that had made it to the floor.

"Very impressive," said Halcyon. "I think that's enough for today."

Pity holstered her weapons and wiped the sweat from her brow. She was tired, but it was a good, glowing tired. The best she'd felt in days. "When do I have to do this for real?"

"When I think you're ready. For now, practice, practice, practice! Here, tomorrow, same time. Until then, my dear"—he gave her a deep bow—"I bid you good afternoon!" He strode off in the direction of his office.

Widmer came up beside her. "So," he said, "what are your feelings on fireworks?"

Stomach quivering, Pity forced herself to look over the edge. Casimir's twenty-odd floors stood solid beneath her feet, but every time a breeze blew, her knees turned to pudding. Cessation spread out below her, dark as a blood blister against the pale desert. The black river of asphalt that had delivered her to Casimir cut through its midst, flowing to the oasis within an oasis.

Could you make it out there alone? A week had passed since she arrived, and though she pondered the question daily, no definitive answer ever came.

Pity turned back to the cool canopy of trees. A perfume of flowers enveloped her as an older man in a crisp suit strode past. She recognized him from the Gallery. Last night he had been entrenched at the tables, throwing hand after hand of dice, only pausing long enough to drink, belch, and grope whoever happened to be within reaching distance. This morning he inclined his head politely at Pity and continued strolling.

She returned the silent greeting and ran a hand over a cluster of flowers, their pale blue petals as soft as silk. The garden covered the entirety of the roof, a lush labyrinth of greenery and stone paths. It was nicknamed Eden, despite being one of the few places where people seemed to keep all their clothes *on*. Of Casimir's many delights—which included lavish dining rooms, a library full of books, and even a cinema hall—Eden was her favorite.

"Morning." Max appeared from one of the paths. "Enjoying the garden?"

She nodded. "It's so peaceful. And I've never been so high before."

He went to the edge. "Ugh, I hate that part."

"So why are you looking?"

He smirked, the silver rings in his lips reflecting a flash of sun. "Not liking something isn't the same as being afraid of it."

"It's so quiet." She gazed out over the city. "Hard to believe what it turns into when the sun goes down. On the commune, days are busy. Nights are as quiet as ... well, as *now*."

"It only looks quiet." Max took a measuring tape from his pocket. "Sorry to interrupt, but I was looking for you for a reason. If you're going to perform in the Theatre, you'll need a costume. So I need some measurements."

Pity eyed the tape. "I hope that means I'll be wearing more than paint."

His mouth turned up at the corner. "Do you want to go somewhere more private?"

She glanced around the nearly deserted garden. "This seems to be about as private as it gets around here."

"Can't argue with that. Stand up straight," Max instructed. "Put out your arms."

She obeyed. Max laid the tape from her shoulder to her wrist. He pulled out a small notebook and pencil and made a notation. Then he measured Pity from shoulder to hip. His touch was practiced, professional, but her stomach fluttered each time his fingers brushed against her. *This is his job,* she told herself. But that didn't quell the sensations kindled within her. She stared straight ahead, face warm.

"You said you weren't born in Cessation," she said as a distraction. "So where did you live before here?"

"I've been around a few places. More than a few."

"Have you been to Columbia?"

"Yes." There was a brusqueness in the reply. "It's not a place I'm fond of."

"Why not? I've heard it's something to be seen."

"Oh, it's a fine place to live," he conceded. "If you have wealth and influence. For everyone else... Well, Olivia wasn't exaggerating when she said you'd have been lucky to find a bed to rent. Trust me, you're better off here." He stepped back a pace. "Uh, I also need to measure your... Well, keep your arms out, please."

Pity's cheeks tingled—red as beets, she was certain. She raised her eyes to the sky as he looped the measuring tape around her torso, bringing it back together at the swell of her chest. She searched for something else to say, but her tongue felt tacked to the roof of her mouth. No secret flirtation or hayloft kisses from the boys on the commune had left her feeling half as flustered. Finally, Max let the tape fall. He took note of her waist and then dropped to one knee.

"Your, uh, inseam," he said.

Was it her imagination or was there a flush to his face, too? Her heart thumped as his knuckles brushed against her thigh. She lowered her arms and concentrated on a puff of cloud. An agonizing moment later, she heard the scratch of pencil against paper.

Max stood. "Done. Wasn't so bad, was it?"

"Not at all," Pity replied, a touch too lightly.

Dense silence floated between them.

"Do you want to go for a walk?" Max said hurriedly.

"Where?"

He pointed over the edge of the building. "There's more to Cessation than Cas."

"Is it...safe?"

"Of course. You're under Miss Selene's umbrella right now. No one will lay a hand on us. They know what would happen if they did."

The Rousseaus? Pity guessed silently. *Or maybe the Zidanes?*

"Right," she said aloud. "I think I'll bring my guns anyway."

Pity kept a hand resting on the butt of one gun as they left Casimir's protective circle and entered the maze of buildings. Her veins thrummed, but more with excitement than with fear. As midday approached, the city was coming to life. The streets were rougher and dirtier beyond Casimir's boundaries, but not what she had expected. The gritty, garish cloak of night had been put aside. Normal-looking folks carried on with normal-looking errands. People greeted one another with smiles, and a pack of children played in the streets.

They walked slowly so she could take everything in. Max bought them skewers of grilled meat from a street vendor and a bag of oranges. He was right—the streets seemed safe enough during the day, and Pity was pleased to see pairs of Tin Men patrolling at intervals. Even when they passed dim doorways that leaked smoke and other ill odors—where jagged men and women lingered, skin sallow and eyes cold—no one gave them any trouble. A few even nodded politely.

Miss Selene's umbrella casts a nice shade, Pity thought.

Max paused before an alley. "Hold on a second."

A moment later, a young boy melted out of the shadows. He was skinny, his clothes faded and threadbare, but he looked healthy enough. Pity guessed he was about ten.

"Hey, Tye," said Max. "Anything interesting going on?"

The boy's eyes flickered to her. "There's a new girl in the Theatre," he said flatly. "People say she's a sharpshooter."

"Smart-ass," said Max. "Anything else?"

"A big group of dissidents came in early this morning. They're camped over by the smoke dens."

"Where'd they come from?"

Tye shrugged. "Dunno. Looks like they seen a fight, though."

"Hmm." Max handed the bag of oranges to him, along with some currency. "Thanks."

The boy faded back into the alley.

"Who was that?" asked Pity.

"One of Cessation's strays. Good eyes." He started walking again. "When I first got here, I knew no one, had nothing but some paints and brushes. I spent my first night huddled in an alley, hungry and cold. Some kids found me. I didn't know what to do, so I painted them a picture on a scrap of wood. They took it and brought me some food. I return the favor now and again."

"That's sweet," said Pity. "So you going to tell me where we're headed?"

"Shopping."

"*Shopping?*"

"What's the matter?" he said. "You don't like—"

A shout sounded ahead of them. An instant later a young man careened around a corner, three Old Reds on his heels. The nearest Red got close enough to shove him, and he went sprawling into a wall. Trapped, he pressed his back to the dirty brick as the pursuers closed in around him.

"Nowhere to go," one of them taunted.

"Please," the young man pleaded. "I don't have anything to steal!"

"We'll see about that." All three pulled knives.

Pity reached for her guns. Max grabbed her arm to stop her, then turned and let out a piercing whistle. One of the Old Reds looked around at the sound. It was the blond girl who had painted the bloody smile for Pity.

"Shit," she said. "Tin Men, incoming."

"What?" The taunter spotted Max. "Oh. Selene's lapdogs." He grinned and raised his hands. The knife disappeared into his sleeve. "We weren't doing anything."

"So move along, then." Pity shook Max off and drew but kept her barrels pointed down. "Go."

"Aw, she wants to play." The blonde giggled. "Good. Pretty girls have pretty guts."

Pity kept her eye on the girl. The way she held her knife was off. *Like she's gonna throw.* She risked a glance back. A pair of Tin Men were approaching at a quick pace, rifles raised, but they were still far away.

The girl flinched.

Bang!

The knife went flying.

Pity took aim again. "Next one to try that loses a hand instead of their weapon."

But as the Tin Men closed in, the gang members bolted. Pity

watched them as they retreated, her guns still drawn, while Max
checked on the young man they had cornered.

"Hey, are you okay?"

The young man—a boy, really, Pity saw as she drew closer—
stared at them, wide-eyed and clearly terrified. She spotted a
bandage around his arm and a cut on his forehead, though neither looked fresh. But he nodded.

"What's your name?" Pity asked.

"A-Ari," he stammered. "I ... I got lost."

Max looked him over, concern tightening his features. "Lost
from where, Ari?"

Tears gathered in his eyes. "I don't ... I'm not ..."

"He's one of them." Pity turned to see that Tye had returned,
though he had already stashed the gifted oranges somewhere.
"The group by the smoke dens."

"C'mon," Max said, signaling to the Tin Men to follow.
"We'll get you back there."

Whether it was the Tin Men's uniforms or Max's calm
authority, Ari obeyed, following closely as Tye led them down
a side street. The buildings turned noticeably rougher, and Pity
kept her hands close to her gun belt. Under Selene's protection
or not, the encounter had left her apprehensive.

"I'm starting to question your definition of the word *safe*,"
she said to Max as they walked.

"Cessation is as safe as it gets for *us*," he said. "Everyone
else ... Well, outside Casimir the gangs run their fair share of
gambling halls and goods trafficking. They know not to cause
too much trouble, and so long as they pay their dues, Selene lets

them be." He paused. "The Old Reds need a reminder from time to time. They're run by a man named Daneko. Let's just say that if he had his way, Selene wouldn't be the one in charge of Cessation."

"Doesn't sound like a very smart position to take," said Pity as they rounded a corner and walked straight into a war zone.

CHAPTER 13

ONCE, WHEN PITY WAS YOUNG, A MAN ON THE COMMUNE took a fall from his motorcycle while out hunting alone. For two days he walked back on a badly injured leg, and that was the only reason she knew what infected flesh smelled like.

It was one of the first things she noticed as they entered the makeshift camp, set up in a sprawling graveled lot between buildings. Unlike the Reformationists' settlement outside the city's gates, here there were no orderly rows and pristine tents. People appeared to have set up where they fell; tarps strung between battered vehicles were the closest things to shelter that Pity saw. Exhausted eyes watched them as they passed, and everywhere she looked she saw bruises, burns, and blood.

"Mama!" Ari ran to a woman hunched over a boiling pot of bandages.

"Where have you been?" The woman stood and embraced him. "I told you to stay close."

"I'm okay," he said, his face half buried in her shoulder. "I took a wrong turn. They helped me back."

With a wary look at the Tin Men with them, she released her son. "Thank you."

"Happy to help," Max said, though he sounded anything but. He scanned the camp, his face grim. "Who did this to you?"

"Who do you think?" Dr. Starr appeared from beneath one of the tarp lean-tos, medical bag in hand. His sleeves were rolled to the elbow, and there were specks of crimson on his forearms.

Max swore.

"Soldiers in black trucks came to our town a few days ago," Ari's mother said. "They told us to be gone by morning. When we didn't listen..." She spat angrily. "CONA bastards. Anyone who won't swear allegiance they still treat like enemies. We only want to live in peace. Is that so much to ask?"

Pity felt the blood drain from her face. "CONA did this?"

"It's not the first time." Without prompting, Starr took Ari's injured arm and began unwrapping the bandage. "Doubt it will be the last."

"But why?"

"They've been expanding west for years," Max explained. "Slowly but consistently. And when they come to a dissident town or settlement they want gone...well, this is the result."

Revulsion coursed through Pity, part of her still disbelieving despite what she saw with her own eyes. *It's not like they'd feature this sort of thing on the broadcasts, though, would they?*

Between the displaced dissidents and the hanged men at Last Stop, she wondered what else those broadcasts didn't show.

Max thought for a moment. "You said they were in black trucks?"

Ari nodded. "With gold markings on the side."

Confusion replaced Pity's disgust. "That's not CONA military, it's—"

"Drakos-Pryce," Max finished. "CONA hires them. Their killers have even fewer scruples than the military. And in return for the dirty work, they get their choice of government contracts, resources—whatever they want." The undisguised vehemence in his voice—a stark contrast to his usual demeanor—took Pity aback. "Does Miss Selene know about this?" he said to Starr.

"Yes." The doctor dabbed some ointment on Ari's arm. "The other medics and I have seen to the worst of the injuries, and there should be a legion of porters arriving any minute with a hot meal."

"Can you stay, too?" Max asked the Tin Men. "Make sure the gangs don't harass anyone else."

One of them lifted his rifle. "We'll keep them in line."

"Thank you again," said Ari's mother. "At least there are some kind folks still in this world."

A smile fluttered and failed on Max's lips as he waved goodbye to Ari and guided Pity away from the camp. Sometime during the exchange, Tye had disappeared again, though she guessed that wasn't what was distressing Max. He moved with a taut, frustrated gait, as if ready to break into a run.

"What will happen to them?" She quickened her pace to keep up. "Will they be okay?"

"Maybe."

"Max, wait!" She grabbed his arm. "Are *you* okay?"

He slowed to a stop. For a moment, his eyes burned with glassy anger, but when they focused on her, his features softened. "Yes, I'm fine. Just...tired of seeing that."

"We could have stayed and helped."

"Selene will send food and medical supplies. We'd only be in the way." He sighed. "Like Starr said, this is nothing new. Most likely they'll patch themselves up, find a new spot to settle, and pray for a quiet year or two before CONA shows up again."

Despite the assurances, Pity ached to do something. If only because the experience of having the world ripped from beneath her feet was familiar now and still too fresh. Thinking of Finn, she glanced back toward the camp and wondered how many people from the dissident town hadn't made it to Cessation.

But he was right. Starr and the Tin Men were there, and more help was on the way. "Which way to Casimir, then? These streets are a maze."

"We're not going back yet."

"What?"

Max brightened a little, hints of his usual persona returning. "I told you there was more to Cessation than Casimir, and that wasn't it. You should see something good today, too."

The camp had left Pity with a sour feeling in her chest, one that would be easier to contemplate behind safe walls. But moments ago Max had looked nearly despondent and now...

If it will cheer him up. "Fine. I guess I still have plenty of ammo if we run into more trouble."

They made their way back to the main streets, soon arriving at a large square building with rows of narrow windows across its front side. Above the entrance, a hand-painted sign read BLACKMARK, flanked by large black Xs. People were coming and going at a steady pace, and Pity was heartened to see more Tin Men. Their presence alleviated some of her worry as she and Max pushed their way through the front doors.

Inside was an electric bedlam that rivaled even that of the Gallery. It was a single open space, the ceiling five stories above their heads. Sunlight streamed through the windows onto a twisted maze of booths and stalls.

"Watch for pickpockets," said Max.

"I've got nothing for them to steal," Pity said, "unless they want a handful of bullets."

"Boots!" the vendors called. "Circuit boards! Vaccines! Spices!"

Though Pity couldn't quite put the battered dissidents out of her mind, BlackMark succeeded in garnering the lion's share of her attention. Compared to the commune's commissaries, it was a cornucopia. She saw dried meats and beans, grains, and fruits of all kinds. There were guns and knives, too, mostly old war-issue stock that had seen better days. As they moved closer to the middle, the booths grew nicer, filled with silks and perfumes, and clothing that reminded Pity of what Flossie's lot preferred.

"See anything you like?" Max picked through a bin of paint cans. He chose one and paid the vendor.

"There's so much! Even if I had any money, this is like looking through a haystack to find a needle I don't need." And it
hardly felt right, ogling the endless goods after coming from a
group of people who'd lost almost everything.

But, she thought, maybe once her wages from the Theatre
started, it would be fun to come back and browse.

"I didn't bring you all the way here only to let you leave
empty-handed. Here, do you like scarves? This one would—"

"Make me look ridiculous?" Pity laughed and turned to
another stall. There, among a selection of leather items, a black
gun belt with silver buckles caught her eye. Unable to resist,
she caught the vendor's attention and pointed. "Can I see that,
please?"

The vendor gave her a dubious look until he spotted the
revolvers at her hips. He turned all smiles. "Of course, miss,
here you are. The very best leather!"

Pity ran her fingertips over the tooled designs. They were
expertly done.

"Try it on," urged Max.

"It's too nice." She began to give it back.

Max stopped her. "Pity, try that belt on. You're getting something while we're here, and I swear it will be that scarf unless
you—"

"Okay, okay!" She unhooked her old belt—her *father's* old
belt, she reminded herself—and handed it to Max. Then she
strapped the black one around her waist and slipped the guns
into the holsters. It fit like it had been made for her.

"How much?" asked Max.

The vendor quoted a figure. Max threw back a much lower

one. They haggled back and forth, but Pity barely heard a word. Grinning ear to ear, she admired the sheen of the leather, the smoothness of the finish. It was the finest gun belt she had ever seen.

And Max was buying it for her.

Finally, the price was settled and Max handed over the money. "You want to keep this?" he asked of the old belt.

She stared at it, one of the few remaining pieces of her past. "No, I do not."

Max tossed it to the vendor. "Don't let me catch you charging an arm and a leg for this one, too."

Her face felt like it might split from smiling. "I'll pay you back, I promise, just as soon as I—"

"It's a gift."

"No. It's too much."

"It's *not*," he insisted. "I don't like having too much money in my pocket anyway. Keeps me honest." He paused. "And after all, we can't have you doing your act looking like a beat-up old drifter."

"I wasn't aware that I *looked* like a beat-up old drifter."

"Hmm, I suppose I should hush up," he said with a smile, "before you decide to test out that thing."

During their return to Casimir, Pity walked a little taller, her spirits lifted by the new gun belt. At first, she thought Max's mood had improved as well. But he seemed to withdraw again as they strolled, a troubled, distant look in his eyes, as if he were seeing somewhere else entirely.

CHAPTER 14

"THE FIRST THING—THE MOST IMPORTANT THING—YOU need to remember," Eva Zidane said, "is to never lose the crowd. If you lose the crowd, you lose the act."

Pity shifted from foot to foot, nervous for her first real training session. As promised, Halcyon had arranged for Eva to work with her, but Pity still had little idea what to expect.

The woman pointed to the opposite end of the ring, where a glass bottle balanced atop a stool. "Now—shoot that for me, please."

Pity drew and fired. The bottle shattered.

"Terrible!" Eva said.

"Why? I hit it, didn't I?"

Eva tipped her delicate chin up. She had striking, earthy features, with olive skin and long-lashed green eyes. When she spoke, there was a hint of an unfamiliar accent, as faded as an old scar. "Is that what you think the Theatre Vespertine's audience comes all the way to Cessation to see?"

Pity crossed her arms. "I aim. I shoot. What else am I supposed to do?"

"Give them a show."

"Yeah, well, it *is* more exciting when my targets aren't sitting still."

"That's not the point," said Eva. "You must find the dramatic in the mundane, capture the attention of the crowd." She pulled a thin blade from her sleeve, turned toward the outside of the ring, and threw. The knife embedded in the wall. "How exciting was that, pray tell?"

Before Pity could reply, Eva twisted in a sudden pirouette. Another blade flew, hitting above the first. She danced forward, her brown skirt spinning as a third and fourth knife landed to each side of it. Finally, she cartwheeled, legs slicing through the air. As she righted, a fifth blade soared. She turned back to Pity, eyes as bright as emeralds. "The *skill* and the *show* are not the same thing."

Pity eyed the cross of blades. "I see what you mean, but I don't think I can do a cartwheel with my guns."

"Then we will find you your own steps. Do you dance?"

"Like a spooked mule."

"You will learn," said Eva. "The act is like a dance. You are one partner, the audience is the other. You must always lead. The audience must always follow. Do you understand?"

"How am I supposed to lead when I need to concentrate on shooting?"

"For you, it should be simple. Your targets are the steps; your bullets are the music. The Theatre will add its own touches, but the most important flourishes will have to come from you. Let's practice. Empty your guns."

"*Empty* them?" said Pity.

"Please. If we are going to dance, I'd rather avoid unintentional injury. I contend with that enough in my own act."

Spin and point, point and spin. Pity obeyed as Eva led her through a strange choreography. She didn't simply aim, she arced her arm in a wide circle, leading with her hips as she moved. Eva showed her how to add grace to every step, embellish every movement. A glide, a step, a hop, a spin—no matter what Eva did, she was the embodiment of elegance.

Pity, however, was not. "I feel ridiculous."

"Well, that is apt, since you look ridiculous." But her tone was patient. "It will come to you eventually."

Along with what else? "Eva?"

"Yes?"

"Have you ever done a Finale?"

She was silent for a moment. "Marius and I have done them together, yes."

"Was it hard?"

Eva pulled out another dagger and stared at it, turning the blade over in her hand. "Killing is rarely easy, nor should it be. But those who end up in a Finale are not people whom you can—or *should*—spare."

Pity holstered her guns. "It's only that I've...never..." She couldn't count the scroungers who'd killed Finn. With no time to think about what she was doing, the grenade had been more luck than intent. While that probably didn't mean much to them—dead was dead, after all—it made a difference to her.

Eva gave her an understanding smile. "Let me ask you— what do you gain by fretting over a moment that may be years in arriving, if it ever does? My husband likes to say that worry is a poor expenditure of life's currency. Right now you should be focused on your performance. You will do that many, many more times than you'll ever do a Finale."

If, Pity didn't bother to add, *I make it past the first one.*

For weeks Pity practiced her showmanship. Sometimes Eva was there; other times she worked on her own. Her body ached constantly as unused muscles were woken and pushed, but it was an invigorating sort of pain, soaked away each evening in her tub. At first, only Halcyon or Max watched her practice, but as the days wore on, more onlookers peppered the stands: Marius, even warmer than his wife; the blank-faced Rousseaus, who never said a word to her; and other Casimir inhabitants she hadn't met yet. It made Pity so nervous that, at first, she missed more shots than ever. But eventually she settled into the performance, finding a certain rhythm in her shooting and the sporadic applause.

Still, she reminded herself daily, a few dozen people were nothing like the real thing.

Halcyon must have thought so as well, because when he announced the next show, she wasn't included in it. Not yet, he told her, but soon. There was no set schedule for the Theatre; instead, it was determined by Halcyon's mood or whoever important happened to be in Cessation at the time.

Pity spent her second show behind the scenes with the other performers, in the spacious passages that ran beneath the stage and stands. There the roar of the crowd was muted, replaced by the frantic hustle of preparations. Trying to keep out of the way, she retreated to the bright alcove that functioned as Max's work area during a show, where Clare Rousseau stood on a riser as he painted glittering fish scales onto her skin.

"I don't know how you do that," Pity said.

"Same way you shoot. Plenty of practice." He dabbed on a last bit of blue. "Okay, that's it. Stand still for a few minutes while you dry." He wiped his hands on a rag and turned to Pity. "How's the act coming?"

"Good, I guess."

They went over to a wall of screens displaying various areas in the theatre. In the arena, a miniature ship of wood and satin sailed upon a sea of blue fog. It was manned by a pack of pirates, drawn closer and closer to an island by beautiful sirens, until the mock ship crashed upon the mock shore.

"Wait..." Pity spotted a familiar face in the crowd. She pointed to a screen. "I know her. That's Maria Alton!"

"Who's she?"

"The governor of my territory. Every time she visited the commune our mayor would trip over his own feet trying to impress her."

Alton sat in one of the luxury boxes. Beside her, in a shirt opened enough to show a hint of collarbone, sat Garland. When he leaned over and whispered something in the governor's ear, she flushed visibly and laughed.

For a moment, Pity imagined herself in the woman's place.

She quickly banished the thought. "Why would she visit a place like this?"

"Besides the obvious?" Max smirked. "Pity, half of Casimir's clientele are CONA officials or corporate agents. More deals get made here than in the halls of Columbia."

"And CONA is okay with that?" Pity watched Maria Alton. Though Garland massaged one of her hands in his, she spoke to another man beside her, the movements of their mouths furtive despite the din of the show.

"Not exactly. But what Selene offers, people want. There's no need for forced propriety or moral smoke screens here. She keeps secrets, brokers connections, and isn't beholden to anyone. In its way, Cessation is as powerful as Columbia." His piercings twinkled in the screen's light. "C'mon, I have something to show you."

He led her to a workroom littered with mannequins and bolts of cloth.

"Wait here," he said, features alight with eagerness. "And close your eyes."

Pity put her hands on her hips but obeyed, content to submit to whatever game Max was playing. His footsteps moved away and returned.

"Okay, you can look."

Pity opened her eyes.

The costume had a simple, striking elegance: a lavender blouse with a darker half corset laced over it, and fitted pants of a supple silvery gray material. Beside the mannequin wearing the outfit sat a pair of high black boots that matched the black leather of Pity's new gun belt.

"I..." Stunned wonder gripped her. "I love it!" She hesitantly ran the tips of her fingers over the purple silk, afraid the slightest touch would mar it. "But how is it going to look on me?"

"Only one way to find out." He gestured to a folding screen set in one corner.

Pity went behind it and shrugged out of her clothes. Acutely aware of her bareness and the thin partition that separated her and Max, she dressed quickly. The costume hugged every curve and angle of her body perfectly. And yet she couldn't help but feel like an imposter, as if it couldn't possibly be for her.

"Does it fit?" Max called.

She tightened her gun belt. "Yes."

"And are you going to come out sometime tonight?"

Her flush turned to one of embarrassment. "I'm considering my options."

"If you don't want to let one person see you," he said, "how are you going to let a thousand?"

"Exactly."

"There's nothing to be afraid of."

Squaring her shoulders, she took a deep breath and stepped out. "I'm not afraid. I'm just...not used to wearing costumes."

Max grinned and set upon her immediately, fussing with the laces of the corset and adjusting the lay of her holsters on her hips. Pity went as rigid as the mannequin.

"The hem of the pants needs to come up a bit, but otherwise..." When he unbuttoned the top button of her blouse, so that more of her neck showed, a shiver raced from her throat to the bottoms of her heels. "There. Perfect. How does it feel?"

Pity took a welcome few steps away, drew her guns, and spun. "I'll have to stand a bit straighter than I'm used to, but... I can work with this."

"Excellent," said Max. "Because Halcyon has already scheduled the next show, a week from now." He paused. "And he wants you to debut."

CHAPTER 15

THE EVENING FINALLY ARRIVED AND, WITH IT, DISMAY.
Pity was to go on after Scylla. From the staging area, she could
hear the hoots and cries of the audience, feel the sensual charge
in the air. A promise of beauty and the threat of death were
Scylla's trade—how could she follow that? She leaned against a
wall, drawing one tight breath after another.

There had been no final, full rehearsal of her act. Halcyon
had said he didn't believe in such things. Still, Eva had worked
Pity for extra hours each day, meeting her early, meeting her
late, in whatever moments the Theatre had to spare.

*Stare into the crowd. Make them think you're looking at
them.*

Move your hips. Don't be stiff.

Smile, but not too much.

The directions had come as rapid-fire as Pity's shots.

As the days raced forward, each night brought a fresh onset of worry. *Why did I ever think I could do this?* she thought, staring into the darkness of her bedroom. *I'm gonna fail and Selene is gonna put me out, and when that happens...*

Her ruminations would go no further. The fear of Cessation was no longer a fear of the unknown. The few weeks she had spent in the city had taught her it wasn't weapons or strength that kept you safe in the world; it was your associations. Your family, your friends, your gang—survival was about who stood beside you.

She couldn't—*wouldn't*—return to the commune. Her mother and Finn were dead.

If Pity failed in the Theatre, she'd be left standing alone.

"Relax," said Eva. "You need to be calm. Focused."

"I'm trying." Each time her heart began to slow, another round of cheers would sound, and the anxiety would come flooding back.

"You want something to help you relax?" Luster pulled out her silver tin.

"Put those away!" Max snapped. "Or she won't be able to hit anything."

"I'm trying to help. Look at how pale she is."

Pity waved them both away. "I'm just nervous." She rechecked the cylinders in her guns for the hundredth time. *Full.* She carried more ammo, but not as much as she would have liked. Every shot counted. Widmer knew how many bullets she had; he would keep track, and she wouldn't run out...she hoped.

"Not to add to that nervousness"—Luster shifted from foot to foot, tiny ankles angling precariously in her high heels—"but so you know, Miss Selene is in the audience tonight."

Pity's gut twisted.

She's come to judge.

I can't do this.

I have to do this.

Backing out wasn't an option. A new act in the Theatre Vespertine was no small event—Halcyon had made that very clear. Announcements had been made; the word spread through the city and its web of associations. There were hundreds of eager bodies above her head, enticed by Scylla but really waiting for her and for whatever she had to show them.

It's not so hard. That's what her mother had said to her, back in the days when Pity missed more shots than she landed. But handgun or rifle, whether they were aiming at practice targets or live game, her mother had always said the same thing: *Stay calm. Sight your target.*

Inhale, aim. Exhale, shoot.

Pity raised one of her guns and pressed the cold steel to her forehead. *Momma, if you're listening, help me shoot straight.* She laughed nervously as she holstered the weapon.

"What?" said Eva.

"I was thinking about my mother. I doubt this is what she had in mind when she taught me how to handle a gun." *Then again,* Pity thought, *her own talent for it didn't get her where she expected, either.*

Widmer buzzed by them. "Saddle up," he called. "Scylla is almost finished."

"Good luck." Luster gave her a quick peck on the cheek. "I'll be watching from the stands." She ran off.

"And I'll be watching from here," said Max.

Pity took a deep breath and let it out, trying to exhale the apprehension smothering her from within. "What if I—"

Max took Pity's hands in his. "This is nothing," he said quietly.

She shook her head. "This is *everything*. I've already lost that once. I don't know if...if I can..." She trailed off, overcome by the truth of the words. She stared at her fingers entwined with Max's. *I don't want to lose any more.*

I don't want to lose this.

"I mean that this is nothing for *you*. Remember when you took that second shot at me, when we found you? You were beat half to death. But when you raised that gun and I saw the look in your eyes, I thought, 'This girl doesn't miss twice.'"

"But I did miss."

"Only because of Olivia. Even so, I felt the wind of that bullet on my cheek." He gave her a loose hug. "You weren't going to miss then, and you're not going to miss tonight."

A smile spread on her face, one she was powerless to stop. "Thank you, Max."

As he released her, Widmer reappeared.

"Scylla is clear," he said. "It's time."

With a final glance at Eva and Max, she followed the engineer into the dim tunnels that crisscrossed beneath the arena floor. Scylla sauntered by, a python hanging lazily about her bare shoulders. "Good luck," she said in a way that sounded entirely contrary.

Widmer led Pity to a round platform. "Stand here," he

instructed. "Halcyon will do his introduction and—well, you know it by now." He clapped a hand on her arm and ran off to get into his own position.

Halcyon's voice rang out from above, his words muted but clear. "Now, a treat! Tell me, Cessation, do you want to see something new?"

The crowd cried out in assent.

"That doesn't sound very enthusiastic to me..."

Pity winced as the air shook with the applause that followed. That she could garner such a response filled her with disbelief.

"You've convinced me! You've convinced me!" Halcyon announced. "Our latest performer comes to us from far beyond the borders of our little hamlet, from the humblest of the humble CONA communes. No serpents for her, no! Instead, only cold, deadly steel. If you ever meet her on the plains, in a dark alley, or simply in passing, beware! She is peerless among sharpshooters, blessed with the lightning speed of a jackrabbit and the accuracy of a striking hawk!"

A striking hawk? Pity rolled her eyes.

"Welcome, all of you, Serendipity Jones—deadliest shot in the west!"

Her platform began to rise. A few feet away, another descended. Halcyon stood upon it. He winked at her. Then the tunnel was gone and the arena surrounded her. Pity blinked. The lights were warmer and brighter than she had expected, and the stands were packed to capacity. Her heart thumped against her ribs as she searched for familiar faces, but it was impossible—there were too many people in the shadowed stands.

She took another breath.

Win the crowd, Eva had said. *Seduce them, excite them, or shock them, but* win *them.*

She scanned the boxes. The one person it wasn't hard to find was Selene, in the largest and most luxurious. She was seated between two men Pity didn't recognize: one with coppery brown hair warmed by the cast of the stage lights, the other older and bald, with a midnight-dark beard and a grim set to his features. Never far, Beau and Adora sat behind them.

The applause slowed to a trickle.

Win the crowd, she thought. *Win the crowd.*

Pity drew both weapons, pointing the barrels toward her feet, and waited. The audience waited with her, voices hushed, breath held.

A moment later, she felt the low thrum of the barrier.

Win the crowd.

Pity raised one gun, pointed it at Selene, and fired.

With a speed that rivaled the shot, Beau was halfway out of his seat as three bullets exploded into blue sparks. Pity flinched at the look on his face. But in front of him, Selene showed no signs of disturbance, her expression placid.

The stands went dead quiet.

Sweat broke out on Pity's brow as biting moments passed. No one spoke, no one even moved.

Then Selene raised her hands and clapped.

Applause erupted from the onlookers, but Pity didn't waste another second to savor her dramatic gambit. Neither did Widmer. The glass globes launched—first to her right, then to her left. Each burst as her shots found them, showering the arena with a rainbow of detonations. The launchers were positioned throughout the stage; one popped up next to her, forcing her to skip backward to find her aim. Widmer was herding her, and she let herself be herded.

One, two, three... She counted her bullets with vigilant precision. When one gun emptied, she'd holster the other and reload, brandishing the weapon to the crowd with a huge smile on her face. They cheered, stamped their feet, and even laughed when Pity decided to play with them, emptying both guns into one section of the stands. *I hope you're keeping count, too, Widmer.*

She fell into an energized rhythm.

Inhale, aim. Exhale, shoot.

Dance.

Flourish.

Pose.

Eva's instruction came to her more easily than expected, bolstered by the cheers every time she hit her target. She only faltered once, her foot catching against the other so that she stumbled. Her shot went wide and a glass globe fell to the ground. Pity just smiled and shrugged dramatically. The audience rewarded her with good-natured laughter.

High above, a cluster of silver, birdlike gliders were released. Pity picked them off as they circled down toward her, reloaded, and then took out the spring-loaded discs that Widmer had rigged to fly up from the floor. Finally, for the apex of her act, nine silver rods descended from the ceiling. At the tip of each was a small golden ball, barely larger than an egg. Pity aimed. As she did, they began to move.

She inhaled sharply. In practice, they had remained stationary. *Dammit, Halcyon!*

The rods spun in an ever-expanding circle, spreading outward toward the edge of the arena. Pity steadied herself. Much faster and she would never be able to hit them. It was now or never.

She aimed.

Bang! Bang! Bang!

One by one, the targets disappeared in a spray of sparks.

As they rained down, Pity sighted her final target: a larger orb that appeared above the center of the arena. When it shattered, she threw her arms victoriously into the air, the silver barrels of her guns sparkling as an eruption of golden flames enveloped her.

Applause ushered her back into the dark. Drenched in sweat, her heart raced. But now it was from elation. They had liked her. Hell, they had *loved* her. Even Miss Selene had stood for the ovation.

I don't have to leave, she thought gleefully. *There's no way Selene would put me out after that.*

When she reached the floor of the tunnels, she found Halcyon waiting.

"Bravo, Serendipity, bravo!" He handed her a single purple rose.

"I-I can't believe—" she said. "I mean, I didn't think I could—"

"I never had a doubt." He dipped his head and was gone again, off to introduce the next act.

She started down the tunnel, half drunk from euphoria and the heady scent of the flower. A male silhouette came toward her from the opposite end. Widmer, she thought, or even Max, come to congratulate her.

But when the figure stepped into one of the lights, it was Beau.

He said nothing as he lunged at her. His hand wrapped around her throat. The rose fell from her fingers as her head thumped against the concrete wall. Stars of pain winked in the edges of her vision. She tried to cry out, but only a faint croak escaped.

Beau jammed his gun under her chin.

"If you ever do anything like that again," he hissed, pale eyes boring into her, "you won't live to see the next sunrise. Do you understand me?" The wrath on his handsome features chilled Pity to her core. He pressed the gun so hard that it bit into her flesh. "Say it! I want you to say that you understand."

He loosened his grip.

"What I understand," Pity wheezed, "is that if you don't point that away from me, we're going to learn which of us can pull a trigger faster."

His eyes narrowed and flickered down to see the barrel pointed at his gut. The corner of his mouth twitched. "Twelve shots, little girl. That's all you've got. I counted. Right now you're on empty."

"Am I?" She held his gaze, jaw set. "I've had a couple of minutes. And I think you'd agree that a smart person keeps their piece loaded in a place like Cessation, right?"

Beau glared at her. Finally, he released her fully and stepped back. He lowered his weapon but made no move to put it away.

"Remember what I said. A smart person also knows when not to press their luck." He turned on his heel and strode off, leaving her slumped against the wall.

When he was far enough away that she knew he wasn't coming back, she raised a trembling hand to her throat. Fear still coursed through her. Her skin was clammy, her muscles weak.

It was a stupid idea, to shoot at Selene. Even with the barrier, she had known that. *But it had worked, hadn't it?*

When she felt strong enough, she straightened and smoothed out her clothes. But before starting down the tunnel again, she flipped open the cylinder of her revolver. Six empty chambers stared up at her. One by one, she reloaded that gun, and then the other.

Only when she had finished did her hands stop shaking.

CHAPTER 16

WHEN THE SHOW CONCLUDED, THE ENTIRE COMPANY ESCORTED Pity to the Gallery, where cheers erupted the moment she walked through the door.

"You were great!" exclaimed Max.

"You were perfect!" upped Luster.

Garland said nothing but threw her over his shoulder and carried her to the bar. By the time he deposited her there, she was beet-red and breathless. Olivia pressed a full, foaming bottle of champagne into her hand. She also slipped her a fold of paper.

I didn't take you as one for dramatics, it read, *but amusing touch. I'll be looking forward to your next show. —S.*

Pity searched the sea of heads. She found Selene in the very back of the room, near her elevator, cordoned off in a spacious, curved booth flanked by Tin Men. Even at that distance, Pity caught the faint nod of her chin.

The last knot within her came undone. It didn't matter what Beau had said, it didn't matter what anyone else said. Selene approved, and Selene's word was law.

Casimir's arms had opened for her, and now they embraced.

Olivia leaned over the bar. "Looks like you had a successful debut."

"I thought so, too." Pity flicked away a bit of foam from the bottle. "But this seems a bit much."

"It's not only for you. It's for them." Olivia indicated the bustling Gallery floor. Performers, patrons, and prostitutes alike were shoulder to shoulder, surrounding the bar and calling out congratulations from the gaming tables and booths. "Since it looks like you're sticking around," she continued, "a word of advice: just because the show is over doesn't mean the performance is."

At that moment, Halcyon jumped onto the bar beside her, boot heels clicking on the wood, purple-and-orange coattails flapping. As if they were still in the theatre, the onlookers quieted immediately.

"My friends…" His practiced voice carrying throughout the hall. "It's not often that we add to our esteemed list of acts. The Theatre Vespertine is as strict a mistress as any of us will ever know—no slight intended, Flossie, my dear—and she is not for those of weak constitution, in either her performers *or* her audience! But tonight we have had the honor to watch our newest, fledgling performer leave the safety of the nest and soar to no less than the expected heights!"

People clapped and hooted. Pity took a long drink from the champagne and raised it to the crowd, who cheered even louder. She looked for Max and found him a few yards away. She wanted to pull him up beside her. He deserved credit, too; without him she wouldn't have had the barest chance in Cessation. But he was too far, pushed away as people jostled to shake her hand and slap her on the back.

Nearby, the two Rousseau boys raised a performer onto their shoulders. More champagne appeared, flying through the air; he caught all three bottles and began to juggle them.

"So tonight," Halcyon continued, "as is our wont and our way, we welcome Serendipity Jones fully into our family. This is the true first day of her life in Cessation, in Casimir—"

As he spoke, the juggler let one of the bottles loose. Halcyon caught it and popped the cork in one smooth motion. The results were explosive. "And in our observed tradition, we baptize her the newest member of Halcyon Singh's Theatre Vespertine!"

Pity shrieked as the frothy liquid poured over her, drenching her hair and running down her back. When she threw back her head and let the champagne pour into her mouth, another round of cheers erupted. She sputtered and coughed as the bubbles caught in her nose, but Halcyon didn't stop until the bottle was empty.

Halcyon bowed. "Congratulations, my dear."

"Thanks, boss." Pity pushed dripping strands of hair from her face.

He stomped on the bar. "More drinks!" he cried. "No one is to stop celebrating until the sun sends the night fleeing from Cessation once more!"

A hand grabbed the bottle she still held. It was Max. He took her by the arm. "Here to save you," he said. "C'mon."

"Good," she said. "I need to go change out of these clothes. All the work you did, and they're already—"

"Afraid not." He grinned. "Tradition. You stay like that all night." He pulled her from the bar and pushed through the throng to one of the booths. Luster, Garland, and Duchess were already waiting, and Eva and Marius, too, though they weren't sitting.

"Excellent job." Ignoring her dampness, Eva gave Pity a hug. "Though there are a few things we'll have to work on."

"Don't pester her, dear." Marius kissed Pity lightly on both cheeks. He was a narrow but handsome man. "Come dance with me instead and leave Pity be. She's done for tonight."

Except she wasn't.

Just because the show is over doesn't mean the performance is.

She slid into the booth beside Max as the congratulations kept coming. Dozens of Casimir's patrons stopped by the table: influential citizens of Cessation or CONA, wealthy traders, even some of the higher-ranking members of the gangs. She was learning to recognize them by sight—Sicarios, Wraiths, Old Reds—but felt no fear seeing them in the Gallery. In Casimir, everyone was friendly with everyone...or else.

At a break in the crowd a man approached the table, a porter a few steps behind him. The porter proffered a tray to Pity, upon which sat glasses and a bottle of wine, a fine layer of dust on its surface.

"Compliments of the gentleman." He deposited the gift.

"I hope I'm not too late to convey my congratulations," said the gentleman in question.

Pity recognized one of the men from Selene's box. Up close he was blandly handsome, with shrewd eyes and an easy smile. His bearing was one of utter ease amid the chaos that milled around him. Behind him, scowling as if he smelled something unpleasant, was the bald, bearded man.

"No," Pity said. "Of course not. Thank you for the wine."

"Patrick Sheridan." He offered a hand. "I hope you enjoy it as much as I enjoyed your performance."

"Okay, Sheridan." The bald man shifted impatiently. "You've spoken to her. Selene is waiting."

"Disregard my new friend Mr. Daneko's rudeness," Sheridan said. "He wouldn't have followed me if he wasn't impressed, too."

Daneko frowned. "I was only interested in getting a better look at the *girl* who shot at three of my people."

Pity sat up straighter, trying not to squirm as the leader of the Old Reds glared at her. She waited for him to say or do something more. *He can't,* she realized. *Not so long as I'm under Selene's protection.* Emboldened by the champagne, she gave him a perky smile. "It was only one, truth be told."

"And from what I've heard of your people, Daneko, they undoubtedly gave her good reason." Sheridan scanned the table, taking in each of its occupants before returning to Pity. "I confess to being curious: what tempts a talented, CONA-raised young woman to a place like Cessation?"

Max tensed beside her. "She might ask you the same question."

"Oh, but I inquired first."

"That doesn't mean she needs to answer."

Pity glanced at Max. His tone wasn't discourteous exactly, but there was a hint of defensiveness, like the flash of a hidden blade.

Sheridan stared at him for a moment with an air of faint amusement. "I think your friend is suggesting I mind my own business."

"It's all right," said Pity. "I'm—"

"No, he's right. I shouldn't pry."

"Sheridan!" Daneko barked.

Sheridan bowed his head politely. "Don't let me distract you from your celebration. Enjoy your evening."

Before Pity could thank him again, the men were gone, consumed by the reveling crowd.

"What was that about?" she said to Max.

"Aw," interjected Duchess, "just because Maxxy's bread is buttered by CONA plutocrats, it doesn't mean he has to like them."

"Is that who he was?"

"Oh, yeah," Luster agreed. "Never seen him here before, but we know the type. Well-dressed, well-groomed, and throwing currency around like it was nothing."

"There're better places they could be spending their money back east." Max scowled. "People who need better food, vaccines—"

"People who aren't *here*." Duchess snatched the bottle and began to pour himself a glass. "And this very fine, very old, and very expensive wine is already open."

Garland stole the glass away and set it in front of Pity. "It *would* be a shame to let it go to waste."

She took a sip. The wine was smooth and spread through her mouth like jam. She nudged Max. "Are we celebrating or not?"

After a moment, his features softened. He accepted a glass.

"I don't see why you're getting worked up about some CONA tycoon." Luster put a hand on Garland's shoulder and raised herself above the edge of the booth. "When's the last time we saw Daneko around here? Look—he, Selene, and Pity's new friend Sheridan are comfy as kittens, surrounded by a bathtub's worth of whiskey and champagne." She lowered herself back down. "Rumor is that they're making peace. Real peace, I mean. Guess it's true."

"Let's hope so," said Max.

"Why?" Garland teased. "We've got Pity here to keep us safe from the Old Reds."

She laughed and took another swallow of the wine. "At this point, I don't think any of y'all should count on me to shoot straight."

"The only thing I'm counting on you for right now is more of this fancy booze," Duchess said. "How about a turn of the room? See who else is feeling generous?"

Beside her, Pity could sense the heat emanating off Max. His arm rested on the top edge of the booth. When she leaned back, they were almost touching.

Pity gave Duchess a content smile. "Thanks," she said, "but I'm fine right here."

"I know I shouldn't jinx it." The words were as thick as molasses in her mouth. "But I can't wait for the next show! I can't!"

The floor lurched.

Max caught her. "Whoa, careful."

"I'm fine!" She closed her eyes, but when she did, it was like she was back in the arena, spinning and twirling. She opened them again. "Okay, maybe I had a bit too much champagne."

"A bit too much? It's a good thing it comes in bottles and not buckets."

"You're one to talk! I didn't see you saying no to any refills."

He tugged at the collar of her blouse. It was sticky and peeled away from her like the skin off a peach. "At least I'm not wearing it."

"I must look like a total mess." She pulled away, stumbling back until she found the wall of the hallway.

He laughed. "You look as good as you did when you stepped out into the theatre."

"Liar." *But it's a nice kind of lie.* When she looked at Max— even the slightly wavering Max before her right now—all she wanted to do was smile. "Where are we?" she said, tearing her eyes away to blink at the door numbers. "All these damn hallways look the same."

"Almost there. You can make it."

She straightened...mostly. "I could make it a mile if I needed to."

"Sure, but lucky for you it's only a few more doors. Here we are—home safe and sound."

Pity punched in the door code, but it wouldn't unlock.

"You're punching in the door number, not your passcode."

She turned back to him, off-balance, but the wall caught her. "Do it for me, would you?" Slowly, she slid down until her backside hit soft carpet.

Instead of opening the door, Max sat down beside her and

sighed in an amused sort of way. "I think you are in for a helluva morning, Serendipity Jones."

"Oh, am I?" Pity moved so that his face was only a foot away. "Well, it ain't morning yet. And you know something?"

His mouth turned up at the edges. "What?"

"It sounds nice when you say my name."

She leaned forward and kissed him. His lips were soft and still tasted of champagne. There was a cold twinge from one of his piercings—a strangely enticing sensation. Max stiffened with surprise, but then he was kissing her back. His mouth moved against hers, his hands finding her shoulders...

He pushed her away. "Pity, stop. I—you're drunk."

"So?" she said. "It's just a kiss. I'm not too drunk for a kiss." She started forward again, but he jumped to his feet.

"I'm drunk, too. We shouldn't. I...can't."

"Fine." She pushed herself up to standing, too. "But tomorrow when I'm sober—"

"Pity, I *can't*."

His tone hit her like a bucket of ice water. She tensed as he took another step backward.

"I...I'm sorry," she said lamely. "I thought you liked me."

"I do!" But Max didn't look at her. He looked at the wall, at his shoes—anywhere but at her. "I can hardly remember the last time I liked someone as much as you. It's...it's just...you're a good friend."

"Oh." *Idiot*, she thought, a cold blade of embarrassment plunging into her gut. She turned to her door and stabbed the code in. This time she got it on the first try.

"Pity, wait—"

"No, I'm sorry." She retreated inside. "I was wrong…mis-read things." She began to close the door and then stopped. "You're a good friend, too. 'Night, Max."

The lock clicked, a final, cheerless knell to the evening. She pressed her forehead against the closed door. *Why did I do that?* All her prior elation was gone; left in its place was a feeling like she had swallowed a pound of clay. Pity ripped off her gun belt and tossed it on the bed, then carefully made her way into the bathroom. The face that stared at her from the mirror was ragged, the last remnant of what might have been a happy glow fading rapidly. Her hair was flat and matted, her eye makeup smudged.

Idiot, she thought again, gritting her teeth as the tears gathering in the corners of her eyes began to fall.

CHAPTER 17

PITY WOKE THE NEXT MORNING TO A POUNDING HEAD and a rebelling stomach. Each beat of her heart brought a fresh stab of pain between her ears as she stumbled into the bathroom, where she threw up bile and scraps of last night's dinner. Afterward, curled on the cool tile, the memories came rushing back, sour as the taste in her mouth.

I think you are in for a helluva morning, Serendipity Jones.

She drank some water and crawled back into bed, then woke for a second time tangled beneath the thick comforter, half suffocated by her pillow, heart pounding from a nightmare she couldn't recall. She downed two more glasses of water and paged the kitchen.

"Hi, it's Pity," she said to the intercom, her tongue feeling

like it was coated in pine tar. She always ate in the common dining area, but today—

Max might be there.

—she wasn't sure she could make it.

"Can you send up coffee and"—her stomach gurgled
menacingly—"plain toast, please?"

There was a good-natured laugh on the other end. "Popular
order this morning."

That done, she lay back in bed and stared at the ceiling.
*So what are you going to do when you can't avoid him any-
more?* It was an inevitability, but the aching embarrassment
was still too fresh. Worse even than the night before—the way
an injury hurt more once the initial shock had passed. Sooner
or later she'd have to own up to her foolishness. The thought
made her queasy in a way that had nothing to do with her
hangover.

A sharp knock startled her from her ruminations. Moving
slowly to favor her still-aching head, she went to the door, mar-
veling at how quickly her food had arrived.

But when Pity opened it, Adora was on the other side.

She looked Pity over with acerbic amusement. "Looks like
the champagne got the best of you last night." She flicked a
folded slip of paper at Pity.

Pity, it read. *Please join me for breakfast tomorrow.* It was
signed with Selene's neat script.

She didn't need to be told the difference between an invitation and an order. "What's this about?"

"Breakfast, I'd imagine." Adora pushed a strand of pink hair back into place. "Someone will fetch you. Early. Don't make her wait."

But when someone arrived to get her the following morning, it wasn't a porter, or even Adora.

It was a Tin Man.

Pity tensed, acutely aware of the weight of the guns against her hips. She had debated them as she dressed, Beau's threat still fresh. Walking into Selene's office armed probably wasn't the smartest idea. Going in unarmed seemed a worse one. And it wasn't as if she had been forbidden to carry her guns around Casimir.

Yet.

The Tin Man glanced at the weapons but didn't say anything, only indicated for her to follow him. She obeyed, a sense of exposure overtaking her as she left her room for the first time since the night of the show. It had been easy enough to hide. Luster had peeked in on her the previous afternoon, but satisfied enough at finding Pity abed, she had promptly returned to her own. Apparently, the whole of Casimir was a little worse for wear following the revelry of Pity's debut.

The Gallery was nearly deserted as they passed through it, only a few cleaning staff salvaging stray glasses and a patron snoozing in one of the booths.

And Sheridan, waiting near the elevator.

He smiled as she approached. "Hello again."

"Good morning." Pity struggled to recall his first name. *Peter…no, Patrick. Patrick Sheridan.*

"Wait here a moment, please." The Tin Man went over to a display set in the wall.

Pity smoothed a hair behind her ear, wondering what Sheridan was doing here. "I should thank you again for the wine. It was the best thing I drank all night."

"One thing among many, I'm sure."

"Unfortunately."

He chuckled—a sincere, disarming sound. "You were celebrating. And from what I can tell, a hangover is practically the morning uniform around here."

But not for you. Sheridan's crisp demeanor rivaled Beau's. "Well, I've tried it on and I can't say I like it."

The Tin Man returned as the elevator door dinged open. "You can go up now."

"Not that I'm complaining," Sheridan said as the doors closed, "but I was under the impression that I'd have Selene to myself this morning. Getting her alone is something of a challenge, it seems. She prefers to conduct business after dark, among her…*distractions.* I, however, do not."

And what business is that, exactly? Pity wondered, recalling what Max had said about all the illicit dealings that took place at Casimir.

"Then again, now that your boyfriend isn't here, maybe I'll have a chance to hear your story."

Pity tensed. "Max isn't my boyfriend."

"I'm sorry. I shouldn't have assumed. It's only that he seemed quite defensive of you."

"It's all right," she lied. A gut-sick feeling stirred in her.

"Max is just a friend. And there's not much to tell. We...I was headed for the eastern cities. Things turned out different."

Selene was watering one of her potted trees as they stepped out of the elevator. "Ah, there you are."

"Sorry, ma'am." Pity spied Adora, spinning lazily in Selene's chair, and Beau, stone-still by the terrace door. "I hope we didn't make you wait."

"Not at all. It's not too early, is it? Sometimes I forget that morning isn't Casimir's forte, but I've always been an early riser."

"I'll confess, Selene," said Sheridan, reaching out to touch the broad, flat leaves of the tree. "All these plants, from all over the world. I don't know how you keep them alive out here in the middle of this barren nothing."

"It's simple." Selene's words came out as ripe as the little fruits on the tree beside her. "Providing one knows what it takes to keep them thriving. Adora, have the meal sent out now, will you?"

Selene led them to the terrace, beyond where Beau stood, half cast in the morning light. He eyed Pity, waiting until Selene and Sheridan had passed before tapping the breast of his jacket. Pity brushed a thumb over the butt of one gun in response.

A pair of Tin Men were stationed outside, one at either end of the large, curved balcony. In the center sat a table set for three—three plates, three sets of utensils on linen napkins, and one white envelope. There was a faint breeze, carrying with it a melodious hum from the city below. Drawn by the sound, Pity went to the edge of the terrace. Below, a dense white mass billowed along the black road that led to Casimir. The Reformationists, she realized, in their pristine white robes, singing hymns. They gathered around the great fountain, their voices strengthening, though Pity still couldn't pick out the words.

Sheridan came up beside her. "Looks like we'll have a serenade. Did you arrange this, Selene?"

"Absolutely not," she replied, though not without a hint of playfulness. "But they're almost pleasant from this distance, aren't they?"

"I'm surprised you let them get that close." He went to the table and pulled out Selene's chair. "Seems like they could be bad for trade."

"They're harmless. A few good souls to help balance out the bad."

Sheridan moved on to Pity's seat. She slid into it.

"Thank you, Mr. Sheridan."

"Patrick, please."

Pity unfolded her napkin and placed it on her lap, burying her hands in it as the food arrived. The others began serving themselves, but she waited, feeling like an extra body at the table. She might have earned her place in Casimir, but she hadn't gotten the seat warm quite yet.

Selene noted the hesitance. "Wondering why you're here, aren't you?" With a sly smile, she slid the envelope over to Pity. "Your first wages. I always make it a point to deliver them myself. Go on."

"Thank you, ma'am." Pity took the envelope and glanced inside. Her fingers stiffened, and for a brief moment she wondered if a mistake had been made. On the commune it would have taken her half a year of solid work to earn the same amount.

"Every cent deserved and then some." Sheridan tore the

corner off a pastry. "I wouldn't mind having your eye for talent, Selene."

"Oh, don't be coy about your own aptitudes." A playful smile spread on Selene's lips. "Pity, Patrick here took next to nothing and spun it into one of the largest non-corporate fortunes on the continent."

"A gift for facts, figures, and faces," said Sheridan. "Little different from what you do here, I suspect."

"If that's the case," said Selene, "maybe you should be coy. Most of my business isn't exactly appropriate for the next president of the Confederation of North America to engage in."

Pity nearly dropped the envelope. "Pardon?"

Sheridan laughed and leaned back in his seat. "A bit premature to announce that, don't you think?"

"Not if I have my way," said Selene. "And I usually do."

So that's Sheridan's business with Selene. Pity had expected black market goods or services, maybe even weapons, but the presidency? How deep did Selene's power run?

"Besides," Selene continued, "it's no secret back east that you've thrown your hat into that ring."

"It might as well be. What little attention I've garnered hasn't exactly been promising." Frustration crept into Sheridan's voice. "One would think two decades would be enough to make people forget which side of the war you were on."

"You were a Patriot?" said Pity.

"Guilty as charged," he replied. "Though barely. I wasn't much older than you when the conflict ended, but . . . well, memories last longer than wars, don't they?"

"That's why it will be all the more satisfying when you win." Selene sipped her coffee as if they were discussing a feat already accomplished. "CONA's first former Patriot leader."

"My mother was a Patriot." Pity felt a pang of familiar grief. "My father never let her forget it, either. Or me, after she died."

"I'm sorry to hear that," said Sheridan.

"She was the one who taught Pity to shoot," Selene explained. "And I think she'd be very proud to see what you've made of yourself."

Pity slid the envelope of currency under the edge of her plate. *I hope so.*

"If there is one thing I've learned in life," Selene continued, "it's that there's no circumstance that can't be overcome. My family was from Singapore, a city completely destroyed in the Pacific Event. We were fortunate enough to be away when it occurred, but it was a mixed blessing; everything and everyone we had ever known was gone. My parents rebuilt a life for us here, piece by hard-won piece. And years later, I arrived in a chaotic, ailing city populated by thieves and predators, and I saw the potential in it." She smirked and gestured around her. "What it offers today draws people from all over the world."

"Okay, you've made your case," Sheridan conceded with a chuckle. "But you're right. For all that's come before, what's important remains in front of us. Speaking of which—Pity, what are you going to do with your newfound fortune?"

The *fortune* stared up at her. "I honestly have no idea," she said. "I haven't had a chance to—"

Over Selene's shoulder, a flash of movement caught her eye. A black orb plunked onto the balcony and rolled to a stop at the foot of the nearest guard.

Pity had just enough time to throw herself to the ground as a thunderous explosion consumed the morning.

CHAPTER 18

PITY WAS FAST, BUT BEAU WAS LIGHTNING. BEFORE SHE hit the stone of the terrace, he tackled Selene, shielding her with his body. The bright morning disappeared, gone in a cloud of smoke.

Pity coughed and blinked away tears. Her ears rang as she pushed herself up, peripherally aware that little damage had been done. The small explosive was a common one, meant to disorient and disarm, not kill.

Except...

The Tin Man was gone, blown off the balcony. Three dull pops sounded behind her. When she twisted around, the other guard was on his knees, blood pouring from his chest. He collapsed as long black snakes of rope fell into view. She stumbled to her feet and looked up to see men in armor and helmets rappelling from the roof. As the first figure touched down on the terrace, she drew. Her shot caught him in the chest. He hit the edge of the railing and fell to the ground.

A few feet away, Sheridan was up, too, but dazed. Beau had his weapon drawn and an arm around Selene's waist, supporting her. A thin line of blood ran down her face.

"Move!" he screamed, dragging Selene forward.

With her free hand, Pity grabbed Sheridan and pushed him ahead of her. She heard more boots hit the stone as they ran. Inside, Beau threw Selene behind the desk, turned, and fired. His shot zipped over Pity's shoulder, hitting a man inches behind her. She hadn't even seen him. She started for the desk, too, but staggered as a series of shots perforated the floor in front of her. This time, Sheridan reached for her, pulling her from the line of fire; clarity had returned to his face. They bolted a dozen yards and dove behind a pair of large stone planters.

Oh, Lord…oh, Lord…

Blood pounded in her veins as she pulled her other gun and clutched it to her chest. "Are you hurt?" Sheridan didn't seem to hear her at first. She kicked him. "Hey!"

"No…no."

"Good. Stay down!" She leaned low and peeked around the planter. Beau was crouched behind the desk, Selene beside him. In the archway to the terrace she counted eight attackers, all carrying rifles. None seemed to be looking her way.

They want Selene.

Beau pushed up his shirt cuff, revealing a dark metal band, and pressed something on it. With a hiss of air, the terrace partitioned off, a latticework of windows appearing where there had been open air a moment before. Two of the men were cut off outside. One of the inside attackers signaled; the others covered him as he peppered the windows with shots. White spiderwebs spread across the glass, but it didn't break.

Six targets, she revised. Eleven bullets left, plus whatever Beau had. And the men were wearing body armor—the attacker Beau had shot was hunched over but still on his feet. She cursed under her breath.

The intruders gave up on the doors. "Drop your weapons and surrender!" one called out. "We'd like you alive, but dead'll do!"

Pity's grip tightened on her guns. *Think.*

Six targets, eleven shots…and body armor. Her bullets would barely put a dent in it. *But it didn't cover everything.* Neck, joints, faces—all hard to protect. She would have to choose her shots wisely.

And if you want to walk away from this—the thought came to her in her mother's voice, not with a parent's timbre, but rather that of a battle-scarred veteran—*you'd better shoot to kill.*

Pity raised herself into a crouch.

"What are you doing?" hissed Sheridan.

"Shhh!"

She peeked out a little farther. Beau spotted her. He shook his head.

She ignored him, leaned out, and fired twice, aiming for the man who had spoken. His exposed face was her target, but the bullets glanced off his helmet. He fell to the ground, stunned.

The other five turned on her and fired.

"Shit!" Pity curled into a ball as bits of stone and dirt

exploded around her, leaves raining down. Then it ceased, though she still heard shots. She scrambled around Sheridan to risk a glance from the other side of the planters. Another assassin was down, a pool of blood spreading around him.

Dead.

Beau hadn't missed. Pity swore again, quietly.

Breathe. Think.

Sheridan pulled her back. "Pity, stop! You heard them—we can surrender!"

She shook him off. "Are you willing to risk your life to find out if they're telling the truth?"

He didn't answer.

Think.

The attackers no longer had the element of surprise. And with the impenetrable glass at their back and no cover, they were exposed. *But they still have the numbers and the firepower.* Pity cocked her guns. *Any moment they're going to realize that, rush Beau and Selene, and then us. Gotta keep them off-balance.*

Nine shots left.

Inhale, aim. Exhale, shoot.

She rolled out from behind the planter, came up on one knee, and fired.

Bang! Bang! Bang! Bang!

A heartbeat later she rolled back, bullets filling the space where she had been. She bit back a scream as a sudden, searing pain lanced through her calf. A red stain spread on the fabric of her pants.

One more assassin was dead. This time her aim had been better, the man's left eye exploding in a telling spray of crimson.

But her other shots had gone wide or hit armor. That left three and the stunned man, who might recover at any moment.

Pity swallowed the dry spit in her mouth and tried to tune out the throbbing pain in her leg. Staccato shots sounded. One of the remaining attackers was firing at the glass again, his partners covering him. As she watched, one pane gave way. Behind the desk, Beau's gaze darted between the exits and Pity. Finally, it settled on her.

He raised his hand and signaled. *Three targets.*

She signaled back. *Five bullets left.*

His features tightened, but he tipped his head back toward the assassins. Chest tight, she nodded.

"Whatever you do," she said to Sheridan, voice brittle with fear, "keep down until the shooting stops."

"Pity." His eyes pleaded with her. "You don't need to do this."

But she did. They were out of time.

The only thing left to do was to end things on *their* terms.

CHAPTER 19

PITY'S HAND TREMBLED WITH THE WEIGHT OF EVERY missed shot as Beau began counting down with his fingers. Blood cascaded through her veins, alternating surges of ember hot and icy cold. She took a deep breath. Across the chasm of floor separating them, Beau looked as calm as a light snowfall.

Three.

Beau, who wasn't injured. Who didn't hesitate and didn't miss.

Two.

Who only needed a few moments.

Pity grabbed the jagged lip of the planter and stood. "Hey!"

She fired double-handed as two of the remaining men snapped toward her.

Bang! Bang! Bang! Bang!

Her first two bullets found their mark, dropping one assassin before he could get a shot off. The third and fourth were less on target but caught the second man's rifle, sending it flying from his hands.

It was the last of the three attackers she knew she'd be too slow for. He spun as his companions faltered, rifle barrel finding Pity as she prayed the seconds she'd bought would be enough.

Fortunately, a sliver of time was as good as an hour to Beau. He charged from behind the desk, firing.

A handful of shots and it was over.

Pity fell to her knees, hands still clenched around her revolvers, waiting for the new pain to come. When it didn't—when the only blood she found on her person was from the first wound—she started to shake.

"Pity?"

As Sheridan spoke, the elevator dinged. Santino and half a dozen Tin Men spilled out, guns raised.

"It's about time!" Beau snarled.

"The alarm just came through." Wide-eyed, Santino took in the scene.

Behind the desk, Selene stirred.

"Stay down for a moment, ma'am." Beau uncovered his wristband again. "Santino, there are at least two more outside. Ready?"

The Tin Men formed up around the terrace entrance. At Beau's command, the windows opened.

Ignoring Sheridan's attempts at assistance, Pity pushed to her feet and limped after them, one thought beating in her head like a drum: *One bullet left... one bullet left...*

But when she got outside, only a single attacker remained—the man she had shot first—his arm clenched to his ribs. She spotted a pair of hooks gripping the edge of the balcony, ropes pulled taunt behind them. Santino was beside them, looking over the side. He slung his rifle over his shoulder, pulled out a knife, and sawed through the ropes. When that was done he peeked out again before turning back, satisfied.

"Pity?" Beau appeared beside her. "Are you okay?"

She blinked at him. Only the faintest flush tinted his sharp cheeks. "I'm fine, thank you." Her voice sounded thin, distant.

"You're bleeding."

She looked down. The bottom of her left pant leg was soaked through; bloody footprints trailed behind her. "Oh. A scratch. It barely hurts anymore."

"That's because you're going into shock. Santino, sit her down before she passes out."

"It's nothing." But the moment the words were out, a buzz began in her head. She holstered her guns, shivering.

"Don't argue." Santino gathered her into his arms and carried her over to the desk. With his knife, he slashed the fabric of her pants. "Looks like it went straight through," he said. "Not too bad, but it'll need attention."

"Sir!" called one of the guards. "Got another warm body here!"

It was the man Pity had hit in the helmet. Some of the Tin Men surrounded him, the others dragged in his cohort from the terrace. The guards bound the attackers' hands behind their backs and deposited them before Selene, who was steadying herself against the other end of the desk.

With a tender touch, Beau brushed the hair away from the cut on her forehead and dabbed at it with a handkerchief.

She waved him away, eyes ablaze. "I'm fine."

"You need to see Starr."

His tone carried something Pity had never heard in it before: *worry*.

"When we've finished here." Selene brushed the dust from the front of her dress. "Patrick? Are you okay?"

Sheridan, to his credit, did not look nearly as bad as Pity felt. His face was flushed, and a line of sweat painted his brow, but he took in the proceedings with restrained aplomb. "I am."

"Good." She addressed two of the Tin Men. "Take him back to his suite."

"Selene, I—"

"This isn't something you need to see. My apologies, breakfast will have to wait for another day."

As the men escorted him to the waiting elevator, Pity made a move to follow.

"Pity, you stay." Selene gestured at the prisoners.

The Tin Men pulled them into kneeling positions and ripped off their helmets. The one from the terrace had pale hair and a ratty face. His companion was older, with a red scar over one eye.

Santino looked them over. "Mercenaries. And not cheap ones, judging by the armor and weapons."

Selene considered the pair. When she finally spoke, her voice was as soft as a kiss. "Who sent you here?"

Neither replied.

"Ma'am," Santino said, "would you like me to—"

"No." The kiss turned to ice. "I'll give you a choice. The first one to tell me who sent you dies right now, quickly. The other will be interrogated for everything else. Hours, days, *weeks*… as long as it takes me to feel satisfied that anything of importance has been disclosed. Do you believe that I will do this?"

One nodded, and then the other.

"Good. Now…talk."

An edged silence fell. Even from the safety of the prevailing side, Pity tensed as anxious seconds passed, a bitter taste in her mouth.

The remaining assassins stared at the floor, eyes blank, as if they were seeing nothing. The one with the scar began to shake. But it was the ratty man who spoke first, one word that looked to pain him more than his injuries.

"Daneko."

"*Daneko?*" growled Beau.

Selene waved a hand, silencing him. Then she took his gun and went to the confessor. Pity turned away as a single shot rang out—worse, somehow, than all the ones that had preceded it. A meaty thump followed. When she found the courage to look back, the Tin Men were wrenching the remaining assassin to his feet.

"Please…wait…He wasn't alone."

Selene signaled for the Tin Men to pause. "What do you mean?"

"Daneko wasn't the one who paid us," the man panted. "I don't know who did, but I overheard him say something to our team leader about help from back east."

"Hmm." Selene stared at him for a moment. "I look forward to hearing the details Santino pries out of you on *that* topic. Take him away." Any hope for mercy—of any kind—evaporated from the assassin's face. "To the interrogation cell, not the regular ones."

Beau accepted his gun back from Selene when they were gone. "Daneko didn't get them into Casimir unseen. Not with that amount of gear."

Selene nodded. "He didn't get them onto my terrace, either."

"They must have had assistance here as well—codes, maps, a way to bypass the surveillance cameras."

"I know." Selene turned back to Pity. She smiled neutrally. "Ugly business, this."

Pity could think of nothing to say. Selene had just executed someone. Maybe not in cold blood but lukewarm at best. *But I killed, too.* It felt unreal, though it had happened scant minutes before. Whatever had burned within during the attack was extinguished, leaving a hollow that clawed at her, trying to fill itself. She stared at the tangle of still forms on the marble floor.

I killed them.

"Santino, take a team," Beau ordered. "I want Daneko here, *now*. We never should have believed him or the bullshit peace he—"

"Beau, relax." Selene pulled out her chair and sat, paying no mind to the fresh bullet holes in it. "We don't need to exert ourselves. Why not have the dogs corner the rat? Send a message to the other gang leaders. Find Daneko, contain him, and send word. If he isn't cornered by sundown, Cessation shuts down."

Her eyes narrowed. "And Casimir is closed until I decide it isn't."

The side door opened. Rifles snapped up, but it was only Adora.

"Everything okay in here?" she said as if she had found them out of drinks rather than surrounded by bodies.

"Everything is fine now, Adora," said Selene. "Get someone in here to deal with this mess, would you? And the one below my balcony as well." She paused. "Beau, why not send a head along with each message. It will add a touch of urgency, don't you think? And, Santino, our new guest will wait a bit. See to Pity." Selene reached across the desk and squeezed Pity's arm affectionately. "Thank you, my dear. I'm in your debt."

Pride joined Pity's stew of emotions as Santino scooped her up again. It was a pleasant addition, though it didn't quite neutralize the others.

"I can walk!" she protested.

"Miss Selene said take care of you, so I'm taking care of you."

"Hold on." For a moment Beau considered Pity, eyes chilly. "That was stupid. You should have waited for me."

She held his gaze, acutely aware of the odds they'd overcome. "They would have gone for you first and then killed me and Sheridan anyway. You had more ammo and you miss less. It made sense."

He glanced at Selene, then back to Pity. "Next time I give you an order, you follow it." He paused. "But Selene is right—you did good."

"Thank you." Pity heard the sincerity in his words.

She could only hope her own belief in them would come later.

"A few more," said Dr. Starr. "Keep still."

On the rigid exam bed, Pity lay on her stomach, a towel draped over her bare hips. The wound had been cold fire by the time Santino got her to the clinic, but thanks to an injection from Starr, the pain had receded to a dull, warm throb. Still, with each new stitch, each pull of the thread, Pity squeezed Santino's broad hand tighter.

"You're almost done, chica." He chuckled. "You've been blown up and shot at, and look at you—green over a few stitches."

Pity gritted her teeth, trying to lose the sensation to the narcotic tide. "It feels weird."

"Not as bad as getting shot."

"Or getting blown up." She looked into Santino's golden-brown eyes. "How many times are you gonna have to get me fixed up?"

"No sé. Seems like you've got nine lives."

"I think I'm down a few."

Santino chuckled again. "Any gunfight you make it to the end of is a good one. I'm starting to think Beau underestimated you. Seems to me you'd be a good hand to keep nearby."

"And here I was thinking how much nicer it is to shoot when you're not being shot at."

"Still, if you ever get tired of the Theatre, say the word and I'll see what we can do."

Pity shifted, uncomfortable with the path of thought the offer led her down.

I killed two men.

Two.

Only two.

She winced as Starr made another stitch, and changed the subject. "Beau, he... Are he and Selene...?"

"It's no secret. Money and power can command good protection. But you want the *best?* There's no better safeguard than someone who is willing to die to keep you breathing." He sighed dramatically. "May we all find un hombre who cares that much, yeah?"

"There," announced Starr. "A little bandaging and you'll be good to go. Try to stay off it for a couple of days, but you can use a crutch if you're—"

"Pity!" Luster barreled into the clinic, a satin robe fluttering about her diminutive frame. "Are you okay? Oh, my Lord—you're shot!"

"She'll live." Starr finished the bandaging. "These, however, will not." He tossed the bloody remains of Pity's pants into the garbage.

"I liked those, too." Her body felt thick and heavy as she cautiously pushed herself into a sitting position. "I'm okay, really. Just peachy. The men that attacked us, though..." She giggled, unable to help herself.

Luster blinked and turned to Starr. "What'd ya give her?"

"Nothing that won't wear off in a few hours. When it starts to hurt again, she can take one or two of these." He put a glass vial of white pills on the exam table. "For Pity, got it? None of these better end up in with your—ahem—party supplies."

"Oh, shush," snapped Luster. "What happened? One of the Tin Men came and woke me, but he wouldn't say—"

"Assassins. They were after Selene. We...we stopped them." Suddenly, Pity's eyes filled with tears. She wiped them away, frustrated. "It's not funny. I don't know why I laughed."

"Oh, honey." Luster's arms enveloped her. "You're just a little messed up right now. What kind of fools would go after Miss Selene like that?"

"Dead fools," Santino filled in.

"Speaking of which," said Starr, his black bag in hand. "I need to give Miss Selene a look over and then...see to a few other things." He tossed a bone saw into his kit.

"Yo también," said Santino, rising. "There's a living fool still left to attend to."

They departed with grim determination.

Luster chewed at her bottom lip. "I can't believe anyone would...How did they..." She shook her head. "You stay put. I'm going to get Max and then we'll get you back to your—"

"No!" Pity cried. "I mean...I'm sure I can manage."

Luster's eyes narrowed. "There something *other* than an assassination attempt that you want to tell me about?"

Pity hesitated. She didn't *need* to say anything. Max was no gossip. Her embarrassment didn't need to be anything other than a regrettable secret, swiftly buried. And yet she spoke anyway. "Um...I...after the show, I tried to kiss Max."

"*Tried* to kiss him?"

"I *did* kiss him. But he...he didn't want to kiss me back."

"Oh." Luster pulled a stool over and sat. "Idiot."

"I know, I never should have—"

"Not you, *him!*" Luster wrapped the robe tighter. "Stupid boy doesn't know what's good for him. No wonder he's been scarce. He's probably holed up in his room painting everything that isn't moving. I swear, he's the only soul in Cessation who doesn't exorcise his demons by drinking, fighting, or—"

"Painting?" A fuzzy realization floated into her mind. "I've never even seen his room."

"Not many have," said Luster. "Look, I love Max. And Garland and Dutch and I are closer to him than anyone here. But sometimes he's so...I don't know. There's a distance to him. And he gets into these moods. Like right before you arrived. I'd never seen him so morose." She sighed. "Then he went off with Santino and Olivia, and by the time he got back, he was his old cheerful self. To be honest, I thought that was because of you."

"Guess not."

Luster nudged Pity's good leg with her foot. "There's nothing to be ashamed of. You're not the first one to be taken in by that sunny smile of his. But whenever anyone tries to get too close... He's never said anything, but I think there was someone before he came to Cessation."

Is that it? He's pining for someone else? Pity felt more foolish than ever. "Oh."

Luster's face puckered. "Don't sound so defeated. You think if there were a happy ending to that story he'd be here now? Life goes on, if he'd be smart enough to realize it."

Pity wiped at her eyes again, suddenly exhausted. "Lord, I'm so stupid. I almost died an hour ago and I'm sitting here talking about *Max.*"

"Well, if you had died, you couldn't have done much about it, right? Max, on the other hand…" She shrugged. "Look, let's get you back to your room and—"

"No," she interjected. "Can you get me some clothes? I want to go to the Gallery."

"Why?"

"Because they're going after Daneko," Pity said, grabbing her guns. "And I want to be there when they drag in the son of a bitch who almost got me killed."

CHAPTER 20

IT WAS PARTIALLY TRUE. THERE'D BE NO AVOIDING MAX now, and Pity wanted to pick the battleground on which she faced him again—upright and resilient in the Gallery rather than lying in bed, looking like an invalid.

As she had expected, Max appeared quickly. Nervousness and anticipation snaked through her, twisting together in a perplexing knot as she stared at him from across the room. But before she could begin to unravel it, Max spotted her, the vague panic on his face relaxing only slightly. He rushed over, breathless, his silver piercings turned coppery by the Gallery's low light.

"I went to the clinic when I heard, and then your room, but you weren't—" He stopped when he spotted her bandaged leg, stretched out on one of the Gallery's cushioned couches. "It's true, you were shot?"

"Yes." She kept her tone even. "It's nothing serious."

He stared, lips parted slightly. "But you—"

"I'm *okay*, Max." A few days ago his concern would have been a balm. Now it grated on her, poked at the invisible wound. *What hurts worse,* she chided herself, *your leg or your pride?* "Dr. Starr patched me up."

"Keep on the way you're going," Garland said as he returned from a trip to the bar, "and you're going to be as patched as an old quilt. Here, it's ginger ale."

Pity used it to wash down one of Starr's pills. Garland pushed in beside her so that she leaned against him. When he dropped an arm around her, she didn't object; his scent drowned out the smell of blood that lingered in her nostrils. Being close to him sent a heady sensation through her, one she doubted came entirely from the painkillers. But guilt stained its edges. She stole a look at Max as Luster pulled him down beside her.

"Better injured than dead." Duchess curled in a chair like a thoroughly cross cat. His fingers dug into the plush arms. "Just think. If you *hadn't* been there, Selene might have—"

"Don't even say it!" Luster said.

Max remained quiet, his face troubled.

Pity told herself it was because of Selene. *Without her it would all fall apart*—that's what Max had said. She understood Selene's sway over the city, but it wasn't until that moment that she realized the fierce loyalty Selene garnered as well.

"Has anyone seen Patrick Sheridan?" She hadn't spared him

a thought since Selene dismissed him, but now she wondered where he was. "He was there, too."

"He's probably hiding in his room," Duchess said, "regretting ever coming here in the first place."

Garland repositioned so that Pity was more comfortable. "He's spending an awful lot of time with Selene."

"They have business," said Pity, unsure if she should say more.

Luster leaned in conspiratorially. "Ooh, what kind?"

"Politics," Max interjected. He noticed Pity's surprise. "What? It wasn't hard to figure out. CONA politicians always have something about them—like a bad smell."

"He's right," Pity said. "Selene says he's going to be the next president of CONA."

"Huh," said Luster. "I know Selene can do a lot of things, but I didn't think she could fix a presidency."

"She can't." Clouds gathered in Max's eyes. "She'd need too much help—especially from the corporations. And even then she wouldn't get it from the one she really needs: Drakos-Pryce."

"Tsk," chided Garland. "Such little faith in Selene."

"It's not that," Max said. "No one back east rises that high without Drakos-Pryce's approval, and they're the one corporation that won't have anything to do with Cessation. They don't like a candidate? All it takes is a scandal here or an 'accident' there, and that candidate is gone. If Sheridan thinks Selene can get him the presidency, he's on a fool's errand."

"Well, maybe Selene knows something you don't." Pity couldn't stop the annoyance that leaked into her voice. "And Sheridan seemed like the decent sort to me."

"Not to mention you saved his life." Luster grinned. "I bet a future president owing you his life is worth a whole lot more than a bottle of wine."

She hadn't considered that. Sure, she had helped save Sheridan, but only in the course of saving Selene. And herself. It had been easier than she would have expected, in the moment. Pulling the trigger. Surviving. But instead of pride she felt bitter guilt.

If those scroungers had cornered both you and Finn, would she be alive?

Pity shook her head. "No. He doesn't owe me anything."

They waited. On the heels of long minutes came longer hours. Silence ruled in the Gallery, a blunt contrast to the usual revelry. A few patrons bent over the gambling tables, quiet and intent, but most remained sequestered in their rooms. As Selene promised, no one was let in or out. The only breaks in the tense stretch came when someone would approach Pity to thank her. Flossie gave her a big kiss on the cheek; Kitty gave her a hug so fierce that she could hardly breathe. Halcyon burst in and out like a tornado, fussing fiercely over Pity and then stalking off to find Starr, declaring loudly that she would be fit to perform again before she knew it.

As the afternoon crawled into evening, Pity dozed against Garland, lulled by his warmth and the pills. Sleep was never far away, but every time she crossed the threshold she heard a pop of gunfire or saw the burst of red from the assassin's eye. Or, worse, heard the thump of dead flesh against marble.

Once she started so hard that she knocked over her drink. Max reached for the glass, but she snatched it away before he could get it. A porter instantly appeared and offered to get her another, sounding like he would have retrieved the moon for her if he could.

"You sure you're okay?" Garland asked quietly.

"Still spooked, I guess." Pity closed her eyes again, chasing the rest that eluded her. *You did good.* She repeated the words over and over, but the more she did, the more they bothered her, like an itch she couldn't quite reach.

A commotion sounded beyond the front doors. Pity roused as they burst open and a tall woman strode in.

"I'll be damned." Luster whistled. "Look who's here."

The woman wore a long travel-stained coat and carried a pack that looked like it had seen decades, both of which she shoved at the porter who rushed to her side. Beneath the coat were a pair of holsters. Pity's interest piqued—only Casimir's inhabitants were allowed to carry weapons into the Gallery, but no one moved to take the guns. At the bottom of the steps, she paused and looked around, flinty eyes scanning the room.

Flossie met her there. "Welcome back, Ms. Bond. It's been a while since we enjoyed your company."

"Him." The woman pointed at one of the young men lounging on a pile of cushions and then at another. "And him."

Flossie waited expectantly.

"It was a long trip," the woman said. "Have them up to my suite in half an hour, with the rest of my gear." She sniffed. "I heard a funny rumor on my way in that Casimir was closed."

"Oh, never for you."

"That's what I said."

Flossie snapped her fingers at the men as the newcomer went to the bar and sat down.

"Who's that?" Pity whispered.

"That," Garland replied, "is Siena Bond. A bounty hunter."

"The *best* bounty hunter," Duchess added, "and someone you wouldn't want to cross."

"Oh, please," said Luster. "She's a sweetheart. Too bad she didn't arrive earlier—she would have had Daneko here in two shakes of a lamb's tail."

"Speak of the devil…" said Max.

A fresh disturbance overtook the Gallery's entrance. Santino entered, leading a small army of Tin Men. In their midst was a handful of Old Reds. One, Pity saw, was the wild girl she had shot at the day Max had taken her to the market. All the mad bravado in her face was gone, replaced by a glaze of cold terror. They marched down the center of the room.

"Where's Daneko?" Pity said as they passed.

"Gone." Olivia brought up the rear of the parade, rifle in hand. She shrugged off the body armor she wore and gestured to Pity. "C'mon. You should be in on this, too."

Pity pulled herself up using the crutch Luster had scrounged. The others began to rise, too, but she waved them away and hobbled after Olivia. She didn't have time to wonder where they were headed; at the back of the Gallery by the elevator, the Tin Men herded the Old Reds into a tight circle and forced them onto their knees. Pity followed Olivia to one side of the assembly.

The elevator opened, drawing every eye in the room. Selene glided out with Beau at her side. The cut on her forehead, now tended, was the only sign of the morning's events.

Santino went to her and said something, quietly.

Selene's expression soured. "And where is he now?"

"Probably headed south as fast as he can," rumbled Santino. "This is on me, ma'am. We thought he was cornered. A few minutes earlier..."

Selene waved him off and stepped forward, regarding the Old Reds displayed before her. After a tense handful of moments, she spoke, her voice carrying through the room.

"You were dead the moment you walked into Casimir."

The Old Reds shifted and shuddered, their movements audible in the chill silence that gripped the Gallery.

"So there is no reason to pretend to know nothing about what occurred here earlier. You will tell me everything, and you will tell me *now*."

None of the Old Reds spoke. Pity kept her eye on the girl, wondering if she was foolish enough to have been in on the plot, but not once did she look up. Her head hung to her chest, defeat and fear like twin weights dragging her down. Selene snapped her fingers at one of the prisoners. Two of the Tin Men yanked him to his feet and dragged him over to her.

"You were one of Daneko's lieutenants," she said.

It wasn't a question, but the man nodded, his face pale.

"Surely you must have something to share."

The man trembled. "I would tell you if I knew something. But I don't. Daneko didn't say one word about...about..."

Beau pulled out his gun and pressed it to the man's forehead. "Truth. Now."

"I swear!" he screeched. "I swear I don't know anything!"

Stern-faced, Selene put her hand on Beau's and guided it away. "I believe you."

Another gesture and the Tin Men returned him to his pack.

"You were dead the moment you walked into Casimir," Selene repeated. "But another stack of bodies does me no good. As of this moment, the Old Reds are disbanded. You and the rest of your gang have twelve hours to leave Cessation. Anyone left in the city come sunrise will sincerely wish they hadn't ignored this brief measure of clemency."

She raised her chin, looking out over the upturned faces that filled the Gallery. "Is that clear? No one is to harm any Old Red in Cessation until the deadline has passed. After that…do what you please. That's twelve hours…starting now."

At that, Selene turned on her heel and headed for the elevator.

"Turn them loose," Beau instructed Santino before following her.

"That's it?" After how Selene had dealt with the assassins, Pity had expected threats, intimidation, even blood—but not mercy. *And why didn't she ask who helped them get into Casimir?*

"Seems like," said Olivia. "Well, looks as if I've got some work to get back to."

"Wait!"

Pity shuffled after, but Olivia outpaced her. She slid over the bar and went immediately to Siena Bond, where she poured brown liquor into a glass until it was at the rim.

"Good to see you, Siena. It's been too long."

"Good to see you, too, Liv." The woman's voice was as dusty as her clothing. "Nearly had to have someone else pour my drink for me. I miss something exciting?"

"Just a little ruckus."

Pity caught up, settling herself a few stools down from the bounty hunter. Up close, she could see that the woman was middle-aged, with a narrow face and cropped, ash-brown hair, fading to gray. But the eyes that snagged Pity's in the bar mirror were bright and sharp. They lingered briefly before dropping back to her drink.

"Good timing, though," Olivia continued. "If you're looking for a job."

"Could be."

"I'll let her know you're available."

Siena drained her glass in one go and stood to depart. "Then I guess I should take what rest I can."

When the bounty hunter was gone, Olivia turned. "Okay, now you can tell me what that look is for, Miss Pity."

Pity leaned over the burnished wood. "Even if Daneko is gone...what about the other thing? The *help*. Why didn't Selene..."

"Shhh." Her voice dropped low. "Because Selene wasn't about to advertise that there might be a traitor in Casimir. Could be anyone: a worker, a Tin Man, even a regular."

Pity stared ahead, at the reflection of the Gallery. The prisoners were gone, but the crowd remained, loosening and unsure of what to do now. It was filled with the faces of strangers, acquaintances, and friends. Max's black-and-blue hair drew her attention like a beacon, and she saw that he was looking at her.

She dropped her gaze quickly. "Then everyone is under suspicion."

"Not as far as they know," Olivia replied. "So keep your eyes open, mouth shut, and those guns close."

CHAPTER 21

KEEPING HER EYES OPEN WASN'T A PROBLEM. DESPITE the madness of the day and Starr's narcotics, sleep visited Pity in slim measure. And when it finally did, it brought frenzied, broken dreams, feverish images impossible to knit together.

Inhale, aim...exhale...

Twelve bullets for twelve men, who shattered into shards of glass when she fired, each one a burst of crimson and wearing Finn's face...Empty chambers, and still the killers came and came and Finn lying everywhere...everywhere...

She awoke drenched in sweat. At first, Pity thought the knock was one of the gunshots that had scored her nightmares. But when she didn't answer, it sounded again.

Slipping a gun from beneath her pillow, she hobbled to the door, ignoring the pains of protest in her leg. "Who is it?"

"Santino. There's someone with me who'd like to speak to you."

The tension in her muscles released. "Hold on."

She traded the gun for a robe and opened the door.

"Pity." Sheridan was with Santino, a rim of red around his eyes. "I'm sorry to wake you."

"I wasn't nearly as asleep as I'd like to have been, Mr. Sheridan."

"*Patrick*. May I come in?"

She moved aside so he could enter.

"Clock's ticking," said Santino.

"I won't be long." Sheridan closed the door behind him and gave her a frayed smile. His shirt collar was open, and the faint sour scent of sweat clung to him.

He looks like he's gotten even less rest than me. "What did Santino mean?"

"Only that in an hour Selene's mandate of protection for the Old Reds expires. From what I gather, Cessation is about to become even more perilous than usual. There's a train departing from Last Stop shortly. I'll be on it."

"You're leaving?" said Pity. "But I thought...your business with Selene..."

"That may be the problem." Worry weaved into his words, turning them reluctant. "It's possible Selene wasn't the only target yesterday. I'd hoped that my visit here would be chalked up to the usual debaucheries, but there are...certain parties who would be displeased with her interference, even for an unlikely candidate like myself."

Pity remembered what the final assassin had said: *help from back east.* Max might think Selene unable to elevate Sheridan to the top of CONA, but perhaps someone else disagreed.

"But before I left, I wanted to thank you," he continued. "If you hadn't been there, things would have ended very differently."

She felt a pang of guilt. "They almost did."

"But here we are, still standing. Us traitorous Patriots need to stick together, right?"

A bit of warmth stirred within her. "My mother was the Patriot, not me."

Sheridan gave her a knowing look. "The other night I asked you what brought you to Cessation. But after learning who your mother was, I'm no longer surprised. I hope you've found whatever it is you're looking for here."

"Thank you," Pity said. "I'm sorry you didn't."

Some of Sheridan's fatigue fell away. "Well, I wouldn't exactly call it a waste of time. It's a shame I can't stay longer."

"Maybe," Pity said as Santino tapped lightly on the door. "But if Cessation is about to hit a rough patch, perhaps it's best that you get moving. While you still can."

The sun had set and pinprick stars had begun to appear in the purple velvet sky as Pity gazed out at the dim, empty streets of Cessation. From Eden, the occasional staccato of gunfire could be heard, and earlier, something had been aflame. She could still detect acrid hints of burnt rubber and wood on the wind, the perfume of the last two days.

Sheridan had been right to leave when he did. With the demise of the Old Reds, the other gangs were carving up their

former territory bit by bit. Santino had assured her it would
calm down soon, but for the moment it remained a bloody pro-
gression. During the daytime, the Tin Men patrolled the city
and kept the peace as best they could, but at night they with-
drew to hold the asphalt moat around Casimir. Like an island, it
floated—safe but isolated.

The danger without was easy to see. It was the troubles
within that still had Pity on edge, coupled with the enduring
memories of what had already passed.

The attack played out in her mind, over and over, intertwin-
ing with the morning of Finn's death until frustration made it
difficult for her to tell them apart. The questionable decisions
she had made, the opportune moments lost. Talons of doubt
targeted her like the assassins' rain of bullets. The more she
thought about it, the more it felt as if each shot had hit her, lodg-
ing somewhere in her gut, festering in a way she couldn't quite—

"What do you think of the view?"

Pity pivoted on her crutch, gun halfway out of her holster
before she could stop herself.

It was Siena Bond. The woman had approached as quietly as
a coyote in the brush. Eden's sallow lights carved hard shadows
into her face.

Pity relaxed. "Sorry."

The shadows cracked as Siena's mouth twitched up on one
side. "Can't blame you for being jumpy, I suppose. So? The view?"

"Not quite as nice as it was a few days ago."

"Ain't that true. When this city is good, it's very good, but
when it's bad..." The bounty hunter put out a hand. "Siena
Bond."

It was as rough as unsanded wood. "I'm—"

"Serendipity Jones."

"It's Pity when I'm not performing."

"Pity, then." Siena gazed out at the dusk-drowned city. "From what I've heard, your show is something to be seen. And those are some nice guns you have, too. Theatre fixed you right up."

"It wasn't the Theatre," Pity replied. "They're mine."

Siena reached for a nearby vine and plucked a flower. "They must have cost a pretty penny."

A vague itch of discomfort ran over her skin. Not a single direct question had been asked, and yet Pity felt as if she were being interrogated. "They were my mother's."

One by one, Siena picked the petals from the flower and let the evening breeze take them. "She give them to you?"

"She would have," Pity said, "if she hadn't died first."

Siena stopped plucking. "Hmm." One petal left, she let the ruined stem fall to the grass. "Sorry. I didn't mean to open any old wounds. Lucky for Selene you know how to use them, though. Olivia tell you about the porter?"

"What porter?"

"The one they found hanged in his room this morning. Used to be an Old Red, though it seems he opted to side with his old boss instead of his new one."

That answers the question of who helped the assassins into Casimir. "Sounds like he made the wrong decision."

Siena chuckled. "Made the right one at the end, though. The last thing you want to do is betray Selene and then have her get her hands on you." She looked at Pity askance. "But you know how that shakes out, don't you?"

Beeks's screams echoed in Pity's memory. "I do." But there was enough weighing on her mind without dwelling on the Finales, too. "You're a bounty hunter, right?" she asked, changing the subject. "Are you looking for someone in Cessation?"

Siena's stony eyes glinted at her, a gaze to set strong men fleeing. There was something disconcerting about the woman. She didn't have the dominating authority of Selene or the dreadful iciness of Beau. Whatever it was about her was more...raw.

"Maybe," Siena replied carefully. "Though I'm considering another offer at the moment."

Maybe? Pity took a step backward, sensing a significance masked by the simplicity of the word. Something hinted at. Her stomach tightened.

No, she thought. *It wasn't possible.*

The better offer was undoubtedly Daneko—so far he had eluded capture, and there were plenty of rumblings about what Selene might pay to see him dragged in dead.

And how much more to bring him in alive.

"'Course," Siena continued, "I'm a patient sort of woman, so I suppose any business I have here could wait." She hooked her thumbs through her belt. "Well, it's been nice talking to you, Pity Jones."

"Nice to meet you, too," she replied mechanically, breathless.

As Siena strolled toward the garden's exit, Pity's blood turned cold. *It wasn't possible,* she thought again. Her father didn't care so much that he'd send a bounty hunter looking for her.

Would he?

CHAPTER 22

"AGAIN!" SHE ORDERED.

A volley of targets launched. Pity picked them off, one by one, reloaded, and took out the next set. Bits of ceramic and glass twinkled in the air and crunched beneath her boots.

Draw. Shoot. Reload.

Draw. Shoot. Reload.

Sweat beaded her forehead as she lost herself in the rhythm, pushing until everything beyond the boundary of the arena was nullified. Here, there were only two things: the target and the shot.

"Again!" She reached into her ammo pouch. *Empty.* "Dammit!"

Widmer popped through one of the hatches in the floor. "Don't you think that's enough for today?"

"No! I just need to get some more bullets."

He cleared his throat and pointed at her leg. A line of blood had appeared, pasting the fabric to her wound.

"I'll change the bandage, then—"

"The generators need a rest. And so do you."

Pity wanted to argue, but his tone left no room for negotiation. By the time she returned to her room to clean up, the small measure of solace she'd gained was already gone. Ruminations floated about her mind like rotten apples in a pond. Any effort to keep them submerged was useless. Push one or two down and another bobbed to the surface.

The men she killed.

The ones she didn't.

The bounty hunter.

Max.

With every moment she spent alone, the thoughts thickened, pressing in on her from all angles. She put on fresh clothes, wanting nothing more than to return to the arena and lose herself again. Instead, she went to the Gallery, only to find it nearly empty, collateral damage from the strife just beginning to recede in the city.

She did a quick scan of the room—no Max. Something in her ached. She hadn't seen him since the day of the attack. But she no longer needed his guidance around Casimir. After saving Selene, its residents now treated her as if she had been around for years, not weeks, and it was a *good* feeling, one that filled the void left by Max's absence.

Or at least that's what she tried to tell herself.

"Pity, thank goodness!" Luster waved at her from the deserted bar. "Relieve this horrid boredom, *please*."

She limped over and settled herself on a stool, stiffening as she spotted Siena Bond at the end of the bar.

"You okay?" said Garland. "You look like a cat that's been rubbed the wrong way."

Pity dropped her gaze from the bounty hunter. "It's been a long few days."

"Ain't that the truth?" Flossie flounced over, lips pursed with annoyance. "You'd think someone had spread a rumor that we're out of champagne." She set her hands on her hips. "It's a good thing Daneko is gone, because I'd kill him myself for the amount of bad business he's caused us."

"They'll be back," Garland reassured her. "They never stay away for long."

"I know. But they won't be back tonight. If y'all don't want to hang around, don't bother." She stalked off.

"Well," said Luster. "That's that. What are we doing for the rest of the night?"

"Whatever it is, can we do it somewhere else?" Pity's skin crawled, as if someone were holding a knife a hairsbreadth away from it. Was Siena Bond watching her? Or was her attention on the half empty bottle keeping her company? In the dim light, it was impossible to tell.

Then again, maybe the bounty hunter had the right idea. Pity glanced around for Olivia, then reached over the bar and grabbed a bottle of bourbon. If she couldn't shoot her troubles away, maybe she could drown them for a while. "And can we start with this?"

They quit the Gallery in favor of Garland's room. Larger than Pity's, the sprawling bed was big enough for all three of them to stretch out on. As Luster flipped through the broadcast channels, searching for a film to watch, Garland slipped on a faded old shirt, torn along one hem.

Settled in the center of the bed, Pity smirked into her glass.

"What?" he said.

"It's just funny. You come back to your room to unwind and put on *more* clothes."

He jumped in beside her with a sly grin. "I wouldn't want you ladies to tire of the view."

Pity rolled her eyes at him, but the humor was welcome. Anxiety still slithered at the edge of her mind, but for the first time in days she felt the grip of tension retract slightly, loosened by a generous pour of bourbon and the relaxed company. At Luster's suggestion, they ordered up dinner and watched a bumbling black-and-white comedy as they ate.

"I wish CONA would make films like this." Luster licked at a spoonful of ice cream. "Might convince me to join up, become a star."

"They do." Pity shifted, trying to find a more comfortable position. Her wound, irritated by her overzealous practice, now ached like an infected tooth. "They'd show them on the commune a couple of times a month."

"Those hokey things they call movies?" Luster laughed. "More propaganda than stories, and no soul at all. Now, this... Would you stop squirming?"

"Sorry. My leg hurts."

"Take one of Starr's pain pills. That's what they're for, right?"

"I left them in my room." *You could always call a porter to go get them.* Pity eyed Luster. *Or...* "I don't suppose there's something in that stash of yours that would do the trick?"

Surprise, followed by impish appreciation, flashed in Luster's eyes. "Aren't you feeling wicked?"

"Don't tease. Not tonight."

Luster, chastened, said, "Well, not *exactly*. But I've got something that'll have you feeling no pain." She pulled out her tin, picked a pill, and offered it.

No pain. Pity reached for the pill, then hesitated. *Is this what you want?* She knew this road. One day, long ago, her mother had started on it and never turned back.

Frustration flared.

I'm not my mother. If the last few weeks had taught her anything, it was that.

She swallowed the pill dry. It left a bitter trail on her tongue.

"And so you don't feel alone..." Luster grinned as she gave one to Garland and took another for herself.

Garland raised his up. "Cheers!"

Quicker than Pity expected, the pain in her leg began to recede. At the same time, her attention started to wander; minutes passed, or maybe it was only seconds. The colors in the room seemed to sharpen as an intense calm spread through her. When she moved her head, she felt adrift.

"See?" Luster's voice poured like syrup. "Better, right?"

Pity nodded. "Doesn't hurt anymore."

Luster tucked her knees to her chest. *She looks like hardly more than a child sometimes,* Pity thought. On the other side of her, Garland looked like anything but. Everything about him was acutely mature—square jaw, high cheekbones, bronze skin. His hair, so naturally dark compared to Max's, gleamed like obsidian.

"Told you." Luster took Pity's calf in her hands and ran a gentle hand over the bandage. "Poor Pity's leg."

Through the fabric and gauze, Pity felt a shiver of electricity run through her. Beneath her, the linens, always soft, now felt like pure silk. Silk that was about to melt into cream. "It could have—*should* have been worse. If Beau hadn't... if I'd only..."

"Stop thinking about that." Garland turned onto his side next to her, head propped on one arm. The other reached out and took her hand, squeezing it reassuringly. "It happened. It's over now."

"That's not how it feels. The last assassin—"

"Isn't your problem to worry about." Luster released Pity's leg and fell back among the pillows. Her hair fanned out around her like dark corn silk. "Whatever's happening to him, he deserves it."

"Maybe."

Garland seemed to move closer to Pity. Or maybe she moved closer to him. It was hard to tell—the feeling of his hand encompassing hers made her thoughts flutter and break apart like leaves in an autumn wind. Comforting warmth radiated off him, and Pity found her eyes drawn to where his shirt had pulled up a little at the waist, a mesmerizing boundary where fabric ended and his skin began.

"Y'know what?" Luster's sat up abruptly, face bright. "I'm tired of lying around. I'm gonna go see what Dutch is up to."

Pity let go of Garland's hand and started to rise. "We can..."

"Oh, no you don't," Luster said. "You need to take it easy, stay off that leg. *Relax*—do you understand me?" With a meaningful wink, she left, closing the door behind her.

Pity turned back to Garland. His eyes—darker than usual, all black pupils—gazed at her. She felt a rush of embarrassment at being alone with him, like this. But it was gone the next instant, flushed out by a more carnal sensation.

"Should we... Do you want to go with her?" Her heart thudded. *Get up,* an apprehensive voice in her head said. *It's time to go.* But a stronger desire kept her right where she was.

"Not particularly," said Garland. "Do you?"

No. "No."

"Then let's stay here." He touched her cheek.

Pity reached up, intending—probably—to move his hand away, but when her fingers touched his wrist, they locked there. When she turned her head, his fingertips ran over her lips. She felt the ridiculous urge to kiss them, but he pulled away too quickly. A moment later, his shirt slipped off.

Pity's whole body pulsed, as if there was too much blood in her veins. She reached out, then stopped.

"It's okay," he said, taking her hand and putting it to his chest.

The skin there was warm, wonderful. She traced the line of his collarbone, losing herself in the exquisite sensation.

What about Max? said the apprehensive voice. Pity's fingers pulled back, as did the rest of her. Something in her gut softened. But a flash of anger followed.

What about *Max?* The soft spot hardened again. *He's not here. And he made it perfectly clear that he wouldn't want to be if he was.* She shoved the thoughts back, drowning them beneath the sensuous, gossamer layer of desire that coated her mind—a desire that reflected only Garland.

Garland, who leaned over and kissed her, instead of pushing her away.

His lips found her mouth, then her neck, and finally the base of her throat. Each caress sent a ripple of pleasure through her. When he began undoing the buttons of her shirt, she helped him. Moments later, her pants were gone, too. Left in only her underclothes, Pity shook with the sudden chill.

Garland kissed both of her knees and then the skin above her bullet wound. "Does it still hurt?"

She shook her head no, too out of breath for words. As he crawled back up the bed, she felt the heat of his breath on her belly. A glorious ache spread through her.

Wait, her last shred of sense cried. "Garland, I can't…we… shouldn't…"

"Why not?"

"Because…I…Well, I'm fertile to start, and I can't…I mean, I don't want to accidentally…"

"Oh, stop." Garland gently nipped the skin of her stomach with his teeth. "You commune ladies aren't half as innocent as you act. I'm sure you can think of a few things that will definitely not put you in any unwanted situations." He moved away a few inches. "But if you want to go back to ice cream and movies, say the word."

Pity threaded her fingers through his dark hair and pulled

him toward her. "I didn't say anything about going back to ice cream and movies." She laughed at the surprise that flashed across his face. But all resistance was gone, burned away by the heat between them. She wanted the touch of his lips again and the delicious feeling they carried—a heady anchor in the typhoon of emotions that tossed her.

The room floated for a while, formless, before slowly turning solid again. Desire burned off, Pity felt other sensations return: cold as well as warmth, pain as well as pleasure. But everything was still too sharp, limned with artificiality. When she sat up and tried to climb out of the bed, she listed sideways into the nightstand, rattling the glasses abandoned there.

Garland roused from where he had been dozing beside her. "What's the matter?"

"Nothing." Pity felt around the floor, looking for her clothes. "I'm going back to my room." The movement made her stomach turn. She regretted the food and drink from earlier—it sloshed around inside her like a lukewarm stew.

"Why?" He yawned. "You can stay here."

"It's late," she lied, having no idea what the time might be. She found her shirt and pulled it on, then reached for her pants and boots. She sat on the edge of the bed. "And...I'm not feeling well."

Garland put his hands on her shoulders. She tensed. "Pity, are you okay? Is this because of what we—"

"*No.*" And it wasn't. Even now, the feeling of his hands was enough to set her skin tingling. *It was a bit of fun. That's all.*

So why don't you feel any better than before?

"I want to sleep in my own bed. That's all."

His hands lingered for a moment before letting go. "If that's what you want."

Pity felt the mattress ripple as he lay back down but couldn't bring herself to turn, to see whatever look was on his face. *If I do, I might want to stay a little longer.*

She stood and headed toward the door. It moved back and forth in her vision as she stumbled forward and caught the handle. No wonder—she had forgotten about her leg. It ached distantly.

"Are you sure you're okay to—"

"Yes." Pity yanked the door open. Light spilled in, far too bright. She blinked. "I'll see you later."

She staggered into the hallway, the door snapping shut behind her. Too late, she remembered that Garland's room was nowhere near hers. She took one corner and then another, realized it was the wrong way, and turned back around. The hall spun; for a moment she lost her orientation completely. Everything looked the same—same corridors, same doors, same patterned carpet. Spotting a stairwell, she entered it, at least certain that she needed to be a few floors down. She gripped the railing as she descended, her injured leg even more untrustworthy than the rest of her. At one landing, she sat and tried to gather herself. A black number wavered on the wall above her head.

Her floor. She smiled.

"Pity?"

The relief disintegrated.

No, not now. She refused to look around, praying that voice was in her imagination, another manifestation of Luster's pill.

But Max was really there. He slid into her vision, a smear of paint on one cheek—reddish-brown, like dried blood.

"Pity, are you okay?"

"Yes, I'm..." She struggled back to her feet. "Just heading to bed."

"Pity, look at me."

She meant to ignore him, but in the next moment found herself staring into his gray eyes.

"Geez, your pupils are as big as dinner plates. What are you on?"

She shook her head. He couldn't see her like this. Not like this, not now. *Go away,* she thought. *Go away, Max.* "Nothing... Luster..."

That scant mouthful was all he needed. "Dammit, Luster. C'mon, I'll get you back to your room."

"No..."

He got on her weak side and put an arm around her.

"No!" She pushed him away. "Stop it—I don't need your help!" A whiplash of anger snapped her vision into focus. Mouth agape, Max looked like she had struck him. It only made her angrier. "I can take care of myself! I don't need you always coming to the rescue!"

Pity grabbed the door of the stairwell, jerked it open, and plunged through.

It was too much. Her feet pedaled forward but wouldn't stop. She struck the opposite wall of the hallway and slid to the floor. The contents of her stomach rose to the back of her throat, and when she closed her eyes, the whole world spun.

Some seconds later, she felt Max take her arms. She didn't

resist this time but couldn't bring herself to open her eyes, either. If she did, the frustrated tears would flow.

"C'mon," he said. "Slow now."

Pity allowed herself to be led. Blind, she became aware of Garland's scent, still hanging about her like a haze. Her embarrassment grew. Could Max smell it, too?

It doesn't matter what he thinks. It doesn't matter at all.

Eventually, she heard a door open and felt the familiar aura of her room. She opened her eyes to find her bed before her.

"Lie down," said Max.

"No."

"You need to sleep it off."

"I don't want to sleep." Pity pulled away and listed toward the bathroom. "I want a bath."

"Are you trying to drown yourself?"

Yes.

"Lie down."

It was too hard to fight. Pity closed her eyes again and let the bed envelop her. A moment later, she felt Max pull her boots off.

"There," he said. "Get under the covers."

"Max..." Her voice sounded distant. Tendrils of unconsciousness tugged at her. "Please...please just go..."

She woke sometime later. The room was as black as pitch. She shifted.

"Pity?"

The voice had come from below. Max was on the floor, she realized, beside the bed. *How long has he been there?*

Staying stone-still, eyes pressed closed, she forced her breaths into a sedate pattern. After a few minutes, she heard Max stand, followed by the muted shuffle of his feet against the carpet. Her eyelids lit up when he opened the door to the hall. The vermilion glow lingered for a few moments—*one breath in, one breath out*—and then faded.

The door closed, and Max was gone.

CHAPTER 23

SHADOWED IN THE UPPER RANKS OF THE THEATRE'S
seats, Pity rolled a bullet back and forth between her fingers,
watching the act below slowly knit itself together. The floor of
the arena was a hectic patchwork of performers and props, but
with a hint of underlying reason to it, too, a pattern working
itself out. By the time of the next show, order would be estab-
lished, she had no doubt, and the act would emerge as another
of the Theatre's mesmerizing creations.

Already she found herself craving the day when all she had
to worry about was pleasing her audience. Onstage, she knew
what to expect, how to react. Onstage, her mother's guns were
as familiar as her own two hands. Nothing escaped her; she
dispatched every one of the Theatre's targets with merciless
precision.

Below, oblivious to her presence, Max adjusted pieces of the blossoming set.

A pang of guilt pierced her.

The arena was simple. Everything beyond it was where her control seemed to fray.

Footsteps approached, dragging her from her thoughts.

"Hi." It was Garland. "Mind if I join you?"

Pity's fist tightened around the bullet. "I was about to leave—"

"No, you weren't." He sat down next to her. "I think we need to have a talk. You've been avoiding me."

"No, I haven't."

"Don't look away like that; it gives away the lie. You've been avoiding me," he repeated, "and you've been avoiding Luster. She thinks you're mad at her."

"Why?"

"Because," Garland said with a mix of patience and amusement, "we've hardly caught a glimpse of you for days. And here you are, hiding in the dark." He paused. "But I don't think you're mad at her or at me."

"Good," she said. "I'm not. Now I've got to—"

"I think you're mad"—he nodded in the direction of the arena floor—"because what happened the other night didn't happen with the person you really wanted it to."

Halfway out of her seat, Pity stopped. She sank back down, defeated. "Dammit, does anything stay a secret in this place?"

He smirked. "Not much. Don't worry. Luster didn't say anything."

"Then how did you—"

"Pity…" His tone turned serious but not unkind. "I've seen how you look at Max. And it's nothing like how you look at me."

Her cheeks burned. "Oh."

Was it really that obvious? There was no mistaking what she felt around Garland. But even now her attention was drawn below, to where Max worked. It was Max who always seemed to rise to the surface of her thoughts, along with that brief moment on the night of her debut when he seemed to kiss her back.

"I'm…" A wave of embarrassment overtook her, so strong it brought frustrated tears to her eyes. "I'm sorry about the other night. I never meant to…"

"Hey, stop. Don't get upset." Garland reached over and pushed a loose strand of hair away from her cheek, a touch that felt more like a comfort than a temptation. "We're friends, right? There's no need to make it any more or less than that." His hand fell away. "But there's something else bothering you, too, isn't there? Luster thinks so, and she's always right about these sorts of things."

I almost died. I killed two men. There's a bounty hunter still hanging around who may have been sent by my father. Max… The reasons jumped to the tip of her tongue, each one good enough to serve to Garland… but all fell just short of the truth.

"I missed."

"What?"

"When the assassins attacked, I missed." A full confession in two words. Her hand tightened into a fist around the bullet. "More than once. More than twice. If it wasn't for Beau…"

Garland blinked at her. "Is that still eating at you? It wasn't the show, Pity. It must have been terrifying—of course you missed a few times!"

"It's more than that!" She stared at the ground, her voice rising uncontrollably. "I could have done more. I *should* have done more. I just *watched* when Finn was murdered...I could have saved her and I didn't. And then the attack on Selene...I'm not helpless. I'm *not!*" Every word pained her to say, as if they were fresh bruises on her soul. "So why does it feel like I am? Why is it so easy in practice and when I'm performing? Why do I only fail when it really matters?"

For a long moment Garland was silent. When she finally looked up at him, she found the warmth gone from his features. In its place was something else, something Pity recognized but couldn't name.

"You didn't fail," he said, his voice hollow. "You did the best you could in the moment. It's just that sometimes...that's not enough."

At first she didn't think he was going to say more. Then he took a breath and let it out slowly. "Y'know, before I came to Cessation, I lived on a settlement. It got sick...really sick."

That's when she saw it—the nothingness. Pity knew it from the commune, a dark souvenir of the war. Women and men who had seen too much, lost too much; some deep part of themselves had withered away, no more likely to grow back than an amputated limb. "Luster told me. I'm sorry."

"So was I. Nothing we tried slowed the epidemic—not medicine, not prayer. My whole family died, and the only thing I could do was dig their graves in the ancestral land my people had barely begun to reclaim. I remember finishing the last one knowing I'd never feel at home again." He shrugged. "So I left. But there was nothing I could have done about it."

"Except..." Pity shook her head. "It's not the same. You didn't make your family sick. But I could have saved Finn."

"Maybe," he allowed. "Or maybe you would have tried and ended up dead, too. Do you think she would have wanted that?"

Pity's jaw tightened. *Run.* That's what Finn had told her to do, the very last thing she ever did. *Run.* "No."

"Everybody loses, Pity—sometimes it's a little, sometimes it's a lot."

Pain shaped Garland's voice. When she reached out and squeezed his hand, though, his wolfish grin returned. For the first time she noticed how it didn't really touch his eyes.

"Can't do anything about the past," he continued. "Today's what we've got. And at the rate you're going, you'll run out of people in Casimir to *not* avoid. It's not really my business, but you can't pretend you're helpless about whatever's gone on between you and Max."

Something unknotted in her chest. *He's right,* she thought. *Max may not care about you the way you want him to, but he's still tried to be your friend. And he's not the one letting a little wound fester.* "Lord, you must think I'm ridiculous."

"I don't," he said. "But I do think Luster is right—you need to learn to relax a little. It's an ugly world, and we need to take what happiness we can, when we can."

"I wanted to ask...the other night..." Her cheeks burned again, and not entirely from embarrassment. "When I said I was fertile...it didn't occur to me at the time that it didn't matter. Because *you're* not, right?"

Garland rubbed his shoulder. "Starr gave me my booster shot a few weeks ago."

"So why didn't we...?"

"You didn't want it to go that far."

Her cheeks flushed. "I never actually said that."

"You didn't have to. Here." He reached into his pocket and pulled out a med injector. "Luster snatched this for you."

"What is it?"

"Same cocktail Starr doses us with. Lasts for six months or so. You don't have to take it, but she thought it might be one less thing for you to worry about."

Pity thought for a moment, then held out her arm. "Go on, do it." She winced at the brief prick, but the pain brought a measure of comfort. *They might show it funny, but these folks care.* Garland was right about Max, too. Of everything that was eating at her, that was the one she had control over.

The question was, did she have the steel to do something about it?

✦

This was no show, Pity told herself, and no battle. She didn't need to rush in. She could collect herself first. In the Gallery, she pulled up a stool and began formulating what to say to Max.

Olivia came over. "Getcha something?"

"Not today, thanks." *You'd best start keeping your wits about you.*

Pity straightened as Siena Bond appeared in the mirror behind Olivia, heading toward them. Over the last few days the bounty hunter had become a too-familiar sight. Pity had spotted her in the stands of the theatre, watching as she practiced, and in Eden, always alone and smoking ugly, hand-rolled cigarettes. But the woman never approached her again or said a single word.

Today, something was different. Siena moved with the deliberateness of a mountain cat, pack slung over one shoulder.

"So?" Olivia said when she reached the bar.

"So Daneko is in the wind," Siena replied. "And I'm on the job."

"Huh. I almost feel bad for him."

"I don't. Not with the bounty Selene's offering." Siena nodded her head at Pity. "Guess I'll have to wait to catch your act, Jones."

"Guess so," Pity croaked, her mouth suddenly parched.

"Next time," said Olivia. "She's not going anywhere."

Siena's mouth crooked up at the edges. "I'll keep that in mind. See ya around, Liv. Jones."

Pity watched until the bounty hunter was gone, a sensation in her gut like a block of ice melting.

Olivia tapped the bar to get her attention. "Are you all right? You look like someone walked over your grave."

"It's just...*her*."

"What about her?" Olivia's brow furled. "Pity, did you do something to cross Siena? Because that's a very bad—"

"I didn't do anything. It's only that..." She glanced back the way the bounty hunter had gone. "What if she came to Cessation looking for someone? And what if...that person was me?"

Olivia blinked at her. Then she laughed.

"It's not funny!"

"Yes, it is," said the bartender. "You can drop that notion right now. Siena is not after you."

"How do you know? You don't know my father! What if he hired her to—"

Olivia raised a hand to cut her off. "Pity, there are two very good reasons why I know your father didn't employ the best bounty hunter on the continent to hunt you down. The first is that if Siena Bond wanted to get you, you'd already be got. You aren't exactly hiding, you know. Or is there a glut of CONA-raised young ladies in Cessation who shoot like the Angel of Death herself?"

"No," Pity said. "I guess not. But—"

"Remember that former occupation I mentioned to you? I know Siena because I spent three years chasing bounties with her before I decided that life wasn't for me and settled in Cessation."

"So what's the second reason?"

"Well," Olivia said, "is your daddy a rich man?"

In the commune, he had a certain luxury, but it was more power than currency. "No."

"Then, trust me. As worn around the edges as she looks, Siena doesn't come cheap. You've got nothing to worry about."

Olivia's confidence was reassuring. And now that Pity'd said it out loud, she had to admit the idea that her father would— *could*—send a bounty hunter after her was a little far-fetched. But if she wasn't the bounty hunter's target, then why had the woman seemed to show such a peculiar interest in her?

One problem at a time, she thought, summoning her resolve. *And you've already got one chambered.*

It was time to pull the trigger before she lost her nerve completely.

Pity found Max in his workroom, sitting on the floor, surrounded by flames. She was nearly upon him before he looked
up from the piles of fabric encircling him—scraps of crimson,
vermilion, and yellow. A shadow passed over his features, there
and gone in the space of a heartbeat.

"Hi," she said.

"Hi."

Oh, good start. Pity swallowed to clear the lump from her
throat. "What's all this?"

He tossed the pieces he had been stitching to the floor.
"Feathers. Or fire. To be honest, I'm not entirely sure yet. It's
something Halcyon has in mind for the Rousseaus, but..." He
sighed. "It hasn't quite come together yet."

"You'll get it."

"Yeah." His gaze remained on the pieces. "Did you...need
something?"

"Yes." She forced the words out before she could reconsider.
"I...I wanted to apologize. For what happened the other night.
And after my debut."

Max stood up. "There's no reason to—"

"Yes, there is. So, I'm sorry. I've been unfair to you. I know
I haven't been acting like it, but I don't mind being just your
friend." She sighed. "In fact, I miss it. And with everything
else that's happened...I guess I don't want to lose that. Heck, I
wouldn't even be here if it wasn't for you."

Max said nothing, eyes glazed with some fusion of emotion

Pity couldn't decipher. His teeth tugged worriedly at one of his lip rings.

"I don't know if that's something you should be thankful for," he said finally. "I promised you'd be safe in Casimir and you almost died."

"That wasn't your fault." She took a deep breath and exhaled. "Or mine. It was just bad luck. And I knew Cessation was dangerous from the beginning. What I didn't expect is how quick I'd come to like it here. The Theatre...and the people." As soon as she said it, the honest truth of it filled her. Despite everything that had happened, everything that she had faced, in no moment had she ever felt alone. In a scant few weeks, the people of Cessation had treated her more like family than her father and brothers ever had. "So can you forgive me for being an ass?"

A faint smile touched his lips. "You didn't even need to ask. Just promise me one thing."

"What?"

"This place—what it offers—can get the better of you if you're not careful."

Fresh embarrassment ignited. "Oh, you can be sure I'm not going anywhere near Luster's pills again—"

"More than that," he pressed. "Casimir, the Theatre, the whole city—it's a puddle on the surface with an ocean underneath. Before you know it, you're overcome. Promise me that if you ever feel like it's getting the best of you—well, get out. I'd rather see you gone than drowned."

Her stomach fluttered, but in a good way. Max had forgiven her. For all the shots she had missed, she was alive, and so was

Selene. And for the moment Siena Bond was someone else's trouble. Bit by bit, the gray clouds that had hovered over her were breaking apart, allowing the light in again. She couldn't change the past—Garland was right about that—but she could be ready for what tomorrow brought.

"Okay, Max," Pity said, her voice barely breaking a whisper. "I promise."

PART TWO

CHAPTER 24

THE NIGHTS, WHICH ALWAYS CARRIED A CHILL ONCE the sun set, turned true cold as winter approached. Still, the warm days disoriented Pity enough that when Christmas Eve arrived, it came almost as a surprise. Less of a shock was the uptick in trade; as the city celebrated its way through an array of winter holidays, customers, vendors, and goods jostled for every inch of free space at the BlackMark.

"Do you think Duchess would like anything here?" Luster rifled through a pile of goods. She tossed aside a stuffed bear and a pair of glittery pants that seemed to be missing their seat. "He's so hard to shop for."

"What about those bracelets over there?" Wedged into a narrow canyon between booths, Pity adjusted the gift-filled satchel on her shoulder. On the commune, some small trinket for Finn had meant saving for months. It was enlivening, handing over money and not feeling a hole in her gut. But one present was still missing. She fingered a set of paintbrushes with dark wood handles.

"Badger hair," said the booth's proprietor. "The best."

She haggled a fair price and tucked them into her bag, hoping Max would like them.

Beside her, Luster crowed with triumph. She held up a book with a bespectacled boy and a train on the cover. "He loves these stories! Thank goodness, because we need to go or we'll be late. Got everything you wanted?"

"I think so."

They pushed their way through the crowd. Despite the press, everyone seemed to be in a jovial mood, and the entire market smelled of cinnamon and vanilla. Somewhere a group of young women were singing songs Pity didn't know but that made her want to join in anyway.

On their way out, Luster bought a bottle of spiced wine. Pity took a long swig, nearly dropping it when a hand grabbed her shoulder.

"What's in the bag?"

She spun, one gun halfway drawn before she realized it was Duchess. Max and Garland trailed behind him.

Duchess raised his hands into the air. "Whoa, it's only us!"

"Shoot him," said Garland dryly. "It'll teach him a lesson."

"Just leave me a pretty corpse!" Duchess begged. "And give me one last drink before I die."

Pity handed him the bottle. "Happy holidays, jackass."

He took it. "And a blissful New Year, bitch."

It was the chilliest day so far, but the sky above was a bright, cloudless cyan as they wandered through a part of the city Pity had never visited.

She slowed her step, falling in with Max, who trailed the pack. "Something wrong?"

Max buried his hands in his pockets. "Why do you say that?"

"Because you don't look very festive."

"I *thought* I did." The tips of his hair were dyed red and green, and a tiny gold bell hung from one of his piercings. It jingled when he moved. He nodded at her bag. "Successful outing?"

"No peeking." Pity pulled it closer. "It's no fun if it's not a surprise."

That earned her a faint smile. "Sorry, I'm not much for the holidays. You seem to like them, though. Good times on the commune?"

"Good enough," she said. "When my mother was alive, anyway. On Christmas morning she used to leave her gift to me outside my door, so it was the first thing I found when I woke up. After she died...well, usually I'd hide out with Finn." The pain of memory came as a pinch—sharp but receding quickly. "What about you? What were they like where you grew up?"

Max kept his gaze straight ahead. "Holidays were..." He thought. "Mostly a reminder of what we were missing."

They came to an intersection of streets. At the center sat a huge dry fountain covered in thousands of candles. The sight was captivating: uncountable hues dripping over the tiers of stone, waxy water frozen in the act of flowing.

"What's this?"

"Memories," said Max. "It's set up every year. Each candle is for a loved one gone."

People were gathered around the makeshift shrine. Many prayed—hands folded, on their knees, with foreheads pressed to the dusty asphalt. A pair of Reformationists stood at a respectful distance, reading scripture to the passersby. As they drew closer, a girl carrying a box of white candles ran up to them.

"Do you want to buy some?" she chirped.

"Miss Selene passes them out to the kids," Max explained. "They get to keep everything they earn."

"That's sweet." Pity bought two candles and added them to the fountain, accepting a lit taper someone handed her. *Finn,* she thought, lighting the first. *Momma.* The second flame sputtered before catching. She stared into it. It was hardly visible in the midday sun, but she could smell the oily scent of the burning wax and feel the heat all around her. *Lord, if you're listening, keep them safe, wherever they are.* She swallowed the lump in her throat. *And you might as well keep Billy and Henry safe, too,* she added, remembering a time before her brothers had taken so much after their father.

Beside her, Luster and Duchess were lighting candles of their own. She turned to see Garland handing the girl some money, but when she offered the box, he waved it away. Max was no longer beside him. She found him a little way off, kneeling carefully among the sea of flames. He had a single candle, which he placed on the ground. As he lit it, his face went stony, sorrow and anger etched in his narrow cheeks. Then the emotions were gone, and he looked himself again.

The lost love Luster suspects? she wondered. *Really lost, then. I was competing with a dead girl.* Guilt prickled, and she chided herself for the petty thought.

The walk back to Casimir was quieter. But it was impossible to stay morose when they found the Gallery decorated from floor to ceiling, a joyous chaos of tinsel, mistletoe, and ribbons. A pair of porters were stringing popcorn and red berries, and there were plates of gingerbread people everywhere. Pity found they came with rather exaggerated anatomy, but they smelled delicious. She took one and broke off a piece without looking too hard at what was getting broken. Tonight there would be a communal dinner for everyone in the Gallery, but on Christmas Day itself Casimir would be shut down. Already most of the patrons had departed the premises for wherever they had come from.

Back in her room, Pity wrapped her gifts in gauzy tissue paper and finished them off with bows. She stared at the pile proudly for a few seconds and then dressed for dinner. By the time she returned to the Gallery, the room was teeming with people, the air thick with body heat and spices and the delicious smells of food. She found the others, waiting patiently to start on the huge buffet that ran down the center of the room.

As the hour struck, the sound of a hundred bells rang out, and everyone got up to fill their plates. The commune had held dinners like this, too. If Pity closed her eyes, it was almost the same—same raucous laughter, same off-color jokes being told. Eyes open, it was a different story, with more color and more skin, but the feeling of community prevailed.

But she felt the voids, too. The puzzle of her new life lacked pieces that had never belonged to it but that *could* have fit. Her mother. Finn. It was easy, pleasant even, to slot in visions of them, to entwine the memory of Finn's laughter with Duchess's, or her mother's tranquil smile with Max's. But it was a fantasy.

Months ago that might have been sorrowful. Now it was bittersweet.

Everyone ate and drank until they were full, waited a bit, and ate and drank some more. By the time the plates were cleared away, the laughter was louder, the jokes even more bawdy. The Rousseaus did flips on the bar and walked the length of it on their hands. Olivia extinguished candles with her whip. Flossie flounced around passing out fluffy white bonbons, popping them into every waiting mouth.

In a nest of sofas and chairs, Pity lounged beside Luster, cradling a cup of mulled wine. Across a table scattered with glasses and cookie crumbs, Garland laughed as Kitty dangled a piece of mistletoe over Duchess's head.

"You gotta give me a kiss. It's tradition," she teased, sloshing champagne from her glass.

"I don't!" Duchess dodged both the splashes and the kisses.

"He's no fun." Garland snatched the sprig away from Kitty and jumped onto the couch next to Pity, grinning. "But I bet Pity is."

She rolled her eyes. "Fine." She kissed him on each side of his mouth.

"That doesn't count!" Luster protested.

"It does where I come from. Two sweet kisses for one smutty one. Yeah, we played this game on the commune, too! Geez, y'all know we do figure out how to make babies eventually, right?"

Duchess shrugged. "I thought you grew them like crops."

Garland waved the mistletoe. "Who wants a turn? Now's the time—don't be shy!"

Max stood abruptly. He'd been quiet all night, laughing when it was called for but offering little to the conversation. At times, Pity had caught him staring into the depths of his drink, as if reading a message there only he could see. She wondered if he was still thinking about his candle.

"I'm going to get some more punch," he said. "Anyone else?"

But before he could depart, a horn sounded. A hush fell on the room.

Across the hall, Selene appeared on a raised dais, resplendent in a cascading silver-and-white dress. Beau stood in his usual place behind her, Adora and Halcyon off to one side. Halcyon wore a suit as white as fresh snow but with a purple top hat. Pity stifled a grin. He looked like a skinny snowman.

Selene clapped her hands together a few times, but every eye in the room was already on her.

"I cannot imagine," she began, voice warm, "that anyone in the world is looking out now and seeing a better family than I see here. Some of you have been here only months, others for years, but all of you bring your own brand of brightness to Casimir, to our home."

Pity leaned back in her seat, smiling. She liked that word and the feeling it carried. She looked around at the people who, not long ago, she would not have imagined turning into a motley sort of family. Her father's face floated to the surface of her mind, but she banished it. She wouldn't think about him today, not when she was enjoying herself so much.

"I don't want to take you away from your celebrations," Selene continued. "But for all our beliefs—those shared and those not—for all our pasts and for all our futures, Casimir is a paradise of prosperity because of all of you. You are the soul of our home. Thank you all."

The cheers that followed were as loud as any Pity had heard in the theatre. As Selene descended the dais, Scylla wandered over, a red-and-white-striped snake coiled around her neck.

"Festive accessory," said Pity.

"Don't you think?" Scylla ran a finger across the serpent's scales. "He waits all year long to be this fashionable." She gestured at the dais. "Pay attention, the boss has a present for us."

Halcyon was calling for quiet again, waving his purple top hat emphatically.

"I wanted to take this opportunity to make a little announcement," he called out, replacing the hat on his head. "On the eve of the New Year, the Theatre Vespertine will hold its next performance." He paused dramatically. "One that will include a Finale!"

Pity sucked in a breath as the room erupted in ferocious applause.

"Who?" said Luster over the din. "Is he going to say who?"

But Pity already knew. The blood in her veins chilled. "The assassin."

"Yup," Scylla confirmed. "Your friend is coming back out to play, Miss Pity."

"They kept him locked up all this time?" Max's brow furled with revulsion. "It's been months! I assumed he was long dead."

"We all did." Scylla petted her snake again. "But he's not, and now we get to have some fun."

Casimir had never been so silent as when Pity woke on Christmas morning. Like the morning after a hard snow, the quiet enveloped the whole building; even the swish of her slippered feet against the carpet seemed a harsh trespass. She had been the first to abandon the party the evening before, sarcastic booing ushering her out of the Gallery. But she had wanted to wake early. Everyone had agreed to exchange presents after breakfast—or lunch or dinner, whatever ended up being the first meal of the day—but Pity wanted to leave her gifts as her mother had done, outside each person's door.

She visited each room in turn until only Max's present was left. Turning the gift over and over in her hands, she considered it, the paintbrushes within clacking against each other. A porter might know where Max's room was, but she still didn't. She could wait, but it hardly seemed fair, now that she had delivered the others.

The basement, Max had said. It wasn't much of a clue. Casimir was huge—it could take her hours to explore its tunnels. But the night he had found her on the stairs, he *might* have been coming up. Though her memories were hazy, she found the stairwell and descended. When she opened the door at the very bottom, cool air carried the scent of iron and damp stone to her nostrils. Surrounded by drab concrete, she made her way through the bowels of Casimir, searching for anywhere habitable. She found nothing—only utility closets and storage rooms. Once a brown mouse scampered across her path.

As she was ready to give up, she came to a junction of halls. To her left, the passage ended abruptly at a large metal door spotted with rivets. Drippy letters were scrawled across its surface: TRESPASSERS WILL BE PAINTED.

Pity smirked. *At least I know I'm in the right place.*

She went to deposit the present. The door was ajar, allowing a dim ochre glow to escape. She listened for a moment but heard no movement within.

"Max?" There was no response. She peered closer.

Even in the low light, Pity could see how spectacular the room was. Murals covered every inch of the walls, bleeding onto the floor and up to the ceiling. Mesmerized by the vortex of colors, she took a few steps inside, the door creaking feebly as she pushed it. She couldn't even begin to pick apart the layers of imagery: spindly trees and bizarre animals mixed in with pure abstract strokes and splatters; a skyline of buildings half covered by a spray of fireworks; a pair of alien eyes looking out from beneath a field of poppy flowers.

As she reached out to touch a bloody sunset, a bell tinkled.

Behind her, on a thick mattress set against the wall, was Max. The only parts of him visible in the mess of blankets were his hair and one hand, hanging limply over the edge of the bed. Beyond the wilted fingers sat a bottle, an inch of liquor left in the bottom.

Pity grimaced. She'd seen Max drink plenty, but there was always a measure of control to his merriment, an easygoing restraint.

This...this was new.

It was a party, she told herself. *He let some of his care fall away and he drank too much, that's all.*

But she knew a sad drunk when she saw one.

Suddenly feeling like a trespasser, Pity began to retreat. Her foot caught a jar full of brushes as she did. It overturned, glass and wood clinking against the cement floor.

Max stirred, his head and shoulders emerging from the nest of bedding. "Pity?" Her name came out thick. "What are you... doing here?"

She held out the package. "It was supposed to be a surprise."

His features pinched with confusion as his gaze moved from her to the gift to the bottle near the bed. "What happened to the rest of that?"

Pity sighed and went to the mattress. She sat down on its edge. "I have a pretty good idea." She overturned the bottle, letting the remaining liquor trickle out. "I think you've had enough of *that*."

Max tried to rise, groaned, and fell back onto the bed. "Yeah, maybe."

"Max...are you okay?"

He blinked at her, eyes fluttering in an effort to stay open. "I'm..." His eyelids gave in and he put his head down. "I'm just tired."

The words carried a weight she had never heard from him before, as if there were anchors attached to them, dragging Max into some unseen depths. All around, the murals drew closer, condensing the dimly lit room until there was barely enough space for the two of them. Powerlessness bloomed in Pity's chest.

You can't fight someone else's demons, she thought, reaching out to pluck a stray bit of tinsel from his hair. *You know that.* But that kernel of knowledge didn't bring any relief.

Slow, even breaths passed between Max's parted lips. Pity started to go, but he roused again at her movement.

"Stay." His eyes remained closed. "For a little bit...just until I fall..."

"Shhh." Pity clutched the gift to her chest, as if it could smother the ache ignited there. "I'll be right here, Max. You go ahead and rest."

She remained like that, surrounded by the manifestations of Max's dreams—or nightmares—until he was asleep.

CHAPTER 25

THE FOLLOWING DAYS FOUND THE ARENA ENGULFED in barely ordered pandemonium. Acts needed polishing, new sets needed constructing, and as a result, Pity found her practice delayed. She waited in the stands, watching the Rousseaus swoop back and forth in the new firebird costumes Max had created for them. It was a scene wildly out of sync with the sounds of hammers and saws and the brassy carnival music being played. The only thing missing from the chaos was Halcyon, normally in the thick of it all, tossing orders around.

Not for the first time, Pity was grateful for the solitary nature of her act and the pragmatic element that called for the arena to be hers alone when she was practicing. But the approaching Finale marred her thoughts. In too few days, the stands would be filled with an audience eager to decide the fate of the assassin.

Offered as executioner for the first time, an undercurrent of unease gripped her.

They want a show, she reminded herself. Not the quick, bland execution she could offer.

"Serendipity! Good, there you are!" Halcyon bounded up the stairs, his long legs taking two at a time.

She stood to meet him. "What's up, boss?"

"Come, come. We have business to attend to."

"What about practice?"

He waved a gloved hand. "It will wait. Selene wishes to see us."

"Why?"

"A mystery we shall solve presently."

Instead of traveling through the Gallery, Halcyon led her to a secluded hallway, then through a trio of doors, each with a keypad lock. In the chamber beyond the last door were an elevator and two rather bored-looking Tin Men, who waved them through without question. A brief ride delivered them into a sprawling suite. It took only a glance for Pity to surmise that they were in Selene's personal living space. Unlike her sparse office, the décor was busier, with an overlapping patchwork of carpets and curved walls speckled with gold-framed paintings. The floor was partially sunken, with a comfortable cluster of sofas at its center.

"Please, have a seat." Selene's words entered before she did, appearing in a doorway, Beau on her heels. "How is the show preparation coming?"

"Splendid, of course!" said Halcyon.

Pity followed him down the steps and sat on one of the couches.

Though Beau remained on the upper level, Selene joined them there. "I'm glad to hear it. We're expecting some important guests, so try to dazzle, won't you?"

Halcyon balked. "I'm offended you'd expect anything less from our sublime syndicate of talent."

"I wouldn't, and I don't." Selene turned to Pity. "Looking forward to the show?"

Pity examined Selene, searching for clues as to why they were there, but the woman was as inscrutable as a blank page. "Of course, ma'am."

"Good, because I have a special request of you." Selene reclined, tranquil as she draped one elegant arm across the back of the sofa. "I want you to perform the Finale."

The placid tone of the request belied the meaning of the words. "But I..." Confusion twisted Pity's tongue. "I thought the audience decided who—"

"These are special circumstances." Selene locked her with a lioness's stare. "After Daneko's betrayal, we sent a message. One that isn't finished yet. This is the next piece."

"But..."

"He won't be armed. It's a simple enough task."

Too simple—nothing more than the pull of a trigger. And yet...

"I want you to do it"—Selene's voice softened—"because you were there, and everyone knows that. You've been here for months now, Pity. Understand that Cessation is an act of its own, one that requires no small amount of balance. We need to make it clear that those who would upset it will not be tolerated. That they will be made an example of."

An example. Pity fought a feeling of being dragged down, the gun belt around her hips ten times the weight it was moments ago. Selene was asking her to kill in cold blood.

No, not *asking.*

"Selene." Nearly forgotten, Halcyon leaned forward, his voice imploring. "Perhaps it's not yet the right time to—"

"It's exactly the right time." Selene's attention remained on Pity. "Can I count on you?"

Was there any other answer she could give? *This is what you signed up for,* she reminded herself. *You were bound to have come up against a Finale eventually.* It had simply happened sooner rather than later.

Too soon. Pity clenched her teeth, desperate to say no—the one thing she couldn't say to Selene.

"Yes," she exhaled. "I'll do it."

Selene smiled, satisfied. "Thank you. Together we'll finish another chapter of this nasty business."

But not the last one. Daneko still eluded capture. There were whisperings of where he might be—in one of the CONA cities, under the protection of a warlord in a South American jungle, even that he was dead—but nothing definitive. And Pity was positive Selene wasn't the sort to give up the hunt over rumors. That reckoning was still to come.

She stood reflexively when Selene did, their audience with her apparently over. "Halcyon, stay, would you? I would like to discuss the Finale details."

"Of course." Halcyon touched her shoulder as he passed. "Pity...take the rest of the day off."

"What about—?"

"Practice can wait until tomorrow morning."

She headed for the elevator as cold understanding settled on her. *I just agreed to kill a man.* In the span of moments, she had gone from entertainer to executioner. Reeling from the imperative, she didn't register Beau until he was beside her, remaining a step behind, as if escorting her.

"Don't overthink it." He spoke so that only she could hear. "It's nothing you haven't done before."

"I know."

"And nothing that needs to hang on you after, either."

She glanced at him, finding less ice in his eyes than usual. Somehow that made her feel worse.

"I'll do what I need to do," Pity said as the doors closed her in.

Despite that bravado, the moment the elevator began to drop, her stomach went with it. She braced herself against the wall as the muscles in her legs trembled.

If the agreement had been in ink, it wouldn't have been dry yet, and already she was searching for a way out of it. The options cascaded through her mind as she descended: she could beg to be released or, at the very least, for fate and the fickle whim of the audience to decide who in the Theatre would do the deed.

But she knew the time to plead had passed.

There was no law but Selene's law. And when the Finale arrived, Pity would be her cat's-paw. But, she reminded herself, the man she'd be killing was a murderer. Someone who had killed not for survival or for principle but for money. He was no better than the men who'd slain Finn or the *admirer* who'd maimed Duchess.

And Pity knew, given the chance, he would kill her, too.

Justice, she thought. *Ugly as it is, this is justice.*

The idea had once soothed her hesitation. But now, propped up before the blaze of the approaching spectacle, the meaning of the word suddenly seemed translucent. Hollow. A definition molded by circumstance.

But maybe that didn't matter.

Justice and murder—in Cessation, they were two sides of the same coin.

CHAPTER 26

DESPITE A FLAWLESS PERFORMANCE, BY THE TIME HER act was over, Pity's thoughts were a tangled mess, broken only by the distant buzz of applause or the rainbow blurs of other performers rushing by. When someone brought her a cup of ice water, she took it without a word. It slid down her throat and into her stomach like a blade. The screens in the preparation area beneath the stage showed the theatre was packed to bursting. Every box, every seat, every bench—full. Tonight's Finale would usher in the New Year, and no one wanted to miss it.

Pity leaned against a table. Hours earlier she had sat in the same spot with Eva, preparing for the evening's show.

Her mentor had minced no words. "You are worried about being chosen for the Finale."

No, actually I'm not. She had swallowed that response. "It's nothing I haven't done before."

Eva's dark-lashed eyes narrowed. "Say what you really mean."

"I am. He tried to kill me. I want him dead."

"A bit of advice for you: do not play poker." Eva ran her knife across a whetstone. "I only want to know one thing: will you be able to perform tonight if you have to?"

"Yes," she had replied, her stomach slithering like it was full of Scylla's snakes. "If I have to."

Would it be worse, Pity wondered, if she didn't know she was going to be chosen? If there was still the chance that she'd end the night with clean hands?

For days she had thought about little besides the upcoming Finale and Selene's mandate. Now she searched the depths of her mind, trying to dredge up the emotions she had felt after the attack on her and Finn, after the assassination attempt and hearing Duchess's story. Pain, helplessness, anger . . . *Hold on to them,* she told herself. *Don't let the rage get away.* But they were oily, slipping away through her mental fingers no matter how hard she grasped.

The only emotion that lingered was dread.

Wherever Selene was watching tonight's performance, it wasn't from a box in the audience, but a familiar face flashed on the wall of screens: Patrick Sheridan. Pity hadn't heard of his return, but the last few days had seen a brisk influx of patrons.

Maybe he'll send you another bottle of wine to celebrate your first Finale.

She shook away the grisly thought as Eva glided over, Marius a few steps behind.

"Almost time," Eva said softly.

Scylla wandered over, too, followed by the Rousseaus and more Theatre members, until Pity's solo watch had turned into a crowd. She looked for Max and found him at the very edge of the gathering, his face bleached white by the glow of the screens. He pushed his way through to her. When he reached her side, he didn't say anything. Pity was glad for it. There were no words to soothe the trepidation that gripped her like a fever.

The last act ended and Halcyon appeared on every screen, his face somber.

"One year ends," he said, "and another begins. But before it does, we in the Theatre Vespertine have one last matter, one final *reckoning* to attend to." He paused, visibly vexed. "No! No, this goes beyond the Theatre, beyond even Casimir. There has been a transgression upon every one of us within the bounds of Cessation...upon our city...upon our *home*. As all of you know, several months ago someone attempted to assassinate Miss Selene."

The crowd booed and hissed.

"This someone—whose name we shall not speak—escaped justice, but thanks to the efforts of our exceptional security forces, one of his minions was not so lucky. Yes, ladies and gentlemen, tonight, in our arena, we have one of the very perpetrators who violated Casimir's hallowed halls with intentions of murder!" Halcyon waited as the crowd worked itself into a frenzy. "It's time to choose," he continued, "to decide who will serve as Cessation's hand of justice!"

Pity tensed as the projections appeared on the ceiling. For the first time, her own face stared down, ringed by images of

Scylla, the Zidanes, the Rousseaus, and others. They began to spin. The first to pop out was Scylla. The crowd cheered. Then came Eva and Marius, and they cheered louder, not knowing it was a sham, a façade.

Another act.

Entertainer. She swallowed hard. *Executioner.*

Either way, this was a price she had to pay.

"Well," cried Halcyon, over the ensuing din, "it sounds like Cessation's justice will have a razor's edge tonight." He threw up his hands. "The Zidanes it is!"

Pity started as if doused with cold water. The breath she was holding came out in a single rush, her shoulders releasing their tension. She hadn't even been offered as a choice. Had someone intervened—Halcyon or even Beau? Or had Selene decided she'd already spilled enough mercenary blood? It didn't matter. However her reprieve came about, she was spared.

I'll do what I need to do. The resolve suddenly sounded so silly, so childish, that a laugh almost bubbled out of her.

On the screens, the Zidanes' picture disappeared, but the others remained. They kept spinning above Halcyon, who grinned his madman grin. "But this is no ordinary criminal, my friends, and so this must be no ordinary Finale! A trained mercenary, an experienced assassin—surely we would not risk any of our beloved family by sending them into the ring with such a creature unassisted!"

Pity's relief turned glacial. Around her, the world went fuzzy. An image of the Rousseaus filled the whole of her vision, eliciting a robust round of applause. But when her face appeared the roar was like that of an oncoming tornado.

The next thing she was aware of was Max's hand on her arm. His mouth was parted slightly, the reflections of the screens rippling over his metal piercings like tiny flames. It was a moment before he found his voice. "You can say no."

"No," she said, anxious blood prickling in her cheeks. "I can't."

I can't.

Do what you need to do.

"Pity?"

It was Eva.

"Come," she said. "We must not keep them waiting."

She shrugged off Max, unable to look at him again as they started for the stage. The other performers called out encouragement, but Pity heard only one word out of every ten, her eyes locked on the black maw of the tunnel leading to their platform. When the cool darkness enveloped them, she roused suddenly, pulling each gun from its holster.

Twelve bullets, she counted, an echo of the morning that had led her here. *More than enough to kill a man.*

But Eva and Marius were with her, too, and the measure of the man's blood was meant to be spread between them. She could guess how.

Selene wants a show.

As the platform carried them into the arena, disorientation rocked Pity, as it had at her first performance. The crowd was still the crowd, she told herself, peering into the shadowy seats. She needed no mock assassination attempt to win them over this time, no false offer of blood. They had already given her their love.

Now, in return, all they were asking for was the real thing.

And if I don't give it to them... She licked her lips. The air tasted different than it had during her act, laced with an unfamiliar ferocity that wouldn't be denied. *If you lose the crowd, you lose the act...and maybe more.*

Halcyon was gone, but his voice remained.

"A sight indeed," he said. "One of our oldest acts and our very newest, side by side. And Serendipity, our savior, our angel with six-shooters—for without her, Miss Selene would surely have been lost. This heinous assassin put a bullet through our darling sharpshooter, leaving her with a permanent reminder of her peril. I say she returns it to him. What say you, Cessation?"

She would have drawn on Halcyon had he been near, for hamming it up the way he was. Instead, she mirrored the Zidanes, smiling and brandishing her guns charmingly, while inside, her muscles felt like they might give way at any moment. Under the pretense of checking her ammo again, she fought to gather herself. Though she couldn't see Selene in the flesh, she knew the woman was watching. The same way she knew that no performance meant as much as this one did.

At Eva's direction, they spread out—Pity moved toward one end of the arena, the Zidanes to the other. Music began, and the floor opened again.

After he'd spent months in captivity—months of interrogations and torture and who knew what else—Pity expected a man half dead already. Instead, save for the dishwater-gray jumpsuit, he looked very much like he had the last time she had seen him. The bones of his face were more distinct and his hair longer, but he must have been fed well enough and allowed to bathe. The only distinct difference was the grim hollowness in his gaze, apparent even at a distance.

Eva signaled and they approached, closing in on him like he was a wounded animal. Eva and Marius drew a knife for each hand. Pity filled hers with ebony grips. No barrier went up, and she didn't expect it to. There was no reason for her to miss.

Twelve bullets.

The assassin considered them individually, turning in a slow circle, as if he wasn't sure where he was or who they were. But when Pity took another tentative step forward and his eyes alighted on her, there was recognition.

And a glint of hate.

She froze, close enough now to see his hands—and fingers— clearly. They ended in red-pink masses. Every one of his finger-nails was gone. Her stomach clenched, hands tightening around the handles of her revolvers. It didn't have to be like this. Surely this man had suffered enough. She could finish it now. Empty her chambers into his chest and call it justice, call it revenge, overzealousness, or anything else she wanted.

When he feinted toward her, she did nearly that. But at the last instant, her fingers froze on their triggers and she danced back instead.

That's exactly what he wants, she realized. He knew he was a dead man and that she was the weak link, the jumpiest of his chosen executioners. *He's a mercenary,* she reminded herself. *A trained assassin.* He tried to kill Selene. He tried to kill *her.*

Pity steeled herself as he crept back, looking disappointed at his failed gambit.

She *could* finish him now. End this macabre farce in a matter of moments. And though she'd be able to name it a lot of things, there was one thing she wouldn't be able to call it...

A show.

He came at her again and she fired. He stumbled back as the bullet struck inches in front of his foot.

Bang! Bang!

With each shot, he jerked away, his movements more and more off-balance.

Bang! Bang! Bang!

Buffeted about like a scarecrow in a storm, Pity almost expected straw to spill out when Eva flitted around his blind side, her blade flashing. But it was blood that flowed, dark and wet, soaking his shoulder in an instant. Then came Marius, with a cut to his forearm. The assassin's cry of pain was barely audible beneath the roar of the crowd. He lurched in Pity's direction again, but she drove him back with another well-aimed shot. The stony calculation in his face was gone, crumbled away to reveal pure animalistic panic. He thought he was done, Pity mused. But, useless as it was, his instinct to survive had kicked in.

Five bullets. Still enough.

And yet, hands moving of their own accord, she found herself refilling the chambers of her guns. She went to the edge of the arena and took her time as the Zidanes continued their volley. To and fro they flew, slicing and stinging, every cut targeted and shallow. Soon the assassin was mottled all over with red.

Pity watched, knowing she should rejoin the fray. Knowing she was being watched, too. But as soon as the cylinder of her gun locked into place, it was as if her muscles had followed suit. *Go,* she willed. *Get back in there.* Still, she couldn't move.

A voice spoke behind her. "You're doing fine."

The words should have been lost, but somehow they had worked their way through the din. She turned to find Patrick Sheridan sitting in the nearest box. He smiled at her, as calm as if she were engaged in some mundane task, while around him the faces of the audience screamed for blood. His gaze seemed to carry the same message as his voice.

You're doing fine.

At the center of the arena, the Zidanes paused. Pity forced herself to take one step forward and then another. The assassin was a mess, bloodied and pale, and swaying on his feet. She could see beneath the tattered jumpsuit, beyond the fresh wounds to skin that was hatched and crossed with screaming red scars.

As she drew closer, Eva and Marius fell back. A lump formed in Pity's throat. *He's a rat,* she thought. They were three cats playing with a wounded rat.

No. Eva and Marius were cats. She was a kitten—one with six steel claws in each paw but still a kitten on her first real hunt.

And now she was being given the kill.

The audience was rabid, screaming and chanting her name, each syllable a ruining beat.

Ser-en-di-pi-ty! Ser-en-di-pi-ty!

Pity holstered one of her guns. She didn't need it.

It was time for the show to be over with.

She stopped half a dozen paces from him. When she raised the gun and cocked the hammer, his legs gave out and he fell to the ground. His head hung toward the floor.

"Do it," he croaked.

No one could hear but her.

"On your feet," she ordered.

He looked up at her, eyes brimming with resignation. Shook his head.

Her grip weakened. His face became Finn's, so clearly that tears clouded her vision. She blinked and the assassin returned. "Get up!"

I can't kill a man on his knees. I can't...

"Do it!" he said again.

Her voice inched toward the scream that was building within. "I said get up!"

He didn't stand, gaze burning with a last, tired defiance. Pity's finger lay tight on the trigger. All she had to do was apply a little pressure.

Inhale, aim. Exhale... She breathed in and then out. Around her the chant continued.

Ser-en-di-pi-ty! Ser-en-di-pi-ty!

Her hand stiffened, but she couldn't muster that last tiny bit of strength.

Do it!

Too many heartbeats passed. She began to shake.

An instant before she gave in, a heartbeat before her arm would have dropped and they would have known her for a weakling and a coward, the man's eyes went wide with surprise. He jerked forward, a thin, scarlet stream spurting from his lips. Startled, she pulled the trigger. A black hole opened on his forehead as a spray of red and gray issued out behind him—a brief, gory halo.

He was dead before he hit the floor.

Across the arena, Eva straightened from her throw, smoothing the front of her dress calmly. Pity nearly dropped her gun when she spotted the hilt of the knife embedded in the mercenary's spine, but a wave of cheers hit her like a slap to the face.

You're still onstage.

She holstered her weapon as the Zidanes came over. Eva gave her a knowing look and took one of her hands. Marius took the other.

Chained together like that, they bowed.

CHAPTER 27

STIFF-BACKED AND COLD AS ICE, PITY EXITED THE TUNNEL, pushing past everyone until she found herself in a shadowed corner. On the floor, a mass of ropes lay piled like intestines. She collapsed onto it and pressed her forehead to her knees, hands clenching and unclenching. She could still feel the jolt of the gun firing. Part of her wished that she could rewind time and empty every last chamber into the mercenary. The rest of her wanted to throw her guns to the ground and never touch them again.

A shadow fluttered at the corner of her vision.

"Pity?" Halcyon stood over her, hat in hand, mouth twitching with a hesitant smile.

Her eyes ached but remained dry. "I'll do better next time, boss." Whether it was a promise she could keep was beyond her at that moment.

Halcyon crouched down next to her, bringing with him the
scent of roses. "It's done," he said, his voice unusually soft.
"Done and over. Over and done. You did very well."

Something in her snapped. "No, I didn't!" She began to
shake again, harder than before. "I couldn't...I tried, but—"

"Pity, stop," Halcyon said. "The beast is fed. The city has been
given its bloody meal and will remain sated for the time being."

The tremors paused. "What?"

He sighed. "A wild animal kept in a cage is still a wild animal, even when it licks its owner's hand and rolls over to show
you its belly," he said. "As long as Cessation is Cessation, and
the Theatre makes it our home, we must pay the city our pound
of flesh. We are lucky to get by as cheaply as we do. When one of
us does what you did tonight, Pity, they do it for all of us."

"I...I don't know if I can do that again."

"And I wouldn't ask you to, but the beast will have thorns on
its rose." He stood. "The others will be on their way to the Gallery by now. May I escort you there?"

"No, please." The thought of the laughter, the decadent joy,
turned her stomach. "I can't. Not tonight."

"Of course not!" Halcyon's usual manner returned. "You
are, understandably, overcome by finally exacting revenge upon
that mercenary scum. I shall carry your condolences with me in
place of your person."

"Thanks, boss."

As he departed, Eva appeared, as soft and quiet as a breath.
She said nothing, only gathered Pity to her feet and wrapped
an arm around her shoulder, an infusion of strength that was
enough to make Pity's stiff limbs work again.

But they had only gone a short way before Adora intercepted them, arms crossed forebodingly.

"She wants to see you."

"I told *you* to kill him."

No conversation. No accusation. Only a statement. Pity perched on the edge of a couch, confined in the plush pit while Selene assessed her from above. It was not unlike being back in the arena, a notion that made her grip the cushions tighter. The show still clung to her, an intangible, greasy film of revulsion and self-reproach. She ached to physically wash it away, but the sanctuary of her room felt a million miles away.

Selene, emanating chill irritation, paced to a bar inset in the wall and began to fix herself a drink. "Not Eva. Not Marius. *You.*"

It happened so fast. "The audience didn't know; no one could tell—"

"I knew," Selene cut in. "I could tell."

"I tried…"

"Not hard enough."

Frustration, flowing like blood from a fresh wound, drove Pity to her feet. "If you wanted me to kill him why were Eva and Marius there, too?"

"Why?" Selene slammed her glass down. "That was a *kindness.* Do you think I didn't see your reluctance? You were afraid—I wasn't going to fault you for that. The Zidanes were with you so you wouldn't be *alone.*"

Speechless, Pity sat again, light-headed as a shiver scraped over her skin.

"And despite that, you still couldn't do it." Selene tapped her nails on the marble bar. "At least Eva had the good sense to cover your shortcomings."

Of course she did. Eva may not have known in advance, but she knew the Theatre—*knew Selene*—and would have understood what her role was the moment the Finale deviated from its usual format. It was Pity who was too foolish to see how the pieces on the board were set up.

"When I ask you to do something, I expect it done. Do you understand that?"

Pity licked her lips. "Yes."

"Then why didn't you shoot him?"

"I..."

"You're young, but you're not a coward," Selene pressed. "You were trained well—you know how to use those guns, and you've killed with them before."

"I-I told you," she said. "I tried...but I couldn't—"

"Then what good are you?"

Pity burned all over, her muscles bone-shatteringly tight. Selene was right. She *was* trained well. *All you needed to do was pull the trigger. Block out everything else and...* Her thoughts would go no further.

"You helped save my life, and don't think I've forgotten that. But I have no use for someone who can't follow orders." Selene stalked over so that she loomed above Pity, her eyes two shards of crystal. "Especially when the next request may not be so simple. Which raises the question, can I rely on you or not, Serendipity Jones?"

Pity searched for an answer but found none.

Silence smoldered between them before Selene spoke again. "You may go."

Pity stood, but a continuing fear kept her rooted in place, unable to believe she was being dismissed with only a scolding.

"This isn't over," Selene confirmed. "I suggest you put some hard thought into what your personal misgivings might be. And whether they truly have a place in a city like Cessation."

The words still seared her skin the next morning: *What good are you?*

She twisted in her sheets, eyes singed sore by tears that wouldn't fall. The prior evening replayed on an infinite loop in her thoughts, alternating between the assassin's plea for death and Selene's reproach. Entwined as the memories were, it was impossible to decide which left her more ill. All confidence was scraped out of her, leaving a hollow pit in her chest.

Another moment that mattered. Another failure. It wasn't about the showiness of it—Selene had never asked for that. She would have forgiven a mundane performance. The only thing Pity really needed to do was follow orders—to be a good, obedient soldier, like her mother. But that was exactly what she had failed to do, jeopardizing everything she had in Cessation.

And yet the thought of another Finale—of being in that bloody spotlight again—set her heart pounding with distress.

A knock on the door split her thoughts like a hatchet.

"Pity?"

Any other voice, save Selene's, she would have ignored. "Just a minute."

She slipped on some clothes and opened the door. Max waited on the other side.

"Hey. You didn't come to the Gallery last night."

"No, I didn't." Pity moved away from the door.

Max accepted the passive invitation to enter, face taut with concern. "I wanted to come find you, but I thought you might want to be alone after…" He faltered. "And Halcyon said—"

"Halcyon was covering for me. I…I couldn't…" She shook her head.

"Pity, what's going on?"

"I messed up." She crumpled onto the bed again, still gripped by the anxious fatigue of the last twelve hours. "The Finale…I messed up."

"What? No, you didn't. He's dead, isn't he? It was—"

"You don't understand. Selene wanted me to kill him. *Me*. But when it came down to it, I couldn't do it. And now she's angry."

Pity continued, not allowing any silence for Max to fill with questions. Bit by bit the story trickled out of her, rising to a flood by the time she arrived at Selene's rebuke. When she was done, Max sat beside her and put an arm around her shoulders. She leaned into him as his warmth overtook her, the most comfort she had felt in days.

"I remember what you said, about the city and letting it get to me, but…" She closed her eyes. "I don't want to leave Cessation."

"You're not going anywhere," said Max. "Selene will cool off. This wasn't a normal Finale. That man tried to kill her. As tough as she is, that's not easy to shake off." His arm tightened.

"And you're too well liked to be kicked out over one little mis-step. By the time the next Finale comes around, you'll—"

She pulled away from him. "Max, I can't do that again. I *can't*."

"What if you have to?"

Pity stood and strode away. "Last night you told me to say no."

"That was when I thought it was the audience choosing you, not Selene. Pity, she'll forgive you for this, but if *she* wants you to perform in a Finale again, you can't refuse."

"Why not?" Her voice rose, beyond her control. "I do my act and everyone loves it, so why do I have to be her execu-tioner, too?"

"Pity—"

"I know what I said about justice, and I know that man would have put a bullet through me without a second thought, but the Finales...they're not right. They're not. A person's death shouldn't be a spectacle, whether they deserve it or not."

"Pity, please." Max stood and reached for her. "I know it's hard, but you can't defy Selene again."

She recoiled. "*You* know? How do you know, Max? You make costumes. You build sets." Talons of anger pierced her throat, strangling her words even as she couldn't stop speaking. "No one is going to ask you to paint someone to death while the audience is cheering you on! So explain to me, how exactly do you know what it's like?"

She might have slapped him. Though he didn't move, the whole of his bearing diminished, the emotional blow landing squarely. Silver piercings flickered weakly as he started to speak, stopped, and finally began again.

"You're right," he said. "I'll never know what it's like to be in the arena during a Finale. And you know I don't entirely agree with what they are, but Selene isn't like CONA. She's not murdering innocents because they want the freedom to make their own choices about their lives." He ran an anxious hand through his hair. "I don't want good people hurt or killed. These aren't good people, Pity. They're the very worst parts of a city whose pieces barely fit together as it is."

"What about Beeks? Did he really deserve to die for being a thief?"

"Beeks crossed Selene." Max's voice was unapologetic but saturated with concern. "Is that something you want to do, too?"

A leaden silence fell as anger seethed within Pity. She hadn't expected sympathy from Eva or Halcyon or anyone else…but Max? She thought he would understand. Instead, he was siding with Selene. Pity longed to lash out, to find any outlet for the resentment swirling within, but before she could, there was another knock on her door.

Crossing the room in two curt strides, she yanked it open. "What?"

It was Duchess. His gaze jumped from her to Max and back.

"Come downstairs," he said. "There's something you should see."

Before they reached the Gallery, the difference in the air was apparent: it hummed, hivelike, with warning. As they drew closer, what should have been a familiar brew of sounds carried an unfamiliar resonance. The halls were scented with something Pity recognized but couldn't quite identify. When they plunged into the near frenzy of the Gallery, filled to the brim with everyone from patrons to porters, she realized what it was: bloodlust.

Cheers and jeers whizzed like bullets, aimed at a far corner of the room. Peeling away from the others, Pity climbed onto a table so she could see above the crowd. In a booth near the bar, calm as a gentle breeze—save for the shotgun across her lap— was Siena Bond. A man in chains sat beside her.

Daneko.

She jumped down and pushed through the crowd.

"Pity, wait!" Max called, but she ignored him, dread propelling her closer. A ring of Tin Men kept the crowd at a manageable distance, though they moved aside for her without question. Pity barely registered this as she stopped a few yards from the booth, her momentum arrested by Daneko's piercing, bitter stare. Defeat clung to him like a stench. He was gagged, and a fresh, ugly bruise covered one side of his face.

"Jones," Siena said pleasantly, as if they were old friends. "I was wondering where you were at. Join us for a drink?"

Pity ignored the bounty hunter's peculiar familiarity. In that moment, only one thing mattered: Daneko's capture and what that meant.

Another Finale.

The vicious celebration raged around them as Pity's heart pounded in her ears. Last night's Finale was suddenly a mere appetizer, a tidbit before the main course in Selene's revenge. Soon Daneko would be in the arena, shrouded in cheers, another of Selene's examples.

"Too bad we didn't make it back before the holidays," Siena drawled. "He would have made a tidy present for Selene, don't ya think? And I hear I just missed your best performance yet." She glanced at her prize. "See what a trouble you are? Would have been easier on all of us if Selene didn't want you taken alive."

"I'll handle things from here."

Pity turned back to see the Tin Men parting again for Santino.

Siena stood to allow access to Daneko. "So long as I'm paid, he's all yours."

"Take him," Santino instructed the Tin Men. "Not to the tombs—one of the special cells. Selene doesn't want anyone getting impatient." His raised his voice so that it carried above the din. "You all hear that? No one is to harm a hair on his head without Selene's say-so."

Pity couldn't bear to listen anymore or watch as the gang leader was dragged away. Whether he went quietly or he was frantic with fear, she didn't want to add the dreadful image to her rapidly expanding collection. She found Duchess and Max behind her, standing at the edge of the crowd, the only ones more interested in her than Daneko. Max took a step forward, mouth opening to speak, but Duchess touched his arm to stop him.

There were a dozen things she wanted to say, a hundred screams of frustration and fear building within. But no words came; they were lost to an understanding, an inescapable realization that she saw painted on Max's face, too.

It was no longer a matter of *if* Selene would ask her to perform another Finale.

It was *when*.

CHAPTER 28

THE SUMMONS THAT ARRIVED THE NEXT MORNING CAME as no surprise.

Occupied with the digital displays set in her desk, Selene didn't look up as Pity entered her office, escorted by Adora. The tight set to Selene's lips showed she didn't like whatever she saw on the screens. As Pity waited to be acknowledged, she stole a glance at Beau, but his expression was indecipherable.

He's not going to be any more help here than Max was, she told herself. *This is all on you.*

Nearly a minute passed before Selene finally ruptured the silence. "Have you thought about what I asked you to do?"

"Yes."

"And?" Dusky eyes flickered up. "Can I trust you to do what I ask?"

Pity knew the right answer—the one she needed to give if she wanted to maintain her position in Casimir—was yes. But no matter which way she tried to force herself to say it, the word stuck in her throat.

"The next Finale..." She had to say something, but every word tripped her like tangled roots. "You want me to kill Daneko."

Selene leaned back and considered her. "Perhaps. But I have a more pressing task for you right now." She tapped a screen on the desk. "After much coaxing, Patrick Sheridan has returned to Casimir."

Sheridan? Pity frowned, confused. *What does he have to do with anything?*

"This took no small amount of effort," Selene continued. "Following the attack, he came under the impression that Cessation, and Casimir, might not be the safest place for him."

Adora gave a snort of laughter. "What a silly notion."

Selene shot her a quieting look. "So I made some...concessions. Allowing a private bodyguard, increased security around him...and you."

"Me?" Wariness trickled down Pity's spine, sickly warm. "I don't understand."

"It was Patrick's idea," said Selene. "His campaign is floundering in the east. He needs my help, but he needs it without anyone thinking that's what he's come to Cessation for. Which is where you come in. As far as anyone will know, Patrick Sheridan is an overambitious, failing candidate, returned to Cessation to drown his shortcomings in gambling, drink, and the Theatre performer he's taken a special interest in."

The way she'd said *special* set Pity's skin crawling.

"None of this goes beyond this room, do you understand?" Selene continued. "Friend or foe, I want whoever might be paying attention to Sheridan focused on his indulgences, the lovely young lady keeping him company, and nothing else."

"What if no one is fooled?"

"Well," Selene said, "you'll have to play your part convincingly, won't you?"

It was meant to be an order—or a warning—but there was something more, veiled beneath Selene's unequivocal tone. Pity studied the woman more closely. The corners of her mouth were tight, her skin slightly flushed.

She's worried, and she doesn't like it. Why? "If you can't get him the presidency, that's all that Sheridan loses." She hesitated. "What do you lose?"

At first, Selene's gaze narrowed to an icicle point. Then it melted, and she laughed. "You *are* learning, aren't you?" Her expression sobered. "I'm afraid it's what *we* lose. When I took control of Cessation, CONA was still licking its wounds from the war, trying to keep its new, fragile society from breaking apart at every unfamiliar turn. Now? The core of CONA's power grows stronger, creeps a little farther west with each passing day. And when they come up against an obstacle?" She let the question hang.

Pity thought of the battered dissident refugees. "They remove it. Or get someone like Drakos-Pryce to do it for them."

Selene nodded. "It's only a matter of time before they turn their gaze to Cessation."

It isn't that Selene wants a pet politician, Pity realized, *it's that she needs one.* Threats like Daneko were nothing compared to CONA. "You want Sheridan to protect the city."

"Yes. In a way I will never be able to. As it stands, we are tolerated. The deals made here, the desires indulged, the secrets kept—they help keep our enemies in the east at bay. But I'd be a fool to think that will last forever." Selene stood, pressing her palms flat on the desk. "Cessation is no backwoods settlement, easily toppled by Drakos-Pryce's little death squads. If threatened, it will fight." She sighed. "And it will lose. But a military movement of that caliber would require approval by the president. My goal is to prevent that from ever happening. Fortunately, as rich and brilliant as Sheridan is, he doesn't have the right associations to gain the presidency on his own."

"Do you?"

Selene blinked at her. The room seemed to chill. *Careful.*

"Max said that only the Drakos-Pryce Corporation can guarantee something like that. And it'll have nothing to do with Cessation."

"Max stays well-informed." Every syllable carried warning. "But Drakos-Pryce isn't the only way to the presidency. There are many, *many* powerful people in CONA who owe me favors."

Pity swallowed, hesitant. "What about Daneko?"

Selene smiled as if she had been waiting for the question. "I'll get to him eventually. *Your* participation in that matter will depend on how otherwise engaged you are."

There it was: the sugar to entice Pity to swallow the bitter. Agreeing to entertain Sheridan was more than a second chance to regain Selene's favor; it was her way out of executing Daneko.

But he won't be the last person to end up in the arena. Her hand twitched, trigger finger curling into a claw before relaxing again. Sooner or later someone else would cross the wrong line and Pity would be back in the same situation. *I can't stop the Finales, but...*

"If I do this"—the words had risen to her lips, escaping before she could stop them—"I never want to perform another Finale."

Selene's face pinched in displeasure. Even Adora appeared taken aback by her boldness.

"You want Sheridan, and Sheridan wants me." Pity wondered if she were digging her own grave, but bloodthirsty applause hissed in her ears, urging her onward. There was no going back now. "I'll do what you want. But if I do it right, I don't want to kill Daneko in the Finale or anyone else ever again." She took a steadying breath. "Seems like a small price to pay in the pursuit of Cessation's continued safety."

Selene didn't respond immediately. A line of sweat ran between Pity's shoulder blades. She prayed her nervousness didn't show on her face.

"Agreed." The word clicked like a bullet entering a chamber. Selene sat back down in her chair, eyes flashing. "You certainly are bold when you want to be, Serendipity Jones. Let's both hope the day never arrives when you wish you had simply pulled the trigger when you were told to."

"Champagne?"

Sheridan served it himself, pouring until the honey-colored liquid nearly reached the brim of the glass. Pity kept her hands in her lap, fingers entwined, and watched the bubbles race to the surface. The festive buzz of the Gallery surrounded the booth they occupied. Its location was discreet enough that they wouldn't be overheard, but it did little to shield them from the stares. Pity felt simmered by hundreds of tiny flames as all around the room people looked without looking, a skill widely mastered in Casimir. It was not unlike her first night in the Theatre, when the audience had been waiting for her show to start. Then, she had been terrified; now, she was irritated. She wasn't doing any more than what half of them did—less, in fact—and it was at Selene's order.

You knew there'd be curiosity. On the heels of her conversation with Selene, an invitation had arrived from Sheridan, asking her to join him that evening for dinner in the Gallery. She tugged the skirt of her dress over her knees, feeling foolish in it.

It's only another costume, she told herself, *the same way this is just another act.*

"How many bottles?" said Sheridan.

"Hmm?" Pity roused to find him beaming a smile at her.

"How many bottles do you think I need to order to make it look like I'm trying to forget a floundering campaign?"

Pity took a bracing sip of her champagne. "If that's the idea, you might consider switching to something stronger, Mr. Sheridan."

He gave her a disheartened look. "This isn't going to work unless you start calling me Patrick."

"I'm sorry…Patrick." Pity tried to force herself to be as relaxed as Sheridan looked. Despite his rapid departure from Cessation after the attack, nothing in his manner suggested a man worried about his surroundings. But that was likely owing to the extra Tin Men in the Gallery, as well as Sheridan's austere mountain of a bodyguard stationed nearby, glaring at anyone who strayed too close.

This is part of the act, she reminded herself. *You need to learn to play this part, same as you did the first time Eva worked with you in the arena.* Unlike in the Theatre, however, where she gave no thought to the specifics of her audience, Pity found her attention continually drawn to the crowded Gallery, anxious to know who was observing them. Selene's orders meant she couldn't tell anyone the truth behind her actions. Not Luster or Garland or Duchess.

Not even Max.

Their argument about the Finales had left Pity with a persistent bee-stung feeling, one that mixed unpleasantly with her current situation. But she hadn't seen him anywhere when she and Sheridan arrived. She silently hoped he wouldn't visit the Gallery at all tonight.

"I want you to know," said Sheridan, as if sensing her troubled thoughts, "that this isn't some kind of ruse; I have no ulterior motives toward you."

"Thank you." Chastened by his contrite tone, she forced a smile onto her face, as if he had just said something incredibly charming. "But what your intentions are and what people are thinking right now are two different things."

"Does that matter to you?"

"I guess not." Even as she said it, she knew it was a lie. *Your pride isn't what's important,* she reminded herself. Satisfying Selene and avoiding the Finales was. "But why me? There are plenty of better choices here."

"None that have saved my life."

"I was saving my life, too. Doesn't seem like enough to hang your trust on."

Sheridan chuckled. "It's more than that, of course. No matter where you call home now, you grew up under CONA, unlike most of Selene's people. And I think you know what it can be like there for a former Patriot."

"I do. At least I know how it was for my mother."

"Do you mind if I ask what happened to her?"

Pity shook her head. "After the war, she cut a deal to keep her neck out of the noose. But like you said before, some people never forget the past. My father included. He hated my mother and he hated me. I left when he tried to ship me off to another commune that needed fertile women."

Sheridan's expression soured. "Is that a regular occurrence on the communes?"

"Regular enough."

"Well, when I'm in control of CONA," he said with a wink, "I'll make sure to put a stop to that."

She eyed him. "Really?"

"You look so skeptical. Of course. It's a small enough thing." Sheridan beckoned a porter. "A bottle—no, two, of the best whiskey in the house. And then champagne for everyone here." He slurred his words slightly, as if already half drunk. "If I can't celebrate success, I'll celebrate failure instead."

"Yes, sir." The porter set off.

He's a better actor than you are. But something in her brightened. Back east, Sheridan's past made him a pariah. Yet in Cessation, home to those who refused to live under CONA's stringent rules, it made him an ally, even a friend. Maybe protecting the city wasn't the only thing he could do. "That's not the worst that goes on, unfortunately. Like the dissident settlements that CONA's been destroying."

"I've heard." His articulateness returned. "It seems unnecessarily brutal to me."

"Most of them were Patriots, too. If you're president, you could put a stop to it."

"So I could." He sighed, but it was one accompanied by a confident smile. "There are many, many matters that will need attention once I'm president. With the combined power of Columbia and Cessation, well, what can't be accomplished?"

"So you really think Selene can deliver what she says she can?" said Pity.

"Maybe." Sheridan swirled his glass so that the champagne glittered like liquid gold. "What I know is that doubt won't get me what I want. And I wouldn't be here unless I thought Cessation could."

It was a relief when Pity was finally able to leave behind the stares and whispers of the Gallery, though not as much as she would have expected at the start of the evening. Despite the unpleasantness of her task, there was an agreeable earthiness to Sheridan. He seemed like a man who didn't take for granted the wealth and power he had gained. As she punched in the code to her door, she realized she even liked the way he navigated Cessation with easy self-control, unlike so many of the other patrons who treated the city like something to be consumed when it suited them and discarded afterward.

"About time."

Pity froze.

Adora lounged on the love seat, Pity's revolver in hand. "I'd begun to wonder exactly how much you were dedicating yourself to your assignment."

"Put that down."

Adora's eyes went wide with false innocence. "I was only looking." She held up the gun, not quite pointing it at Pity but not putting it down, either. "Very pretty."

"Put. It. Down." Pity gauged the distance between her and the weapon's twin, still in its holster.

Too slowly, Adora's arm lowered. She deposited the gun next to her on the couch. "You're wound awfully tight, you know. I unloaded it first. I'm not stupid."

Pity crossed the room and snatched the revolver away. She checked the chambers. They were empty. "What do you want?"

"Everything." Adora sat forward so that her elbows rested on her thighs, her chin cupped in her hands. "What you ate, what you talked about—spill."

Of course. Not only did Selene want Pity to pretend with Sheridan; she wanted her to inform on him as well. Did she see Sheridan as anything more than a game piece, being moved around on a board of her own devising? Or Pity, for that matter?

Who cares? she told herself. So long as Selene kept her promise about the Finales, she was welcome to the information. Pity returned the gun to the holster beside its mate, making sure to remain between them and Adora, just in case.

Then she began to talk.

CHAPTER 29

THE DINING ROOM AT MIDMORNING WAS A JOLTING clockwork of bodies. Some were winding down after a long night, others gearing up for the new day. Pity felt stuck somewhere in the middle. Even after Adora left, her thoughts had kept her awake. An early morning practice, rescheduled to accommodate her new responsibilities, had left her in a state of exhaustion rivaled only by her hunger. The night before, she'd been too unnerved to do more than pick at her food.

As she looked for somewhere to sit, she spotted Max and the others, along with Chloe and Carine, two of the Rousseau girls. She stopped, wondering if it was too late to turn around. But Luster had already seen her and was beckoning.

You can't put this off forever. "Mornin'."

She took the seat between Garland and Duchess, who eyed her

as she sat. Across the table, Max looked up long enough to give
her a half smile that fell somewhere between polite and unsure,
then returned to the paper before him, filled with swirls and patterns. When Chloe tapped decisively at one of the designs, he
discarded the paper for a fresh piece and started re-creating it.

"Really? That's all we get?" Duchess said. "Half of a 'Good
morning'?"

"What were you expecting?" Pity buried her nose in her coffee mug, the last shred of hope that last night's events would be
overlooked gone.

"I don't know, maybe something about how cozy you suddenly seem to be with Patrick Sheridan."

When Max looked up sharply, Pity's stomach tightened.
Apparently, he wasn't caught up on Casimir's latest gossip.
Remember what Selene said: play your part well. "There's not
much to say. He asked me to dinner. I said yes."

"Leave her be," said Luster. "It's none of our business if Pity
wants to share a meal with a patron. Especially Mr. Sheridan.
He seems like a real gentleman."

"He seems," Max grumbled, "like a politician."

The vinegar edge to his voice cast a pall over the table. On
either side of him, the near-mirror images of Chloe and Carine
traded a glance and got to their feet, departing with only the
sounds of rustling cutlery. The others looked as if they were
considering doing the same.

"I thought he was done with Cessation," Max continued.
"Or does he still think Selene can make him president?"

"No," Pity lied, feeling the heat rise to her cheeks. "He's here
blowing off steam because his campaign isn't doing well."

"Is that the *only* reason? Does he want to see you again?"

The air seemed to thicken around them. Pity ached to blurt out the truth. At the same time, his flagrant disapproval grated on her. Luster was right. It wasn't anyone else's business who she spent her time with. Especially Max's. So what did the truth matter?

"As a matter of fact, yes." She fought to keep her voice calm. "He's invited me to dinner again tonight. And he wants to see the city. We're going on a tour of it tomorrow." She prodded her food with her fork. "He's not so bad, y'know. You might even like him."

"I doubt it."

Frustration churned within her. "Easy to say when you don't know the first thing about him. Sheridan fought in the war as a Patriot. That's why he's doing so poorly. And unlike most of the CONA folks who come here, he wants to improve things between the east and the west. Not just have some fun and go home."

Max scoffed. "Are you sure about that?"

"What do you mean?"

"Well, he can say anything if he knows he's not going to win. Did you ever think that maybe he's just telling you what you want to hear?"

The bitterness in his tone hit her like ice water. "It wasn't like that at all!"

"Maybe." Max's mouth twisted into a humorless smirk. "But if he *were* elected, he would do what he was told, by Selene or whatever corporate puppeteers were tugging on his strings. He'd be lucky to be allowed to pick the color of his tie."

Pity bristled. "For someone whose tune was all about getting me to give Cessation a chance, you're awful quick to dismiss Sheridan."

"Because I know people like him and where they come from."

"Really?" She stood up. "Because it seems like you've forgotten that it's where I come from, too."

Garland put a hand on her arm, but she shook it off.

"I've lost my appetite," she snapped, and stalked out of the dining hall.

So much for worrying about whether anyone is fooled.

As much as the new, unwanted attention needled her, it wasn't as vexing as her quarrels with Max. First the Finales and now Sheridan.

And one of them isn't even real.

The thought hung on Pity all through the day and night, though she tried to put it out of her mind. *If Max knew the truth, he'd understand,* she reminded herself over and over. This was her chance to escape the Finales, to never have to play executioner again. *And this isn't going to last forever.* Sheridan would be gone eventually, and if Selene did work her magic, he'd be able to help protect one thing Pity knew Max genuinely cared about: Cessation.

But nothing she told herself stopped the lingering frustration.

This time, she decided, she wasn't going to let the divide grow between them. And while she couldn't tell him the truth, there were other options.

She found him in the theatre, touching up the paint on some faded sets.

"Get up," she ordered.

"Excuse me?" He stood and wiped his hands on his pants, adding to the existing kaleidoscope of stains.

"You're coming with me."

He looked at her like she'd lost her mind. "Where? I'm in the middle of—"

"No questions." She crossed her arms. "The sets will wait."

"But Halcyon—"

"You trust me, right?"

His brow furled with confusion. "Of course I do."

"Then come with me."

Pity led him into the Gallery, up the stairs, and to the front entrance.

"Pity, really, where are we—oh."

Max stopped as he spotted Sheridan, limned by the midday sun streaming through Casimir's exterior glass doors. Santino and the bodyguard stood on either side of him while, outside, a sleek black vehicle idled.

"Well…" Sheridan looked equally surprised, though he hid it quickly. "Good morning."

"You remember Max, right?" Pity said quickly. "He was the one who showed me around the city when I first arrived. I thought he could come with us."

Beside her, Max tensed. "No, I shouldn't. I'd only be in the—"

"Of course." Sheridan's face lit up with a smile. "Please join us. I'd be delighted to get to know one of Pity's friends better." Bodyguard in the lead, he headed for the waiting vehicle.

But Max didn't move.

"This isn't funny," he said so only she could hear. "I don't want to go with...with the two of you."

"One hour," she said. "That's all I'm asking. Get to know him a little. Is that asking so much?"

He frowned and stared after Sheridan, teeth tugging at one of the rings in his lower lip.

The gesture weakened something in Pity's gut. "Please?"

Aversion filled his gray eyes, but he nodded. "Fine. I'll try."

Outside, Pity slid into the vehicle's sprawling backseat, beside Sheridan. Max unenthusiastically joined them, while Santino took the front passenger seat. Sheridan's bodyguard drove. His name was Elgin, but Pity had privately nicknamed him Hook, for the shape of the thick pink scar on the back of his head. He steered them away from Casimir and onto Cessation's main avenue.

The city, awash in the bone-dry daylight, encompassed them. It was only the second time Pity had seen Cessation from a wheeled vantage point, but she could still recall the concurrent feelings of her awe and Max's enthusiasm when she'd first arrived. That moment stuck out in stark contrast to the current one. Next to her, hands knotted in his lap, Max looked like he'd bitten into something sour.

"Where to first?" Santino called back. Unlike Max, there was a pleasant set to his features, as if he was enjoying the outing as a guest, not charged with Sheridan's protection. Pity felt a flutter of jealousy at his ability to keeps his emotions sorted. Any interrogation—no, *torture*—Daneko was being subjected to was his duty, yet he appeared his usual temperate self. "A loop of the city, yeah?"

"An excellent idea," Sheridan agreed.

They made their way to Cessation's main entrance, where Hook turned onto an avenue that ran between the Reformationist settlement and the city's boundary. As they passed, the group's members dutifully fell to their knees in prayer.

"Ever persistent," said Sheridan with a hint of amusement.

"Has the camp gotten bigger?" Pity eyed the tents. They seemed more numerous since the last time she'd seen them, sprawling further into the desert. She turned to Max, but he only shrugged halfheartedly in answer.

"They come and go like the tide," Santino said. "When the heat comes back, they'll recede again."

As they traveled around the perimeter of the city, a heavy silence fell. Trapped between Sheridan and Max, Pity searched for a way to break it but couldn't think of a single thing to say. *Maybe this wasn't such a good idea,* she thought. Discomfort hung in the air like incense.

"So," Sheridan said finally, "you're with the Theatre, too, Max?"

"Yes." Pity jumped on the opening. "Max makes the costumes and sets. He's very talented."

"As I've seen. I know Pity is a relatively new addition, but how long have you been in Cessation?"

At first, Max didn't say anything, his gaze locked on the window. He sat on the side away from the city, and beyond him, the desert stretched relentlessly toward a pale horizon.

When he did reply, his voice was cool. "A while."

"I remember when he first came to Casimir," Santino rumbled. Hook turned again, and they reentered Cessation from another side, plunging back into the jungle of concrete and color. "Even skinnier than he is now. Hard to believe he'd survived the streets on his own."

"Impressive," said Sheridan. "Then you must know the city well. What would you suggest seeing?"

Max finally turned toward them. "Pity says you used to be a Patriot. Maybe you'd like to visit some of the people you fought with, like the Ex-Pats." His voice tightened. "Do you know that CONA's military shoots them on sight? Or maybe you'd prefer some of the dissidents CONA has driven from their homes."

"Max!" Pity hissed.

"No," Sheridan said. "Let him speak. I know there's more to this city than what goes on in Casimir. And I'm sure there are as many mixed feelings about visitors like me as there are about Cessation itself in the east."

"Something like that," Max muttered. "Then again, there's nothing here I could show you that compares to the slums in Columbia."

Pity's jaw tightened. *This was a terrible idea.* "That's not Patrick's fault."

"Maybe not," said Max, any trace of politeness gone, "but I'm guessing he hasn't done anything to help the people there, either."

She started to scold him again, but Sheridan took her hand, cutting her off.

"He's right," said Sheridan. "Columbia is no utopia. And I haven't done as much as I could." He paused. "Tell me, Max, if you were in my position, what would *you* do?"

The air seemed to chill. Max's mouth thinned. Rueful eyes

glared at Sheridan, then flickered down to where Sheridan's
hand overlapped Pity's. "Please stop. I'll walk back from here."

"Sir?" said Hook.

"Stop the vehicle," Max ordered again.

"It's okay," said Sheridan. "Do it."

He was out the door the moment they stopped. Pity was
in pursuit before anyone could object, slamming the door
behind her.

"What is wrong with you?" she cried.

A dozen yards from the vehicle, he spun to face her. "This
was a mistake. I never should have come."

She balled her fists. "You're right. I thought you'd at least
try to give Sheridan a chance, but you're clearly unwilling to do
even that."

"I don't like him," Max spat. "And I know what you think,
but I don't trust him."

"Why? What has he ever done to you?"

"Nothing! He's...he's just..."

"Exactly!" She couldn't stop herself from yelling. "He's done
nothing to deserve how you're treating him. And if you'd actually talk to him calmly instead of treating him like a monster,
you might realize what kind of good he could do for Cessation
and Columbia."

Max began to speak again, then stopped. He threw up his
hands in frustration. "I'm going back to Casimir." Without
another word, he stalked off.

Pity stared at his back for a few seconds, hating every step he
took away from her, but she couldn't bring herself to call him
back. Then he turned a corner and was gone.

She returned to the car, her entire body tight with anger.

"Is everything okay?" Sheridan looked past her to where Max had disappeared.

"Fine." Pity crossed her arms bitterly. "Max needed to get back to the theatre."

"Ah." Sheridan accepted the lie graciously. "For the special performance tomorrow night, of course."

Special? Her mouth went dry. "What? No one told me about a show. I didn't think there'd be another one until—" Her heart kicked at the inside of her chest.

Until Daneko's execution.

"Relax, chica." Santino had noticed her distress. "Selene has some important guests arriving." He looked pointedly at Sheridan.

"Yes," said Sheridan. "As much as I enjoy your act, tomorrow you won't be performing. You'll be in the audience, with me."

A measure of cool relief washed over her. Tomorrow's show was about pure entertainment, then. Or at least as pure as the Theatre Vespertine ever was. There'd be no Finale.

Not yet.

But Sheridan was wrong. She was performing.

It was simply a different kind of act.

CHAPTER 30

A DIFFERENT KIND OF ACT.

The words ran through her mind over and over as the spotlights swept around the arena, searing the edges of the audience. Though they followed the Rousseaus as they flew through the air, Pity felt as if they kept settling on her. She repositioned herself in her seat, doing her best not to draw any more attention. As it was, she felt as if thousands of eyes were trained on her instead of on the performance taking place.

Beside her, Sheridan leaned over. "I neglected to say you look lovely tonight."

"Thank you."

"So how does it feel to be on this side?"

This entire city is a stage, she wanted to say. *There is no "this side."* Still, there was a distinct sense of wrongness she couldn't shake. She watched as Christophe and Chrétien executed a synchronized set of aerial flips, her insides echoing the maneuver. *I should be below, with Eva and Marius and—*

Max.

—the others. I should be out there, in the arena.

"Different," she replied. "It reminds me of the first time I saw the show."

And my first Finale.

She startled as Sheridan placed a hand on her forearm and gave it a brief, affectionate squeeze.

Settle down. She forced out a soft smile for anyone who might be watching.

As the Rousseaus' performance ended, the lights dimmed, casting the emptiness before them in a velvety gray glow. No music played. In the center of the stage a single spotlight remained, as if waiting for someone. Pity's blood began to pulse in her ears. The pungent tang of fearful sweat filled the air. Though Santino had told her otherwise, she was sure that Daneko was about to appear, to rise out of the dark pit to meet Selene's justice.

Ser-en-di-pi-ty! Ser-en-di-pi-ty! The wicked chorus played in her memory. *Ser-en—*

No. She gripped the arms of her seat. When Halcyon appeared to announce the next act, she relaxed. There was no Finale coming. Tonight, the beast would not be fed.

Pity's hands ached by the time the final round of applause sounded. She obediently took the arm Sheridan offered as the audience quit the theatre for the Gallery. The crowd was thick and perpetually shifting, a maelstrom of glitter and smoke and flesh. She scanned the Gallery as they entered, spotting Luster at a gambling table, an arm around a patron. Garland and Duchess were entrenched in some kind of dice game, while Olivia worked the bar, slinging drinks to Flossie and Halcyon.

Max was nowhere to be seen.

Something akin to relief filled her as they navigated through the mess. After the failed trip through the city, it was better if Max kept his distance. The thought of him watching her all evening—judging every word or laugh she traded with Sheridan—scalded her with annoyance. He'd revealed a side of himself that baffled her no matter how she tried to fit it into her existing perception of him, as if he were a puzzle she'd thought she'd finished, but that was now missing crucial, clarifying pieces.

They settled into their private booth, already stocked with a plethora of fine food and drink, and attendants ready to fetch anything that might be missing. Pity accepted a glass of wine but left it untouched. Her head was already swimming uncomfortably, her veins humming with anxiety.

Smile. You're still onstage.

She sought out Luster again, desperate for a friendly face, but as her gaze skimmed past the bar, a knot of patrons loosened to reveal a solitary figure.

His back was to her, but she knew him before he started to turn.

Max.

Their eyes snagged on each other's.

Something was different.

Pity didn't need to be close to see it—it was painted on him in the set of his shoulders, the curve of his mouth—but she couldn't give it a clear name, either. He had a look like a bird halfway through molt, a serpent with its skin half shed. More of him seemed to fall away as they stared at each other, until she wasn't sure who it was she was looking at anymore. The urge to shove her way through the crowd, to shake off whatever it was that was gripping him, nearly carried her to her feet.

"Pity?"

She turned back to find Sheridan watching her.

"Is something wrong?"

Beneath the table she dug her fingers into the seat cushion. *Fine. Say you're fine.* But before the lie reached her lips, the cacophony of the Gallery dimmed and disappeared. In the center of the room, Halcyon stood on a table, calling for attention. Pity took advantage of the distraction and looked back at Max, but he was gone. She caught a glimpse of him, disappearing through one of the arched exits.

"Friends." Halcyon's arms swept through the air. "Tonight you experienced a sampling of the notorious, illustrious Theatre Vespertine, an unrivaled wonder throughout the world. But..." He flashed a teasing smile. "Your experience was incomplete, lacking a certain *visceral* element for which the Theatre is particularly known. Yes, yes—anyone who attended our show at the turn of the year can tell you about that which I speak."

The edges of Pity's vision dimmed as her view of Halcyon sharpened, too bright a figure even among the surrounding vibrancy.

"But do not despair," he continued, "for fools have been in high supply of late. I know many of you have been anticipating this very announcement, so wait no longer. One week from today the traitor and criminal Daneko will join the Theatre

Vespertine as our guest in the show's Finale, to meet the justice he evaded for far too long!"

Cheers erupted. Pity heard them only as muted static as blood pulsed in her cheeks.

Halcyon remained where he was, whipping the crowd into a frenzy, but for an instant his gaze fell on her. What the look carried—whether warning or commiseration—she couldn't discern.

Around them, the macabre revelry grew.

It was midnight by the time Sheridan decided to retire, and an almost feverish sensation gripped Pity as they left the chaos behind. Inside his suite of rooms, the windows were thrown open. The cool night air was a balm against her flushed skin. She leaned against one of the room's plush chairs, sharing the weight of her body, sore from too much worry.

Sheridan loosened the collar of his shirt. "You look tired."

Exhausted was more accurate. A whole day and night of practice couldn't have left her as drained as she felt then. She smiled weakly. "It's getting late."

"You might tell that to everyone downstairs." His fingers worked the buttons of his cuffs. "You know, there aren't too many who leave that room behind them when they go. Cessation gets into the blood like a strong drink, it seems. No matter how much one satisfies the desire for it, sooner or later the craving comes back. I see it in the faces of the visitors while they're here, and in their faces when they're back in the east. But you? I don't see that same fixation in you."

She had no reply to that so said nothing.

He came to her, lifting her chin with his fingers. She recoiled at first, surprised by the intimate gesture—here, where there was no one to see them—but braced herself as his face hovered above hers, searching for...what?

"Good night, Pity," he said at last. "Get some sleep."

Though she was relieved at being released, threads of adrenaline coursed through her veins as she entered the nearest stairwell and started to descend, leaving her unable to fathom sleep. In the wake of Halcyon's announcement, the silent weight of the dark was the last thing she wanted. At the same time, she had no desire to return to the wondering stares of the Gallery, and the only things she'd find in the theatre were ghosts.

One week for Daneko to live.

One week in which Selene would decide whether or not Pity was to be his executioner.

We made a deal, she told herself. *I'm doing what I said I would.*

But it hadn't exactly been a deal, had it? Selene didn't ask, she ordered. Pity was the one who had laid down a price.

In the end, you sold yourself anyway.

Pity knew what she stood to gain from their agreement. What she wasn't sure about yet was how much it was going to cost her.

She reached her floor. And yet something kept her descending, her feet unwilling, unable, to stop. When she reached the basement, she stumbled into the tunnels, pausing long enough to rip off her pretty, horrible shoes and toss them into the dark. She padded along barefoot through the dark maze of concrete and pipes, half blinded by a glassy membrane of tears.

Even so, she found her way.

The door was ajar, as it had been the first time she had seen it. She didn't pause to knock, and the metal hinges screamed as she opened it.

Max turned as she entered, wary as a surprised animal. "Pity?"

She started to speak, but whatever words she had been about to say caught in her throat. She was unable to comprehend what she was seeing. Max had a paintbrush in one hand but wore clothes that had no business in Casimir: sturdy boots and a battered, resilient coat. At his feet, streaked by his lank shadow, was a traveling pack.

"What are you doing?" The words shot out of her. She moved closer to see what he was painting. A patch of white now covered one of the existing murals—a blank, lifeless void in the calamity of color. On it was writing.

I'm sorry. Two words, scrawled in midnight blue, but with plenty of room for more.

"Max, what is this?"

"N-nothing," he said. "What are you—?"

"It's not nothing!" She kicked the pack. "What are you doing?"

He straightened, his features hardening. "Something I should have done a long time ago. I'm leaving Cessation."

"The *hell* you are!"

Startled by the pure ferocity, Max dropped the brush. He took a step back before catching himself. "Go away, Pity. I don't know why you're here in the first place, but go away. And if you care at all, keep this to yourself until I'm long gone."

She held her ground. "I'm not going anywhere," she said, her tone like chipped porcelain, "and neither are you until you tell me why."

"I..." Max shook his head. "I can't." But his voice wavered.

She stared at him, fists clenched. Then she went to the wall and dragged her palm across it.

"Don't!" He lunged at her, grabbing her wrist, but it was too late. The beginning of his note was obliterated.

"Why did you do that?" he cried. "Why...why are you here?" He released her, face crumpling with pain. "Dammit, Pity, why do you always turn up right when I'm trying to leave?"

The blaze within her flickered out. A stifling silence rose between them, so thick that Pity's ribs began to ache. She fought for each breath as she stood steadfast before Max, equally bewildered and torn apart by the battle raging within her, the one that had driven her here in the first place.

An agonizing minute ticked by.

Only when she'd made her decision did the air seem to lighten.

She went over to the door and closed it.

"What are you—?"

"Please, just listen." Her back still to him, she leaned against the cool metal, trying to slow her pounding heart. "I made a deal with Selene."

Another moment of quiet passed. "What...what kind of deal?"

She turned toward him. "One where I'd hang off Sheridan's arm, pretend to be the reason he was back in Cessation." Once she began, she knew there was no going back. The words tumbled out of her. "Do you understand? It's not real—a misdirection, in case whoever sent the assassins for Selene tries again."

Max's brow pinched with confusion. "But Daneko—"

"Was working with someone in the east. Sheridan thinks he was a target, too. He hasn't given up on being president, and Selene needs an alliance with him in order to protect the city. I agreed to play my part, and in exchange…" She swallowed, her mouth dry with anxiety. "I'd never have to do another Finale."

"This is about the Finales?"

She nodded. "I wanted to tell you, but Selene ordered me not to."

At this, he paled. "Pity, you shouldn't have—"

"*I know.* But back in the Gallery…and yesterday…the way you kept looking at me…" She couldn't finish.

Across the room, Max went as still as stone. An invisible maelstrom of emotion seemed to envelop him as he worked to parse her confession, an echo of his earlier affliction in the Gallery. Unable to watch it, her attention fell on the traveling pack. She was anxious to know what he'd meant earlier about leaving, but too petrified of the answer to ask.

Max took a deep breath and closed his eyes. When he opened them again, it was with a determined air.

Her heart leapt as he reached for the pack…

…and stopped. He straightened again, resolve shifting to desperation.

Instead, he took a step toward her.

Driven by her own longing, she closed the distance between them, paint-stained fingers curling into his shirt as she pressed her face against his shoulder. The scent of him filled her: paint, linseed oil, an earthy warmth like wheat fields baking in the summer sun. The mix went to her head, better than any drug or drink, so much so that at first she didn't feel his arms close around her.

"Pity..."

"Don't." She turned her face to his. "Whatever you're about to say...just don't. I don't care."

His eyes flickered over her, seemingly afraid to alight on any one place. But his embrace tightened, grounding her, making her feel solid for the first time that evening. He pressed his forehead against hers, the heat of him neutral, as if they shared a single skin.

As they stood like that, a silent tableau cast half in shadow, the rift between them vanished. This time, Max's lips sought hers, the world around them receding as Pity returned the kiss, desire rising within her like fever.

Within heartbeats, there was no Selene, no Sheridan, no Cessation...

Only Max.

CHAPTER 31

PITY DOZED, TRYING TO REMEMBER WHEN SHE HAD ever felt so perfectly warm. Max's head lay against her shoulder, each exhalation of his breath tickling the fine hairs of her neck. Beneath the blankets, their limbs entwined. The sensation of his skin against hers was so calming that she didn't want to move, didn't want to disturb anything. Occasionally her hand rustled through the dark spikes of his hair, but mostly they were still.

She had no idea how long they had lain like this before Max rose up on one elbow and looked around sheepishly. The comfortable quiet shifted to one tinged by hesitance.

"I think your dress is ruined," he said finally.

The garment hung limply off the edge of the bed, dark smudges marring the fabric. Pity also saw a streak of blue on her forearm and several across Max's chest and shoulders. She suspected she would find plenty more like them were she to lift the blankets and look. "I don't care. If I have to wear a costume, I'd prefer the one you made me for the Theatre."

A spiteful shadow crossed his eyes. "Your arrangement with Sheridan and Selene—does she really need him that badly?"

"Selene seems to think so." Pity took a deep breath. "And I tried to remind myself of that, and the fact that we'd made a deal. But with whatever everyone was thinking about Sheridan and me, and then tonight—with Halcyon announcing the next Finale...and you—it was too much." She shook her head. "Something came over me. I didn't even mean to come here."

"Are you...upset that you did?"

"No." She sat up to face him. "Are you...upset that we...?" Searching for any hint of regret in his face, she couldn't finish. *A mistake,* said a fearful voice. *He's going to say this was a foolish mistake.* The thought made something within her begin to crumble.

Max looked away, as if working out some complex reckoning. Then he raised his head again and leaned closer. The light touch of his lips coupled with that of his fingers, which entwined with hers.

"No." He kissed her again. "No, I am not."

A smile overtook her, dumb and insistent. "Still, I shouldn't have cornered you like that."

Max kissed the base of her palm, heedless of the dried paint there. "It feels like all you ever do is corner me."

She felt a twinge of dread. *You're going to have to ask*

eventually. "Max, where were you going?" He tensed. "And what did you mean about me showing up whenever you're trying to leave?"

"That...Forget it, okay?"

"Oh, not a chance." She held his gaze, fed up with things left unsaid. "There's no way I'm letting you get away without an explanation. *Especially* not now."

Max sighed. "I knew you were going to be trouble," he said. "I knew it from the moment you tried to kill me." He let go of her hand. "Home." He said it in a way that sounded like the complete opposite. "I was going home. Now and when we found you."

"I don't understand."

Max drew his knees to his chest and worried one of the rings in his eyebrow. "If I explain, you have to swear not to say a word of this to anyone else. Not Luster, not Eva, not even Selene. *No one.*"

The reluctance in his voice was like a darkened doorway— one that if she stepped through and turned on the light, there would be no way to turn it off again. But she had to see what was on the other side. "I promise."

"Swear it."

"I do," Pity said. "On my mother's guns. I won't breathe a word to anyone."

But she could tell it wasn't her promise he wanted—whatever he held inside, it scared him. The worry was etched into his brow, the set of his jaw, and the way he was breathing, as if he wasn't sure he was getting air or not. Seconds ticked by: one... two...three...

"I lied to you," he said abruptly, as if to get the words out before he could reconsider. "About my life before Cessation. I wasn't poor, and I didn't move around. I grew up in Columbia. My family had—*has*—money. A lot of it."

"That's it?" She almost laughed again, but the haunted look in his eyes cut it off. "What are you doing here, then?"

"Living my own life," he said. "Doing what I want and not only what I'm expected to. You should understand that."

"Of course I do," she said. "But if that's what you want, why would you go back?"

He looked away from her. A full minute passed, one in which each second lengthened and expanded, only to settle on Max's shoulders like invisible weights.

"Because," he said quietly, "I promised that someday I would."

A chill settled on Pity. She pulled the blanket tighter, thinking back to the day at the fountain and his single candle. "What was her name?" She couldn't help it. If Max was telling the truth, she wanted—*needed*—all of it. "And how did she die?"

If he was surprised that she had figured out that much, it didn't show. "Sonya," he said. "She was murdered."

The admission was a fresh wound on an old injury, seeping from him. His eyes went red around the edges.

She didn't want to ask but couldn't bear not to. "Did you love her?"

"We weren't really old enough for that, but..." He stopped, considered. "Yes, I guess I did."

Pity felt something twist in her chest. "Are you...still in love with her?"

Max shook his head. "No. No, just…just listen, okay? I don't know how else to tell this but straight through."

He lay down again, the mattress creaking under his weight. Pity slid back beside him. Hesitantly, she laid her head on his shoulder. Max wrapped an arm around her, chasing off the goose bumps that had broken out on her skin.

"She was no one…" he began softly.

CHAPTER 32

PITY HEARD THE GRAVITY IN HIS STORY, HIS RELUCTANCE to tell it, in the very first words.

"She was no one," Max repeated, as if reacquainting himself with a particular definition of that statement. "Her mother and father worked in our house, and sometimes she hung around the servants' areas when she wasn't in school. I had seen her, but I never really *noticed* her until the day I caught her reading in our library.

"When she saw me, she...she *begged* me not to say anything, to not get her parents in trouble. I remember thinking that she shouldn't have touched the books without permission. But I also remember being embarrassed that she was apologizing so...profusely. Like she was afraid of me. So I asked her if she wanted to stay and read for a while, to keep me company."

Pity stared at the bare plane of his chest, trying to ignore the ache in hers. "That was kind of you."

"I'm not sure it was," he replied. "I just wasn't sure what I was supposed to do. My only 'friends' were like me, and I only ever saw them at whatever ridiculous event was being thrown that week. You think the scheming in Cessation is something? It doesn't compare to what goes on in Columbia. At every meeting, every party, my parents' associates would parade around like peacocks while at the same time acting as if they had a knife at their ribs. It was brittle, exhausting. Even as a kid I hated it.

"Sonya was so far from that world. She went to a good school, on a special scholarship. She'd read anything she got her hands on—physics, art, philosophy. That's how it started. We'd read together, on the pretext of studying the same topics. But mostly we talked. She told me about the pieces of Columbia I knew nothing about: the slums; the shortages; wages that would cover rent or food or medicine, but not all three; jobs that paid well, but only because they were dangerous.

"At first my parents didn't care. Maybe they thought I was just having some fun with her. Then one day we snuck out to a rally for better working conditions. It was unlike anything I had ever seen before—thousands of people coming together. So many were struggling to live, but that didn't dampen the undercurrent of hope. One group was painting a mural with some slogan. I don't even remember what it was, but I picked up a paintbrush to help and…lost myself. Before I knew it, I had covered an entire corner of wall with the ugliest flowers you've ever seen.

"When I got home, I was so energized, so optimistic. I

thought I had seen the truth on both sides, which meant I could make others see it, too. When I told my parents..." Max stared at the ceiling. "They told me that Sonya wasn't a proper companion for me...and punctuated it by firing her parents."

Pity shifted beside him. *That was the world you tried to run to. Not Max's—Sonya's. That's what would have been waiting for you in Columbia.* When he didn't continue, she took his hand in hers and squeezed. "What did you do?"

Max took a deep breath. "What I should have done was never see Sonya again. What I did do—what *we* did—was leave. Sonya knew about some movements in the northern cities. I had access to plenty of funds. We thought we'd be long gone before anyone even knew we'd left.

"In reality, we made it a day and a half before my parents' people found us. They dragged us out of the old barn we had crashed in after a day of hitching rides. Sonya was screaming... I think I was screaming, too. They separated us. When I asked where they were taking us, they said home."

Max stopped again. This time a full minute passed before he continued.

"When I saw my parents, they were livid. There was a lot of yelling, mostly on their end, about what could have happened if anyone had found us, found out who I was—kidnappers, ransom, or worse. They didn't want me to see Sonya ever again. I told them that they couldn't keep us apart forever. After that, I became a prisoner, someone on my heels at every minute. And Sonya, she..." Max's voice broke.

Pity threaded her fingers through his hair again as if doing so would somehow draw his pain into her.

"They fished her body out of a river. The story was that she had lost her scholarship and was so upset that she jumped from a bridge." A pair of tears drew wet lines on his cheeks. "I knew it was a lie. And my parents knew that I knew. It wasn't a suicide—it was a *lesson*."

Frost blossomed in her chest. She thought of her father. As nasty and indifferent as he was, there were domains of cruelty he'd never come close to.

"A few months later," Max continued, "when things had calmed down, I left for good. It wasn't easy, but I did it, keeping my head down and away from the obvious paths. For months I had no idea where I was going or what I was doing. I just kept moving. Finally, with the last of my money, I bought a ticket on the TransRail and rode it to the very end. After that..."

"Cessation," Pity finished.

"Yes," he said. "The end of the world."

"I'm sorry." Pity's voice chased away the grim silence that had descended. *Sonya. Finn.* Their roads to Cessation both bore grave markers. "But none of that explains why you want to go back. I'd think you'd want to keep as many miles between them and you as possible."

Max turned onto his side so their faces were only inches apart. "Because Sonya wanted to change things, make them better for everyone. I decided I'd do it for her. I thought sooner or later my parents would find me, no matter where I hid. And when time passed and they didn't, I decided I'd return one day and use their influence to do everything she—*we*—had dreamed of." He took a strand of Pity's hair between his fingers. Stared at it. "There were times I tried to leave. I always lost my nerve. A little longer, I reasoned. What did it matter? Then, when Santino and Olivia went after Beeks, I volunteered to go along as a helping hand, figuring I'd have them drop me at the TransRail. Save the pain of good-byes, y'know? But then we caught Beeks, and I still hadn't done it. And then…after that…"

"You found me," she said.

"Yes."

And you decided I needed you more than you needed to go home. She sat up. "So I was just a reprieve, an excuse for you to stick around Cessation a little longer."

"What?" he said. "No!"

Pity twisted toward him. "Really? Because it sounds like you were looking for any excuse you could find to avoid going back."

"You needed help!" Max protested, looking at her like she was some strange animal he had never seen before.

"I did. *Then.*" Heat rose in her face. "But that was months ago and you're still here. What made you decide you had to leave now?"

"Isn't that obvious?"

"No, it's *not.*"

"You and Sheridan!" His eyes smoldered. "I couldn't stand the thought of you and him, especially with you mooning over how much he cared about fixing CONA and helping the dissidents and…" He stopped. "And because no matter what I do I can't keep my mind off you. It wasn't so bad with Garland, but now…"

Pity flushed. Of course he knew about Garland—how

couldn't he? Her voice rose with anger and embarrassment. "Then why have you been keeping away all this time? Acting like I'm hardly anything to you?"

With a noise of exasperation, Max jumped to his feet and strode away. "Haven't you been paying attention? When I go back east do you think I can take anyone with me? My parents already murdered one person I cared about. Do you believe they'd think twice about another? Dammit, Pity, the closer you are to me, the more danger you're in!" He stood resolute in the center of the room, fists knotted at his sides.

Well, that's not fair, she thought. It was hard to stay angry with him when the light and shadows fought their own battle on his naked body. The dark was winning on his lean shoulders but giving way at the angles of his hips. She rose to meet him on the same ground, letting the blankets fall away as she crossed her arms over her chest. "If you haven't noticed, I can take care of myself."

His gaze flickered over her.

"And no matter what you say, you don't really seem to be in a hurry to leave." She padded over to him.

"I have to go back," he said. "Sonya..."

"Is dead. Like Finn. But the difference is that I know Finn would want me to be where I'm happy, not where I thought I had to be, out of some stitched-together obligation. And Sheridan *wants* to be in Columbia. Why not swallow your pride and do what you can to help him from here? You know this world as well as anyone."

"It's not enough."

"What *would* be enough? Tell me." She squared her shoulders.

"Actually, look me in the eye and tell me that leaving Cessation—leaving me and Casimir and everyone else—is really, truly what you want. Not what you think you *should* do but what you *want* to do."

He stared at her. His lips trembled and parted, as if he was about to speak, and then they closed, as did his eyes.

She wrapped her arms around his neck. A moment later, his hands found her waist.

"Tell the truth," she said. "If you could ask Sonya what she would want for you, what do you think she'd say?"

"I think..." She could hear the struggle in his voice: affection and longing fighting the years of calcified guilt. "I think she'd tell me to stay right here, with you." He buried his face in her neck. "I don't want to go back there."

She tightened her arms around him. "I know," she said. "I know."

He kissed her again. Softly at first, and then with a growing hunger. The chill that had begun to settle on Pity's skin disappeared. They tumbled back into bed, burying themselves in the blankets and trading kisses back and forth until Max stopped suddenly.

"What about Sheridan?" he said, breathless.

"What about him?" Pity said. "I keep up the act. I have to or else Selene will put me in the ring with Daneko. You said it yourself: I can't cross Selene."

"I know, but..." He trailed off.

"You're still jealous!" She laughed.

"It's not funny."

"No, none of this is, but it's been eating me up, and I don't know what else to do. Max, I want to stay in Casimir without being ordered to murder someone whenever Selene feels slighted. Is that so much to ask?"

She tried to kiss him again, but he held her back. "It's only... I don't like you anywhere near him."

"I know. But if Selene can get him the presidency, he can keep Cessation safe. Isn't that worth it?" She smiled. "Look, if it makes you feel better, I promise that whatever I have to do to help Selene keep him here, it won't look anything like this."

She pressed her lips against his, then hooked a hand around his neck and fell back, pulling all of his delicious weight down on top of her.

CHAPTER 33

THE TARGET EXPLODED, SENDING A SPRAY OF VIOLET powder into the air. As the wind took it, carrying it over the edge of Eden, the onlookers clapped. Pity took aim and sent three more to the same fate. More applause. By the time she obliterated the remaining setup, the far end of the makeshift range was a rainbow haze, drifting slowly to the city below.

"Marvelous!" A patron clapped Sheridan on the back. "You'd best stay on this one's good side, Patrick."

"I'm doing my best." He shot her an enamored, effortlessly convincing smile.

It was supposed to be a party, though by Casimir's standards Pity wouldn't name it that. Barely a dozen people stood beneath the crisp, cloudless sky, lingering around tables set with

refreshments or reclining on padded sofas. While numerous
Tin Men did their best to blend in with the garden, Eden was
otherwise closed off, the usual selection of Casimir's workers
excluded.

If it was a party, Pity figured, it was an intensely private one.
But hope stirred. Whatever promises and pacts Selene was making on behalf of Sheridan, they seemed to be bearing fruit. There
was an elite air to these particular guests, a flavor of confidence
only exuded by those comfortable in their power.

"Yes, her talent is peerless!" Halcyon flitted about like a
gigantic hummingbird, extolling the virtues of the Theatre to
anyone who would listen. "Serendipity never fails to astound."

"That's nothing." Pity set to reloading her spent weapons.
"The targets aren't even moving."

"She's right." Nearby, Selene lounged beneath a trellis of
bougainvillea, sunshine dappling her charcoal sundress so that
she resembled some kind of wildcat. Adora sat beside her, doing
nothing to hide her boredom, while Beau stood watch over them
both. "Halcyon, why don't you and Pity show everyone something a little more exciting."

Halcyon's face brightened. "I have just the thing. A moment's
preparation, please." He beckoned a Tin Man and whispered to
him. The man ran off.

Meanwhile, Sheridan resumed conversing with a pair of the
special guests. Earlier, he'd quietly offered Pity some of their
names, but she'd promptly forgotten them. It was hard to focus
on details like that. Or anything. Sheridan was still her charge,
but it was Max who dominated her thoughts—his smile, the
glint of his rings, the feeling of his body against hers. It was like

a fog had settled upon her, a warm, early morning haze that left her feeling like there was nothing else in the world.

Her cheeks warmed, followed by the rest of her. For days she and Max had spent every free hour together. Hours that passed like minutes, while the ones when they were parted stretched into eternities. Impatience gnawed at her. Even now, he might be in her room, waiting for Sheridan to discharge her from the tedious service. No one, save for Halcyon, had said more than a handful of words to her all afternoon; it was clear that she was regarded as little more than the entertainment.

"Aha!" The Tin Man returned with whatever Halcyon had requested. "My dear, if you would take up your position once more?"

Pity obeyed as he headed downrange, wondering what trick he had up his sleeve.

"I'm sure you've all enjoyed Serendipity's exhibition so far," Halcyon announced, turning so that he faced her. "But what is any act by the Theatre Vespertine without a touch of danger?"

With a dramatic flourish, he raised a pack of cards, fanned it out, and picked one.

Nervous understanding stirred in Pity's stomach as he held it up between his index and middle finger: the ace of spades.

Too risky. She shook her head slightly, but Halcyon remained as he was, the card held less than a foot from his head. She turned to Selene.

"That won't do." Selene stood and swept over to Halcyon. "Let's show the people something they've never seen. Right, Pity?" She snatched the card. "It will be just like your first show."

The stirring turned to cold fear. Around them, the guests'

attention piqued, accented by whispers of disbelief as Selene raised the card in the same manner as Halcyon.

"Selene, no." Sheridan laughed. "I don't think anyone needs more proof of Pity's talents."

"Oh, it will be fun."

Beau marched over to her. "Absolutely not. I can't let this—"

Selene put up her other hand, cutting him off. "Go on, Pity. Don't keep us in suspense."

Pity couldn't move. Couldn't breathe. Beau hovered near Selene, the clash of dissent versus deference clear on his face. But it wasn't Beau's approval that mattered. And unlike at Pity's first show, Selene was giving her permission to shoot.

Her hand tightened around her gun. The shot was challenging, but not impossible. No more than what she did every time she performed in the Theatre. But if she missed? A realization picked its way to the front of her mind—if she missed outright, Selene would think it was on purpose. Yet even if she tried her best, there was always the chance that Selene would end up short a finger or two . . . or worse.

Selene waited, a patient smile on her lips.

It's a test. Another demonstration of submission. Beeks, the Finales, Sheridan . . . one trial after another, and there was only one path that would give Pity what she wanted.

Obedience.

She lifted her gun. Aimed.

Numbness washed over her as Beau's hand lifted. For a sliver of time, Pity anticipated a flash of black, followed by pain as his bullet pierced her. But his arm stopped mid-movement. His hand tightened into a fist and dropped to his side again.

She hesitated, praying he would interfere.

Knowing he wouldn't.

The ice of his stare pressed on her, as did the nervous anticipation of the onlookers, but she forced it all away, until only
two things were left: Selene and the card. The spade centered in
her vision; every grain of her concentration focused on it, raven-
black in the sunlight.

Pity took a breath and exhaled.

Bang!

The card bucked in Selene's hand. Instinctively Pity knew
she had made the shot the moment she pulled the trigger, but it
wasn't until Selene brandished the target triumphantly that her
tension released. The guests applauded in delight.

Selene glided back to Pity, Beau shadowing her, and held
the card out. A neat hole pierced the spade. "See? Not so hard.
Wasn't that a good shot, Beau?"

"It was an unnecessary shot."

Pity winced at his tone, though she didn't think it was
directed toward her.

"Oh, I think it served its purpose." Selene gestured at Sheridan, already entrenched in conversation again. "He seems satisfied, don't you think?"

"I certainly hope so, ma'am."

"As do I. But Casimir wouldn't be what it is if I counted on
hope to tell when a patron was pleased." She handed Pity the
card. "You've done well so far. Let's keep it that way, shall we?
No unpleasant distractions."

"I'm sorry, ma'am?"

"The upcoming show. I've already spoken to Halcyon, and I

think your talents are of better use where they are right now."
She smoothed her dress. "So let's not be worried about any *other*
performances, okay?"

It took a few seconds for the words to sink in. *No performance.*
Selene was releasing her from the Finale. Brilliant relief coursed
through her. She fought the grin that rose to her face, losing momentarily before regaining her composure. "Yes, of course. Thank you."

"Well?" said Selene. "Back to work."

Pity obeyed, returning to Sheridan's side. When he touched
her shoulder affectionately, she looped her arm into his, smiling
like a woman besotted.

It wasn't so hard to do, so long as she thought about Max
while she did it.

To her delight, Max was waiting for her when Selene's party
finally concluded, well after the velvet cloak of evening had
descended. He jumped up from her bed as she entered the room,
enveloping her in his arms.

"I finished in the theatre hours ago. Where have you been?"
There was a new vibrancy to his demeanor, as if a film of despair
had been ripped off, leaving a fresh version of him behind. "He
didn't want to keep you any longer, did he? Did he treat you okay?"

"Stop it." Pity pushed him away so she could collapse on the
bed. "He was so busy rubbing elbows he barely acknowledged I
was there. Selene made me shoot her, though."

"Good...wait, *what?*"

"Give me a minute and I'll tell you all about it. You were
careful to make sure no one saw you come in, right?" Fiction or

not, she was supposed to be with Sheridan. Rumors of Max in and out of her room at odd hours were the last thing she needed.

"I can be as sneaky as you, y'know."

She felt her boots loosen and her socks disappear, and then Max's hands were massaging her bare feet. It felt delicious, but she laughed. "You're doing that at your own risk, y'know. I don't know what's filthier—my feet after standing around all day or your hands."

"Well, if we're both so filthy," he said suggestively, "maybe we should hop in the bath and clean up."

It was a welcome suggestion, but if Pity had to describe what went on after that, *clean up* would not have been the words she used.

"Don't go." She yawned, eyes blinking. "It's early."

"No, it's not." Max pulled on his shirt. "If I don't stitch up those last backdrops this morning, Halcyon will pitch a fit."

She slid out after him, shrugging on her robe. "Let him."

Max embraced her, a gesture she felt she'd never tire of. It was like being wrapped in a favorite blanket.

"Not all of us are big, shiny stars of the Theatre." He released her. "I'm only a worker bee, and I do what the queen—or king, in this case—says."

He peeked out the door. Pity followed and grabbed his hand as he slipped into the hall.

"Fine," she said, "but give me one more kiss before you go."

As his lips touched hers, Pity thought she saw a flash of pink over his shoulder. But when she looked again, the hallway was empty.

CHAPTER 34

"OH, HEY, YOU LOOK FAMILIAR." LUSTER PEERED CLOSER. "Can't quite place your face, though."

"Ha, ha." Pity climbed onto the barstool beside her. Around them, the Gallery's energy was sluggish, only a handful of the gambling tables occupied.

"You look tired." Luster sipped at a mug of coffee. "Funny, since you seem to be going to bed plenty early."

"Morning practices. That's all."

"Really? Then why didn't Halcyon deliver this himself?" She brandished a folded square of orange paper.

Pity snatched it away.

Serendipity, it read, *despite your respite from tomorrow evening's performance, please join me in the morning. I've had the most brilliant idea for your act! Devotedly yours, Halcyon.*

"Hmm, he must have forgotten."

"Serendipity Jones, you are the worst liar I've ever seen!" Luster leaned in conspiratorially. "And every time I've caught a glimpse of you lately, there's been a big, silly smile on your face." She cocked her head. "You know what? Come to think of it, someone else has been walking around with a fresh glow..."

"Shh!" Pity's cheeks blazed, fear coursing through her. She looked around, but no one was within earshot. "Keep your voice down! Okay, I admit it! Max and I...we..."

Luster laughed, a great whooping cry. "I knew it, I knew it, I knew it!"

"Be. Quiet," Pity said through gritted teeth.

Luster settled, with a grin so wide it nearly split her face. "It's about damn time. Tell me everything. Well, not everything, but tell me what finally happened. And what about Sher—"

She broke off.

Pity followed her gaze. Adora stood a few feet away, arms crossed.

"Miss Selene would like to see you," she said. "Right now."

Adora led her to the suite's elevator, snapping her fingers impatiently at the guards as they reached it.

"Wakey, wakey, boys. Look sharp," Adora snapped. "Or at least pretend. Pity? Guns. Leave them here."

"What?"

"Leave your guns"—Adora accentuated each word—"here."

She'd never been barred from carrying her guns in front of Selene before. Fingers dumb with reluctance, Pity yanked at her belt strap. She removed it and handed it to one of the Tin Men.

"Watch those," Adora ordered, a little cat's smile on her

lips. "But don't play with them. Pity doesn't like it when you do that." She motioned for Pity to enter the elevator.

When it opened again, Selene stood before a window, her back to them. Adora cleared her throat and sat on a couch, eyes wide with expectation, something Pity had seen plenty of times before.

It was the look of someone waiting for the show to start.

A nervous sensation grew within her, as if a nest of ants had settled in her stomach.

Selene's voice, when it came, was low. "Have a seat."

Pity took a few steps forward, one eye trained on Adora. "Is something wrong?"

Selene's figure turned partway, so that the light of the noon sun glazed the edges of her form. "Sit," she said again. It was not a request.

Pity went down the stairs and obeyed.

Selene moved closer so that she stood above them. "Sheridan. What did he tell you?"

"About what?"

"When is the last time you were with him?"

"I...yesterday. At the party."

"You were supposed to stay with him." A streak of red entered Selene's voice. "To report back on whatever you observed."

"I did. I was there whenever he wanted me—"

"And what about when others wanted you? From what Adora has told me, you've been spreading your attentions around."

Her skin prickled, a frost of fear blooming. "Miss Selene—"

"I gave you a task," Selene spat. "Play your part. Keep Sheridan content—and observed. Instead of doing that, you're off with Max—*Max*, for goodness sake—and now Sheridan is leaving!"

Pity stiffened. "What?"

"He sent word this morning." A vase of white flowers sat on a table nearby. Selene went over to it, plucked a dead leaf, and crumpled it in her fist. "He's leaving and you're carrying on however you please."

"That's not true! I did exactly what you told me to do!"

Selene tossed the ruined leaf away and snapped her fingers at Adora. "Look!"

Adora pressed a button set into the arm of the sofa. A screen flickered to life on the wall, cleverly hidden among the paintings.

"What—" Pity began. The sound was muted, but the headline scrolling beneath the picture of Sheridan was all the explanation she needed.

DRAKOS-PRYCE ENDORSES DARK HORSE PRESIDENTIAL CAN-DIDATE PATRICK SHERIDAN.

"Do you understand now?" Selene demanded.

"Yes," Pity said quietly. This had nothing to do with Max. "Drakos-Pryce decided to back Sheridan. He doesn't need you anymore."

"Drakos-Pryce didn't *decide* anything. They would never give away support like that for nothing. Sheridan must have been hedging his bets from the beginning, dealing with them behind my back." Her expression darkened. "Drakos-Pryce would never suffer a president indebted to us, so they indebted him first. Either way Sheridan gets what he wants. The minute he's elected they'll probably have CONA's forces on our door-step, ready to reduce the city to ash."

"He…wouldn't…" She fixated on the broadcast again. *Selene or Drakos-Pryce—if what he wanted was the presidency, what did it matter who handed it to him?* Cold dread pierced her gut. Maybe Max had been right. What if Sheridan had told her only what he thought she wanted to hear?

No. Sheridan had been a Patriot once; he wouldn't turn on the people he'd fought with. And he knew the city's power. He wouldn't want to see it destroyed. "But Drakos-Pryce could back whoever they wanted and still get rid of Cessation. Why Sheridan? It doesn't need currency. What else does he have to offer?"

"That"—Selene signaled for Adora to turn off the broadcast—"is something I don't know."

For the first time since coming to Cessation, Pity heard real fear in Selene's voice. Anxiety pricked at her temples. Selene's confidence had always seemed adamant, unshakable. And yet, in one move, Sheridan and Drakos-Pryce had undone her.

"We can't let him leave," Selene continued. "Not yet. Your romance might have been an act, but he likes you. Trusts you. I need you to convince him to remain in the city while I figure this out."

"How? Hold him at gunpoint?" Pity's blood burned with frustration. "And if what you're saying is true, what happens if Drakos-Pryce—or CONA—gets wind of that?"

Selene paced across the room, thinking. "You're right. I may not be able to keep him here, but he's president by my hand or not at all." She stopped and turned back to Pity. "So you are going to leave with Sheridan. Once you're in Columbia, find out how Drakos-Pryce got their claws into him. Then, when the opportunity presents itself, kill him."

Pity sucked in a breath. "What?"

"Perhaps a lovers' quarrel of some sort?" Adora offered.

"Yes," said Selene. "That will be believable, given the circumstances, and won't be blamed on Cessation. Yes, that will work."

"No!" She stood. "I won't do it."

"It wasn't a request."

"I can't." The thought of putting Sheridan in her sights made her whole body clench. "He might have betrayed you, but he didn't betray me. Find another way."

Selene approached again. Her hand shot out, grabbing Pity by the chin. "He betrayed all of us." Her voice was poison spread on silk. "Does he know about Max?"

Pity shook her head.

"Good. Then tell him whatever you have to—that you're tired of the Theatre, that you've really fallen in love with him—I don't care. Just make sure you are with him tomorrow when he goes. Or"—her grip tightened, fingers digging into flesh—"the next Finale will be yours to deal with."

Pity's gut clenched.

"And instead of Daneko, I'll make Max its star."

The air went out of her lungs. *No.* "But he hasn't done anything wrong..."

"So?" Selene let her go. "Neither did the porter who hanged himself after Daneko tried to kill me. He wasn't the one who helped the mercenaries into Casimir, but I knew word would get out, and a living, unidentified traitor is worse than a dead, known one." An acid smile etched on her lips. "A piece of advice, Pity: Whatever your weaknesses are, don't let them show. And if they do show, find a way to make them go away. As it will turn out, that poor boy's death was a cover-up by the real conspirator: Max."

"Max isn't a traitor!"

"No, of course he's not," said Selene. "But if I put him in that arena and say he is, who is going to question it?"

Pity's hands dropped to her sides, but found only air instead of steel. "You wouldn't."

"Do what you're told and you won't have to find out. And if you think you can get to Max first, forget about it. He's already in the tombs, where he'll stay until I'm sure Sheridan isn't a problem anymore."

Pity gritted her teeth, her whole body petrified by anger. "How can you do this? I did everything you asked. I helped save your life!"

Selene turned away. "My life is only worth something in Cessation. And if the city isn't safe, none of us are."

"But...but..." Pity grasped for something, anything. "You said that Casimir is a family! Max is family!"

"He is," said Selene, "but this family is big. And I'll do what I need to in order to protect it, including making sacrifices. Now go. And if you need inspiration to do whatever it is you need to do with Sheridan, just picture Max"—she glanced back over her shoulder at Pity—"in the spotlight, and how those soulful gray eyes will look the moment before you pull the trigger."

The moment the Tin Men gave her back her guns, Pity ran through the halls, not caring who saw, to the nearest stairwell.

Then it was down, down, almost tripping over her own feet, until she reached the tunnels. For a brief moment she had no idea where she was. The same dingy pipes and concrete branched out in every direction. She picked a tunnel and began running again, taking corner after corner until, miraculously, some part of her brain forced her in the right direction.

His door was a gaping mouth, wide-open.

"Max!" She ran inside.

He wasn't there. The lights were on, the bed its usual tangle of blankets. In the center of the floor lay a fold of orange paper, debris incongruous in an otherwise empty landscape of concrete.

As if it had been dropped in surprise.

Trembling, she picked it up. It was nearly identical to the one Luster had delivered to her, a request from Halcyon to report early the next morning, to make last-minute alterations on some sets.

She crumpled the paper in her fist. Other places Max might be crackled through her mind—the theatre, Eden. But she knew exactly what had happened to him.

Selene didn't make empty threats.

Pity collapsed onto Max's bed, swallowing a scream. Hot tears ignited as his scent filled the air around her. She wiped at them angrily.

I did everything. The words kept beating through her head. *I did everything I was asked.*

Regret diffused through her. If only she'd never gone to Max, confessed the deal she'd made. He might be gone, but he'd be safe. Instead, she'd crossed Selene, and Max stood to pay the price.

I won't do it. Nothing in the world would make her hurt him. But even as she had the thought, she knew it didn't matter.

If Selene forced them both into the arena, only one would walk out, or neither. And no one would intervene—not Halcyon, not the other performers, maybe not even their friends. After all, Beeks had been part of their family, too, and there had been no objections to his death.

Only cheers.

What do I do?

Every minute that ticked by was one less to find a solution to her grim predicament. But no matter which way she turned the situation, looking for a crack, for a way out, she found nothing. No one would defy Selene to help Pity, and if Sheridan departed Cessation, so would any chance she had to save Max.

There was no choice—she needed to go with him.

CHAPTER 35

EVENING FELL LIKE THE LIGHTS IN THE THEATRE, AS IF the world was setting the stage for her performance. Downstairs, the Gallery was beginning its nightly upswing of debauchery, but outside the door of Sheridan's suite, it was quiet. Pity heard a ghost or two of movement, a muffled voice, but nothing more. She stared at the number on the door, hands at her sides, where her guns should've been. For once she was glad for their absence. Even if she succeeded in convincing Sheridan to take her along, she couldn't fathom the thought of murdering him.

It felt like an hour passed before she found the strength to knock.

Hook's massive form filled the portal. "What do you want?"

"Is Patrick in?"

Her voice dripped with honey, but he gazed down at her as if she were a bug that had flown into his drink. "No."

Pity smiled wider, praying the dread didn't show in her eyes. "Can you check again? I really need to talk to him."

"I said—"

"Let her in." Sheridan's voice came from within.

Hook moved aside. In the suite, suitcases and trunks were piled near the door. Pity felt her smile crack. He really was leaving.

"Pity." Sheridan sat in an overstuffed chair, a drink in one hand, shirt open at the collar. "I didn't expect to see you."

She glanced at the baggage. "I heard you were leaving."

"Yes. Some business came up back east."

"I know." She alighted on the arm of a sofa. "Congratulations, Mr. President. Still, I thought you'd at least say good-bye."

"You're right." Sheridan sat a little straighter. "I've been rude. I expected you'd be relieved to be rid of me. No more pretending."

Tell him whatever you have to. "Who says I was pretending the whole time?" Her gut ached, but Pity made herself look back at Hook with an affected sulk. "Do you think we could have some privacy?"

Hook glowered, but Sheridan waved a hand. "It's okay. Go on and make sure everything is ready for tomorrow."

The bodyguard reluctantly vanished into one of the adjoining rooms.

Sheridan got to his feet, ice cubes clicking against the side of his glass. "Drink?" He went to the bar and poured her a glass of wine.

"Thank you." Pity took the glass and sipped, summoning her

courage. "I can't believe you're leaving so soon. We were just getting to know each other. Then again, as soon as I heard, I thought... well, it's silly."

"What is?"

No use dancing around it. She chewed her lip, doing her best to look cautiously excited. "I thought maybe I could come with you."

"Oh?" Pity searched Sheridan's face, looking for surprise, interest—anything—but his faint, placid smile remained unchanged. "What about the Theatre? You've got quite a following in Cessation. Why give that up?"

Earlier she had searched for the right lie, something that Sheridan would never question, only to settle on the truth instead. "I never meant to end up in Cessation. I wanted to see Columbia and all the cities in the east." A sick feeling stirred in her gut. "And the Theatre is going to execute Daneko tomorrow night. I don't want to do it, or any of the Finales. I never did."

In her mind, she saw the arena. But instead of Daneko, Max stood in the center, lights glinting off his piercings and a glaze of terror in his eyes. A cold sweat broke out on her skin. "You're going to be the next president of the Confederation of North America. There must be something I can do to help. I mean, I'd make as good a bodyguard as anyone you'd find there." Her fingers tightened around her glass. "And like you said, us Patriots need to stick together, right?"

Sheridan moved closer, regarding her like she was a novel curiosity. The smile turned into a smirk. "So you want to come with me to Columbia. Be my... bodyguard? Hmm, I didn't realize you enjoyed our time together so much."

Pity nodded, not trusting her voice.

He leaned in, until only inches separated their faces. Pity's hand shook as she tried to set the glass down on a side table, anticipating his response. A yes signed his death warrant. But a no...

"Cut the shit," Sheridan said. "Why are you really here?"

The glass slipped from her fingers and slid off the table, wine splashing onto the carpet. "What?"

He straightened and moved away. "Did Selene send you?"

"No! I came on my own."

He retrieved his own drink from the bar. "You're a bad liar, Pity."

"I don't know what you're talking about." The words caught in her throat like chunks of food. "I...only want to come with you."

"That I believe," he said. "But I don't believe for a moment it's of your own accord. You look like you're going to be sick."

The shaking spread, overtaking her. She slid onto the couch, eyes downcast. One foot overlapped the wine stain, a scarlet bruise on the beige carpet. She stared at it, unable to think. Sheridan had seen through her in an instant. He would leave without her, and Selene would make good on her threat.

Max. Her breath hitched.

Sheridan loomed over her. "Selene sent you."

It wasn't a question this time. There was no use denying it. "Please," she said, hating the word immediately, loathing the begging tone in her voice. "Please, you can't go."

"There's no reason for me to stay anymore."

"A few more days. Talk to Selene, let her try to finish what she started for you. That's all I'm asking."

"And if I don't," said Sheridan, "what is Selene going to do
to you?"

"I..."

"Pity." There was no anger in his eyes, only a curious kind
of concern. He put a steadying hand on her shoulder. "You can
tell me."

Pity took a deep breath. "Not me."

"Then who?"

She hesitated, but only for a moment. What did it matter at
this point? The act was over. "Max."

His hand tightened. "Max?"

"Ow." Pity shifted away, but he grabbed her arm and hauled
her to her feet.

"Has Selene done something with him?"

She blinked at him, not comprehending.

He shook her hard, once, like a dog with a rat in its teeth. "Is
that why you're here?"

She ripped her arm away and retreated. "Why? What does he
matter to you?"

Sheridan spun and pitched his glass at the wall. It shattered,
sending crystalline shards twinkling through the air and leaving
whiskey dripping down the wallpaper.

Frozen with bewilderment, she could only stare as Hook
rushed into the room.

"Sir?"

"I'm fine!" Sheridan barked. He kept his back to them, his
tense frame slowly relaxing. "An accident. Please leave us alone."

"Sir, I don't think—"

"*Go.*"

Sheridan turned to her as the bodyguard obeyed, his cool demeanor returned—save in his eyes, which shone with an intensity Pity had never seen before. *What is happening?* She moved behind the sofa, keeping it between them. First Selene had turned on her, now Sheridan was losing his mind over... Max? It didn't make any sense. Sheridan barely knew who he was and only knew him through her. Max was no one to Sheridan, a painter in the—

The room lurched. She grabbed the couch to steady herself, overcome by a sensation like ice water flooding her veins.

No one.

But Max wasn't *no one,* was he? His parents were powerful enough to worry about kidnappers, to send a retrieval force after him, and to get away with murder.

No. Please, no.

Tears formed in her eyes, the adrenaline in her blood an elixir of utter helplessness. She didn't want to ask the question, but already drowning in half-truths and lies, she wanted—*needed*—the answer.

"Who is Max?" She swallowed, her mouth dry. "And what does he have to do with you and Drakos-Pryce?"

Seconds stretched like hours as Sheridan considered her. "He never told you about his life before Cessation?"

"No, not...all of it."

Sheridan laughed with honest, but hollow, amusement. He collapsed into his chair and stared at her, uncharacteristic indecisiveness etched on his face. Pity waited, every fiber of her being aching to escape, and knew there was no way out of the quicksand dragging her down by inches.

"Pity," he said finally, "this is very important. Put the games aside and answer me truthfully: can I trust you?"

The meaning carried clearly: he was already trusting her. And if he needed to do that, it meant his situation, whatever it was, had turned desperate. But could she trust him? She eyed the door Hook had disappeared through, aware that he was probably listening, ready to intervene at a moment's notice.

If she tried to leave now, would Sheridan let her?

Leave and go where? She thought of Selene's eyes, laced with anger, and heard her orders. Selene was willing to serve up both Pity and Max to achieve her ends. *She's no friend of yours. Not anymore.*

And maybe Sheridan wasn't either, but she saw no other choice.

"Yes," she said. Then again, louder: "Yes, you can trust me."

"Good. You may be a terrible liar, but you're no fool." One hand rubbed his temple as he sighed. "Your 'Max'? His real name is Edwin Khristos Maximillian Pryce." Sheridan paused. "And he is the one and only child of Alanna Drakos and Jonathan Pryce."

CHAPTER 36

PITY SAT AS HER VISION NARROWED, THE EDGES TURNING DIM.

Max...How was it possible? Drakos-Pryce was more than a powerful corporation. It was an empire. How had Max managed to elude that for so long?

"Are you sure?"

"Yes," said Sheridan. "Facts, figures, and faces—those are my talents. I never forget them, though years and the dye and piercings did a good job of obscuring his features." He registered her confusion. "In all my time in Columbia, Drakos-Pryce might have never turned their eyes toward me, but, oh, I watched them. The deals they made. Who they talked to at parties and who they didn't. And even the skinny, bored little boy they ignored more often than not."

"He said he hated the parties." The words trickled out of her as she fought to process her bewilderment. One thing was clear, though: the payment Sheridan had offered up in return for the corporation's endorsement.

"For years he was assumed to be abroad—hidden away until he was old enough to join his parents' business. I should thank you. If not for your debut, I might never have noticed him that evening in the Gallery." He leaned toward her. "Pity, where is he?"

A sour taste filled her mouth. "Locked up, where no one can get to him. Selene won't let him go unless I go with you."

"And...?"

"And kill you."

"Ah." Sheridan was silent for a moment. "What happens to Max if you don't?"

Again, Pity's eyes fell to the scarlet stain. "She'll tell everyone that he was working with Daneko, put him in a Finale, and make me kill him. And when I refuse to do that..."

"Yes, I understand." Sheridan's tone turned jarringly light. "Well, since I'd rather not be killed, and you would rather not kill Max, I think we are both on the same side."

Were they? "It's too late. You need Max, and he's in Selene's hands."

"But she doesn't know what she has." He paused, pensive again. "Or what is happening around her."

She looked up. "What do you mean?"

"Pity, what if I told you that Selene's plans no longer matter?"

A new kind of dread ignited in her belly. The territory they were traversing had changed suddenly. "I-I don't..."

"Selene isn't as universally beloved as you might think. And she's a fool if she thinks anyone would believe Max an accessory to her assassination attempt. Even if I didn't know he was the prince of a cutthroat corporation, I never would have tried to acquire his assistance."

At first she thought she misheard. "But it was Daneko who—" She stopped. The *help* in the east. "Oh, Lord, it wasn't Daneko who tried to kill Selene. It was *you*."

"Oh, Daneko was involved," Sheridan said. "But as my cat's-paw. He was more than willing to sell Selene out if it meant he'd take over the city, even if only as my proxy." He chuckled. "It was a bit ambitious—I see that now. But how could I have known that my plan would fail simply because Serendipity Jones came to breakfast?"

Pity stood, freezing in place when she realized she didn't know what she was doing. More than trust, this was a confession. Sheridan had tried to murder Selene.

Sheridan, not Daneko.

Her thoughts cast back to that morning. To the assassins who had offered to take them alive and Sheridan's words before the final rally: *You don't need to do this.* At the time, she'd heard it as the sentiment of a man believing surrender would save his life. Now she realized he'd never been in danger to begin with.

Be careful, she thought. *Be very careful.* "Why? Why would you do all this?"

"I told you: Cessation is the power in the west," Sheridan said. "Like Columbia is in the east. Together they form a conduit through which authority over the entire continent flows. Selene is partially right in her machinations. I want Cessation... though not with her."

The blood drained from Pity's cheeks. Finally Sheridan's intentions were illuminated. It was one thing for him to be allied with Selene. But singular control over CONA and Cessation was unprecedented, each city a bastion of influence that could be used to covertly benefit the other. Sheridan would effectively command the entire continent, with an amount of power unseen since before the Pacific Event. *This was what he had wanted all along,* she thought, *why he made a deal with Drakos-Pryce.* Even if he'd once thought Casimir's secrets and sway could gain him the presidency, he'd never intended to let Selene live.

"But without Selene," she said, "there's no Cessation. It will all come apart."

Sheridan sniffed. "A useful fiction that has served Selene well. But any old soldier can tell you that when a general falls, the troops will fall in line so long as a strong leader is there to replace him. Which is where our friend Daneko comes in."

Our friend? "The city hates him."

"This city will accept whoever gives them what they want."

"Selene is already doing that, remember? He'll be dead come midnight tomorrow."

"No," said Sheridan, with a sly smile. "Selene doesn't know it yet, but there will be no show. Daneko will be free well before that, and her reign will be over."

Pity tried to swallow, but her mouth had gone as dry as chalk. "How?" That one word nearly took the breath out of her, and a moment passed before she could continue. "She's more careful now. Casimir is a fortress when it needs to be. And you'll never be able to get to her, not with Beau and security around her."

"Don't concern yourself with Selene. As to Casimir, tomorrow the Reformationists will march on it. But this time hidden among them will be a force of my own, courtesy of Drakos-Pryce. Once they get inside, it will only be a matter of time."

So it hadn't been her imagination. The camp *had* gotten larger since the last time she saw it. It was so perfectly simple— the Reformationists were fanatics, but peaceful ones, who wouldn't raise suspicion. "They'll never get past the front door."

"That's been taken care of, too." Sheridan paced across the thick carpet. "I told you, I'm not alone in this."

Who? Not a single name came to mind. Instead she thought of the aftermath of the assassination attempt—Casimir's anger and tears on Selene's behalf. Would it have been the same if she hadn't survived? Pity wanted to believe it would, but Casimir was a place of safety and luxury far beyond the normal reach of its residents. Maybe Sheridan was right; maybe everyone would fall in line so long as a firm hand still held the city.

"And when Casimir is ours, Max will be, too. You two will be together again before this time tomorrow—if I can count on you to keep this quiet. Please, Pity, I need your help."

No, you don't. Sheridan would make his play with or without her—she had no doubt. But finally she saw a glimmer of light, the opening she was searching for. If Sheridan freed Max, maybe there was a way for the two of them to escape, beyond the reach of Selene or Drakos-Pryce or anyone else who threatened them. It was a slim chance, but what choice did she have?

A dark thought thrust its way to the forefront of her mind. "There's going to be resistance."

"I know," Sheridan said. "It's impossible to promise that no blood will be shed, but I promise no one will be harmed when it can be avoided."

She tried to picture it: Sheridan's men storming Casimir and the chaos that would ensue. But her thoughts kept twisting to Max, so close—only a few stories below her feet—and yet as unreachable as the moon. Something in her hardened. She couldn't let the weight of her mistakes fall on him.

I'll do what I need to, Selene had said.

Well, so would she.

"Yes," Pity said. "I'll help you."

"Good," said Sheridan. He guided her gently toward the door. "Now, I want you to go to your room. Selene is probably having you watched. Pack enough to make it look like you're accompanying me east and then return here." He gave her an encouraging squeeze of her arm. "Be quick. The wheels are in motion, Pity. There's no stopping the train now."

The sentiment echoed in her ears as she left the suite, tangling with the thoughts ricocheting through her mind. All this time, from the very moment Sheridan stepped foot in Cessation, he had been planning. And Selene, for all her calculations, had missed the threat of him entirely.

That's why he fled after the assassination attempt. His life wasn't in danger until Selene survived and the possibility she might discover his involvement arose. But by then he knew about Max, the ace up his sleeve with which he could leverage Drakos-Pryce. And while their sham romance had been a misdirection, it was one meant to keep Selene worried about the unknown threat in the east instead of the one standing at her very door.

Adora appeared around a corner, blocking her path. "Well?"

The single word cracked in Pity's ears like a shot. For a heart-beat, she forgot the original objective of her visit to Sheridan and the plot she already had a part in. Adora waited, a smug smile on her face. Pity imagined throwing her against the wall, removing the expression with a well-placed fist. Instead, she stared straight ahead, blood burning in her veins.

Selene still thinks she's got the upper hand. Well, she can go on thinking that.

"You can tell her it's done," Pity said. "I'm going with him."

CHAPTER 37

THE JOURNEY BACK TO HER ROOM WAS A FEVER DREAM.

Get what you need, her mind screamed when she finally made it there. *Get what you need and get back to Sheridan.* She fought to stay attentive, to focus on the instructions like a target. But her limbs moved like clay as she changed into traveling clothes. *Move. Don't think. No matter what is about to happen, you need to protect Max.* She didn't think for a moment that she could trust Sheridan once Max was freed. And she wasn't about to allow Max to be handed over like currency.

We'll escape. Get out of Casimir, Cessation, and then… then…

No plan came to her, but she'd have to worry about that later. Getting to Max was her first priority. She grabbed her gun belt, the beautiful thing he'd bought for her. It felt like eons ago.

Instead of putting it on, Pity froze, mesmerized by the glossy black leather and the weapons it cradled. An almost electric sensation crawled down her spine.

It's going to be a bloodbath. Casimir wasn't going to roll over. People would resist. Fight.

That's how wars go. She heard her mother's voice suddenly, thick and sullen. *People fight, people die.*

But Pity didn't have to do either. She strapped on the gun belt. All she had to do was walk away for a little bit, and Max would be safe.

All she had to do was stand by and let others die.

And who is it going to be? This time she heard Finn. *Luster? Duchess? Garland? How many friends do you want to lose, Serendipity Jones?*

She tried to ignore the thoughts, but they burrowed out of the earth of her mind like worms during a rain.

I can warn them. Tell them to stay hidden in their rooms. But if she did that, they would alert Selene. And Selene would kill her and Sheridan, maybe even Max. And probably not in that order. Even if Pity convinced them to obey her without question, who else might die? Which lives were worth Max's, and how many of them?

All of them, the selfish part of her said.

None of them, said another, and that part sounded too much like Max.

Her skin crawled with frustration. *He wouldn't let this happen,* she thought. *He wouldn't risk losing the friends—the* family—*that had embraced him when he'd had no one.*

She was the one about to do that.

Max would tell Selene. Max would stop it all.

"Dammit," she hissed, because the decision wasn't Max's.

It was hers.

But if she went to Selene, tried to bargain Sheridan's betrayal for Max's life, would Selene even believe her? She wanted Sheridan in her grasp so badly. *She'll think every word out of your mouth is a lie to save Max.* And even if she did believe it, what would happen to Max when Selene discovered who he was? He would be in more danger than ever.

But at least Casimir would be safe.

What is it going to be? she asked herself. *Stand up, take a risk...or stand by and watch the slaughter?*

"Dammit, dammit, dammit."

With a last, decisive yank on her gun belt, Pity flew out the door and into the graveyard silence of the hall. By the time she reached the end, she was almost running. Consumed by her thoughts, she rounded the corner and collided with an unyielding mass of flesh. The impact sent her sprawling to the ground, but when she looked up, cool relief coursed through her.

"Santino!"

"Pity?" He yanked her back to her feet as if she were made of straw. "Where are you headed in such a hurry?"

"Thank goodness!" She dropped her voice. "I need to talk to Selene. *Now.*"

"Why? What's wrong?"

"I'll explain when we get to Selene. But she's in danger. We're *all* in danger!"

"Pity, chica, relax." Santino pressed his hands down on her shoulders, then gestured behind him, to a pair of Tin Men she hadn't even noticed. "They'll take you to Selene. I'll get more men and meet you there."

Pity's hands tensed into fists. "You need to hurry!"

"I will." He turned to the Tin Men. "Take her up the restricted way. And don't let anyone near her."

They parted, Pity and the Tin Men heading for the nearest elevator. Her body ached with anxiety as they traveled. Distant sounds of laughter and music echoed in her ears. The Gallery was doubtless in full revelry, unaware of the danger that was camped just beyond the city limits, readying to strike.

And Max... did he have any idea what was happening? Why he was imprisoned?

Pity roused from her ruminations as they entered the elevator. It jolted beneath their feet and began to descend.

Down. She tensed. *Not up.* "Where are we going?"

"The restricted way," grunted the Tin Man to her right. He stood a step in front of her, the other, a step behind.

The floor numbers ticked lower. "Is that through the basement?"

"You'll see when we get there." He didn't quite manage to keep the note of irritation out of his voice.

Instinct kicked in, and Pity went cold. Santino hadn't asked what she knew or how she knew it.

He trusts you, she tried to tell herself. *That's all.*

But the icy feeling spread. *I'm not alone in this,* Sheridan had said. What was Santino doing near her room so soon after she had left Sheridan?

Pieces began to slot together.

Santino was too late to stop the assassination attempt.

Daneko narrowly slipped through his grasp, and he was the one who took control of the gang leader as soon as he was captured.

At every juncture, what appeared to have been innocuous timing on his part suddenly seemed as precise as a clock.

And now he knows you were going to warn Selene.

She sucked in a sharp breath as understanding gut-punched her. It must have shown on her face, because when the Tin Man who had spoken glanced back at her a moment later, his eyes were hard. But it was the flash of movement behind her—reflected in the polished metal wall of the elevator—that stirred her from the paralyzing realization. She reached for her guns and turned—

—a fraction of a second too late. The prick of a med injector registered right as her limbs went dead, a cry of surprise misfiring on her lips. One of the Tin Men caught her as she fell—she knew only because she stopped moving. She felt nothing. She was a doll, nothing but rags and stuffing.

The elevator stopped and opened. Her head lolled at an awkward angle, and Pity found herself staring out at the vast, deserted garage.

"Get the truck," said the man holding her. "Hurry, she's heavy."

The other Tin Man rushed off, his boots thumping on the concrete. Pity blinked; she had that much movement still. But even her sight was beginning to dim around the edges. Her thoughts jellified, and she wasn't sure if they had been waiting for a minute or an hour when her captor carried her a few feet forward and out of the elevator.

"What's taking so long?" her captor called. His voice echoed faintly.

There was no reply.

With an angry scoff, he lowered her to the ground. Her head knocked against the floor, jostling her sight back into focus. But she was facing the elevator, the whole of her vision filled by its metal panels. The Tin Man's reflection was a watercolor blur.

Get up! She tried to move, but nothing happened. The world distorted more as tears filled her eyes. She blinked them back. *Dammit! Get up! Reach for your guns!*

Fresh footsteps sounded.

"Stop!" the Tin Man ordered. "Turn around. This isn't any business of yours."

Another blur appeared in the panels.

"I mean it! Not another step forward or I'll—"

There was a sharp, airy pop, followed by a heavy thump that Pity recognized all too well. Only one blur stood in the wall of the elevator now. Her sight started to fray again, the world churning as someone rolled her onto her back.

A weathered face stared down at her, framed by flickering spots.

Siena Bond.

The spots turned to clouds, and everything went black.

CHAPTER 38

PITY WOKE TO AN EBON HAZE, FOLLOWED BY THE SLOW resolution of sensations: the jerking, heaving feeling of vehicular movement…odors of exhaust and tobacco. She blinked. One side of her vision glowed faintly, and after several moments a silhouette resolved before her.

"Where—" The thick, croaking sound surprised her. "Where am I?"

"Getting your voice back, huh?"

Siena.

"That's a start."

Pity still couldn't move her limbs, but with some effort she turned her head to her right. The glow she saw was the horizon, a narrow strip of vermilion just beginning to chase the night away.

Dawn?

Panic gripped her as she fought to orient herself. Cessation was gone. They were in the desert. As she struggled to formulate why, the vehicle they were in slowed and stopped. Siena turned off the engine and flicked on a light in the ceiling, casting everything in pallid yellow.

"Where are we?" Pity demanded, her mouth tacky. "Why did you—"

"Relax, kid. You may be talking again, but it'll be a little while before the rest of your body follows suit." Siena pulled out an ugly hand-rolled cigarette and placed it between her lips. But when she lit it, its scent was as fine as any of the cigars Pity had smelled in Casimir. "Thirsty? It's dry as old bones out here."

Pity nodded, a movement that seemed easier than a minute ago.

Siena pulled out a canteen and lifted it to Pity's lips. The water was warm and faintly metallic, but she swallowed several mouthfuls, letting it run over her parched lips.

"Where's Cessation?" she said when she was done. Twin poisons of fear and anger coursed through her veins as her memories regathered. *Santino.* It made her ill to think about it. The big, friendly man who had saved her life on the plains and carried her to Dr. Starr when she was shot—a traitor. And if Santino could turn coat, who else might have? "We need to go back. *Now.* It's a matter of life or death."

"Always is." Siena sniffed. "But we're gonna have a little chat first, and it seemed smart to do that somewhere no one would interrupt us. You wanna tell me what was going on with those Tin Men?"

Pity narrowed her eyes. "You wanna tell me why you stopped them?"

"Okay, I'll give first," Siena said. "I saw you get into the elevator. Something was off, that was easy enough to figure. Good thing I've been keeping an eye on you."

"On me?" A shiver ran through her as her old fear surfaced. "Did my father send you?"

Siena snorted in a way that might have been a laugh. "No, but maybe your momma did."

"*What?*" Pity would have jolted straight up had she been able to. Instead, her arms jerked weakly in her lap. "My *mother?*"

"Uh-huh. 'Cause that's who I thought I was seeing that day I rolled in and you were there: Joanna Jones, in the flesh. 'Cept you were younger than I ever knew her." Siena reached out and took one of the guns from Pity's belt. She rubbed the pad of her thumb over the inlay on the grips. "Beautiful as the first time I saw them, though they've lost a bit of that new shine." When she saw Pity's confusion, an amused smile deepened the lines around her mouth. "Geez, girl, didn't your momma ever tell you where she got these?"

"She said some of the Patriots gave them to her, after the war."

"Close. Though she lied about the 'after' part. She must have stashed them somewhere safe before she got caught. Joanna was always smart like that. Everyone in our squad had their special weapons, our good luck charms, we used to call them. Had myself a pretty shotgun, though it's been gone a few years now."

"Your squad?"

"Joanna didn't tell you a damn thing, did she? The Reapers."

Pity's heart thumped against her ribs. *Finn's dumb story.* "No. My mother said she guarded supply depots."

"There are a lot of dead folks that would attest differently, were they able."

"But..." Another piece of what Pity thought she knew shifted out of alignment. "Why didn't she tell me? And why didn't you say anything sooner?"

Siena returned the gun to its holster. "There's one answer for both those questions," she said, "which is that going around bragging that you were a Reaper is a good way to find a noose around your neck, or worse. There's still a high bounty on them. Hell, that job's been offered to *me* a few times." She flicked ash onto the floor. "Truth is, I'm probably the only person who could find any of the Reapers still left on this earth." Her voice turned nostalgic. "That's how we ran things, you see. One person in command, and that one the only link between us and the Patriot command. If the one fell, our next in command would make him or herself known. Otherwise, no one knew us from any other group of guerrillas that ran with the Patriots."

"My mother—"

"Joined up a few years before the end of the war," Siena said. "She was the most natural sniper I had ever seen, as good as anyone with twice her years. But we were on different missions when the turn came. I heard she got captured but not what happened after."

It wasn't a question, but Pity knew Siena wanted an answer. "She was in a prisoner camp for a while. But CONA couldn't execute or jail everyone, so she bargained herself into a spot on an agricultural commune, with a marriage and the promise of children."

"And?"

"And the marriage was hell, but she had three kids anyway and spent the rest of her years walking the wall and drinking herself toward a fall and a broken neck."

A fog of silence fell.

Finally, Siena spoke again. "That's a poor end for a woman like Joanna Jones."

Pity nodded in agreement, not trusting her voice for the tightness in her throat. With concentration, she found that she could now raise her right arm. Weak as an old woman, she wiped at her eyes. As she did, Siena opened the door and stepped out into the desert, pacing off into the receding darkness.

"Hey! Come back!"

But Siena ignored her. Abandoned, Pity assessed her surroundings, angling her half numb body as best she could. There was a good-sized space in the rear of the vehicle. She saw a cot, a supply of tins and water, and an arsenal that rivaled that of a small commune. There were nonlethal instruments as well—flash grenades, shock sticks—and a variety of restraints. She smelled gun oil and steel and, underneath, the gut-quivering perfume of old fear.

A Reaper.

Pity fit the piece of information into the memory of her mother, the missing bullet in the chamber. She remembered her mother's eyes, so caring sometimes, so haunted at others. *By how many dead men?* No, it was never ghosts that had haunted her mother—it was the cage she had found herself in.

A poor end...

She shook the thought away. There was nothing she could do for her mother, and if they didn't move soon, it would be the same for Max and Casimir.

Agonizing minutes passed before Siena returned. "It's been my experience," she said, climbing back into her seat, "that folks who have fallen afoul of Selene's Tin Men aren't typically in a rush to return to Casimir. You want to tell me exactly what's going on?"

With Santino's betrayal as fresh as a new wound, Pity's tongue twisted with the urge to stay silent. There was no one in Casimir she could trust now—only herself and Max. "No."

"Okay, let me try that another way. Where's your boyfriend? The real one, not the one you've been pretending with."

Though she thought her surprise spent, Pity felt the breath go out of her again. "How—" She shook her head. "Take me back to Casimir. *Now*."

"You're in no position to make demands. Where is he?"

"Nowhere you can get to him."

The bounty hunter chuckled. "You might be surprised. I'm not going to ask again. That young man is a very large payday, and even Joanna Jones's daughter won't be keeping me from it."

"Too late," Pity snapped. "He's already been sold away. Or at least he was until Selene took him captive."

"Shit." The amusement fled from Siena's face. "So Selene found out Sheridan was planning to snatch a treasure out from beneath her nose?"

"You know about Sheridan?"

"Of course," said Siena. "He hired me to help get the boy safely back to his parents."

"You're *helping* him?" Pity fought the stiffness in her limbs, pushing herself up with the power of rage. "Betraying Olivia and everyone in Casimir for money? Don't you care about what's going to happen to them?"

Siena blinked at her. "What are you talking about? Sheridan's paying me for control and transport—that's it."

Pity deflated at the honest confusion in Siena's face. She fell back in her seat, exhausted. *You were ready to betray them all, too,* she reminded herself. Maybe her reason was better than greed, but that wouldn't matter to the folks caught in the crossfire.

"He contacted me while I was after Daneko," Siena continued. "Said to let him know when I was headed back to Cessation, that he had a sensitive retrieval job for me there. Didn't much care to tread on Selene's toes, but the price was right. I was supposed to keep an eye on the boy and be ready to move when Sheridan was." She paused. "Suddenly that doesn't sound like the wisest deal I've ever made. How sideways is this, kid?"

"Very." Pity closed her eyes. Siena Bond, another one of Sheridan's pawns. Drawing the lines was getting easier: while Daneko and Casimir's traitors solidified their control of Cessation, Sheridan and Siena would finish the trade with Drakos-Pryce. "Those Tin Men weren't Selene's, not anymore. I was trying to warn her when they got me."

She let the story spill out of her, revealing the truth behind the botched assassination and Sheridan's new plans, and praying that Siena would see the urgency of the situation. She was a part of Casimir, too, in her own way.

When Pity was done, Siena reached behind the seat and

brought out a bottle of bourbon. She took a long swallow, then offered it over. "Want a draw?"

Pity shook her head. "Were you listening to what I just said?"

"I heard you." Siena took another sip. "I never thought I'd be around to see the day when Selene's ship sinks, but it sounds like she's got some rats on board, all right. Big ones, too."

"But we can stop everything if we go back now!" Beyond the windshield, the horizon was a steadily growing blaze.

"Oh, I'm going back," said Siena. "But what happens to Casimir isn't my concern. I've got a job to finish. Your boyfriend is still worth a lot of currency. Though I think I won't be splitting it with Sheridan anymore. I'm not partial to being used like that."

Pity gritted her teeth. "To hell with you, then!"

Siena's lips thinned sourly. "Well, you got your mother's mouth, that's for sure. Look, if you want to play the hero and try to save Selene, that's fine by me. But I'm collecting my bounty one way or another. From what you're saying, I need to get Max out of Casimir quick. You can go along with that or not."

Frustration gripped Pity with more force than the fading paralytic had. *This doesn't change anything. You were going to get Max away from Sheridan; you'll find a way to get him away from Siena, too.* But doubt rose in her like the growing dawn. "You'll never get him out in time, not now."

"Oh, I think I might." Siena lit another cigarette, exhaling a milky cloud that glowed with the dawn. "But I don't think you're gonna be keen on how."

CHAPTER 39

PITY'S STRENGTH RETURNED, AS SIENA HAD PROMISED.

Not that it mattered, she mused, feeling the tension of her restraints with every bump and shimmy of the vehicle. She was bound, wrist and ankle, and a thick strip of cotton was lashed across her mouth so she couldn't cry out. Her guns were gone, in Siena's possession now. And the arsenal a few feet away might have been across the world; a chain around one foot kept her tethered to the cot.

It's all come apart at the seams.

A day ago she was trading kisses and promises of later with Max. It felt as if a month had gone by since then, and every minute that passed was one less chance to stop the approaching danger. Was the Reformationist camp stirring yet, making preparations for their unwittingly insidious march later that morning? And what about Casimir? How many of her friends were awake?

How many would be dead before the sun went down?

She glared at the back of Siena's head. The bounty hunter was whistling, a cheerful tune that got under Pity's skin like a flensing knife. She would have told Siena to shut the hell up if she could. She would have said a lot of things to Siena Bond.

"MMMmmmmm!"

"Calm down. We're almost there."

Pity went slack and stared at the ceiling. Was Max doing the same, in whatever cell Selene had him in? Part of her anger belonged to him as well. *Edwin Kyros*...No, that wasn't it. Whatever his name was, he'd failed to tell her the full truth. She was going to let him have a piece of her mind, too, when she got the chance.

If she got the chance.

Suddenly, the world dipped and the light in the vehicle changed. They stopped. Siena climbed in back, Pity's gun belt slung over her shoulder. She carried a bit of black cloth in one hand.

"Sorry 'bout this, kid," Siena said, and she pulled a hood over Pity's head.

Darkness, again. The bounty hunter unlocked her chains and led her from the vehicle.

Pity inhaled and exhaled as slowly as she could, the air inside the hood humid as they crossed the garage, not to the elevator this time but to a door. Pity heard the hinges as the door swung open and then shut behind them.

"Mmmm-hmmm."

"I know where to go," said Siena. "Not too many places in Casimir I ain't been."

Pity worried the gag between her teeth. Her heart was a hammer in her chest. She counted her steps to try to stay calm. *One, two, three...* Just like her shots in the Theatre. *Four, five, six...* Her heartbeat began to slow. She told herself to think of Max and how each step brought her closer to him. Wherever they were going, it was deeper than the garage and Max's room. Somewhere none of Casimir's own would wander into, much less patrons.

Somewhere no screams would be heard.

They stopped. Pity heard a fist bang against a metal door.

"Open up," called Siena.

A sliding sound was followed by another voice. "Ms. Bond? I'm sorry, I wasn't told you were coming."

"Let me in. I have a prisoner I need to lock up for a spell. Dangerous one."

There was an air of hesitation. "This isn't a good time—"

"Oh, are you havin' a tea party in there?" Siena banged on the door again. "You wanna call Beau on down and we can all lift a cup while you explain why I had to wait out here so damn long?"

"No, ma'am—"

"Then open the hell up."

Pity began to think the guard would turn them away, but then she heard hinges squeal.

Siena jabbed her in the shoulder. "Welcome to the tombs. Now move!"

Inside, Pity's blood began to pulse again. It was lucky she

was gagged or else she would have started calling for Max then and there.

"Your prisoner doesn't look very dangerous."

Pity turned her head toward the sound. The guard was no more than a few feet away.

"Not now, but she's not someone you'd want to meet with a gun in her hand."

Siena ripped the hood off. Pity blinked at the light, her vision clearing in time to see the bewildered look on the guard's face. Over his shoulder, the line of cells that made up the tombs ran down a dimly lit hall.

"But that's—"

"Serendipity Jones, fastest shot in the west," Siena said. "Or whatever nonsense it is that Halcyon likes to spew. Thing is, she ain't so fast right now."

The guard stared at Pity, perplexed. She gave him the best grin she could manage through the gag.

"But I am." Siena thrust a shock stick into the guard's gut. He doubled over and crumpled to the floor.

"Mmmmmm!" Pity struggled against her restraints.

"Hold on!" Siena checked the guard, then shoved the shock stick back into the satchel she carried. She pulled a knife from her belt. "Don't move."

Pity felt the cold touch of the blade against her cheek as it sliced the gag away. She spit. "I still don't see why that was necessary."

"I said you got Joanna's mouth, didn't I? Didn't trust you to keep quiet and not blow it."

Siena cut the ropes around her wrists. The moment she was free Pity bolted down the hall.

"Max?" she called. "Max!"

The first five cells were empty.

"Pity?" In the sixth, a pair of hands appeared on the bars.

"Max!" She laughed and wrapped her hands around his. There were dark circles under his eyes, which brimmed with confusion, but otherwise he appeared fine. The anger she felt about the piecemeal truth of his past evaporated. "Are you okay? Are you hurt?"

"No, but..." His gaze darted over her. "What's going on? No one would tell me anything or let me talk to Santino or Halcyon or—"

"It's my fault!" She tightened her grip on him. "Sheridan was leaving and...Selene threatened..." Pity hesitated. "Sheridan betrayed her. She threatened to put you in a Finale if I didn't go along and kill him."

Max's features twisted with disbelief. "Selene wouldn't do that. *She wouldn't.*"

"She would and she did," Pity said. "But that's not our biggest problem right now. Daneko wasn't the one behind the assassination attempt, *Sheridan* was. And his forces are gonna storm Casimir and take it and...and...Santino is in on it, Max. Him and others, I don't know who."

Max jerked toward the bars, blood draining from his cheeks. "When?"

Pity felt a brief fluttering of pride that he didn't question her at all. "Any time now. Siena—hurry up with the damn door!"

"That's why you got the gag!" came the reply.

But a moment later the cell door clicked and slid open. Pity threw her arms around Max, burying her face in his neck before raising her mouth to his. The taste of him briefly washed away the fear, filling her with desperate warmth.

"Save it for later, Jones!"

They broke apart.

Siena stood outside the cell, dangling Pity's gun belt in one hand. "I give these back, we gonna have a problem?"

"Not so long as we're in Casimir. Beyond that, I can't promise anything."

Siena smirked but tossed her the weapons. "I'll take my chances."

"What did you say about my mother?" She strapped the belt on. "As good as anyone with twice her years?"

"Look, I don't know if you realize this," Max interjected, "but I've been locked in a cell for the past day. Invasion aside, what else did I miss?"

Pity opened her mouth and then closed it again, not knowing the right words. "Max..."

"Or is it Maximillian? Or Edwin? Or Khristos?" Siena said. "That's a lot of names, even for a rich boy."

Max wavered, his whole body seeming to go slack. Pity grabbed his arm to steady him as he stared at Siena, his face ashen.

"Sheridan made a deal with Drakos-Pryce," Pity explained. "The presidency...for you."

For a moment, Max looked like he was going to be sick. Then anger flashed across his features, there and gone like summer lightning.

"Decision time, Jones." Siena put a hand on the sawed-off shotgun holstered at her hip. "You coming or not? We can't linger here any longer, and I want to be gone before the bullets start flying upstairs."

Max shivered once before finding his voice. "No. We can't go."

"I'm not in the habit of leaving that choice to my bounties," said Siena.

Pity took his hand in hers. "I'm not gonna let her take you back there. I swear."

Max raised her hand and placed it over his heart. "Yes, you are. I'm sorry, Pity, but sooner or later this was going to happen."

"No!"

He ignored her and turned to Siena. "I'll come with you, willingly, but only if we go to Selene first. No word about my parents. We warn her and Beau, and then we leave. Pity comes with us, and on the way we get her somewhere she'll be safe. You got that, Pity?"

"I sure as hell do not!" She ripped her hand away. The look on his face splintered her hopes of escape into shards, which buried themselves in her heart. "So that's it? You're just gonna give in?"

"No," said Siena. "He's making the best play he can, given the circumstances. Fine. You're still no one. I suppose I can make Selene understand that Pity was half out of her mind with love when she broke you out of here. Me? I was only going along with an old friend's daughter to make sure she didn't make a mess of things."

"No!" cried Pity. "No, I do not agree to this!"

Siena ignored her. "But you stray one inch from my sight and the deal's off. Understand?"

"No, he doesn't!"

"Please, Pity." Max kissed her again. "I'm sorry."

"The hell you are!" She balled her fists, nails biting into her flesh. "The hell with both of you!"

Siena sniffed. "Before you really do lose your mind, maybe I should point out that my job ends the moment I deliver Mr. Pryce here back to his parents. After that, no reason you two lovebirds can't be together, so long as you don't mind being together back east."

"No reason?" Pity surged out of the cell, fury emanating from her so thickly that even Siena Bond moved aside. "Then maybe you should ask Mr. Pryce what happened to his last girlfriend."

They locked the guard in an empty cell and returned to the basement tunnels. Siena brought up the rear, keeping Max in her sights as he trailed Pity. Every time he got close to her, she quickened her step, refusing to look at him.

He touched her arm. "Pity, c'mon. Talk to me."

"There's nothing to talk about." She stepped out of his reach. "We need to hurry."

Max grimaced, matching his pace to hers. "I know you don't understand, but I only want you to be safe."

Pity stopped and shoved him away. "*Safe?* I was ready to do anything—*anything*—in order to keep you safe. And it doesn't mean a damn thing because I'm gonna lose you anyway. *That's what I understand.*"

Max's eyes searched hers, too surprised to fight back.

"Not the time," Siena warned.

"Time for what?"

They turned to the new voice. A few yards away, at an intersection of tunnels, stood Luster.

"Shit," said Siena.

Pity stepped away from Max. "What are you doing down here?"

"I've been looking for you two!" She stalked over to them. "You never came back after Adora fetched you, and then Max disappeared, too, but neither of you were in your rooms last night!" She paused, looking nervously at the bounty hunter. "I got a bad feeling. I was checking Max's again."

Pity locked eyes with Siena.

"Rats on the ship," said the bounty hunter, easing a hand into her satchel.

Pity's pulse quickened. There was no way to know whom Sheridan had gotten to. *No, not Luster.* She wouldn't believe it. Luster loved Casimir as much as anyone. She would never endanger it.

You would have said the same thing about Santino a few hours ago, she reminded herself.

The gun was out of her holster in a heartbeat. Luster shrieked as Pity threw her against the wall and pressed the barrel to her shoulder. "Whose side are you on?"

"What? Pity, why are you—"

"Whose...side...are you on?" The words boiled out. She moved the gun so that it was pointed at Luster's temple.

"Stop!" Max lunged at them, but Siena held him back. "What are you—?"

"Quiet, Max." This time Pity's voice was deathly calm. Luster's terrified face floated in her vision, tears streaking down her glittering cheeks. "Tell me whose side you're on."

Luster trembled. Her mouth opened to speak, but nothing came out. The silence dragged on until finally, a specter of a word escaped from between her lips: "Yours."

Pity's arm went limp. The gun fell to her side and she stepped back, anger smothered. A bone-deep desire to sit down right where she was blossomed, to close her eyes and pretend the last twenty-four hours had been a nightmare.

Luster raised a hand to her mouth but remained rooted in place, her eyes wide and wet.

"That doesn't mean much," said Siena.

"I know." In that moment Pity didn't think she could have raised her gun again if she tried. Luster was her friend. As foolish as it was after everything she had learned, it was a truth Pity refused to let go of. "But it means enough."

She holstered her weapon and grabbed Luster by the shoulders. "Listen to me and don't ask any questions. Go find Garland and Duchess, and then the three of you hole up in your room. Go fast, and don't stop to talk to anyone. Do you hear me? Anyone!"

Luster's face crumpled with fear. "Why, what's—"

"There's no time to explain." Pity squeezed tighter. "Barricade the door and don't open it for anyone. Not the Tin Men, not Santino, not anyone except for one of us or Selene herself. No matter what you hear. Promise me."

"I..." Luster nodded. "I promise."

Pity began to let her go, then wrapped her arms around her friend and hugged tight. *I'm not losing everyone,* she thought. *I refuse.* "Go," she ordered again.

They waited until Luster's delicate footsteps were out of earshot.

"You better hope she's not scampering off to Sheridan," Siena said.

"She's not." Pity prayed it was true. "Let's go."

They came to a stairwell and ascended. A few floors up, Pity ducked her head out into a hall. "It's clear."

"Are we going through the Gallery?" Max whispered.

"No." She thought for a moment, trying to orient herself. "We can't. Sheridan said the Gallery was taken care of. It's a good bet the Tin Men there now are Santino's. We have to go the other way, through Selene's rooms. Down here."

They came to the long hall. As soon as Pity saw the first door, she swore.

"I don't suppose you have the codes," Siena said.

Stupid. In her panic, she had forgotten all about the locks. Fighting the urge to slam her fists against the thick steel, she searched for a solution. But she was no engineer. *Should have paid better attention during all those hours with Finn in her workshop.*

Max punched in a few combinations at random. Each was met with an angry flash of red. "We can turn back, go through—"

"No." An idea materialized. "Siena, give me your bag."

The bounty hunter raised an eyebrow but handed it over. Pity fished out the shock stick, said a silent prayer, and jammed it into the keypad. There was a flash and a hiss, followed by a spray of sparks. Then a heavy clunk. Max grabbed the handle.

The door opened.

Not quite as elegant as what Finn could have done, but…

"Not bad, Jones." Siena herded them both through, into the hall with the second door. Pity repeated the process but hesitated before the third.

"There's a pair of guards on the other side," she whispered. "We don't know whose side they're on."

"Not ours." Siena pulled out a pair of tranquilizer guns. "Pity, lock. Max, you get the door. I'll take care of the guards. Ready on three. One, two…three!"

Zzzzt. Click.

Max yanked the door open.

Thwip. Thwip.

Thud. Thud.

Pity peeked around the corner. The two guards lay motionless on the floor, tiny darts protruding from their necks. Beyond them, the elevator doors stood open.

"Last chance to get out of here," Siena said to Pity. "Assuming they're trustworthy, your friends are probably safe by now. No need to risk a fight if it can be avoided."

Pity felt temptation's barbs under her skin, but Max seemed to sense her thoughts.

"No, we see this through," he said. "Or you can forget about me coming quietly."

Siena toed one of the drugged guards pointedly but stashed

her tranquilizer guns. "A deal's a deal," she said. "Best not come up on Selene with weapons drawn. Beau has always been one to shoot first and ask questions later."

The elevator seemed to move slower than Pity remembered, the hum of the hydraulics the only sound as each floor came and went. *Almost there,* she told herself. *It's not too late…it can't be.* Selene would hear them out, and then Casimir would turn the tables on Sheridan's borrowed mercenaries. She prayed that the Reformationists hadn't decided to march early.

The elevator shuddered and stopped. A moment later the doors opened, revealing Selene's living room.

But there was no Selene.

Adora sat on one of the couches, her back rigid. She looked over as the three of them spilled into the room.

Halcyon stood behind her, a gun leveled at her head.

CHAPTER 40

PITY DREW.

"Don't!" Halcyon's arm stiffened, his normally jovial face sagging with panic.

Fingers on the triggers, Pity aimed one gun at Halcyon and the other at Adora.

"Which one of you?" Her gaze swept back and forth. "Which one of you is a traitor?"

Halcyon didn't answer, his brow beaded with sweat.

Adora scoffed. "You know, I really thought you had half a brain in that country head. Max, you want to tell your girlfriend not to shoot me, please?"

"Don't listen to her!" Halcyon found his voice. "Lower your weapons...uh, please!"

"Lower yours." Siena stepped into Pity's peripheral vision,

her shotgun raised. "If you ain't a traitor, then we've got her plenty covered."

When he didn't move, Pity felt a sick slither in her stomach.

"Boss, please." The pleading grief in Max's voice made the feeling worse. "Halcyon, put down the gun."

Halcyon's jaw tightened. "I can't."

"You lying, conniving son of a bitch!" Pity was moving before she knew it, descending the steps to the sunken floor, advancing on Halcyon. "How could you?"

He retreated back several steps and swung his weapon toward Pity. "Don't come any closer!"

"How could you?" She stopped a few feet away, both barrels trained on him. First Santino and now Halcyon. The betrayal seared like a hot iron.

"This wasn't supposed to happen," he said, his words weak. "You're supposed to be...Max...I...." He trailed off.

"What is he talking about?" Max said.

Realization came to Pity in a flash of orange. *The notes.* "He means this wasn't his part in the plan. We were supposed to be in the theatre this morning. I'm right, aren't I? You were going to get Max and me together and then deliver us to Siena, weren't you? Max so Sheridan could fulfill his deal and me so he had a way to force Max to cooperate."

He didn't respond, but the truth was painted on his features. "I—"

"You better be about to speak one hell of an explanation."

The gun dropped an inch. Halcyon smiled, sad and sheepish. "The Theatre," he said simply. "I only wanted to share it with the world. I wanted to share *you* with the world, Pity—you and the rest of them. Selene refused to acquiesce, but Sheridan, he promised me..."

Pity holstered one of her weapons and closed the gap between them, grabbing Halcyon's wrist and twisting the gun out of his grasp. It fell to the couch as she brought up the butt of her other gun, smashing it into his face. He cried out and fell to the steps. Blood gushed from his nose.

"Pity, dammit!" Max appeared beside her. "That was the stupidest thing I've ever—"

"He wasn't gonna pull the trigger," she said icily, staring down at Halcyon. "Even if he had the guts to do it, he wouldn't shoot one of his best acts. He betrayed Selene for the Theatre."

Halcyon groaned. Red dripped over the lower half of his face and onto his suit.

"Well, aren't you clever." Adora picked up the gun beside her like it was a dead rat and tossed it to Siena, who added it to her arsenal.

"You're welcome!" spat Pity. "What did he tell you?"

"Nothing. He arrived a few minutes ago, pulled a gun on me, and told me not to move. I listened." A perturbed expression tempered Adora's manner. "But Daneko—"

"What about him?"

"Daneko supposedly said he needed to see Selene right away—something important about Patrick Sheridan's departure, but he'd only tell her." Adora eyed one of the doors, a tinge of apprehension creeping into her voice. "They were bringing him up from his cell."

"Does that open into Selene's office?"

"Yes."

"We need to get to her first. Casimir is about to be attacked. Get up!" Pity ordered Halcyon, who obeyed reluctantly. "Siena, Beau or not, Santino might be in there already..."

"And we're not going in like fools." The bounty hunter smirked. "You don't need to tell me how to take a room, Jones."

They went to the door. Adora paused in front of it, her hand on the knob.

Pity readied herself. "Halcyon, you next. Don't you make a peep, either, *boss*."

"I harly thing I neeh to." He pressed an orange handkerchief, now mostly crimson, to his broken nose.

"Shut up. Siena and I will follow you. Max, stay in back."

Behind her, she heard him take an apprehensive breath and let it out. He put a hand on her back—a simple touch, familiar and reassuring. The memory of him, his arms around her, the feeling of his lips on hers...Her muscles threatened to give out. Pity gritted her teeth and stood straighter.

Now was not the time to lose her steel.

Adora opened the door and went through. Halcyon followed, and then she and Siena, smooth as dance partners, their guns raised.

Pity had only heartbeats to take in the scene. Selene sat at her desk, Beau and Santino to one side of her. Daneko was on his knees in front of the desk, hands chained behind his back, with a trio of Tin Men for guards.

And behind Daneko, with Hook, was Sheridan. His hands were tucked in his pockets, a disarming grin frozen on his face.

Whatever was being said faded like the last notes of a song.

Beau.

Pity turned to him and their gazes locked. His eyes bore into hers. Her muscles tensed. Fast as lightning, he pulled his gun—

—and aimed it at Sheridan. "Nobody m—"

There was a hollow crack as Santino brought his shock stick down on Beau's head. He collapsed, gun flying from his fingers and across the dark marble. Pity sucked in a fearful breath as Adora bolted to Selene's side. In unison, Hook and the Tin Men pointed their weapons at Pity and Siena.

"Hold your fire! No one fires a shot without my say-so." Sheridan's command carried easy, presumptuous authority. For the first time Pity clearly saw the man who had fooled them emerge. "Everyone just...relax. You two as well," he said to Pity and Siena.

"Yes," said Selene. "Everyone contain themselves and tell me right now what is—"

"Shut up, Selene," said Sheridan.

No one moved, save for Beau. Facedown and dazed, he tried to push himself up. Sheridan pointed and Santino raised his stick again, bringing it down in a wide arc. It connected with Beau's calf. Even from across the room, Pity could hear the wet snap. Beau screamed.

"Santino!" Selene yelled. "Stop! Stop right now!"

Santino ignored her, his attention on Beau, who was still trying to rise. "Stay down, jefe."

His club fell once more, breaking Beau's other leg. This time he didn't scream, only let out a strangled bark, and fell to the floor, still. Santino grabbed Beau's wrist, pulled off the alarm band, and threw it away.

"You..." Selene's voice was pure acid. She started for Santino, but Adora stopped her.

"If she reaches for her console, put a bullet in her," Sheridan instructed the Tin Men. "Well, this is *not* how I planned things to play out. Put your guns away—now. And raise your hands."

"Not a chance," said Pity.

"Do it, Jones." Siena lowered her weapon, placing it at her feet. "We're outgunned here."

Sheridan grinned. "Wise. But I suppose a bounty hunter with your years would be. Listen to her, Pity."

Defeated, her arms felt like iron as she slid her guns back into their holsters and put up her hands.

"Thank you." Sheridan sighed and shook his head, pointing. "You...you are trying, Pity. All you had to do was leave quietly. I wasn't even mad when you changed your mind—I can forgive an emotional moment. But instead of going along with my men you had to—"

"Going along?" Hot rage coursed through her. "They drugged me!"

"Serendipity." Selene's voice sliced through the charged air, quiet but imposing. "What did you change your mind about?"

Pity nodded at the gang leader. "Sheridan was working with Daneko all along. He's behind the attempt to kill you, and now he's trying to take over Casimir. He..." She faltered. "He promised to free Max if I helped him."

Selene's expression didn't change, but frigid fury radiated off her. She turned to Daneko. "I assume this is the 'vital information' about Sheridan that you were about to confess?"

A sly smile slit the gang leader's face as Santino approached him and unlocked his chains. As he stood, one of the Tin Men passed him a handgun. "Close enough. Oh, Selene, I have pictured this moment a thousand times while I suffered pretending to be your prisoner. Your reign is over."

"He's right." Sheridan went and picked up Beau's weapon. "Cessation is mine now, Selene."

"Ours," said Daneko.

"Of course. Even now, *our* forces are approaching. In a short time, Casimir will be under our control."

Selene scoffed. "Even if you kill me, you couldn't hold it for a day."

"Oh, I'm not alone." Sheridan beckoned Halcyon, who slunk over, never once looking in Selene's direction. "I've got the Theatre Vespertine. And I've got a new head of security, who in turn has enough Tin Men to allow my forces access to Casimir. Which will happen any minute now."

Selene's face hardened.

"It's true," Pity said. She let her hands drop a few inches as she spoke. "They're marching now, hidden among the Reformationists."

"And when that's done, Daneko will take your place, and I will return east to claim mine."

He glanced at Pity, as if daring her to reveal Max's secret. As if it mattered now. Her jaw clenched, but she said nothing.

"Enough," said Daneko. "Kill her."

"No!" cried Adora.

"Oh, relax," Sheridan said. "Nothing needs to change for you, Adora. I know value when I see it. Step away from Selene, and you can keep your position. That's a pretty good offer, isn't it?"

Adora crossed her arms. "Mr. Sheridan, you can take that offer and shove it up your—"

"Take it, Adora," Selene said, too calm. "Say yes. It's a good deal."

Pity didn't miss the note of resignation the words carried. Adora's impassive visage shifted to angry confusion.

"No," she said.

"Take it," Selene commanded.

"I said no!"

"Here," said Sheridan. "Let me make the decision a little easier for you." He raised the gun and fired.

Adora lunged to push Selene out of the way, but a fraction of a second too late. The spray of bullets tore through both of them, their bodies tumbling to the floor in a bloody tangle. Adora's head lolled to the side. She coughed once, a bubble of blood forming on her lips before she went as still as Selene beneath her.

The world turned static gray, like the moments before a bad storm. Pity's ears buzzed. She blinked and the buzzing turned to screams.

Beau. His ghostly pale face was twisted with horror. He reached for Selene, still yelling.

"Good Lord—Santino!" Sheridan cried. "Shut him up."

Santino pulled out his knife.

Pity dropped her arms and drew.

She fired twice before she had a chance to think, or to aim. Santino's shoulder and side exploded in crimson. He cried out and dropped the knife, which fell beside Beau. In the corner of her eye, she saw Daneko raise his weapon. The shot rang out as Max collided with her, knocking her to her knees.

No. Daneko had missed her, but she felt the bullet hit anyway, a shard of terror right through her heart.

"You idiot!" Sheridan screamed.

"Shit!" said Siena.

The bounty hunter dove on her shotgun and came up firing. She caught one of the Tin Men in the chest. Through tears, Pity saw Halcyon's purple form dart away as Hook shoved Sheridan behind him. She unloaded one revolver in their direction, hardly looking where she fired. The other arm she wrapped around Max, who lay on his back, a ruby stain spreading across his gut.

She heard a second shotgun blast and a scream, and then Siena was beside her.

"Move, Jones!" she screamed, grabbing the collar of Max's shirt.

Siena dragged him behind the desk as Pity drew her other gun and covered them. Bullets whizzed like angry wasps as Hook, Daneko, and the remaining Tin Man fired at them. Pity took aim. An instant later Daneko's gun went flying, scarlet strings of meat where his thumb had been.

"Ahhh!" Pity felt a line of pain blaze up her arm as she tumbled behind the desk.

"You hit?" Siena was on one knee reloading, her head low.

"A graze." She gritted her teeth, filtering out the pain. All she could see was Max propped up against the desk. She scrambled beside him, boots skidding on the dark, bloody marble. His chest was rising and falling with rapid breaths, his face blanched.

"You stupid—" Her voice hitched. "Why did you do that?"

Max gave her a weak grin. "Do I really need to answer?"

She ripped his shirt away to reveal an angry hole leaking blood.

No.

"We have to stop that!" Siena drew a handgun and fired around the desk. "Here!" She reached into her bag and pulled out a square packet. "You know how to apply a field dressing?"

Hands trembling, Pity grabbed the packet and tore it open. She positioned the patch over the gunshot and pressed down.

"Uggnnn!" Max's head drooped, eyelids fluttering.

Pity slapped him. "Don't you dare! Stay awake!"

Max's gaze came back into focus. He lifted one hand and put it on top of hers, where they pressed against his stomach. "I'll hold it."

"No!" She kept her hands where they were.

"Yes!" snapped Siena. "Get those guns reloaded and firing or that patch job won't mean a damn thing."

Reluctantly, Pity pulled away, wiping her palms on her pants. When she wrapped them around the ebony handles again, they stopped shaking. Siena was right. Max's only chance lay with them getting out of this.

Pity reloaded her guns and peeked around the desk. She was on the side farthest from Sheridan and the others, with no line of sight. A few yards away lay Adora's and Selene's bodies, Beau and Santino beyond them.

Somehow Beau had gotten on top of the injured Santino, who was trying to shake him off. Beau's face was as gray as old ash, but he hung on. One arm was hooked around the bigger man's neck. The other held Santino's knife. As Pity watched,

Beau plunged the blade into its owner's neck. A grisly fountain erupted. Santino bucked once more and went limp, red spreading around him as Beau slid off. Before she could tell if he was still conscious or not, she saw a rustle of movement in the foreground of her vision.

Selene. Pinned beneath Adora, she stirred briefly before going still again.

Pity pulled back behind the desk. "Selene's not dead."

Siena laughed, firing wildly. "Not yet."

Desperate, Pity squeezed off a few shots over the top of the desk. "We're pinned. What do we do now?"

"Well," Siena said, "I think a prayer wouldn't be amiss."

CHAPTER 41

MAX FOUGHT FOR EACH BREATH. THE ONLY COLOR left in his face was the silver of his piercings.

Pity reloaded again. *Lord, if you're listening, please...*

"We're not dying here," she said aloud. "Not in this damn office!"

"The minute we pop up from behind here, they're gonna unload on us. Four against two." Siena snuck a look. "Five. They gave Halcyon a weapon."

"Four and a half, then," said Pity. "And Daneko will be shooting left-handed." She paused. "Not the worst odds."

"Not the best, either." Siena wiped at her brow with the back of one hand. "Though none of them are crack shots."

"With a little luck, we might be able to..."

"Yeah." Siena checked her clips. "Not like we've got much choice."

"No," said Max. "Pity, don't."

"You need help," she said. "We can't wait."

Sheridan's voice boomed out like a crack of thunder. "Pity!" he yelled. "It doesn't have to end like this. Throw out your weapons and come out with your hands up. I promise you won't be harmed."

"Horseshit!" Siena answered. "Why don't you throw down *your* weapons instead?"

Sheridan ignored her. "How's Max? You know I want him alive as much as you do, Pity. All you have to do is come out."

Pity pressed the grips of her guns to her temples. "We can't trust him," she said quietly. "Siena..."

"No," Max pleaded.

"On three," said Siena. "One..."

Pity gripped her guns tighter. *Twelve shots,* she thought. *Make every one count.*

"Two..."

The door to Selene's suite flew open. No one came through, but from their vantage point, Pity could see Olivia and a cluster of Tin Men a few steps within. Olivia brandished a pair of flash grenades, then pulled the pins and arced them through the doorway toward Sheridan and the bodyguards.

Pity threw herself down beside Max. She squeezed her eyes closed and covered her ears as twin explosions rocked the room. She scrambled up a moment later, ready to fire, only to lurch to one side, disoriented by the shock waves. She steadied herself in time to see the elevator door closing beyond a haze of smoke. Sheridan, Daneko, and the others were inside.

Olivia ran into the office, her rifle raised.

Pity swung around. "Stop where you are!"

Olivia pointed her weapon at the floor. "Don't! Rifles down, all of you," she ordered the Tin Men behind her. "Pity, we're here to help."

"How did you know we were here? And how do we know you're not with Sheridan, too?"

"Luster. She said you told her not to trust anyone, but she knew about my time with Siena, so she came to me."

"Relax, Jones." Siena holstered her weapon. "You vouched for your girl, and I'm vouching for Olivia."

"What about them?" Pity indicated the guards behind her. "Santino's turned some of the Tin Men. Those two over there were with him!"

Olivia's eyes went wide at Santino's name, her mouth dropping open in protest. But it closed when she spotted his body. She went over to the dead Tin Men. "These were Santino's men, all right, brought on by him in the last six months, no more. Everyone with me has been with Casimir for years." Her voice thickened. "Shit...Santino."

"He's dead!" Pity shoved her guns back into her belt. "And we need to get Max to Doc Starr!" She returned to his side. Her heart skipped a beat when she saw that his eyes were closed, but they fluttered open and fixed on her. "Hold on," she said. "Just a little while longer."

"For you?" Max winced as Siena got an arm under him. "Sure, why not. Selene...is she?"

"Check her!" Pity cried. "She was moving a minute ago. Beau's alive, too, and..." She froze.

Selene was sitting up, Adora's body cradled in her lap, her face half buried in the young woman's hair. Their respective masks of rigid confidence and casual indifference were gone, and for the first time, Pity saw the resemblance that had been hidden beneath them. Adora must have looked more like her father, but it was there nonetheless.

Her eyes met Selene's.

We do learn so much from our mothers. Selene had said that at their first meeting, hadn't she?

The mask returned. She held a hand on her neck, and one side of her was soaked with blood from at least two more wounds Pity could see.

"Help her!" Olivia ordered two of the Tin Men.

Pity turned back to Max. Siena and another Tin Man had him standing, but the patch on his stomach was soaked through. He raised his head weakly. Pity went to him, grabbed his face in her hands, and kissed him. Hard. She lingered there, on lips colder than they should be, terrified to break away.

It felt too much like a kiss good-bye.

"Pity," he whispered when they broke apart. "If Sheridan is working with my—with *them*..."

"I know."

"Go. Stop him," said Max.

"Don't die on me."

"I won't if you won't."

Pity smiled, unable to keep the tears from leaking out. Then she stepped back and drew her guns again. "I'm going after Sheridan. His forces are still coming. If we can get him, maybe we can make him call off the attack." She started toward the elevator. "Siena?"

The bounty hunter shook her head. "This ain't my business anymore—he is. Oh, don't look so hurt. I'm gonna keep hell from coming for him if I gotta fight it myself. This bounty's too good to lose."

"Fine," she snapped. "I'll go alone!"

"Not alone." Olivia fell in beside her.

Pity nodded at her. "You keep him safe," she called back to Siena.

"Serendipity," Selene croaked.

They paused. Selene had her good arm slung around a Tin Man, who was working to apply dressings to her wounds. Pity waited, but Selene didn't say anything. She didn't need to. Adora lying at her feet was enough.

In the elevator, Olivia checked her rifle as they descended, each floor they passed beeping quietly, like a slow heartbeat. "What was that about Max and a bounty?"

"I don't want to talk about it." Pity busied herself by inspecting the wound on her arm. Blood oozed and it burned like hellfire, but she could manage. "The guards on the front doors are probably Sheridan's, too."

"Maybe," said Olivia, "but you didn't think I ran to your rescue without raising the alarm, did you? Casimir should be on lockdown by now."

As they got closer to the Gallery, faint pops echoed.

"Ah, shit," said Olivia. "I guess I was a little too late."

They spun to opposite sides of the elevator as the doors

opened. Bullets sliced through the air where they had just been, piercing the back wall.

Pity slammed a fist into the control panel to keep the doors open. "I'll cover you. Stay low!" She leaned out and fired, glimpsing chaos as Olivia scrambled forward and threw herself behind a gaming table.

A pair of Tin Men—who must have been Sheridan's—had control of the doors at the front of the room and were firing at anyone who approached them. Others, whose side was unclear, were scattered throughout the Gallery, along with prostitutes and patrons and anyone with the misfortune to have gotten caught in the crossfire. Bodies were scattered about. Some were moving; others lay motionless. One man was slumped over a table, a drink in his hand and his head half gone.

Pity took a deep breath. A slurry of scents filled her nostrils: gunpowder, whiskey, blood. Perfume that smelled of lilies. She let it out, then bolted from the elevator. Shots whizzed by her, but the main action was toward the front of the Gallery. What had come at her and Olivia were probably strays, but there was little comfort in that; stray bullets were indiscriminate in their targets.

She tumbled behind an overturned chair a few yards from Olivia.

"What a damn mess!" Olivia aimed her rifle but lowered it before pulling the trigger. "I don't know who I'm supposed to be shooting at!"

"We need to find Sheridan." Pity went first this time, ducking low and weaving through the luxury playground turned battlefield. She slipped behind a booth and then motioned Olivia forward.

"Pity!"

Flossie crouched a few yards away behind a couch. She had a tiny gun in her hand and one leg stretched before her, its lacy stocking streaked with crimson. Mad rivers of makeup ran down her cheeks. Beside her was a trembling young man whose name Pity didn't know. Beyond the safety of their barrier lay Kitty, her eyes wide-open and lifeless.

Pity felt a stab of grief in her gut but pushed it away for later. "Flossie—are you okay?"

"No!" Her bosom heaved with every breath. "What the hell is going on? One minute I see Halcyon, Sheridan, and Daneko come out of Selene's elevator. Not ten seconds later a bunch of Tin Men spill into the Gallery, ordering everyone to stay where they are. Then suddenly everyone is firing at everybody else, like we're in the middle of a damn war!"

"Did Sheridan make it out?"

"No." Flossie wiped at her face, leaving a smear of blood. "He got caught in the middle of the room somewhere. That bodyguard of his is down, though—somebody's shot caught him in the throat."

"We can still get him," Pity called to Olivia.

"Better hurry." Olivia peered over the table she was behind. "The front doors automatically locked when I raised the alarm, but it looks like Sheridan's forces are trying to get in. The doors'll hold, but not forever. If I can get outside with some Tin Men and flank them..."

"Go!" she yelled at Olivia. "I'll take care of Sheridan!"

"On your own?"

"If they break through before you get outside, he's the only one who can call them off." Pity stared at Kitty—the sweet, pretty young woman who had tried to snatch holiday kisses from Duchess. The low burn of anger that had been coursing through her exploded suddenly, fury hot and vicious cold at the same time, and tinged with guilt. If she had gone to Selene sooner, none of this would have happened. Adora was dead. Beau, near enough. And Max…

"I'm not letting him get away. Not after all this." She waved a gun. "Go!"

Olivia eyed the bar. "That's my way out. There's a trapdoor into the tap cellar. Cover me!"

Pity fired, one gun after another, as Olivia sprang up and dashed to the bar. She threw herself over it, bullets turning the polished wood into splinters. Pity aimed in the direction the bullets had come from until her cylinders were empty.

"Y'all keep your heads down, Flossie," she said, reloading. "I need to move."

Flossie brandished her tiny gun. "Be careful!"

Pity ran for a row of marble statues and then weaved toward a cluster of tables. She searched the Gallery, but she couldn't see Sheridan.

No sense in playing it coy. "Patrick Sheridan!" she yelled as loud as she could. "You still alive?"

For a long moment there was silence. No answer, but no gunfire, either. It was as if the whole room held its breath.

Then: "I'm here."

It came from a booth not twenty yards away.

"Tell your men to stop shooting!" She poked one barrel through a gap in the tables, looking for movement.

"Are you going to tell yours to do the same?"

"They're not mine. They're Selene's, remember?" Pity paused. "She's still alive, by the way! You ought to work on your aim."

More quiet followed, and she could hear the sounds of pounding on the front doors and distant gunfire. But in the Gallery there was silence.

"You're lying," Sheridan said finally.

"Nope." She looked around and saw people darting toward the exits, taking advantage of the cease-fire. *Keep him talking. Give them time. Give Olivia time.* "She's alive and pissed off. I don't even want to know what's going to happen once she gets her hands on you." No response. "You thinking about it, Patrick? Maybe if you give up now she'll make it quick—"

A shadow fell upon her.

Daneko. His right hand was wrapped in someone's silk scarf, but his left held a gun, as dark as death itself.

Idiot, she had enough time to think. *Distracted by your own distraction.* Pity raised her weapons, but it was too late, he had the drop on her and—

BOOM.

Daneko went flying backward in a mist of scarlet.

Pity twisted around and found Siena standing nearby, shotgun smoking. She threw herself down beside Pity as gunfire erupted again.

"Good timing!" Cold terror followed relief. "Max! Is he—"

"Still alive?" Siena snapped. "Yes. And irritatingly insistent that you stay that way, too."

"You don't care at all, of course."

"Don't get smart. Where's Liv?"

There was a sudden flurry of activity from the front of the Gallery. A mob of Tin Men flooded in through the front entrance, Olivia at their head. The ones who had held the door all dropped their weapons, save for one, who bolted.

Olivia cut him down before he made it a dozen paces. "We've got them surrounded!"

Pity cried out with triumph, a sound that caught in her throat as she spotted Halcyon and Sheridan disappearing into the halls of Casimir.

CHAPTER 42

PITY WAS IN PURSUIT IN AN INSTANT, NOT PAUSING TO see if it was safe or when Siena yelled after her. She darted through the carnage, leapt over a body, and made it out of the Gallery in time to see the flutter of Halcyon's coattails down a side hallway. She ran to the corner and took a quick look around it. Empty.

She turned and ducked barely in time as Sheridan appeared at the far end. Plaster exploded above her head. Pity righted herself and took aim, but he was already out of sight. She waited a moment, ready, but he didn't show himself again.

She took the next corner more carefully, catching another glimpse of them. Heart beating so hard she felt like it might come out her ears, she trailed them through Casimir's maze of hallways. She thought she heard Siena calling somewhere behind her, but she didn't stop as more gunshots erupted ahead.

A minute later she came across a Tin Man slumped on the floor, a trail of blood on the wall behind him.

She checked for a pulse.

Nothing.

Everyone stay in your rooms, she prayed, continuing after them. Sheridan was desperate now, and there was no telling what a desperate man would do.

The theatre, she realized. That's where they were headed. *Halcyon must have some emergency way out. He'd be a fool not to.*

Cautiousness forgotten, she ran, bursting through the doors of the theatre as the two men reached the arena floor, Halcyon leading.

"Stop!" She propelled herself down the steps, firing a pair of warning shots.

The bullets struck the floor between them. Halcyon kept running, but Sheridan stumbled and fell to the floor.

"Wait!" he cried, but Halcyon disappeared through a door at the edge of the arena, slamming it shut behind him.

As Sheridan scrambled to his feet, Pity took aim again. "Don't mo—"

He spun and fired. Pity dove into the stands, bullets slashing around her. She screamed as her injured shoulder collided with the edge of a seat, the gun flying from her left hand. Razor-sharp pain streaked down her side. She gritted her teeth and searched for the weapon, but it had disappeared among the stands.

Dammit. She tried to lift her arm, but it barely obeyed. One-handed, reloading was almost impossible.

Six shots left.

She flinched as another shot splintered the wood of a seat a few yards away.

"Did I get you, Pity?" Sheridan called.

"'Fraid not." *Sound strong. Don't let him know you're hurt.* "You're not that good of a shot, Patrick." Pity wormed her way down the aisle on her stomach. She had the high ground, but right now he'd pick her off the moment she stood.

"What are you doing here, Pity?" Between the seats, she could see him backing toward the door as he searched for her, face taut with fear. "Why aren't you with Max? That wound looked pretty bad to me. He might be dying right now."

She slid along faster. The end of the aisle, and a better line of sight, was only a few yards away. *He's goading you. Don't listen.* But in her mind she saw the blood seeping out of Max's stomach, his too-pale face. A red haze of anger settled on her. She gripped her gun tighter.

"There might still be time to get to him," Sheridan said. "If you throw down your weapons now and come out, I promise not to shoot."

But he didn't wait for an answer. Reaching the door, he tried to open it.

It was locked.

With a cry of frustration, he turned and fired at the latch.

Pity pushed herself up. In an instant, Sheridan was in her sights.

Inhale, aim . . .

As her finger tightened on the trigger, the haze dissipated. For all that he'd done, for every corpse he'd left in his wake, she couldn't bring herself to shoot him in the back. She stood instead, keeping him in her sights as she tucked her useless arm to her side. "Even if you get that open, where are you going?"

Sheridan swung his weapon back to her. But he didn't fire.

Be careful, said a voice in the back of her head. *He's doesn't have much left to lose.* "Halcyon abandoned you. Do you know a safe way out of Casimir without him?"

Silence answered her question.

"You're not getting out of here, Patrick." Wondering whether she'd lost her mind, Pity holstered her gun and raised her empty hand. "Santino and Daneko are dead. Your mercenaries failed to take Casimir. You've got only one chance left: surrender."

He stared at her, uncomprehending. "I don't understand."

"If Max dies, you're dead, too." The barrel of his gun followed her as she made her way down the stairs. With each step she expected to feel the sharp sting of a bullet through her flesh. But Sheridan didn't move a muscle. "Whether Selene kills you, or you escape somehow and Drakos-Pryce finds out the part you played in his death."

She reached the arena floor and made her way toward him. He mirrored her movements, until they stood in the center of the arena, a dozen paces separating them.

"But if he survives…" She tried to swallow the lump in her throat. "We tell Selene who he is. She can use him as a hostage, force Drakos-Pryce to keep up their endorsement of you."

It was bad coin, but it was all Pity had left to trade. Siena wouldn't be happy, and maybe Max wouldn't, either, but there were worse prisons than Casimir. Assuming he wasn't dead yet.

"Selene wants to protect Cessation," she continued. "That

hasn't changed. And she is nothing if not brutally practical. Offer her that and *maybe* she'll let you live."

Sheridan shook his head. "No…Selene would never trust me."

"She doesn't have to trust you," Pity said. "She only has to control you. Think about it: You still get the presidency. Selene gets you. Max remains in Cessation with me. We'll all have what we want."

"It won't work." But there was something new in his demeanor. Hope, she prayed. "Too many people know I tried to kill Selene."

Her mouth twitched into a smirk. "This is Cessation, remember? Selene's word is law. Folks will go along with whatever she tells them to go along with." She paused. "It's too late to undo what's been done, but maybe you can cut a deal with Selene and still do some good, like we talked about. Become president. Protect Cessation, stop the raids on the dissident settlements, give the former Patriots a voice in the—"

Sheridan laughed. Pity stiffened as he leveled his gun at her head. "I knew you were gullible, but do you still believe all that nonsense? To hell with the Patriots and whatever scraps of them are left. The war is over. They lost. And the only useful thing that ever came out of their continued defiance was Cessation." A desperate, manic smile split his face. "But you're right about one thing. Selene *is* my only option now."

Her skin crawled with terror as he took a step forward, eyes like daggers. "I'll take my chances with her, but not with you. Not again." His voice dropped to a hiss. "And just between us, I'm finished with this place. If I do make it back to Columbia alive, I want you to know that the first thing I'm going to do is convince Drakos-Pryce to raze this entire godforsaken city to the ground."

He pulled the trigger.

A white-hot tremor of terror surged through her, so encompassing that caustic moments passed before Pity realized no pain accompanied it.

Sheridan tried again.

Nothing.

Slowly, deliberately, Pity drew her own gun, never taking her eyes off him. "You should have kept better count of your shots."

Sheridan tossed the weapon away. "I guess so."

"Me?" Her voice sounded distant as she aimed her barrel at his chest, like someone else was speaking. "I've got a full cylinder. Six shots I can put into you. One for Max, one for Kitty, one for Beau and Adora. Hell, even one for Selene. And that still leaves one for me, for all the times you've almost killed me now."

"I surrender." His face, his voice—the entirety of him was subdued. He put up his hands. "You don't want to kill me, Pity. I may have been wrong about some things, but not about you. You're no cold-blooded killer. Take me to Selene."

She glared at him, gun growing heavier as indecision threatened to drag her to a floor that knew spilt blood as well as a battlefield. Sheridan had lied and manipulated her, even tried to kill her. Because of him, Max might be dead. If Selene allowed him to leave the city, he would still be a threat.

And if she didn't . . .

The darkened stands leaned in around them like the walls of a grave. Stretched beyond bearing, something within her ruptured.

A person's death shouldn't be a spectacle, whether they deserve it or not.

"I don't want to kill you," Pity said, voice shaking. Tears welled up and threatened to spill. "But if I did, I'd only need one shot."

"I know," Sheridan said, nodding with relief, "I kn—"

She fired.

The gunshot echoed like a firecracker through the empty arena. Eyes wide with surprise, Sheridan looked down at the crimson stain blossoming on his chest. A moment later, he pitched forward onto the ground, his heart's blood pooling beneath him.

Soon, even that stilled.

Pity left him where he fell, a faint roar lingering in her ears as she departed the theatre, like the ghost of a thousand rounds of applause.

CHAPTER 43

"DO YOU WANT THE GOOD NEWS FIRST?" SAID DR. STARR. "Or the bad?"

"Don't draw it out, Doc." Siena crossed her arms. "He alive or not?"

Pity stared at nothing, thankful Siena could ask the question she couldn't.

Olivia had already come and gone with other news: Beau was badly injured but would recover. Sheridan's mercenaries were dead, captured, or hightailing it out of Cessation. Halcyon had managed to elude capture for a few hours but was eventually found trying to bribe his way out of the city. The contamination of the Tin Men was a trickier situation, and everyone who had joined on in the last year was under scrutiny.

But when it came to Max...

Pity longed to split from her skin, which seemed a size too small and shrinking. Her arm, bandaged at her side, had throbbed like a bad tooth, keeping time with the minutes that ticked by. And yet the moment Starr walked in the door, she was struck by silence, too afraid to even look at his face for what she might see there.

"He's alive," said Starr. "That's the good news."

Pity's stomach quivered. *Thank you, Lord.* But the smile that had formed crumbled a heartbeat later.

"The bad news," he continued, "is that while I've done what I can, a fragment of bullet lodged near his spine. If I try to operate, there's a good chance he'll lose the use of his legs, assuming he makes it through the surgery at all. I'm sorry. Even if I had the experience for the procedure, I don't have the right equipment or resources here."

Pity catapulted to her feet. "So you're going to do nothing?"

"I didn't say that." Starr crossed his arms. "What I'm going to do is put him in a stasis container and let Ms. Bond take it from there."

She felt the blood drain from her face. She turned to Siena. "You told Selene."

"Didn't have much choice. She overheard enough to start putting it together anyway." Siena put a hand on her shoulder. "You knew it was going to end like this anyway, kid. If he stays here now, he's dead. But back east—well, if there's something Drakos-Pryce has, it's resources."

Pity shrugged away. "But if she knows who he is—"

"He's no good to her in the condition he's in."

"Not to mention she's already given her blessing for Ms. Bond to take him," Starr added.

"But...he..." Pity searched for another argument but found nothing. *If he stays, he's dead. If he goes, he'll live.* "Fine. But I'm coming with you."

"Dammit, Jones, that's—"

"I'm not leaving his side until he's where he needs to be. And if you try to leave me behind, I'm gonna follow you all the way to Columbia." She stared down the bounty hunter, her jaw set.

Siena sniffed and shook her head. "Somewhere your mother is laughing her ass off."

She strode out of the room.

"Can I see him?" Pity said to Starr.

He shook his head. "I've already induced stasis—couldn't risk the fragment moving around. However," he said with a note of annoyance, "if you're keen to talk to someone else who should be resting and recovering, stay put." He held the door as he departed.

Selene entered. Her neck and shoulder were bandaged, and she walked with a cane, but a stately air still clung to her like a warning. She sat down gingerly, regarding Pity much like she had at their first meeting.

A minute of sharp-edged silence passed.

"I'm sorry about Max," she said finally.

That she sounded sincere didn't dampen the fury that blazed within Pity, a pyre for the trust she had once put in the woman. "You would have done it, wouldn't you? You would have put him in a Finale, just to make a point—to show how much control you have."

"I don't make empty threats," said Selene. "You know that. I did what I believed needed to be done." She paused. "You really love him, don't you? Sometimes I forget what it's like to love like that, thinking of only one and not a thousand."

"You would have tried to make me kill him."

"For the benefit of that thousand, yes." Selene sighed. "But that would have been my sin to carry, not yours."

Something in Pity's chest tightened. "Sheridan..."

"Speaking of sins? What *were* you thinking about when you killed him? Max... or Cessation?"

"I was thinking about *both*." She felt the quake of the shot again, saw the blood spread. "Sheridan wasn't going to give up. If he couldn't control Cessation the way he wanted, he would have seen it destroyed." A wave of exhaustion crested over her. "I didn't want to kill him. But I didn't want him to have the chance to hurt anyone else, or for you to have a chance to..."

"Put him in a Finale?" Selene finished.

"Yes."

She smiled humorlessly. "Right and wrong isn't so easy, is it? Sometimes the choices we make are a little bit of both." Selene sighed again. "It's been a while since I felt like a fool. I saw Sheridan only as an ally, not as a threat. But I made my choices, and you made yours. And we both paid the price."

Genuine sadness filled Selene's face, unlike anything Pity had seen in the woman before. Her anger receded slightly. "Adora. I'm sorry. Who knew?"

"That she was my daughter?" Selene closed her eyes, mouth thinning. "Only Beau, though I think Flossie had her suspicions. I thought if I kept her a secret I wouldn't have to be afraid for her in the way you were afraid for Max. That I could keep her from ever being a target or a pawn." A tear rolled down her round cheek, there and gone in moments. "If only she had said yes to Sheridan. I could have died content with that."

"Except she didn't," Pity said. "She was too loyal. And you've got no one to blame for that but yourself."

It was a bitter shot to take, and her only reward was a slight pinching of Selene's expression. But Pity didn't need to read the woman's mind to know her bullet had hit its target. Fresh guilt might have found her in that moment had there been any room left for it among the churn of emotions fixing to shred her to pieces. Even an insincere apology felt beyond her tolerance.

"So what's going to happen?" she said instead. "When CONA finds out about Sheridan...what I did..."

"What *you* did?" Selene stood and steadied herself on the edge of a table, her complexion a shade paler than before, her cloak of strength slipping a little. "Patrick Sheridan, along with many others, was *tragically* caught in a raid executed by an over-zealous branch of the Reformationists." As weak as she looked, a sly smile broke on her lips. "Who, of course, have been receiving support from anti-Cessation elements in the east for ages, despite Cessation being outside CONA control. There are plenty of witnesses who will confirm this." The smirk receded a bit. "It came at a high price, but this may actually quell our enemies for a time."

A high price...Pity stared at her boots. *It was too high.* "And Drakos-Pryce?"

Selene scowled. "When it comes to Alanna Drakos and Jonathan Pryce, they're getting what they wanted. And I have enough trouble to deal with on this side of the continent. I would appreciate if, as far as they know, no one in Cessation had any idea who Max was."

"No one did."

"Let's hope *they* believe that," Selene said. "Max, you crafty little...Between losing him and Halcyon, the Theatre will never be the same."

"What about the Theatre...now that Halcyon...?"

Selene carefully made her way toward the door. "The Zidanes can manage things for the time being." She looked back at Pity. "I even suggested that it might be time to retire the Finales, but when the other performers found out what Halcyon had done, they seemed inclined toward one more. A Finale for the Finales." She paused. "It wasn't exactly our deal, but given what you paid out for the sake of us all...well, I don't like owing debts."

Pity tried to muster some sympathy for Halcyon but found little to spare. "Eva and Marius will do a good job."

"I know. And once Max is seen to, will you come back here?"

"I think..." Pity closed her eyes. Pools of blood spread across her thoughts. "Max made me promise him, once, that if this place ever started to get the best of me, I would get out. I think, for now, that's what I need to do."

"I understand." Selene reached the exit. "But for all of our... disagreements, you've earned your place. Now and in the future, there's a home for you here."

Silence stood vigil as the gray container was loaded onto the train. No matter how many times Pity told herself it wasn't a coffin, that Max was alive inside, the sight made her gut ache. Siena and Olivia stood beside her, and the rest of their party behind them. Dozens had accompanied them to Last Stop like an honor guard, tears flowing freely for both Max and Casimir's dead.

Olivia squeezed her uninjured shoulder reassuringly. "He'll be fine," she said. "Max is tougher than he seems. As for Siena, she takes her coffee black with sugar, and watch her around the bourbon while she's on the job."

"She's only coming along this once," grumbled Siena.

"And I'm not going to make her coffee," said Pity.

"Uh-huh." Olivia stepped away. "Black with sugar, watch the bourbon. I'll see you when you two roll back around this way again."

As she disappeared into the crowd, Luster, Duchess, and Garland came forward.

"Take care of him," said Duchess, embracing her. "And don't forget to bring me something nice from Columbia, okay? But nothing yellow. Or with feathers."

Despite it all, Pity laughed, a sound cut off as Garland swept her off her feet and kissed her. Before she had a chance to react, he released her, winking playfully. "That was for Max, when he wakes up."

"Riiight."

Luster's eyes were bloodshot and wet. She stared, began to speak, and burst into tears.

When Pity put her good arm around her, she hugged back so tight that Pity felt every ache and pain all over again. "What I did back in the tunnels…I'm so—"

"Don't even say it," Luster begged. "I know. And don't stay away forever. Neither of you. Whatever he is back east, Max is one of us. You make sure he knows that."

Suddenly Pity's cheeks were wet, too, no matter that she thought she had cried all the tears she could that day. "I know," she choked out, wiping them away. "And I promise—"

"Jones!" Siena now hung from the door of the train. "You coming or not?"

Pity took a deep breath and started toward the bounty hunter. But with each step, a piece of her sloughed off, remaining with the people watching her go. This is what it is, she realized, to leave someplace you belong. To leave a home.

But home is on that train, too, and he needs to get moving.

"Go on," called Luster. "It's just a few miles. We'll see you when we see you."

"Just a few miles," Pity echoed and climbed onto the train. "Hardly anything at all."

EPILOGUE

FROM THE DRAKOS-PRYCE COMPOUND, PITY COULD see all of Columbia, spreading down the coast in both directions. She stepped closer to the picture window, so near that her breath left a fog on the glass. It was beautiful—majestic and stern, its gray spires reaching into the clouds. Just as she'd always imagined it would be.

"Taking their damn time." Siena paced across the room for the hundredth time. She'd been jumpy since they arrived in the city, and it was getting worse with each passing day. "Not enough space here," she had said one night, talking into her liquor. "This city leans in on you like a chest cold."

A week ago a dozen stern guards in black suits had met them at the train station and immediately taken custody of Max. Siena and Pity were escorted to a hotel, set up in rooms so luxurious that even Casimir looked drab by comparison, and told to wait. Since then, Pity had spent hours wandering the city, gaping at the soaring buildings and glittering glass. She had seen the museums and art galleries, the artfully landscaped parks, even walked along the sandy beaches, bare feet treading through the lapping waves.

Have you ever swum in the ocean?

Max never felt far away. Every moment she was aware that this was his world, the one he had so desperately avoided. And remembering that, she made herself look, really look, until the cracks in the gilded veneer showed themselves: the uniformed people whose heads hung low as they left the pantheon core of the city at day's end; the beggars and veterans camped beneath bridges and overpasses; the angry graffiti scrawled in the alleys. It was all there if she looked hard enough.

Finally, the summons came. A sleek black vehicle carried them over a long bridge to an island, where it deposited them in front of the largest house Pity had ever seen. They were led through its echoing halls to a plush, sprawling sitting room.

An hour had passed since then.

No news was good news, Siena had told her. Payment depended on Max being returned alive. If he had died, the bounty hunter assured her, they would've been booted from their cozy digs.

That fact didn't comfort Pity as much as she wanted. Her fingers worried at the fabric of her pants, her guns left behind at the hotel. "Do you think something is wrong?"

"Nope," said Siena. "Our time ain't worth what theirs is, that's all."

Moments later, the door creaked open. Pity straightened. She tried not to look as nervous as she felt, but her chest was tight, her stomach fluttery.

Jonathan Pryce entered first. He was a tall, narrow man with hazelnut-brown hair streaked silver. Piercing eyes caged behind delicate, rectangular glasses swept over Siena and then Pity. Alanna Drakos stood a head shorter but seemed bigger than him somehow, with striking green eyes, a joyless mouth, and thick, dark hair pulled back with combs. Between them, Pity could just see Max, a composite with every sharp edge removed.

"Ms. Bond," Alanna Drakos said. "Lovely to finally meet you."

Her tone suggested otherwise, but Siena nodded civilly. "Mrs. Drakos, Mr. Pryce."

"Who is this?" said Jonathan Pryce.

"My new assistant," said Siena simply. "Serendipity."

"What a pretty name." Max's mother barely glanced at Pity. "I'm sure you'll be happy to hear that our son is doing nicely. Our doctors assure us that with a few months of close attention, he'll make a full recovery. We owe you our thanks."

Pity let out the breath she had been holding. "Is he here?"

"That's good news," Siena interjected, shooting her a warning look. "And you can thank me all you like, so long as you pay me, too."

Jonathan Pryce adjusted his glasses. "Your payment was transferred a few minutes ago."

The bounty hunter smiled. "It's been a pleasure, then."

Pity cleared her throat.

"I hear you," said Siena. "One more thing, if you don't mind.

My assistant here was hoping to have a word with your son before we go on our way."

They stared at her, Alanna Drakos with one dark eyebrow raised.

"Just for a few minutes." Pity gave them a disarming smile, mimicking the one Finn used, the one that had always gotten her whatever she wanted. "Some of the folks who knew Ma—your son out west, they gave me messages to pass on to him. Good-byes they didn't get to say, that sort of thing."

Her heart thudded as they considered her. A look passed between them, but finally Alanna Drakos nodded.

"As long as you're quick," she said. "He's still quite weak, you understand."

"Yes," said Pity. "I understand."

Alanna Drakos kept a half step ahead of Pity as they traveled through the house. Her heels clicked against the stone floors, reminding Pity acutely of Selene's office. She wondered how much of the truth Alanna Drakos knew about her son's injury. The story they had told was the same one concocted for Sheridan's death—that rogue Reformationists had stormed Casimir, killing dozens before they were finally turned back. Rumors and half tales had reached Columbia before they had, and Pity had been amazed to see how quickly the explanation was accepted. Certainly Max's parents knew it was a fiction, but they also seemed content to keep their part in the affair secret.

"Did you know my son?" Alanna Drakos said abruptly. "During his time away from us?"

"Yes." Pity chose her words with care. "He saved my life once." Twice, in truth, but it didn't seem wise to point out that the bullet he'd taken had been meant for her. "If it weren't for him, I wouldn't be here right now."

"Hmm." Alanna Drakos sped up her pace.

"Your son has a good heart, ma'am."

She stopped in front of a door, eyes as hard as emeralds. "Be quick." She turned the handle.

The room was large, white, and almost entirely empty. One wall was glass, looking out into a small courtyard filled with flowers and trees. On another was a display, streaming the afternoon's news broadcasts. Opposite that was a bed, surrounded by machines that beeped and clicked and hummed. Pity saw all of this and none of it.

Max lay in the bed.

She barely recognized him at first. His hair was shorter, the blue spikes gone. All of his piercings had been removed. But when his eyes opened and alighted on her, familiarity returned. They stared at each other.

"Darling," his mother said from behind her. "This young woman asked to have a word with you."

"Pity." His voice cracked.

"Hi." She blinked, desperate to keep the tears away.

"Thanks, Mom," he said, and waited.

For a moment, Pity feared that his mother would remain, but then she heard the click of the door as it shut. She ran to the bed.

"What are you doing here?" Max hissed as she crouched down beside him.

Pity wanted to kiss him so badly that her whole body ached. If she could have thrown her arms around him and healed every inch of him with love, she would have. Instead, she took one of his hands in hers and squeezed. "Who do you think got you here?" Her face felt like it would split from smiling. "You're alive," she said, finally believing it. "You're okay."

Max squeezed back weakly. "I told you I would be. And you…you're okay…" His face went grim. "You *are* okay, aren't you? I saw the broadcasts. Sheridan is…"

"Dead," she interjected, her words wooden. "An unavoidable tragedy."

He didn't ask her to elaborate. She filled him in on the other details, good and bad, elated to be talking to him. When she was done, they sat quietly, surrounded by the lifeless sounds of the medical machines.

"You can't stay," Max said finally, his voice thick.

"I know. Siena's been paid. We'll be heading out pretty soon."

He nodded several times, as if forgetting when to stop. "I…"

"You're going to get better." Pity tightened her grip on his hand. "You're going to get yourself strong again, and then I'm coming back for you. Do you understand?"

"Pity—"

"I'm coming back unless you tell me that you don't want me to. Tell me that, Max, and I'll stay away forever."

He stared at her, eyes wet, a small, sad smile on his lips. "I don't want you to go at all."

She stood. "Then hurry up and get well. For me. And to hell with your parents or anyone else who tries to get in my way. I've had dissident drifters, trained assassins, and mad politicians try to kill me, and I'm still here."

She leaned over and kissed him on the lips, not caring if they were being watched. Max returned the kiss eagerly, reaching up to place a hand behind her neck and pull her closer. When they separated, Pity kept her face a few inches from his. "I don't care if I'm in Cessation, Columbia, or at the ends of the earth, so long as I'm with you."

"Same here," said Max. "I love you, Serendipity Jones."

"I love you, too, Max," she said. "Or whatever your name is."

He laughed.

The door opened again. Pity turned to find Alanna Drakos staring icily at her.

"I trust you're finished now," she said.

"We are"—Pity smiled at her and reached down to give Max's hand one more squeeze—"ma'am."

"Then I'll show you out."

"Your son has a good heart," Pity said again as she passed through the door, low so that only Max's mother could hear. "It's in the right place and with the right people. You should make sure to remember that."

Siena was waiting for her in front of the house, smoking one of her ugly cigarettes and leaning against a marble pillar. "Say what you needed to?"

"Yes. For the moment."

"Well, where to now? Or are you still getting your fill of Columbia?"

Pity shook her head. "No, I've seen as much of it as I want to." She thought for a second. "Finn talked about New Boston. Think you can find any jobs up that way?"

Siena blew a cloud of smoke at the city. "I suppose I could. North it is, then."

"North," echoed Pity. And after that, maybe south, or in

whatever direction fate and the bounty took them. But one day...She turned and stared at Columbia, and at the sun that was beginning to drift lower in the afternoon sky. Beyond it, past the farthest edges of her vision, was another city that, down to her core, she knew she would never be able to leave behind entirely—and didn't want to.

One day, west again.

Read on for a BONUS
short story featuring Selene!

PIECE BY PIECE

A Selene Story

That they blindfolded her was the biggest insult. As if she didn't know where they were going. As if knowing that the leader of the Golden Jackals conducted his business in the stately, if slightly dilapidated, old courthouse was some well-kept secret that she had yet to ferret out. *Golden Jackals*. If she hadn't been blindfolded, her captors might have seen her roll her eyes as they dragged her up staircases and through echoing halls. Finally, they deposited her in a lumpy chair, only then taking the time to loosen the dark fabric obscuring her vision.

She was in an office. A rather small one.

And across a pitted and cigarette-burned desk, Kluge grinned a pulpy, insipid grin at her.

He was not a handsome man. His lips looked like two plump

earthworms had affixed themselves to the doughy flesh of his flushed, pockmarked face. But luckily for Kluge, attractiveness wasn't a prerequisite for a gangster. Neither was taste. Which is why she was trapped in a moldy-smelling office over-appointed with garish bits of statuary and gold wall hangings that didn't quite hide the graying plaster behind them.

She raised a hand to fix her hair, only to find it was still coated in blood, now tacky. Her dress was smeared with it, as well.

Her *white* dress. She sighed. There'd be no saving it.

Kluge's smile contracted slightly as he, too, took note of her disheveled appearance. One of the strong-arms who had delivered her leaned close to Kluge and whispered in his ear. The pleased expression wilted further. He folded his hands in front of him on the desk, as if to be sure they wouldn't do anything...untoward.

"I told them not to hurt you. As a *courtesy*."

She leaned back in the chair, gripping the arms, not caring if she left streaks of blood on them. They'd be at home with the other stains. "Your lackeys failed to inform me of that when they set upon me."

"You *stabbed* one of my best men."

"So I did." She shrugged. "To his credit, he was very quick. And the knife didn't go nearly deep enough to be fatal."

"I suppose Dante should count himself lucky, then." Kluge chuckled. "I told them: 'Don't hurt her. And don't underestimate her, either.'"

Now it was her turn to smile.

"Would you like a drink?" He removed a bottle and a pair of glasses from a drawer. Fine-cut crystal, though one had a chip on the rim large enough to see from where she sat.

"No, thank you." She raised her stained hands. "I *would* take a damp towel, if it's not too much trouble."

"Chelios?" Kluge waved a hand as he poured a measure of tea-colored liquor. One of the men set off. "See? Civilized. Like I knew we could be. To be honest, I considered razing that garish little parlor you call a business to the ground and having your whole crew shot up, but that's so..."

"Unimaginative?"

"I was going to say barbaric. And we're supposed to be moving beyond that, aren't we? The war in the east is over. Everyone is building and rebuilding. It's time to settle our disagreements in a more constructive manner."

"I agree entirely. In fact, that's why I came to Cessation."

His glass paused inches from his mouth as he considered her, a gaze that did its very best to convey that it already knew everything worth knowing. "You've been here how long now, Selene? Just under a year?"

"That sounds about right." Eleven months, three days, and seven hours. Maybe eight. She wasn't exactly sure how much time had passed between when Kluge's goons had stormed her place of business and now.

"And in that time you've done quite well for yourself. *Tch,* a little slip of a woman like you. I honestly expected you'd be dead...or worse...within a few weeks' time."

"Maybe you should take your own advice about underestimating people."

Kluge's lips pressed into a curdled sort of smile. "Better late than never." He took a sip of the drink. "The Broken Bones. Nora Le Roux and her people. Even those bootleggers from down south. Small fish, but they're all swimming in your little pond now."

"I wouldn't call it little." Neither would he, which is exactly why he did, of course. "And you forgot the Poison Lilies. They work for me now, too."

His ruddy cheeks flushed deeper, though he did an admirable job of feigning disinterest. "As I said, small fish. But enough is enough, Selene. I don't think you understand what kind of city Cessation is. A bag of vipers is still a bag of vipers, even if you make that bag from velvet and trim it with pretty gold embroidery. What are you doing here? Go back east—back to dinner parties and ribbon-cutting ceremonies and the sort of backstabbing that doesn't involve anyone ending up with an actual knife in their back."

Chelios returned and presented her with a wet cloth. She took her time with it, cleaning thoroughly between her fingers, under her nails, until not a speck of blood remained. All the while, Kluge watched her.

When she was done, she folded the soiled cloth into a square and returned it. "Thank you," she said to Chelios, before addressing Kluge again. "I know exactly what kind of city Cessation is. What it *will* be. And I am not going anywhere."

Kluge's fingers tightened around his glass. "Everyone, out."

Chelios looked from Kluge to Selene and back. "Do you think that's a good idea? She's—"

"Declawed." His tone was strained, irritable. "Go. I can

handle her." When his guards were gone, he placed his empty glass on the desk and spun it once, twice. "I've been polite. I've been courteous. And now I'm warning you now that my patience is running out. Last chance—leave the city."

Selene entwined her hands in lap. "Don't think that your civility isn't acknowledged and appreciated. But I am just getting started with Cessation."

Kluge's eyes darkened. A long minute of silence stretched between them. "You know," he said finally, "I'd almost like you...if you weren't such a pain in my ass."

"Why, thank you. I suppose this is the point where you tell me that if I don't leave, I have to join up with you. That I'll get a fair cut of my business, and all I have to do is swear fealty to the Golden Jackals and make sure the payments arrive regularly and on time."

The worms plumped with confidence and then spread, so that she could see the line of yellow teeth behind them. "Normally? Maybe. But to be honest, Selene, there's something about you that's far too...ambitious." He opened the drawer again and pulled out a folder. "So I went another way. To be honest, I couldn't stop wondering, 'Who is this woman? I've seen flowers less fragile than her, and yet she waltzed into one of the most dangerous places on the continent and set up shop before the first whiff of her perfume had faded.'" He slid the folder across the desk. "So I had Dante do a little digging."

"What a pity that you wasted his time like that."

"I was beginning to think so, too," Kluge agreed. "Until he struck gold."

Her fingers tightened around one another.

"It wasn't easy, I will give you that. But once he discovered your real name…" He laughed. "I'm honestly amused. Giving up all that to come *here*?"

She didn't move. Didn't meet Kluge's gaze. He was bluffing. Or attempting to siphon information to fill in the gaps of whatever he thought he knew.

"It's a shame about your husband, though. From what I hear he was highly regarded on both sides. There were rumors…may I ask what happened?"

He wasn't bluffing.

"You may." He already knew, of course, he only wanted to twist the knife of that memory a little. Still, a waver crept into her voice. "It's a common story. The war ended for most of us, but not for him."

"My condolences." He tapped the folder with one finger. "At least you still have…well, why don't you take a look at what else Dante found?"

No.

The blood drained from her face as a shiver ran through her. It wasn't possible…she'd been so careful. She'd disconnected, covered up, erased…

And yet.

Hands cold, she took the thin file and opened it. Inside was a single photograph.

A girl.

Taken at a distance.

But close enough to see the magenta ribbons braided through her hair.

"How…" The word squeaked out. She licked her lips and took a breath. "How did you get this?"

He leaned back in his chair, chest puffed like a self-assured rooster. "It's funny. You don't think anyone should underestimate you, and yet you seem to believe the rest of us have no more savvy or sense than a common hustler."

"If you've done anything to her—"

"Nothing more than snapped that photo. Which I will hang on to when you leave the city, which will be within the hour. And to keep you in your place once your pride shakes itself off, when you set up your new enterprise elsewhere—and let's not pretend that ambition of yours will call for anything less—you will send me a cut. We'll call it a guarantee of safety." The worms pursed with satisfaction. "Do you understand?"

She closed the file and set it back on the desk. A different kind of cold ran through her now.

"Yes…I understand completely."

"Good." He stood. "I knew that we could settle this. Don't look so sour, doll. Time comes we all learn our place. Speaking of, it's about time for you to get going, don't you think?"

"Yes." A deep breath smoothed the tightness gripping her chest. "Yes, I do believe it's right about time."

"Chelios! Get back in here." The lieutenant reentered, trailed by two more guards. They surrounded her. "Give her five minutes to get what she needs from her place and then see that she leaves the city immed—"

"I was wrong to underestimate you."

Kluge's face crumpled, as if he was half-surprised that she was still there. "What?"

"I'm admitting my mistake," she continued. "I think it's important to be able to do that. But even though I underestimated your resourcefulness, I was correct in judging that you'd overlook something important."

His eyes narrowed. "And what's that?"

"That there's always one."

Kluge's forehead furled with confusion.

"Always," she continued. "In every organization. Someone who isn't quite happy, doesn't quite feel like they're getting what they want. The trick is knowing how to spot that someone...and how to appeal to them."

He snorted, amused. "You're wasting your breath. My people are well paid. They're loyal."

"Are they? It's probably easy, at the top, to overlook the subordinate who'd bring their family to the city, if only it was safe enough for them. Or the person whose closest friend is still in the prisoner camps. Or even someone who simply has the foresight to see an unsustainable system for what it is."

A faint pop sounded nearby, quickly followed by another. Kluge's gaze flew to the door.

"Loyalty," Selene stood, "is a commodity as much as anything else. There's always at least one who is willing to sell it for the right kind of currency." She gestured. "Though in your case it was quite a lot more than one."

Chelios and the men with him raised their guns and pointed them at Kluge. His eyes flew from them to Selene, his face turning redder with each passing second.

"'Time comes we all learn our place.' Isn't that how you phrased it?" She slipped around the chair and stood behind the men. Somewhere below, more gunfire sounded. "A little misleading, though. There's no place left for you in Cessation, Kluge."

"You little bi—"

"Or anywhere."

Kluge's hand flew under the desk. He brought up a handgun as his men fired at him. Bullets took him in the chest and shoulders, throwing him against the back wall, though he managed to squeeze off a single shot. It went into the ceiling, raining plaster down upon them all. His body was already lifeless as it slid to the floor, leaving behind a trail of red.

"Selene!" Anna, her head of security, appeared in the door to the office. She yanked off the helmet of her body armor, releasing a sweaty blond braid. "Are you okay?"

"Of course." Bits of plaster clung to her. She brushed them away. "Thank you, Chelios. You and your associates were perfect. I look forward to working with you all. Now, while I wrap up here with Anna, why don't you finish downstairs? I'm sure your former employer had some caches of currency or goods that, were they to disappear before my people have a chance to search properly, wouldn't be missed."

"Yes, ma'am," said Chelios, with a last glance at what was left of Kluge. He and the men departed.

"Are you sure you're okay?" Anna's examining gaze crawled over her, from head to toe. "You look pale. Did he do anything to—"

"I'm fine, really." A chill still raced through her veins.

Careful. She'd been so careful.

"Look, I know this is how you wanted to play this, but one

person can only be so lucky. And once the rest of the gang bosses see what's happened here, there are not going to be any more polite chats—just bullets and blood. We need to have a talk about getting you a dedicated bodyguard. I know someone. He's not particularly charming, but he *is* a crack shot and you'll—"

"Later." She went to the desk and searched through the drawers until she found what she was looking for. "Dante. The one I stabbed."

"We have him. He's a little ornery right now, but seems like the sort to see clear, once he recovers."

"He won't."

"Excuse me?"

"He won't." Selene picked up the file and removed the photo again. "Recover. Make sure of it." She flicked the lighter she'd taken from Kluge's desk and held the flame to the corner.

"Understood," said Anna. "What's that?"

"It's nothing." And everything.

In a world filled with secrets, it was the only one she needed to keep.

She held the photo as long as she could, watching the paper curl and blacken, the magenta ribbons bubble and burn. Finally, she let it fall to the desk, where the fire finished its meal, leaving behind a scorch mark on the wood beneath it, like a shadow of someone no longer there.

ACKNOWLEDGMENTS

I have to start by thanking my agent extraordinaire, Laura Zats. Without her guidance, input, and ideas, *Gunslinger Girl* would not be what it is today. I am incredibly lucky to have an agent with her passion for books (not to mention her excellent taste in both tea and beer).

To Aubrey Poole, thank you for your hard work and patience as we kicked this funky little act into Theatre-ready shape. This has been an amazing experience, made all the better by having a supercool editor like you!

Endless gratitude to James Patterson for this incredible opportunity, as well as the entire team at Jimmy. Special thanks to Sabrina Benun, Erinn McGrath, and Gabrielle Tyson, plus everyone on the managing editorial and production teams—I know how much work it takes to put a book together and I appreciate it more than I can say. And to Tracy Shaw and Jeff Miller: this jacket is more fabulous than any author has a right to hope for!

Thank you to my family for always supporting and encouraging my hobbies (even when you didn't quite understand them), not to mention buying me lots of books growing up. (Lane, you are my favorite nephew!)

To Katrina Kruse: in addition to being the best foodie friend ever, you help me keep my sanity on an ongoing basis. Not enough gratitude in the world for that.

To Jadah McCoy, thank you for giving this book one of its very first—and very needed—injections of confidence. And Elizabeth Briggs—what can I say? Being part of Pitch Wars was one of the best things that ever happened to me; thank you for all the time and work you put into *Gunslinger Girl,* as well as your continued support. And more thanks to the entire Pitch Wars community (especially the class of 2015) for its dedication to writers and readers of all kinds.

The final round of gratitude goes to a group of people whom I could go on about for pages. My writing group is the *best* writing group in the whole wide world, and I will break out the fighting words for anyone who tries to claim otherwise. To Kat Black, who was there with me at its inception, your unwavering positivity and experience have been invaluable. To Kyle W. Kerr, thank you for all your help in managing the group; I look forward to all the books we'll produce from our Parisian apartment overlooking the Seine (someday). Robert Davis can be summed up in one word: *awesome.* Special thanks to Natalie C. Anderson, who probably read more versions of *Gunslinger Girl* than anyone else. To Victoria Sandbrook Flynn and Lura Slowinski—who could ask for better beta readers? And much love and thanks to Clare Fitzgerald, Gillian Daniels, Jess Barber (sorry about Finn), Lauren Barrett, Emily Strong, Caitlin Walsh, Nyssa Connell, Eric Mulder, Andrea Corbin, Julia Gilstein, Jay O'Connell, Michael Hilborn, Angela Ambroz, Seth Gordon, Elizabeth Brenner, and all the others who have passed through our ranks. May all your futures be filled with fabulous books and no murder closets!

JAMES PATTERSON

BRINGS YOU THE MOST

THRILLING DYSTOPIAN

SERIES SINCE

THE HUNGER GAMES

Twin sisters Becca and Cassie are inseparable—until one is kidnapped and sent to a jail where she must fight to survive.

NOW THEY'LL DO ANYTHING JUST TO STAY ALIVE.

READ

AND LOOK OUT FOR

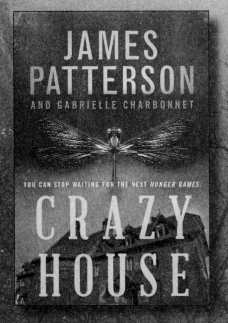

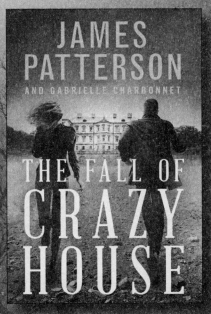

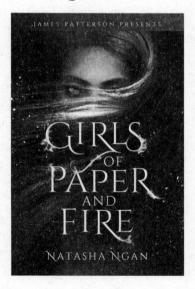

ABOUT THE AUTHOR

Lyndsay Ely is a writer and creative professional who currently calls Boston home. She is a geek and a foodie, and has never met an antique shop she didn't like. *Gunslinger Girl* is her debut novel.